L'Affaire

L'Affaire

by

Diane Johnson

MICHAEL JOSEPH
an imprint of
PENGUIN BOOKS

MICHAEL JOSEPH

Published by the Penguin Group
Penguin Books Ltd, 80 Strand, London WC2R ORL, England
Penguin Group (USA) Inc., 375 Hudson Street, New York, New York 10014, USA
Penguin Books Australia Ltd, 250 Camberwell Road, Camberwell, Victoria 3124, Australia
Penguin Books Canada Ltd, 10 Alcorn Avenue, Toronto, Ontario, Canada M4V 3B2
Penguin Books India (P) Ltd, 11 Community Centre, Panchsheel Park, New Delhi – 110 017, India
Penguin Group (NZ), cnr Airborne and Rosedale Roads, Albany, Auckland 1310, New Zealand
Penguin Books (South Africa) (Pty) Ltd, 24 Sturdee Avenue, Rosebank 2196, South Africa

Penguin Books Ltd, Registered Offices: 80 Strand, London WC2R ORL, England

www.penguin.com

First published in the United States of America by Penguin Putnam Inc., 2003
First published in Great Britain by Michael Joseph 2004
1

Copyright © Diane Johnson, 2003

The moral right of the author has been asserted

This book is a work of fiction. Names, characters, places and incidents are either the product of
the author's imagination or are used fictitiously, and any resemblance to actual persons, living
or dead, business establishments, events, or locales is entirely coincidental.

Set in 12.5/14.75 pt Monotype Garamond
Typeset by Rowland Phototypesetting Ltd, Bury St Edmunds, Suffolk
Printed in Great Britain by Clays Ltd, St Ives plc

A CIP catalogue record for this book is available from the British Library

ISBN 0-718-14744-8

To Carolyn Kizer,
who introduced me
to Prince Kropotkin and *Mutual Aid*

Acknowledgments

My grateful thanks to the many people who helped me with ideas and information, moral support, and advice with the manuscript – patient friends, John Beebe, Marie-Claude de Brunhoff, Robert Gottlieb, Diana Ketcham, Carolyn Kizer, Alison Lurie and John Murray. Also to Dr Alain Gruber, who knows about the moon-bleaching of tablecloths, and CK Williams for putting me on to the Allen Tate translation of Baudelaire that I have attributed to Robin Crumley. Many thanks too for the wonderful support at Dutton from the editors Carole Baron and Laurie Chittenden.

I should note that French inheritance laws, often revised, may have changed in some details by the time of publication.

It is because America has consented neither to sin nor to suffering that she has no soul.

– André Gide

The destiny of France is to irritate the world.

– Jean Giraudoux

PART I
Hotel

Les Affaires? C'est bien simple.
C'est l'argent des autres.

– Alexandre Dumas fils

I

All of Europe had been fascinated for the past few days by televised images of avalanches descending in the wake of storms on certain ski resorts and pretty villages in the Alps. Caught for the screen by cameramen safely distant, the snowy plumes were as beautiful as waterfalls or clouds, and thrilling, too, in that it always stirs the human heart to watch nature assert her propensity for malicious destruction.

Despite the usual preventive measures taken with dynamite and seismograph, some ancient chalets were engulfed completely, some modern structures of concrete were imploded in a bizarre fashion never before studied. In one place, inhabitants were killed with the power of a tidal wave or volcano; in others, the possibility of life beating faintly in an air pocket under an eave stimulated massive rescue efforts organized from the Austrian, Italian, and Swiss Alpine patrols as well as the local French ones. Yet, with characteristic resolve, ski lifts stayed open when they could, and skiers, having booked their precious *vacances d'hiver*, still ventured resolutely out onto the slopes that were open.

Unaware for the moment of the dangers at the higher reaches, Amy Ellen Hawkins, a dotcom executive from Palo Alto, California, had defied the usual injunction never to ski alone. She was trying out new parabolics, an innovation since she had last been on the slopes, and she had thought she had time for a run or two while the light was good, even though the snow was already falling. In the several days she had been here, the terrible weather had mostly impeded any skiing at all, and now that her jet lag had worn off, she was too restless and eager to stay indoors any longer.

Amy was an experienced skier, but wished to be better. She had chosen the Hôtel Croix St Bernard in Valméri, France, for a couple of weeks' stay as part of a personal program of self-perfection, an almost superstitious way of placating the gods for her recent good fortune. Humbly, she would seek mastery of deferred skills like skiing, cooking, and speaking French, and she saw no reason she should not approach them with the discipline and effectiveness that had marked her career in the decade since she left college.

By the time Amy reached the top of the chair lift that swayed up the mountain above the hotel, the cell phones of the liftmen still higher above were crackling with warnings. Visibility had already deteriorated markedly, the new sort of ski turned out to have an independent wish to turn despite her, requiring an effort of understanding she had not expected, and the terrain was steeper than an intermediate/advanced slope would be at Squaw Valley, with strange intervals when she could not determine whether she was going down or up – not a whiteout exactly, but an eerie one-dimensional landscape that seemed to have no undulations or contours. A cool-headed person, she kept her nerve, reminding herself of the reassuring facts of gravity. If she was sliding, she must be going downhill, and she allowed her skis to carry her. Now, face stung with snow, she was just thankful to have finally made her way in the failing light down the difficult slope on which she had found herself and was stashing her skis by the entrance to the ski room at the Hôtel Croix St. Bernard, shaken and sobered by this immediate lesson and suddenly aware of the reverberations of what sounded like dynamite in the distance.

She saw that though it was still early afternoon, many people had come in already, forty pairs of skis or more were wedged into the wooden grid, poles jammed into the deepening snow. (The amenities of the hotel included the van from the station, a ski room where boots were warmed, a technician, and the custom of arranging the guests' skis outside next to the ski run in the mornings.) Unlike Amy, the other guests seemed mostly to be Europeans and must know something about the weather that she had missed. She looked back at the slope she had just struggled down, now hardly visible in the snowfall, and it occurred to her she had narrowly escaped death.

'Miss Hawkins!' It was the man who had been referred to as 'the baron' who was greeting her, scraping the snow-packed bottoms of his boots against his bindings and frowning at her. She knew who he was, but was startled that he knew her name. With her good memory for faces, she had already begun to sort out the people who had been in the hotel van with her coming up from Geneva, or in the ski room when she got outfitted. This was an Austrian, or maybe German, baron. Also in the ski room this morning had been an English publisher and his family, an American man – Joe, a pair of elderly women from Paris, and two Russian couples she had not spoken to. Most of the people at the hotel were French or Germans, mysteriously alien, to her great satisfaction.

'People have come in early,' she said, feeling herself flush at being faced with this censorious person. Amy sometimes felt reticent, though she was not timid. Her success in corporate life had come about the way some actors who stammer and blush in private life come to power and authority onstage. In private, her sweet smile was found pliant and endearing. She was also modest and sociable and, now, surprisingly rich, as had happened to not a few in her same year at Stanford.

'Indeed. The warnings are posted everywhere.' The baron rolled his eyes at the hopeless naïveté of her observation, from his expression wondering if in behalf of local tourism he ought to take this woman in charge. 'Didn't you see them? They're written in English as well as French.'

'Oh yes, of course, I hurried in, but I wasn't sure of the route,' she said. She was still shaken by her adventure, and by the fact that she hadn't seen the warnings, though she had scrupulously read the posted times for closing of the lift she had been on, not wanting to miss the last ascent. She usually didn't make mistakes, it was a point with her. She was also a little irritated by his suggestion that signs would have to be written in English for her to understand them.

Of course that was more or less true. She was about to protest that, A. she could read French, somewhat, and B. thank you, but her tendency to reject authority didn't extend to ignoring posted warnings about avalanches,

6

any more than sharks or riptides, she simply hadn't seen them. Instead, she said nothing, and smiled her pretty, candid smile.

'The pistes are plainly marked.' His tone was still censorious. Her kind of beauty, he was thinking, was peculiarly American, the beauty lent to a face by an optimist's temperament. Optimism however unwarranted. He could see she was a person with high hopes. In looks she might also have been an Austrian *mädchen*, with her thick braid of caramel-colored hair, bright cheeks, and a dimpled face of unusual sweetness. Her half-breathless alert quality must come from an awareness of the constant possibility that her high hopes could be dashed. It was essential in his line of work, property development, to be good at reading faces and perceiving dashed hopes.

The Croix St Bernard was a cheerful, fashionably simple, family-run hotel with some of the affectations, and prices, of a grand one, quiet and discreet, standing apart to one side of the central pistes on a road of private chalets, distant from the après-ski scene of the village itself. From hints given in the brochure, Amy had gathered that it was the choice of diplomats taking a break from Geneva, the occasional adulterous couple, well-off families with young children who like an early night, assorted Eurotrash eccentrics bored with the relentless pace found in the larger hotels, and above all, those who wanted to take the fabled cooking classes offered by the hotel's celebrated chef. All this she had inferred from the photographs and promotional material, and thus had chosen it for her stay, for the fun of mingling with people of a kind unknown to her. To be accurate, she didn't choose it so much as agree to it – it had been suggested by a Madame Chastine, a Parisian connection of Amy's friend Patricia, when Pat's aunt and Géraldine Chastine were both at Wellesley. Amy was disappointed that her two friends Pat Davis and Marnie Skolnik, who had been coming with her for the skiing and cooking, had cancelled, each for different reasons, leaving her to come alone. But she acknowledged to herself it was probably best in the long run, as without them she would concentrate better and learn more. There was also the fact that no one knew her here, so their disapproval would not count should she do something that might shock at home – a common justification for travel.

She was also glad no one here would know how well she was fixed. Though she was delighted with her money, it embarrassed her too; it had led to a modest celebrity in Palo Alto, and even to an extent in San Francisco, and she would not want here that odd sensation of being recognized even in a restaurant she'd never been to before.

Valméri itself was a conglomeration of chalets, luxurious hotels, cable cars, and Poma lifts slung across a narrow valley below Alpine peaks of stupefying grandeur. The architecture of local ski stations varied from the harsh rectilinear buildings of the International style to the kitschy pseudo-Swiss, which was the preferred, more expensive, and best-appointed option; Valméri was in the Swiss style, built by the English in the nineteen-thirties.

Amy and the baron stamped into the ski room, where

the ski attendant was listening, frowning, into the telephone, and other skiers, ranged along the benches taking their boots off, seemed to be waiting in silence for some announcement from the television set in the corner. The rescuers being interviewed on television had an air of slightly self-conscious heroism, knowing their own lives to be endangered by the still unstable snow conditions and ongoing snowfall. Men in red parkas stood beside helicopters and patted Rottweilers on leashes. In other valleys, during this disastrous week, fourteen Austrians were known to be dead, an unknown number of Swiss, three in France so far, and thousands of tourists were expected to be pinned in the Austrian Alps by the weather conditions and blocked roads.

Amy waited politely until a Russian lady extricated her feet with a grateful sigh from her enormous orange boots and carried them off to the warming rack. The baron was now leaning in with the ski attendant at the telephone as if news would come with volume audible to bystanders. The atmosphere in the ski room, Amy now saw, was one of attending a collective fate, as at a soccer match. A flush of wonder and happiness filled her when she thought of the dreadful weather and the wonderful acts of community Europeans were capable of, with their evolved, socialized governments and sense of noblesse oblige – not that she wanted socialism in America. But she admired all these trilingual people hushed in their concern about the fate of motorists on the road to Valméri, though of course Americans in the same circumstances would be concerned too.

'They are afraid the road will collapse the other side of

Les Menuires,' said the ski man finally. Amy looked back outside but the sky was calm slate, against which thick distinct flakes gathered their numbers and danced off in a mounting wind without seeming to land on the already deep snowbanks.

'Is the storm worse? Is there something to do?' she asked the baron.

'No, no, there are road crews. But I have to get to Paris tonight on the six o'clock train.' He frowned. Gallic shrug from the ski attendant, who called the baron 'Otto.' There was a general discussion of the condition of the local roads, making Amy feel amazingly lucky to be safely here.

Now the face of the young hotel manager, Christian Jaffe, appeared at the door. Something in his expression added to the hushed mood of expectancy that today replaced the ebullience with which skiers normally came in, pleased to have survived another day, high colored from the cold and exertion, laughing. Jaffe's pale face struck the others as it did Amy, as something luminous and portentous, his indoor pallor startling next to the bronzed cheeks of the skiers. Perhaps it was also the slightly mortuary effect of his business suit among the parrot-colored ski garments, yellow or red or blue, or in Amy's case pale silver-gray.

Talk fell off, but when Jaffe didn't see whom he was looking for, he ducked out again and the talk rose up, questions about the weather, something needing tightening, a boot problem, a cacophony of languages. The hill was closed now, lifts shut down, and there were rumors of other avalanches in the adjoining valley of Méribel. Skiers stood in their boots in the lower lobby outside the ski room watching through the windows as the snow continued to fall. Two Russian girls spoke an odd, thick English to the ski man, English being the only language they had in common with him, in wheedling tones, cajoling a better forecast for tomorrow. Thinking of the baron, whom she had found out was Austrian, Amy resolved that after she learned French she would go on to German. A language related to English, how hard could it be?

2

The rumor had reached the Hôtel Croix St Bernard from its origins with an Italian ski patrolman assisting in the avalanche rescue efforts, that the new cataclysm today had been triggered by the vibrations from low-flying American warplanes on their way to refuel in Germany, presumably to do with the ongoing overflights of the Middle East, bombings of some unlucky Balkan country, or another of the numberless adventures the surly super-power was conducting. Such an airplane theory seemed plausible. Vapor trails were often seen to mar the sky above the snowy crags and silent peaks of Valméri, the noise sometimes catching in the canyons and rever-berating like dynamite all the way to the lowest valley. The physics of vibration, intensely studied by the snow seismologists, without enhancing their ability to predict the action of a given snowfield, were perfectly consistent with this rumor. Skiers were often enjoined to silence as they traversed a treacherous slope beneath a fragile cor-nice. If a whispering skier could unsettle tons of snow, how much more could powerful jet engines? The planes were the major topic of conversation in the lobby, along with the rumor that a family staying at this very hotel had been among today's victims.

As was the custom every Sunday, the management had invited all the guests for a glass of champagne before dinner. Amy, veteran of numerous compulsory corporate seminars on dressing for the message, had long ago conquered any concern about what to wear to cocktail parties; she had put on black pants and a blouse that she thought neither seductive nor dowdy, and brushed and rebraided her hair. She was reluctant to appear, by making too much effort, as if she was looking for men, since emphatically she wasn't; on the other hand, attention to appearance was a desirable form of social cooperation, a subject that interested her intensely in the abstract.

Drinks were served in the lobby, from a long table covered with a white cloth or by waiters from the dining room walking among the guests with little trays. A hot fire in the large fireplace drove people from its immediate vicinity to cluster nearer the door, where the owner, Chef Jaffe, and Madame Jaffe in her Tyrolean-style suit of loden-green, greeted and chatted, helping the guests to get to know each other, and trying to deal with anxious questions regarding avalanches.

This was the first general social occasion of the new week, so most people didn't know each other, and stood with expectant, cooperative smiles. Amy looked around. One or two little old ladies glowed with diamonds, making her think of cat-burglar movies. Over there, a very heavy Russian wife was astoundingly bemedalled, decorations up and down her bosom. Amy had her usual sense of cocktail party hopefulness, knowing intellectually that the room would be as full of fools and bores as any party, but always with the belief that among these particular people some would be worldly, kindly, and friendly, and that kindred spirits would emerge. Why wouldn't they? She struggled to suppress a surge of love for them – not these particular people, but for the powers of human organization, our gregarious natures, the kindliness of our impulses to share food and talk to each other, the sweetness of agreeing to dress up for others. Sometimes she saw these activities as products of the struggle for power, as Darwin might have, or at least Herbert Spencer, but for tonight she was touched by the sight of humans wishing to be liked by others and to make them lovely things to eat.

She saw this cocktail party and parties in general as aspects of mutual aid, a subject of her passionate interest since high school, when she had joined the Mutual Aid Club, an extracurricular activity frankly designed to embellish the chances of getting into good colleges, in this case by taking pets, small children, and CD players to old persons' homes to cheer the elderly residents. The faculty advisor was a Miss Steinway, and Miss Steinway had in her own youth come under the influence of the works of an old Russian anarchist, P. Kropotkin, whose idea was that contrary to the teaching of Darwin, the human species had progressed not through competition but through mutual aid; that this was true of other species, too, ants and baboons and all sorts of creatures; that whereas individuals might compete for food, successful species had insured survival by developing highly elaborate forms of cooperation, and that in imagining every being locked in a struggle for survival of the fittest, Darwin had it wrong or had been misinterpreted.

Amy had already decided that at the end of this European period of narcissistic self-improvement, she would establish and fund a foundation for propagating the ideas of Prince Kropotkin. But that was eventually. For now, she accepted a soft-boiled egg – no, it was an eggshell filled with eggy custard, with caviar on top – and smiled around her.

'Like Queen Victoria,' a man said to her, with a kind of Kentucky accent, looking with her at the bemedalled Russian. She recognized him as the American who been in the van from Geneva with her. She had also seen him in the ski room, but he did not appear to ski. Anyhow, he would solve the other cocktail-party problem, whom to talk to, for one must not be standing by oneself, a rule he evidently also believed in, edging nearer. This man would do, attractive and open-looking. 'Joe Daggart,' he said.

She smiled at him. 'I took an oath, coming over, not to talk to other Americans. Should I break it?'

'What have you got against Americans?' he asked.

'Well, nothing, naturally. It's just that I know them already,' Amy said, noticing his glance at her shoes. 'Since I am one, I want to meet other people. But I'll count you as an other.'

He worked in Geneva, but often came here to stay, for the skiing and food. Companionably, they waded into the assortment of people, introduced themselves, smiled, agreed that the day had been unusual. It was disconcerting to notice that people switched into English when either she or Joe Daggart spoke, when they had been talking some other language to each other, but of course it was necessary, if she was to talk to them. Joe, she noted, could speak French. Her disadvantage strengthened her resolve to get to work on languages.

In general, everyone was nice, though there were one

15

or two moments that surprised, even daunted. 'Isn't it awful, so much smoking?' she had said at one point in a low voice to Joe. 'Why aren't they all dead?'

'It's typical French bravado. Since Americans think it's bad for you, the French have to show us what sissies we are.' He spoke loudly enough that all could hear, and looked around him combatively.

A nearby woman took him up. 'French cigarettes don't cause cancer, you know. Cancer is caused by the additives put there by the American tobacco companies. This is well known, only of course the tobacco companies don't allow this fact to be published in the United States.'

'Really?' Amy wondered, thinking that it could even be true.

The speaker was a glittering woman with dark auburn hair, wearing high heels with her narrow evening pants, and she introduced herself as Marie-France Chatigny-Dové. This conversation led directly to another faux pas on Amy's part.

'I think you are quite right, you two, to come in here as if nothing had happened. Of course it isn't your fault,' said Madame Chatigny-Dové presently.

Amy didn't understand what she was talking about, and her blankness must have shown. 'The perfidy of American tobacco companies?'

'American planes yet again dropping things willy-nilly, not caring who might die on the ground,' explained another woman, in a mid-European accent. 'Quite an irony that one of the people buried in the snow actually was an American. I'm sure your pilots didn't think of that beforehand.'

'The avalanche,' said someone else by way of explanation, seeing Amy's baffled expression. Amy, somehow thinking they were joking, laughed good-naturedly. Her laughter produced an array of astonished expressions on every nearby face. Americans laughing at how they have killed innocent skiers! Yet again, they might have added, for no one had forgotten an Italian incident of some years before. The red-haired woman turned and hurried over to Baron Otto, as if appalled to be in the presence of someone as callous as Amy.

'*Mon Dieu,*' other people said. Amy quickly understood her gaffe; these people seriously believed U.S. airplanes had set off an avalanche.

'It can't be true,' she protested. 'No one who knows anything about physics could believe … I don't believe it.' It occurred to her that loud noises were routinely used to set off avalanches.

'There have never been avalanches this early in the season. How else can you explain it?'

'I saw them myself, saw the cornice tremble just after they came over.'

'It can't be true,' Amy insisted, but people had moved on, turned away, withdrawn. She found that her heart was pounding irrationally. Why had she so stupidly laughed?

'If we live over here long enough, finally we come to appreciate other Americans,' said Joe Daggart at her elbow. 'Our jokes, shared status of pariah.'

She turned to him gratefully, but what might have been a promising and instructive conversation was soon interrupted or augmented by the intrusion of another man, who now languidly strolled up to them. She had seen him in the lobby and guessed correctly from his height, purplish cheeks, and shock of pinkish-white hair that he was British.

'Robin Crumley,' he said. 'I couldn't help but overhear you speaking American. You know, divided from us by a common language.'

She tried to guess his age – late forties or even fifty. He wore a sort of sagging pinstripe suit, and had a high, slightly quavery voice. He had said he was a poet, or perhaps he had said 'the poet,' but it was hard to imagine him saying his poems in that voice. Crumley dismissed the unpleasant little moment that had just passed. 'Pay no attention to them, my dear. For all his vaunted rationality, the Frenchman is a compendium of received opinions, unlikely to think for himself.' Amy smiled gratefully at this assurance. 'I know the Venns,' he added. 'Him, slightly, a terrible business. He is an Englishman.'

'Oh?' said Amy. She had not heard of the Venns.

'Quite surprised to see them here. I'm travelling with the Mawleskys. Prince de Mawlesky. Over there. Did you meet them?' He nodded discreetly toward a small couple standing at the drinks table, each of the pair with shining dyed black hair. Amy hadn't met them, but they had been pointed out – people had not failed to mention the hotel's small store of princes and barons. They had for Amy a sort of stagy unreality, making her think of *Masterpiece Theatre*. But of course these people weren't actors, they actually existed. Somehow there was a warming satisfaction to being in the same place as titled people, the better to verify the existence of European history, the reality of alternative social structures, the arbitrariness of being an American at all, when but for the discontent of some ancestor you might have been speaking French this minute, or Romanian or Dutch.

She herself might have been speaking Dutch; some of her ancestors were Dutch, back in the time of Peter Stuyvesant, though who knew what had been mixed in since. Her family had no tradition of remembering Europe at all, but in her Palo Alto set, European ancestors were somewhat unfashionable, and the idea of finding your European roots had been attacked as incorrect Euro-centricity, and worship of a passé civilization of wicked colonialists; but she was interested in finding out about them. She hoped to combat the national failing of being too uninterested in history, though part of her agreed – why dwell on history when it couldn't change anything?

It would be interesting to meet a prince, she decided, but what would you say to him?

'Where did you ski today?' she asked Mr Crumley.

'Ski? *Moi?* I don't ski, dear, but I have a taste for the snow, a feeling for the magic mountain, for the health-giving properties of mountain air.'

She wondered if he were ill. The idea cast him in a romantic light, a poet in the Alps for his health. He looked quite sound, if elderly. She wondered if he drank, which she had observed all English people to do quite a bit, at least the ones who came to Palo Alto. Robin Crumley swooshed two champagnes off a passing waiter's tray and handed one to her.

'And you, a Yank obviously, what brings you here?'

'Well – the skiing.'

'How tiresome, it means you'll be away all day and

you won't have lunch with me. However, some night you must join the Mawleskys and me for dinner. So hard about the Venns. Still, they are alive, if barely, and that's something. Of course, heaven knows for how long. Buried alive, always a fate for which I have had a particular dread. Skiing is for fools, really.'

3

Kip Canby, another of the guests, also American, an attractive, open-faced boy of fourteen, had not been paying attention to the snow or sky. He felt himself in a spot, having to deal with his nephew Harry, a baby aged eighteen months, while Harry's mother and father were skiing. Kip had no skills as a baby-sitter. He was thinking a nice hotel like the Croix St Bernard should have some toys, a playpen, whatever would be needed for a kid, but there was nothing. Of course, he hadn't asked.

The others had not come in yet. He'd volunteered to baby-sit because he was conscious of his brother-in-law Adrian's generosity bringing him along on this trip. Now, four o'clock, Adrian and Kerry weren't back, and little Harry was crying and bored. Kip bobbled him around on his knee and said things like 'Now, now, buddy,' and 'This is the way the farmer rides' to no avail. Eventually he put on his Walkman and ignored Harry's whines, but as the afternoon dragged along, he was obliged to address the matter of a bottle for Harry and some cereal for Harry, and eventually, changing Harry. Ick.

At four forty-five, Adrian and Kerry still hadn't come back. Kerry was his sister, Adrian her elderly husband, surprisingly spry for someone his age – he was still on the slopes, and evidently had fathered Harry. Kip found Adrian self-involved and demanding, like many old persons, but Adrian was nice to him, and Kip was sensible of that.

Kip's own room, damp from the shower steam, now smelled like dirty Pampers and talcum powder. Adrian and Kerry had a suite for themselves and the baby, but Kip had felt uncomfortable there, their stuff all around, and had thought Harry could crawl around in his room while he read or something. He called their room yet again. He had no special apprehensions, was puzzled more than worried. As the light fell outside the window, and the snowdrifts turned a gray-blue, his room darkened.

Later he put on his Walkman again and took Harry out into the corridors. Harry had only recently learned to walk, and occasionally doddered into the walls or sat down with a plop, so that the back of his coverall was sopping from where the carpets were wet with the snow off people's shoes and boots. Kip found it hard to walk as slowly as Harry. People smiled at this nice boy Kip, for being in charge of a little tot.

They dawdled up and down the green-carpeted corridors of the lobby floor. Harry raced, fell, giggled with mad baby merriment. Outside the cardroom, Kip saw that Christian Jaffe, the chef's son, who managed the front desk, was following them, tentatively, wearing a grave expression, the expression of an adult who was facing the need to discipline you. He saw that Christian Jaffe was probably only a little older than he, maybe nineteen. Behind Christian was one of the daughters, the plain one, hands clasped at her waist. Kip knew something was wrong, and that it involved him and Harry. He picked up Harry and waited.

'Monsieur Canby, there has been some bad news,' Christian said. 'I suggest we go upstairs. Come up to the office.'

Kip obeyed, not asking what the bad news was, not wanting to hear it yet. He had a crawl of apprehension in his stomach. It must have to do with Kerry and Adrian. The daughter reached out her arms to take Harry, and without words they moved up the stairs, past the pool table and coffee lounge, into the small room behind the front desk. The daughter saw Kip installed in a chair, then left, carrying Harry.

'This is very bad news,' Christian said. He sat down and faced Kip. 'Mr and Mrs Venn have been taken in an avalanche. We were just telephoned.'

'Taken?'

'Swept away. Excuse me, my English.'

Kip heard this without grasping it. Taken or swept? 'But I just saw them. They were going to have lunch, they were just there on La Grange,' a simple run down to a cluster of houses at the bottom of the western slopes. Well, a couple of hours ago.

We never know where an avalanche or other act of God might capriciously, or purposefully, strike us, said Christian Jaffe's look.

'Are they dead? Is that what you're saying?'

'No, no!' cried Jaffe, happy to be able to adjust the bad news upward. 'They are still alive, thanks, God, but their condition is not so good. A helicopter is coming to take them to the hospital in Moutiers. Has done so.'

Now Kip felt his face getting red with relief, Kerry not dead. He realized that he'd been expecting bad news all afternoon, dread resonating with the distant echo of dynamite along the snowy ridges. But broken legs had been more in his mind. 'Where?' he asked, as if it mattered.

'They didn't explain. They found them a few hours ago, but we weren't notified because the rescuers had no idea what hotel they were staying in. They – we always advise avalanche detection devices when people are skiing *hors piste,* but – but they weren't skiing *hors piste*, they were quite low down, I only heard that they weren't *hors piste*.' A quaver of concern suggested anxiety about the liability issues.

'But will they be okay?'

'They – I gather the condition of Monsieur Venn is – grave. They were buried in snow for an unknown length of time, many minutes, an hour.'

Kip's eyes stung. This was bad. He didn't know how to feel or react. He felt the weirdness of Adrian and Kerry buried like corpses in the snow. Was it really them? Should he go and look at them? His stomach turned – he bet that they wanted him to identify Adrian and Kerry. He sat, jammed with thoughts and amazement. At least Kerry wasn't dead.

'I guess I should go to the hospital,' he said finally. 'If that's where they are.'

'Yes, I thought you would want that. We'll try to make it down to Moutiers. My sister will look after the child.' Christian, evidently having ready a recitation of what they were prepared to do to help, some lesson learned in hotel school about service, concern, humanity.

In the car, Kip asked Christian Jaffe over and over to tell him the story, exploring the phrases for additional information, but Jaffe knew no more than had been told. Dug out of the snow, Adrian more dead, Kerry more alive, some delay in notifying the hotel because at first there had been no way of telling where they were staying.

'But they found a ski to go on, with the rental number, only one ski, but they could trace it.'

The hospital was small, a nineteenth-century building that might have been a school, or one of the sanitoria where the tuberculous came in the old days. A couple of people sat in the hallway on folding chairs. On the wall a large three-dimensional map of the region. At the far end of the corridor, through an open door, Kip could see lights and hear electronic beeps, intensive care noises familiar from television and from when their mother had died.

With Christian Jaffe, he approached and paused in the doorway. A figure nearest them, mounded in wraps, could be Kerry. Another machine sighed in the corner under another mound of dark blankets. They entered. There were no doctors, just a couple of nurses pottering with the tubes and watching the monitors. It seemed the consultations were over, the measures implemented, the accident victims were now absorbed into the routine of the nighttime shift. No one stopped them coming closer.

The nearer figure was Kerry. Kip stared and stared at her closed eyes as if to warm them awake with his mounting hot panic. He felt some obstacle to grasping this, a thick, shocked feeling. He could not believe her eyes wouldn't open, conspiratorially, when she realized it was him looking down at her. But she was like a stone, machines wheezing around her. The other mound must be Adrian.

Maybe he shouldn't look at her. People hate it when you look at them asleep. There were several nurses, coming in and out, looking at him, but no doctor talked to him. Kip wondered what he should do, perhaps sit there beside her into the night? But the nurse urged him out after only a few moments.

Christian Jaffe, smoking in the corridor, pulled up his collar, and with a motion of his head meant to include Kip, moved toward the exit at the end. He looked anxious to start back. 'The late seating will be beginning, I ought to be there,' he said. 'The guests will have heard by now of the accident.' Such news introduced collective excitement and anxiety, with the resulting increase in food-related complaints, and wines sent back, and general querulousness.

Kip wondered where the doctor was, and why no one had talked to him, the brother. He looked around for the doctor or someone to talk to. He didn't speak French.

'She's not going to die or anything?' he asked Christian Jaffe. 'Could you ask how she is?'

Jaffe spoke to the nurse just coming out. '*Non, non,*' the woman said. Kip understood that much, though not the rest.

'She says she is in a stable coma, but she is still very cold.' This sounded contradictory to Kip, but what did he know? He guessed she meant Kerry was not going to die and that there was no point in sitting there. A doctor stepped into the hall and shook hands with Jaffe. Turning to Kip, he said in English, 'Monsieur Venn is not good.

His brain shows very little activity. But he is very cold, and so it is too soon to say. Madame Venn is much younger, and also was the first to be rescued, and there we have more hope.'

Kip's stomach unknotted with relief. Kerry okay. He didn't really care about Adrian. Christian Jaffe spoke again to the doctor.

'Madame Venn is your sister?' the doctor asked.

'Yes.'

'Then you perhaps know who will be the appropriate person to make the decision – uh – decisions – in the case of Monsieur Venn? A member of his direct family?' Kip had no idea, and it only came to him later in the car what the Decision might be. But Kerry would get better and be able to make the Decision for herself.

In the car, the questions in Kip's mind, as numerous as the snowflakes that hurled themselves against the windshield, almost cancelled themselves out, leaving an anxious blankness, a passive resignation as cold as a field of snow. Kip saw that the person in charge was him, Kip, there was no one else, but that didn't mean he knew what to do. With their parents dead, he and Kerry only had one relative, an uncle in Barstow, California. She also had Adrian and Harry, but he, Kip, only had Kerry, though now he had responsibility for Harry, who would probably cry all night. What would they do? He looked at Christian Jaffe, grimly driving up the narrow winding road against the increasing snowfall and the dark, and he knew he would have to decide himself what to do.

Presently Jaffe spoke: If there were people who should be notified, if they needed to be present, the hotel could accommodate them, or arrange it. 'Their own doctors, perhaps, or their lawyer.' But of course Kip didn't know who those functionaries might be. Christian Jaffe suggested he look through Adrian's papers. Kip said he would; but he knew he would feel funny about it.

4

Maida Vale, London, W9. A pleasant first-floor flat in a large Regency house with white columns in front, over-looking an oval garden common to the rear. Large comfortable chairs in loose beige covers, the sofa faintly tea-stained on the arms, magazines and books stacked around in disorderly but readerly fashion, a small bronze sculpture, the potted plants of ornamental pepper and African violet neat in the window, a stereo, a BBC voice announcing the shipping forecasts, an indolent spotted cat, a slight rattling of the panes as the weather worsened. An English scene of mingled elegance and penury.

Cruciferous cooking smells. Posy and Rupert are having dinner with their mother Pamela, as they try to do every so often since Pam has been alone, not that she demands it, she is plenty busy. Gammon, sprouts, cauliflower, and mash, the smelliest dinner in Pam's repertory, theirs by request as it took them firmly and comfortably back to childhood, before the family trouble. They always asked for it, there being nowhere in London, now so foody, where you could get such nursery dishes. Pamela herself was foody and cooked out of Prue Leith and the *River Café Cookbook*, but in their childhood had only known how to boil things, and had had ideas about what was appropriate for children.

Posy Venn was a large, beautiful young woman of

twenty-two with high color, a cascade of shining, unruly chestnut hair, English skin and ankles, and the air of slightly heartless confidence that goes with having been good at games, school, driving, amateur theatricals, her summer job as credit manager for a chain of boutiques, and everything else she had turned her hand to. Rupert, her brother, referred to himself as an ordinary mortal next to Posy. To others, they seemed very much a pair, both handsome, ironic, ambitious. Rupert worked in the City, not enthusiastically, and was the elder of the two by three years.

Posy, although the younger, had moved into a flat with two other girls. Rupert, however, still lived at home. Though he planned to move out soon, inertia and the distraction of his new job had delayed this. Having him at home was all right with Pam as a temporary measure, though she had begun slightly to resent that her new freedom, though unasked for, was impinged upon by maternal duties now that she was in a position to start life anew.

This was not a secret but more the source of jocular remarks: 'Rupe, at least mow the garden lawn,' or 'Earn your keep, boy, and take this out to the bin.' Luckily, Pam and Rupert got along, as Rupert was equanimity itself, always believed by his mother to be hiding depths of turmoil but also artistic talent. He wrote delightfully, was rather good at the piano, and appeared to have no ambitions at all. After university he had taken a business course, suggested and paid for by Adrian, and was now installed with a midrank-sounding title at Wigget's as a bond salesman. Unfortunately for him, he was rather good at this, so that bond selling became part of his family's definition of him. He had a wide circle of friends, no particular girlfriend, and was everybody's extra man, which seemed to suit him.

They brought their vodka tonics to the table, which was set in the corner of the living room, while Pam finished in the kitchen. They heard the phone ring, heard her high, clear voice, scales of agitated tones punctuated by exclamation, murmurs in a descending register. These notes, too, had their reverberations in childhood memories. They exchanged sympathetic glances; their mother was excitable. She came in. Her eyes were bright with an unreadable expression. It was the moist look she had worn when they were little and had a surprise or big news for them.

She sat down, touched her glass but didn't lift it, shook her hair (she had the English prematurely white hair worn shoulder-length to emphasize the freshness of her skin). They saw that she was not calm.

'Your father. It seems he's been killed, or practically,' she said in a stifled, overcome voice. Rupert and Posy stared, too shocked to comment, maybe not believing her. 'In hospital in France, but not expected ... not expected ...' Her voice caught.

She stopped, sipped a little of her drink, and tightened her face, the fate of Adrian Venn being nothing to her now, officially. She briskly repeated what she had been told. An avalanche in the French Alps. He had been buried alive, and pulled out almost dead. His new wife had perhaps been with him – the person calling hadn't said. Huge avalanches. They were still rescuing people.

She looked out at the dark garden. It was an hour later in France, they couldn't still be digging.

'My God,' Rupert said, hearing the banality of this simple exclamation, but what else was there to say? He contemplated the finality and the more than poetic justice, the malign retributive nature of fate. He could see that Posy, too, was thinking of the horror of their father buried alive in an icy grave. Their father was nothing if not fully alive, vital, irascible, unpredictable in this as in everything that had come before.

Posy sniffled, feeling she ought to cry. 'Who was it that called?' she wondered.

'Someone – Alpine rescue people, I suppose. Spoke English.'

'How did they know about us?' Posy insisted. Practical Posy, Adrian had always called her. A sob caught in her sternum.

'I don't know,' Pamela said. 'Someone asked if I were Madame Venn.' She was not, but had been.

'Well!' she went on in a moment, against the silence of her stunned children. 'Do you feel like eating? We might as well eat. We can talk. You'll have to go over immediately, you know. Are you all right?'

Posy felt tears come even with the rise of an inner reservation. Was she all right? She had not got over her anger at her father. She glanced at cool Rupert, who also looked rather blinky and hot eyed. All three had mixed feelings about Adrian Venn, but none extended to wishing him dead, especially in a horrible way. It was as hard to believe as any accident, or harder, their slightly grotesque elderly parent lost in an avalanche, the stuff of anecdote.

They had heard he was going skiing with his young wife and their baby. It had provoked their bitter mirth. Now they sat in somber amazement. All were thinking of Father's beautiful château, which housed his press and publishing business, and the vineyard – *vignoble* – the whole side of their lives that took place in France. They talked of how they had loved the summers in Saint Grond the whole time they were growing up, and thought, but didn't mention, how they always ignored Father's unseemly capers with the college girls who came to pick the grapes – one of them, one year, Kerry Canby, from Eugene, Oregon. 'In those days when we thought of France, it meant summer and life,' cried Posy.

'And now, it appears, it is to mean winter and death,' Rupert said. They thought about this harsh formulation. Soon Posy went off to her flat to pack her suitcase. Rupert sat with his mother a few moments longer before going upstairs to do the same.

5

There was very good food at the Croix St Bernard. Cooking lessons were given on snowed-in days and in summer by the ambitious chef Monsieur André Jaffe, and meals were elaborately served by local young people training as high-class waiters, in tailcoats and jackets handed down from one generation of *stagiaire*s to the next with the minimum of alteration, which gave them a look of being ill at ease in their clothes.

Despite the unusual day, vibrant with crisis and the distant booms of TNT, these waiters were now beginning the preparations for dinner, polishing glasses and placing the cheeses, still in their wrappings, on the cart, and the guests began to move into the dining room. By now, all had heard the rumor that one of their number had been caught in the stirring avalanches of the afternoon, had listened with interest to the versions that swept through the lobby during cocktails. In the bar, others, fascinated, watched on the overhead TV set near the bar the televised rescue efforts in Méribel, the images strangely brighter than the actuality of the dark sky outside.

'Since skiing is not ever without drama, this catastrophe seems to me only a little more sobering than the concussions, fractures, and plastered sprains that people regularly turn up with,' Robin Crumley was remarking to the *princesse* as they passed to their table. Of people staying there for any length of time, some would eventually appear in the dining room in plaster casts and on crutches, to the surreptitious pitying and slightly triumphant glances of those still intact. 'I notice that nothing impedes them from the delicious food,' he added.

In the dining room, a process of elimination confirmed what people had heard, that it was Mr and Mrs Venn, he a British publisher, who had been overtaken on a slope normally considered quite safe, the snow possibly dislodged by airplane noises. They had not at all been *hors piste*, they were returning for the day and been struck by an unexpected small slide that had carried them into the well-marked depression known as Hilary's Hole, named after an unfortunate Englishwoman who had been lost there and dramatically rescued some years before. Though as a single traveller she was placed at a table alone, Amy Hawkins gleaned all these details from Joe Daggart as they walked in, from the hovering waiters, from the walls, as it were – and felt natural, human concern.

Venn, a man in his seventies, was near death. The much younger wife, in a coma, was also still alive, and the two had been helicoptered to Moutiers. The young man at that table over there, with the baby, was one of their party, but evidently had not been skiing with them, luckily for him. The waiters hovered anxiously around him, set up the high chair, warmed a bottle for the baby. The boy sat in a trance, in shock, apparently. A sturdy-looking youth of fourteen or fifteen, pleasant face – maybe a relative, maybe the old man's son by another marriage? He wore the somewhat scruffy sport coat and used-looking tie of a boy who went to a boarding school somewhere.

A profile emerged of the victim, for he was a relatively well-known figure, flamboyant for a publisher, and well off, perhaps rich, several times married. An Englishman who had founded, in the Luberon, the arty press Icarus, which had made its name at first, in the nineteen-fifties, by printing works not allowed in England, published by Maurice Girodias at the Olympia Press in Paris; later by introducing remarkable facsimiles of famous rare editions of Blake or Dalí or Breton or even Gutenberg.

The victim was located by means of a glove that had floated on top of the crushing snow mass. He was not carrying his wallet, but his Barclay card was in the zipped pocket of his parka, and the twenty-four-hour help number was able to assist with details of his identity and give his rescuers an address in England, and this was the reason relatives in England had heard about it first and were already on their way. Barclay had not offered a way of finding which hotel he was staying in here in Valméri. Luckily, the skis, only one of which was found, were marked with the name of Jean Noir, a ski shop he had rented his equipment from. The trouble was, many hotels in the area used the services of this agency, so it had taken some time for the shop to track down the renter . . .

Yes, it was through the magic of the computer that relatives somewhere else heard first of the catastrophe that had befallen Venn.

It was known there were older children, other wives. What a tragedy for them all. How unwise for a man of that age to be out skiing!

There were other details, repeated from one party to

another around the room. 'His face was covered with an ice carapace formed from his breath freezing; his breath had suffocated him.'

'His hands were extended before him, as the sinners of Pompeii had tried to avert the fiery ash, or perhaps he had tried to claw against the filling trough of snow the force had tumbled him into.'

'Beneath the icy mask his face had the congealed resignation of a mummy.'

Kip took Harry up to Kerry and Adrian's room, where the crib was, and stuffed his little limbs into some sort of too-small pajamas with feet. He didn't know if Harry was too young for a story. He started to tell him 'The Three Bears,' but Harry wanted to climb down off his knee and wouldn't listen, and began to run around. Kip plunked him into the crib, where he cried for a little while, without conviction, and fell asleep sucking his thumb. Kip supposed turning on the television would wake him up, so he sat there in semidarkness awhile in silence. But he didn't like sitting there with his thoughts of Adrian and Kerry, remembering the horrible cauls of tube and mask over them. With a sense of life boiling downstairs, or ebbing in the hospital, when he thought it was safe, he tiptoed out and down to the comfortable stone-walled lounge, one floor below the lobby.

Here in the center of the room stood a circular bar, from which waiters filled their trays, and around the perimeter, banquettes and low coffee tables invited the guests to loll or mingle. The walls were still festooned with pine branches from Christmas. It was here people stood around after dinner with their coffees, moving on to brandies, and beyond to whiskey sodas, and a small combo of musicians or a pianist played cocktail tunes and café oldies.

Kip felt the friendly, pitying smiles. 'Terrible thing,' a man called out as he went by. 'Reinhardt Kraus from Bremen,' said another man, sunburned and bald, standing near him. 'My wife, Berthilde. Terrible thing.'

Everyone wanted to know what had happened, even though they seemed to know already, and when Kip began to tell what he knew, others drew nearer. 'Still in the hospital. They have to thaw them out very slowly. My sister is still unconscious but she might be all right. My brother-in-law is not doing too well . . .'

It was comforting but embarrassing to feel their interest. Maybe it was only curiosity, but it seemed like kindness that animated the smiles. It was if he himself had done some big heroic deal. Mr Kraus asked him if he'd like a beer, and he said yes. But when it came he didn't drink it, he remained standing near the fireplace, its warmth like the emanations from the people in the room. Their languages rose around him unintelligibly. Though they spoke English to him, left to themselves they spoke German, or French, or Slavic languages he'd never heard before. It was a babel of sympathy and concern. Sometimes English leapt to his ears from among the murmurs and formed phrases – still in a coma, unconscionable neglect by the piste keepers and ski patrol. He had the sudden thought that the hospital couldn't call him if anything happened – could they? Did they know where he was? Who he was?

Christian Jaffe was coming toward him, so Kip asked him these questions.

'They know you are here. We are all in communication,' Jaffe said. 'Members of Mr Venn's family are on the way.'

With an air of authority, Jaffe answered the questions of the guests who crowded around him. Kip had known that Adrian had other children beside Harry, that Adrian had been married before, but he didn't know to whom. He felt sort of relieved to think others would be coming to back him up, and to look in their turn at the cold, moribund figures. He wouldn't be alone.

But his head was spinning with new problems, that he'd have to sleep in Kerry's room tonight or else bring Harry down to his, which would mean transporting all that baby gear. With this, it was as if he had pulled out the one thought that had held back the barrelful of other worrying thoughts, so that the other thoughts now came rushing out – about Harry's clothes and how to pay the chambermaid if he could get her to help tomorrow, could he put it on the hotel bill, how many days would Kerry be in the hospital? Beneath all these thoughts was the main fear about Kerry, and, of course, Adrian, two immobile forms encircled by gurgling tubes and an eerie blue light in a strange Alpine hospital in a land where he could not speak to anybody.

So he was really relieved when the next person who spoke to him was the pretty blond woman with long braided hair he had seen in the dining room sitting by herself. That had seemed funny to him. Mostly when people sat alone, they read a book or something, but she just sat

39

in a sort of calm glow he had liked, compelling attention. Other people looked at her too. He thought she might be a foreign person, but now when she spoke, her voice was reassuringly American.

'Hi, I'm Amy. I was just wondering if I could help you in any way.'

6

Amy Hawkins was in the process of changing her life. In a man it would be called a midlife crisis, but she was too young for that, and for her it was more an adventure, and a meditated series of philosophical decisions regarding which things were truly important, such as the meaning of it all, and the uses of charity. Till now, her main existential affair had been with the company she had helped start, and realizing this had opened her eyes to the fact that life was fleeting by with so much else left to do, and soon she would be thirty.

Like many such revisionist moods this feeling came on after a life change: she had found herself unemployed. The company had been sold, she got an enormous sum of money, and now had to find other things to do. Two of her colleagues – the techie geniuses Chris and Neal – had found roles in Dootel, the company that had bought them out, but her own contribution – administrative oversight, writing the speeches, suggesting policy – was not definable or even transferable. As their good idea had taken fire, it had also been helped along by organizational strategies garnered from her taking an MBA course and two years of law. Not to mention her initial investment of ten thousand dollars. The ideas, the creativity had been her friends', but the start-up money hers, the practical tactics hers too, and also occasional design suggestions, which they took more often than they realized. She had been important, she felt, her role becoming more and more responsible as the company grew.

Though in some ways she knew she had come miles since it all started, in other ways she felt she had gone nowhere. When it all began, she was still gawky, a nerd herself, impatient to come into beauty and power, but now that she had, it was too late to reverse her secret earnestness or lose the common sense that had kept her useful in the practical affairs of a modest start-up. It was her common sense that had prompted her prudently to cash out her stock and options at the top of the NASDAQ, at the moment their company was acquired by Dootel for almost a half billion dollars.

At first, a slight estrangement had existed between her and the other founding partners, Chris and Neal, over the size of her share of the buyout, which by contract was huge but they thought morally unwarranted. Things had been a little strained with Neal anyway since Amy and he had tried living together for a brief time, one of several serious affairs that had not worked out but had not distressed her much either. In the end, there was so much money that no one could complain. But Amy, unlike Chris and Neal, was faced with the lack of a new role. Of the two other partners, Ben had already invested in large tracts of land in Patagonia to set aside as a nature preserve, and Forrest had turned to extreme sports.

Amy had travelled some – to the Greek islands, for instance – but it had not taken her long to realize that such trips were mere diversions and made no permanent alterations in her character, at least that she could feel.

True, she now had an impression of, say, the difference between Ionic and Doric, but could have got the same from photos and books. She herself had not been changed, any more than by her several relationships with perfectly nice men who had not, somehow, touched her. She was embarrassed by her money, had not yet learned how to feel about it, and could not forget that *nouveau riche* was a term so dismissive that for English speakers it had been left in the original French, like terms for other harsh concepts – *coup de grâce*, or *savoir faire*.

Eventually, she supposed, she would learn to be rich, but for now she hoped to grow from a corporate drone into being a better, more aware human being, more creative at her work, a better woman in the area of domestic accomplishments she hadn't had time for but felt she would enjoy, skills like skiing she had always wanted to improve. She would pay more attention to her friends and relatives, develop more disciplined personal habits, and perhaps have a baby (big question mark).

She'd been accused of frivolity when she announced that before taking up a new job as director of her personal foundation, she planned to spend some time in Europe learning to cook and speak French. Frivolity was what she hoped for. She wasn't troubled by the shallowness of these pursuits; looked at one way, everything was shallow, and from another perspective everything had innate interest and the power to enlarge. For now she was in the perfect zone of receptivity. Above all, her resolutions concerned the acquisition of knowledge, or rather, culture, in its broadest sense, though she was under no illusion that she could do more than a crash course.

What had caused her sudden consciousness that she lacked a sense of the world was not entirely clear to her, but she dated her quest for self-improvement from a chance remark overheard in an antique shop. She'd been in Seattle, with a morning to kill before her plane, and was browsing in the old streets near the art museum. A part of town in transition – upscale book shops alongside pawnshops and gun dealers, English antiques, vendors of clocks and nautical instruments, local designers. In one shop, the owner was talking to someone else, Amy was listening, couldn't help overhearing.

'Why is this stuff so overvarnished like this, it's ruined,' said the woman who had come in a few minutes before. 'You have some nice English pieces here, but they're ruined.'

'That's how they like it around here. It's the dot-commers. They don't know anything, and they think it ought to be shiny. So we revarnish it.'

'That's horrible,' mourned the woman. 'Can't you explain it to people? Concepts of the original, concepts of restoration?'

'No one has taught them anything. If it weren't for Martha Stewart the whole culture would be down the drain. It's amazing the things they don't know. They don't know ironing, or how to set a table. Their mothers didn't teach them, their mothers worked. Their mothers didn't know!'

'They can afford people to teach them. Consultants, decorators.'

'They don't know what they don't know, so they don't think of asking.'

This was no instant epiphany for Amy, it had merely stimulated her to wonder who 'they' were – presumably people of her own age who had made money in the dot-com world, as she had herself. More tantalizing was the question of the knowledge they, or she, didn't have, the questions they didn't ask. In a way this didn't trouble her – it was obvious there was a lot of stuff she didn't know and questions she hadn't asked. She knew what she needed to know. But it was interesting to wonder what these two blue-haired women knew, or felt they knew, that she didn't. Things about antique furniture, yes, but their tone, and the reference to the housework guru Martha Stewart, implied a wider store of lore usually purveyed by mothers, equated with culture itself, endangered at that. And Amy didn't know any of it.

From then on, daily, the world brought her new evidence of her lack of culture, her ignorance and in-experience – and that of her colleagues, for sure. She thought they were worse than she because they didn't think of asking big questions. She felt in a way that it was her patriotic duty to refute by her own example the things people were always saying about Americans, that they were too self-absorbed and had no head for history, nor any culture to speak of.

It was this that had brought her to her idea about about promoting mutual aid, both the idea and the great book by that name. Prince Kropotkin's simple observation had always excited her, never mind the political implications. Their teacher, Miss Steinway, hadn't stressed them or per-haps hadn't detected the protosocialist ideas that would have alarmed the parents of the nice young ladies in her charge. Or maybe not. As the author of *Mutual Aid* was a prince, Prince P. Kropotkin, how subversive could he have been? Of course the idea of mutual aid was more complicated than just charity or simple cooperation. It implied a whole philosophy, a rooted behavior. The pioneers had shown it at barn raisings and sewing bees. (Prince Kropotkin had not mentioned these superb American examples that had allowed her forebears to conquer adversity and eventually everything else.)

And Amy had been raised to believe in giving something back, so ever since high school she had had in mind that she'd like someday to devote her personal resources – money, in particular – to furthering the work of mutual aid by making P. Kropotkin's writings better and more generally known. She thought something along the line of the Gideon's, a copy of his great work in every hotel room. This and other activities would be the focus of the foundation she had established and would run when she got back to California, when she was herself a better-rounded person.

Promoting mutual aid, like personal roundedness, seemed a manageable, definable goal, a worthwhile and virtuous goal, a goal she believed in, setting aside P. Kropotkin's totally ridiculous political philosophy, which, however, had probably been appropriate for his day and Russian nationality. She herself yielded to no one in her enthusiasm for the kind of American capitalism that had rewarded her brainy, creative friends and even herself for her useful but stolid role in their fortunes. America was the best country, hands down, but it didn't have everything, and nothing precluded your trying to

46

acquire some of the delightful features Europeans seemed to have built into their lives, like the long, long ski runs. You just didn't find these in Aspen.

'Tell me what happened,' she said efficiently to Kip. 'So far it's all rumor.'

'Number one, you'll need a baby-sitter,' she decided, when he had finished telling her about Kerry and Harry and Tamara, the cross chalet girl. Kip was disappointed she herself didn't offer to baby-sit, for she radiated competence, but even so his eyes stung with gratitude that there was another American who would know what to do. He could have cried, but he knew he was too old.

7

Amy had already had breakfasted and was putting on her ski clothes when the phone rang. It was her worldly and kindly advisor, Géraldine Chastine, the friend of her friend Pat's aunt, calling from Paris in a state of excitement. She had just read in the morning paper that Adrian Venn had been buried in an avalanche. Adrian Venn was someone Géraldine knew. Had Amy heard any details?

It had not crossed Géraldine Chastine's mind that anyone she knew could be caught in an avalanche, even less that the avalanches would change the life of her daughter Victoire. But a shock lay in store for her when she turned on the TV news that morning. Of several people engulfed in the Alpine catastrophes, Adrian Venn was famous enough to be mentioned by name as a headline: 'Noted English Publisher Among Victims in Alpine Slide.' She felt a pulsation of some note of satisfaction.

She was surprised at her own reaction. Now she found that as she stared at the TV and searched on other channels for more details, she was breathing shallowly, rapidly, like an animal, her cheeks scalding. The memory of her brief time with Adrian Venn was suddenly resurrected with the same visceral distress he had caused her then. Venn had provided her with her sole experience of being hated, of being mistreated, of being exposed to sarcasm and derision, of being bruised and slapped, all this thirty years ago but as present to her now as it had been then, though it had lain hidden for all the time in between. She could once more hear his English voice with its sneering imitation of her accent, uttering cruel remarks about her housekeeping, personal things.

She was glad her husband, Eric, was at the office, he would be bound to notice how shocked she was, not at the death but at being pulled into this state by something she had long since thought behind her. It had been inside her all this time, probably poisoning her and bringing on cancer, as evil emotions were known to do. Her life was in peril, in a way, unless she could evict these feelings. She struggled to master them at once.

The unforgettable thing was that she, her person, had disgusted him. Once he had asked her to bathe, though she had just bathed. 'All women smell horribly,' he had said once. 'Not just you. You haven't noticed? Females. Men just overlook it, they have to.' Other smells had upset him too – ineffable intrusions of the material world on his consciousness otherwise focused on words, beauty, drawings, or books. Even then he had been specially fascinated by calligraphy, and poems in shape of words, and the strange forms of exotic alphabets.

She had never told anybody about this shame, and had only borne it for a few months. Being asked to bathe was something she had never forgiven, it pressed on her breast even now. And because of this passage in her life, she had always felt herself to have had a shameful past, had felt this shadow of distance between her and other women of her age and class and background. No, it wasn't Victoire's birth that had given her this shame that drove her even now, it was that she had had the bad judgment to have taken up with Adrian Venn.

Now, though she had not known herself to be a vengeful person, she found herself thinking, Good: if he dies, Vee will have some money.

Because her father had been a diplomat in America, Géraldine had gone to college there, and had now developed a sort of professional specialty, acting as a personal organizer and counselor for the many American women who came to Paris wishing to change their lives, learn to cook, acquire French, or simply meet Frenchmen, after unpleasant and/or lucrative divorces back home. There were a lot of these, along with the odd widow, and because all of them needed to find Parisian gyms, personal trainers, language teachers, and cookery schools, Géraldine had made a good thing out of it. She was now well known in both the French and the American communities in Paris, and trusted.

At first she had advised people from simple good nature – she had good connections and liked being of help. Because of this, her classmates at Wellesley had begun to call on her, or direct their friends to call on her, with increasing frequency. She had always been glad to help; she understood the personal dissatisfactions and the specifically Paris-based projections of hopes for a new life that brought a certain number of Americans to Paris each year to reinvent themselves. When the calls had become too numerous for her to handle, gradually a fee structure had evolved. It had shocked some of them a little, at first, to be asked to pay for friendly advice from a friend of a friend, but they came to see it as reasonable.

As her business expanded, Géraldine brought in some American women living in Paris to help her. She knew Americans who were going away leaving apartments to rent, knew the directors of cooking schools, knew interior decorators of both nationalities, penniless teachers of French, and so on. By now she had a little Mafia of American women who had shops, or did personal shopping, or interior decoration, or taught Pilates System exercises to the newer arrivals, who were always so relieved to be able to avoid speaking French. This activity kept her busy and surrounded by friends. Putting people together with people they should meet suited Géraldine's motherly and worldly nature, and made a little money, though Eric was well off, was an executive at L'Oréal, a cosmetics firm.

Géraldine had often sent people to Monsieur Jaffe's cooking school at the Hôtel Croix St Bernard in the summers − for instance, very recently she had sent another American woman there for the skiing who had had a wonderful time. So she knew the place would be perfect for Amy. She had understood something about Amy's situation from her school friend, who on the telephone seemed a bit reserved about *l'Américaine* in a way that hinted at much: 'She's a girl who has done very, very well, and thinks she'd like to spend six months or so over there. She's apparently done so well ... I guess she thinks she's earned a little time off ...' Of course, neither of them really knew how well was well, or, more to the point, what the girl's taste was.

Even before meeting Amy, she had marshalled her troupe of decorators and real estate ladies to begin preparing Amy's apartment in Paris, for it was in the Paris phase of Amy's sojourn that Géraldine expected to do her the most good. First of all she had called her friend Tammy de Bretteville, who had a private real-estate consultation business serving other Americans, primarily on the Web. 'Be on the lookout for an apartment *de standing,* with a couple of bedrooms. An American friend is sending me a darling girl – at least she sounds darling, and she'll be needing something, I'm told she will want something *quite* nice.'

'Will she lease or buy? If we find something right away, Mr Albinoni would be free in March to do the kitchen,' Tammy said. 'I'll pencil in March.'

'Louis Which?' Wendi Le Vert, the interior designer, had wondered about the general emphasis of the decor.

'*Tous les Louis,* I would think,' said Géraldine, 'with contemporary accents.' When she finally met Amy, briefly, at the Aéroport Charles de Gaulle where Amy was to change planes for Geneva, though she thought her lovely looking, so dimpled and creamy-skinned, she also understood that Amy had no taste of any kind, and it was this she wanted to remedy. Amy interested her – the girl's unpretentiousness, evident intelligence, and somewhat unfilled mind, a remarkable tabula rasa ripe for European impressions and perhaps emotional experiences. Géraldine's clients were usually hoping for a sentimental adventure; but she had not detected in Amy the usual restless qualities that signalled such a need.

Géraldine knew that Adrian Venn had published Chef

Jaffe's cookbook in his glamorous series about French regional cookery, so she easily deduced that Venn had been staying at Chef Jaffe's hotel. Now, with the excuse that she desired to be reassured about Amy's health, given the catastrophes, she had rung Amy. Marvelling at the way Europeans all knew each other, Amy told Géraldine what she had heard, confirming that two of the guests, a Mr and Mrs Venn, had been caught in an avalanche and were in the hospital, an atmosphere of horrible gloom had swept the whole valley, and so on.

'Oh, *mon Dieu,*' Géraldine said, again and again.

Eventually, returning her attention to her charge Amy's own welfare, Géraldine asked about the après-ski action, for this inevitably interested single women in their life-changing modes. Was there anyone attractive or friendly? But Amy firmly dismissed her questions. Yes, there had been a cocktail party, there appeared to be some unattached men, but she was not at all interested in meeting people, certainly not men, that was the last thing she wanted.

'My current male friend is fourteen years old,' she said, and explained about the plight of the little brother, all alone, a teenaged boy for whom she planned to do what she could to help.

In Paris, later in the morning, the worldly and well-connected Géraldine heard more about the disaster from Baron Otto von Schteussel: in the rest of the Haute Savoie, the west slope of the village of Belregarde had lost four of its eight houses, though all the inhabitants, week-enders, had survived by not being there. Because of being on the train, the baron had not heard the most recent news of the fate of anyone staying at the Croix St Bernard, but he knew three permanent residents had died in luckless Pralong, four kilometers away – this was the slide that had been captured on Antenne Deux at the moment of its *déclenchement*, so that all of France had seen the eerily slow-motion grace with which the monster slab of snow detached from its lofty site and slid in one mass toward the unfortunate valley, in a sheet, like a pane of glass or building facade in a demolition scene, sending a giant plume of snow a half kilometer into the air, simulating the spray of some magnificent vessel.

'Nothing about the Venns? Monsieur Venn?' she asked.

'No, no, not when I left.'

Despite all the disruptions caused by the storms, the baron had succeeded in reaching Paris last night, and had come by appointment to Géraldine's for coffee and a real estate chat this morning. A large blond man, he had a cheerful, florid face and spoke good French with a British accent, no trace of the Germanic. He had earlier sent her his card with its string of seedy-sounding Austrian honorifics, Graf, Baron and whatnot – she didn't believe any of them, but they looked splendid on a business card. During his frequent business trips to Paris, Otto never failed to importune the Chastines on a certain real-estate matter; he worked for a multinational developer, and was constantly writing to them about a proposed luxury complex the corporation was hoping to build in Belregarde. Géraldine's husband Eric's family had a little chalet in that village, and now Otto had come to make another offer to buy it, in the hope that minds had changed since avalanches earlier in the week had swept into Belregarde itself.

Géraldine was naturally concerned about that, though she didn't ski and so had never cared about the place in winter – picturesque though some found it – stone chimneys chugging smoke over ice-dripping roofs and the straw and dogshit embedded in the ice of the paths, people wearing violent purple anoraks. She loved the mountains in summer, with the wildflower walks and climbing. The baron Otto's company had already bought up several chalets, including some that had been flattened in the avalanches of yesterday. He talked enthusiastically of the future. 'Of course you would keep the right to reserve one of the best deluxe mountain-view units in the new complex,' he was saying. The situation reminded Géraldine of movies she'd seen in America, westerns, when the little family that refused to move was to be swept away by the dam/railroad/mining development the villains were representing.

Baron Otto had accepted a second cup of coffee, which he now finished, and, mentioning another engagement, stood to take his leave. He hoped to see his several prospects this afternoon and head back to Valméri by the late TGV, removing the need for another hotel night in Paris. 'Naturally the local architectural style will be respected – none of the cement horrors you see at other stations. Allow me to leave the sketches with you.' The sketches showed pitched shake roofs, wooden balconies with fretwork decoration, symphonies of geraniums blooming from window boxes of the clustered condominiums. They would see each other in the mountains over Easter no doubt, they'd discuss all this again, hello to Eric. Otto's wife, Fennie, had sent her best wishes.

Baron Otto, experienced in sizing up clients and investors, had always pegged Géraldine perfectly, a well-groomed woman in her late fifties, early sixties, even at this hour in the morning dressed smartly for the day in stockings and winter beige suit, hair tinted reddish blond, glasses on a string. She obviously had a native business sense, but he was not sure what drove her or explained her somewhat tense manner, for her position was that of a comfortable bourgeoise. Today she seemed a little more agitated than usual, struggling to maintain a serene and courteous semblance of attention to his words, which he could see weren't playing. 'The avalanches have apparently spared us,' she pointed out. 'We weren't in the path at all.'

'The global warming is supposed to produce many more of them,' Otto warned.

'Not in my lifetime anyhow.' Géraldine didn't care about global warming. She had withdrawn her attention from politics before the advent of environmentalism and had not caught up with its mood.

'I believe you have a young American friend who is staying at the Croix St Bernard this week. Do you think she might like to buy a condominium in the Alps, or somewhere? Might it be within her ... budget?' Otto asked.

Though it was a part of Géraldine's character to bring buyers and sellers together, to facilitate, to explain people to each other, her indignation rose with her sense that he might try to influence her protégée Amy. She still had not heard where Amy's money came from, it was a mystery, for the girl had neither the manner of an heiress nor any palpable métier that could explain it. Probably she'd had a lucrative divorce, that was usually it. But whatever the size of Amy's fortune, Géraldine saw it as her duty to protect her from the sharks who were already encircling her. And, of course, to advise her about how a fortune should be spent.

'I believe I may have met her. She has a certain unfamiliarity with Alpine conditions,' Baron Otto went on.

'She seems quite eager to spend some time in Europe,' Géraldine agreed, and the baron's peony-bright face brightened even more. 'But I should tell you, I am already making arrangements for her in Paris. I do not think you need trouble about her.'

'Maybe she'd like to have both something in Paris and something in the mountains?' He was thinking that he had always found Madame Chastine, for a *française*, uncharacteristically frank about money, and he would appreciate information – in case he could be helpful to Miss Hawkins.

'Mademoiselle Hawkins will be better off with an apartment in Paris than a chalet in Valméri, Otto,' said Géraldine firmly, 'and I will thank you not to try to suggest otherwise.' She made herself clear.

When the baron had gone, she rushed to watch more of the morning television news, anxiously studying the pictures and waiting for the phone; but she didn't think that any of the sticks and rubble shown sticking out of snowdrifts could be theirs, and no one had telephoned from Belregarde with bad news. Not that she would have minded terribly, and there was insurance. There was nothing more about Adrian.

8

Géraldine had sometimes regretted that her daughter, Victoire (also called 'Vee' as in *vie*, 'life,' or as in 'victory'), alone among the children of people she knew, had taken the step of legal marriage. Mostly, marriage was out of fashion among French young people. Some were exploring the advantages of the quasi-marriage called PACS now being offered by the state, but, no, Vee had wanted marriage, white dress, assembled friends. Perhaps her bridegroom Emile had also wanted this, had liked a liaison with a solid bourgeois French family. His own had come to France only a month or two before his birth. They were Tunisian doctors, Christians who had been living in southern Senegal when warfare among local tribesmen had sent them fleeing to avoid massacre. He often had to recite this pedigree to avoid misunderstandings about his religion.

Géraldine worried constantly about Victoire; Victoire, on the other hand, thought of herself as a fortunate person. For one thing, she had recently got an apartment in one of a group of buildings designed as a social experiment under Mitterrand by a famous architect to show that public housing need not be grim: a verdant courtyard planted in box and willow, elegantly trimmed, big sunny windows, a secure gate and elevator code. Vee and Emile and their two children, Salome and Nike, had three comfortable rooms, plus kitchen and bath, or shower, rather, for there was no tub, well located off the boulevard Général Brunet near the Métro Bozaris. True, it was public housing, but many if not most of their friends from university lived in worse conditions. Architecture students were forever being found in the courtyard of the building, sketching and photographing this admirable place.

It was the sweetness of Vee's nature and temperament that made her feel lucky and thankful, even when the evidence was against it. There were moments when she herself questioned her luck, but she was unquestionably lucky about the apartment, and her children, less so about the omnipresent back pain, which the doctor felt would disappear in time, and mostly the problems with Emile. In general, Vee was too busy ever to feel low. Bilingual, she ran an English-speaking play group for bilingual toddlers and kids whose families wanted them to learn English, she played the flute in an ensemble, and was active in the parents' association of Salome's *école maternelle*.

Her love for her children and passion for her husband were her conscious life definitions, her project. Not that she was a deluded, self-sacrificing young woman, she told herself, not at all. You decided freely on the values that would motivate your life, and because you were doing as you pleased, you were free. She valued freedom, temperamentally and intellectually. It was *willingly* that she ran the play group, which also did keep the wolf from the door, and she had a government supplement from the social security, and occasionally was paid for a flute gig, so even the most consternated sighs from her parents didn't make her feel sorry for herself. In fact, she had a merry disposition, and graceful fair looks to go with it, like the dancing women on posters by Chéret.

The dashing Emile had more or less deserted Vee and the children, though they were not officially separated. He rarely dropped by. Well embarked on his career as a public, telegenic intellectual, a career that, however, didn't bring in much money, he was exploring connections to Islam despite his Christian upbringing – he and Victoire had been married in the church of St Roche – and had even recently been quoted as saying he was looking into the issue of four wives. He had made this pronouncement on TF 1, people told her, with his charming smile that said he didn't mean it. Sometimes, when he was home, he was irascible, and kept reminding Victoire that she was lucky he had not yet pronounced the words 'I divorce thee.' This tried Vee's cheerful nature but didn't surmount it. She knew he couldn't help saying dazzling, outrageous things, his mind hurtling along over steeple and minaret without descending to connection and explanation. His cleverness, and his dark curls, made him fascinating to most people. When she thought of him, her heart surged toward him, and when she thought of their lovemaking, her blood stirred as though a magnet passed across her skin.

Sometimes when he did drop by, it was during the day, when the children were at school, and he wanted a quick fuck. She was always happy for an hour or two afterward, and sang around the house. Such was the case today.

Emile was there when she had to leave the house to go pick up the children; he was dressed and drinking a cup of tea when Victoire's mother, Géraldine, called with the amazing news that Victoire's father was near death in an Alpine accident, meaning, apparently, not Eric Chastine but someone else altogether, someone Emile had never heard of. Emile waited till Victoire got home with the children to tell her the amazing news, a biological father he had never heard she had, near death.

Victoire didn't seem much interested or distressed.

'You never told me your mother had "been with" a man when she was not married,' Emile said, his note of self-parody striking her. She never knew whether he believed, or was mocking, some religious idea.

'Probably they were married,' she said, quite amazed at this reappearance of a father who had barely before been mentioned. 'It is not the kind of thing I could ask.'

'Your mother thinks you should go there while he is still alive, to say "farewell,"' said Emile, who always seemed to put words into quotation marks, to emphasize his scorn or dissent, or amused reservation. 'To say "adieu."'

'I've never seen him yet, why would I now?' said Vee. 'If Maman wanted me to meet him, why didn't she say so years ago?'

'He is your father, "apparently."'

'I'm completely indifferent – sorry for him, of course,' she added. 'An avalanche, how horrible. But I'm not a hypocrite to show up at someone's bedside at the end when I never went before.'

'To oblige your mother? It is she probably who would like things put to rest, made final. Like to think her daughter has "seen her father," that he has seen his beautiful child, that certain "memories renascent" . . .'

'Oh, *s'il vous plaît*, Emile,' laughed Vee, whom Emile always made laugh. 'You'll stay with the children, of course, while I dash down to the ski slopes.'

Emile frowned at this practical side of it. 'Your mother would stay with them.'

Géraldine had suggested to Emile on the telephone that Vee should go to say a last word to her father. Later, when Vee brought the children over for their regular Tuesday-afternoon visit and Géraldine had embraced the darlings, her mind having stayed on the news she had transmitted to Emile, the moribund state of Venn, she again broached the idea that Vee should meet this phantom parent while there was time.

'It's unthinkable, Maman. How could I feel an interest in someone who never saw me and had no interest in me, technically my father or not? He was never part of my life, and I'm not going to be part of his death. Think how hurt Papa would be. Eric – my real papa.'

Of course Vee had always known that Eric was not her biological father, but this had never been import-ant, so completely had Eric been a wonderful parent to Vee, Vee to him a devoted, bonded daughter, the two passing through all the appropriate and healthy stages of a daughter-father relation leading in time to Vee's appropriate transfer of love to her husband, etc. (Eric had been less pleased than Géraldine with Vee's choice of Emile Abboud as a husband. Géraldine could at least see his powerful charms.) Géraldine also understood that loyalty was big on Vee's list of virtues, these days especially because of her problems with Emile. Vee didn't discuss her marital problems with her mother, her pride wouldn't let her, but she clearly thought that loyalty was a virtue above all others and rewarded eventually from Above.

'You'll be sorry one day, not to have said goodbye. Not to have ever laid eyes on him,' Géraldine insisted. 'Eric doesn't mind. He thinks you should go. And the girls should meet their grandfather.'

'I hope all *my* illegitimate children will rally round my deathbed,' said Eric, coming into the room. He had been half listening to the conversation. But Vee didn't think this was funny. Her face assumed the expression of angelic blankness she always wore when her mind was resolved or resolving. She had the fair ringlets and wide blue eyes of *putti* in paintings, and the same manner of looking away from the central subject at something else outside the frame.

'Anyway, the children. And the play group, and I'm playing for a Rameau festival. And how could I be some-one called "Vee Venn," it sounds like an herbal tea. Anyway, I have no wish to torment myself with sadness at the deathbed of a perfect stranger. And aren't there real children? Think how they would feel with me intruding into their grief.'

'I think there are real children. They would be your half-brothers and sisters. The more reason you should meet them.' She could be talking about a stranger she had never met. Vee was struck, as she had been by other women her mother's age, at the detachment they seemed to feel from their own biological histories, as if they couldn't remember being in bed with vanished figures, couldn't remember giving birth.

'*Non, Maman, pourquoi?*' said Vee, in a definitive tone of voice. When Vee had gone, Géraldine telephoned Emile at his office – she didn't know where he was staying these days. Luckily, he was there. She was fond of Emile, they got along and understood each other. She urged him to go to Valméri and look into the situation, and he, with surprising graciousness, said he would.

9

When he woke on Tuesday, Kip remembered his dream. He had been dreaming of their parents, of a time in his childhood when they had scolded Kerry for something he had done. In the dream it was a red stain on a rug, like spilled wine, and he dreamed of his mother's face glaring at him as Dad said, 'All the same, Kerry, you should have watched.' He should have watched her – was that the message of the dream? Kip was a good athlete, was on the snowboarding team at his school, and longed some-day to compete in the Olympics, and so hadn't been poking along with Kerry and Adrian, at the stately pace they skied. Now he saw he should have stuck with them. He would have spotted the avalanche, and said 'Look out.' He pictured them standing frozen in terror as the beast rolled at them, himself urging them to safety.

When he opened his eyes, he had felt a moment of relief that the dream was not real, then a rush of sick dread when he remembered that the reality was worse. It was morning. Harry was not in his crib. Kip bolted from the sofa, but almost immediately heard noise in the bathroom, and rushed in there. The chambermaid, an Australian named Tamara, was holding Harry's bottom over the washbasin cleaning him, his fat little legs churning.

'Didn't you even hear him? He was shrieking up a storm,' she said. 'So I came in.'

'God, no, I didn't hear him.'

'Yeah, well, plain you're not his mum. Everyone else could.'

Tamara rather crossly helped him get Harry ready – diaper, little terry-cloth suit, little shoes you had to shove on his feet – and they went in to breakfast. He could see that it was going to be easier to deal with Harry at mealtimes than other times. Stuck in his high chair, with stuff to smoosh around on his plate, he was a cheery, cute baby, drawing smiles. No one spoke to Kip this morning about Kerry's state, but people looked at them as they had last night, with sympathy and admiration.

There ought to be a phone number he could call this morning, or some word from Christian Jaffe. The normalcy of things made Kip uneasy, dining room full of people in ski clothes ordering their coffee and piling their plates from the breakfast buffet. He filled his plate with ham and some yogurt, stuff both he and Harry could eat, and got two glasses of orange juice. He decided they would finish breakfast before trying to find out anything about Kerry. If she were worse, they would have told him, or wakened him in the night. But he couldn't shake a feeling of sick dread.

When they had spent as much time as possible over breakfast, Kip lifted Harry out of his high chair and they walked into the lobby. Kip was hoping to see his new friend Amy, perhaps with the baby-sitter she had suggested. Even from the dining room they could hear stout voices asking questions in English in the foyer in demanding tones. New bags were piled by the front desk. A tall, handsome couple stood by the sofa, evidently waiting for their room to be ready, and Christian Jaffe was coming toward Kip waving his hand toward these new people.

'Mr Canby, here are Monsieur and Mademoiselle Venn. This is Mr Canby, Mrs Venn's brother.'

Hearing their names, these Venns looked at Kip and especially at Harry. They mustered polite smiles, and the young man explained that they were Adrian Venn's children. The term seemed to exclude Harry.

'So nice to meet you,' they said vaguely, with reflex courtesy. 'Is that the baby?' asked the man. Kip felt a momentary hope that these people were here to help with Harry.

'Our little brother!' said the woman in a slightly acid tone. She was a bit scary, Kip thought, big, solidly beautiful, with scornful eyes. When Kip led Harry over to them, their unconscious first response was to shrink away, peering with distaste at the cute little child, symbol of Father's betrayal.

'I'm sorry, you are who, actually?' said the man to Kip.

'Kerry's brother.' Now Kip could see they were in a state of high agitation, not meaning to be rude. Posy's objections to some transaction with the desk rose and swirled around Christian Jaffe – why couldn't they get into their rooms? They had driven all night. They were still in shock from the sight of their father, down there in the terrible little hospital, no more than a corpse, how had it happened? Christian Jaffe murmured reassurances, rooms had been prepared or would be, all would be well.

'Do you know how my sister is this morning?' Kip

ventured to ask them, but the highly intimidating Posy didn't know, hadn't noticed her, hadn't been told.

Could she be dead? But they would know that, would have been told.

Posy looked theatrically around, saying with a wail, 'This is all so unbelievable. Unbelievable. Unbelievable.'

The Venns turned to their luggage – Christian Jaffe himself bore it away – apparently finished with Kip. In her room, Posy unpacked her valise and carefully put things in the drawers, like someone planning a long visit. At first she had thought they should be staying nearer the hospital, but now she was glad to be in this cosier ambiance, with an optimistic, smiling woman at the desk, and the sound downstairs of healthful stamping of snow off boots, the rattle of skis being donned outside, skiers returning joyfully to the slopes. They would get Father sorted out.

She was tired. They'd driven all night, taking turns at the wheel, having to change over to the wrong side of the road at Boulogne. French roads were so straight, the same defect as the French character, revealing a Gallic lack of imagination, a repellent literalness. She and Rupert had been quarreling over what was probably going to happen next. Father would or wouldn't be awake, he would or wouldn't be glad to see them, the new girl-wife would be there (of Posy's own age), and the famous and embarrassing baby. They touched on one especially delicate matter: If Father should die, would he have already changed his will to include the baby, or made it totally in the baby's favor and that of the new wife? But they were embarrassed talking about such things, and guiltily dropped the matter almost as soon as it came up.

They had gone directly to the hospital before coming to the hotel, so they already knew the reality, Father in a coma with no prospect of recognizing them, at least not very soon, and the teenaged boy the only person looking after the baby, and the girl-wife in a coma of her own. Posy saw it would be up to her and Rupert to decide what must be done, but she felt this as an imposition. She struggled against anger. Her father had had no compunctions about going off with the American bird and putting them all out of his life, and now he needed them back in it. Of course they would do the right thing.

Of Pamela's two children, Posy had been the more censorious about Father, the more rebellious, and the more irritating to him. Perhaps this made her sadder and more frightened now. She had never been able to please him, while he had completely approved of Rupert, for instance of his present job in the City selling bonds. 'A good thing to have a practical money person in the family,' he had said, expressing surprise that it was Rupert, and thereby conveying that he had expected it would be Posy who would have such a soulless, mercenary career. Rupert had read history and philosophy, and had seemed headed for a donnish life, tutoring or writing, except he was rather fond of parties and London life too. Pamela had been worried at one point that he might be gay, but Adrian had scoffed and said he himself had been just like Rupert at that age. All the same, they were relieved when Rupert for a time was seeing something of Henrietta Shaw and some other nice girls.

Now, they none of them quite understood what Rupert did, but it involved bonds, and sitting at the computer all day. He hated it, really, should have gone on to read law, should have gone to Australia to work on a sheep ranch, or signed onto a freighter. Pamela had said that a strong, active young man like Rupert ought to be outdoors, and when asked by his father what he saw himself doing – this was when he had been seventeen or so – he had been unable to think of anything whatsoever. Venn had laughed and said that probably meant that Rupert would write a novel, but Rupert had no literary aspirations either. Posy could imagine writing a novel, but she knew that Father, the great publisher, would never take it seriously.

She sat on the bed and telephoned her mother in London, to recount things as they had found them. 'The doctor says there isn't much hope, and that he probably won't wake up, but they haven't quite finished warming him.'

'How do they do that?'

'They've covered him with blankets, and I think they put warm salt water in his veins, something horrible like that. I didn't quite understand the doctor, his English was rather . . .'

'Dear God,' said Pamela, thinking that it was redundant to ill-wish someone who was so badly off; one was left with nowhere to stand, tipped off balance. Her innate kindness, and the good memories of twenty-three years of marriage, however much of a philanderer he had been, softened her tone momentarily.

'The baby is cute, but he doesn't look anything like Father,' Posy said. 'There's a boy taking care of him, the younger brother of the wife. It's quite a strange situation.'

'Probably I should call his solicitor,' said Pamela, whose heart was very hard toward that individual, Trevor Osworthy, who had acted for Adrian during the divorce, against herself. 'Or, at least, a British doctor.'

'Could you, Mummy? Maybe you could even get them over here today. I'm afraid it may be – you know. Over.' At this her voice broke, reassuring her that she was indeed capable of feeling some more decent emotion than the superficial exasperation that seemed to be rising in her.

'I'll call Mr Osworthy. Give me your number there.'

Posy finished unpacking and went down to the lobby again. It seemed odd to her to be attending a tragedy when the world outside the hotel seemed so full of health and cheer. The hotel guests were suited up in vivid Gore-Tex parkas, booted, chatting in the lower lobby. The youthful personnel of the hotel, wearing plain morning faces, scurried through the corridors with the guests' skis and dry cleaning. She and Rupert faced the grim duty of returning to the hospital, when anyone would rather have been on the slopes. She envied the bronze skins and air of mindless health emanating from one and all, the same people to be seen in their bikinis in summer – she had twice been to Cannes and Nice in the school holidays, and had felt the bad luck of being a pale, large-scaled Brit who only had limited holidays, next to these slim, carefree people who had, apparently, nothing to do, and all the time they needed for pleasure and laughter.

Again at the hospital, they saw no change in Father, who had been lying just like this when they had seen him earlier in the morning, so unmoving he might as well be dead, preserved like Mao or Lenin, except for the wheezing of the machine and the almost imperceptible rise and fall of his chest. The color of his skin was not altogether alive, but not altogether dead, his eyes were closed serenely. Posy could not believe that thoughts weren't streaming across his interior mind.

Oh, ha, isn't this ironic, she imagined his mind's voice saying, lying here in the power of all those I have wounded, who are now assembled together to wreak their collective vengeance because I am helpless, off in another realm. They did love me, I see that now, I shouldn't have abandoned them. Aren't you sorry now, Venn, foolish sod, to have forsaken poor Posy, poor Pam? Oh, and poor Rupert, of course.

'I think that by late this afternoon or tomorrow, things will be clearer,' the doctor said, interrupting her reverie. 'But you must be prepared. I would like to speak to Mr Venn's family this afternoon, say at five,' he said.

Kip had the idea of taking Harry to the hospital to see his mother, in hopes that the voice of her baby would penetrate her coma, as on *General Hospital*. Harry's voice might melt through the ice in her brain. He had weighed the question of whether the fright to Harry of seeing his mom frozen and inert would outdo the good to her of hearing her baby; and concluded that since Harry was so little, even if he recognized her, he'd forget the weird sight of the tubes. Anyway, he had to take Harry with him because he didn't think he could ask Tamara to sit anymore, and had no money to pay her besides. He also didn't think he could ask Christian Jaffe for another ride to the hospital, but there was a shuttle to Moutiers that ran often. Harry was cute in his bunny-eared snowsuit, and people laughed when he chased a dog at the bus stop.

Standing at the bus stop keeping Harry out of the road, Kip was scared, even more scared than yesterday. Something about the ordinary Alpine morning slowly lightening the gray sky, a trace of sun piercing the clouds, the mighty peaks looming all around, dwarfing the merely human village, the cold – it all made him feel desperate whereas yesterday he had only been shocked.

The hospital, by daylight a frayed nineteenth-century mansion with remodelled windows and doors, seemed inadequate and retrograde, but there was a reassuring, professional smell of antiseptic and medicine. Today no one stopped Kip from walking into the intensive care room, where nothing had changed. In the daylight, he could see that the covers mounded over Adrian were an ugly pale green. Kerry was more lightly covered in folded sheets. A third person in another bed had been placed between the two Venns, and a nurse was doing something to this new person's machine. She looked at Kip and said *bonjour*. A fourth bed was occupied too. He wondered if these were also avalanche victims.

It seemed to Kip that today Kerry looked somehow rosier, was more alive looking, though really there was no sign she was coming to, she lay as still as ever. The noise of the machines was more terrible today, wheezing and beeping, gasping and strained, the monitors pale like old black-and-white TVs. Some of Kerry's clothes were folded over the foot of her bed, as if she were at camp. Kip held Harry up and said, 'Say "Hi, Mommy."' Harry stared and said nothing. 'Hi, Mommy,' Kip repeated. After a few more promptings, Harry said, 'Hi,' in a wee voice.

Kerry didn't react, didn't budge. 'Hi, Kerry, it's me, and Harry's here to see you.' Kip went on like this as long as he could bear to, until he began to feel as if he were berating her, so resolutely still did she lie, refusing to listen or react. When the nurse wasn't looking, he held Harry closer, his hand over Harry's tiny hand, and together they patted Kerry's arm. 'Hi, Mommy,' squeaked Kip in Harry's voice.

'There is not much change today,' said the nurse. 'But she is definitely not worse.'

Kip tried putting Harry down, but had to pick him up again when he saw the dangling bags of urine and rolling carts and other things Harry could push over or pull off. When he had stared long enough at Kerry's inert body, he turned to leave, his notion of correct behavior warring with his wish to be out of there. What could you do in a sickroom, anyhow, and what good did it do to just sit there, which wasn't really an option with Harry there, but you did hear that talking to coma victims helped them.

'So, bye for now, Kerry, I'll come back later. Harry says bye-bye. Harry says you'd better wake up soon, Mommy. Uh – bye, Adrian,' he added, remembering that Adrian had no one to talk to him in his coma, in case it made a difference, though the brother and sister could do it, but did they know to?

In the hall the doctor approached him. Kip felt wary – the doctor hadn't sought him out before. 'If you could be here when Monsieur Venn's children next come, I would like to speak to all of you together. Perhaps late this afternoon? Say at five?' Kip was about to protest that he wasn't a family member, but he saw that he sort of was, on Kerry's behalf, maybe even on Harry's behalf, in case there was something he had to represent Harry's opinion about. Kip promised to be there, but he felt full of dread.

As they left the hospital, the Venn brother and sister were coming in. It seemed to Kip that as Harry was their half-brother, they ought to take a turn with him, but he could see from their grim, distraught faces that they weren't going to. In the chill of their unconcerned glances at Kerry, Kip felt his and his sister's isolation. Kerry wasn't the object of these people's concerns, Kerry was just collateral damage, he himself a forlorn emissary of a small state whose fate was incidental. He foresaw that no one but he would lift a finger or make an inquiry in Kerry's behalf. No one would ask whether she was getting good care or if she ought to be taken someplace else or what she was like, a sister sometimes nice, sometimes horrible, like all sisters he had ever heard of. He saw he'd have to fight for Kerry, but he had no idea how.

For a while, they walked around Moutiers. There was a newsagent and some little restaurants and not much else. He wondered how old you had to be to drive in France. He didn't have his license yet but he knew how to drive. What was he going to do with Harry for a whole day? Ski school? How old did you have to be to learn how to ski? He'd seen some really little kids in the ski school, tiny toddlers with short little one-foot-long skis, going like bombs, but none of them was as small as Harry.

Eventually they took the bus back to the hotel. The doctor's words, so portentous and uninformative, stayed on Kip's mind all afternoon, even when he managed to stash Harry with the chambermaid Tamara for a nap after lunch, and make a couple of runs down the *boucle blanc*. He told himself that his not making a couple of runs wouldn't help Kerry. On his board hurtling downhill, he could feel free, unencumbered, outrunning tragedy. Once he saw his new friend Amy, who was supposed to be helping him, but she was talking intently to a ski instructor at the bottom of the lift and didn't see him. Kip thought she was incredibly foxy. Someday he would be a ski instructor. It was a well-known perk of being a ski instructor that women would do anything you wanted.

'You know what it's about,' Posy had said to Rupert at lunch, talking of the doctor's summons at five.

'Perfectly. We're going to have to decide whether to pull the plug on our father,' Rupert said.

'Of course we couldn't possibly.'

'How can we know? We haven't heard the medical details. Maybe it would be a kindness, or maybe . . .' His voice betrayed the poorly mastered panic she felt herself. She saw that he had shaved and cut himself since they arrived, and had stuck a little tissue on the place.

'This is so – so extraordinary. What a thing to happen,' said Posy. 'Father has always been just a bloody whole lot of trouble.' She dabbed at tears and tried to sound calm. It was true. Growing up, their lives had always been organized around his comings and goings, trips to France, purchases – new car, new place in the country, boat, once even a racehorse – the sorts of things that would suddenly be sold. When he and Pam had divorced, a sort of boring lull had oppressed them, and she had thought it was Father they missed; perhaps it was only the excitement.

'This cheese is remarkable,' sighed Rupert, unwilling to talk any more about it all. 'They do cheese better in France.'

'I like France, I've always liked France,' Posy said, looking around at the comfy dining room, with its pink tablecloths, flowers, displays of porcelain edelweiss, and glass cases along the walls featuring Chef Jaffe's signature china.

'Except for the French,' Rupert said. It was an Englishman's obligatory rejoinder.

'Even the French,' Posy insisted, suddenly in a better mood, her spirit armed by the wine against the sorrow and pain they had come to France to experience. 'The doctor was nice.' Though she didn't like doctors.

'Doctors are always nice, it's their duty, even French ones,' Rupert said.

'I think doctors are foul,' declared Posy.

At four Kip came in from the slopes, checked on Harry, who was napping under the glowering supervision of Tamara, and started again the cumbersome bus trip down to Moutiers, hoping vainly that the English brother and sister would offer him a ride. He had been too shy to remind them that he, too, had been sent for, and they had not approached him at lunch. They had sat together at a window table, seeming to have little to say to each other, though Kip could see them sometimes waving their hands and shaking their heads in a burst of animation. They never, that he could see, looked at him or even at their brother Harry.

The meeting was in Dr Lamm's office, and the doctor was just coming in, perhaps had himself been delayed. His office was a small, windowless room behind the nurses' station, where extra chairs had been brought. The Venn brother and sister were there, another man Kip had never seen, who laid his overcoat, Burberry lining carefully folded out, over the back of his chair, and a man in hospital green. The doctor took off his white coat, which gave the impression that he was eager to be off home, though his tone was stately and somberly unhurried. Posy and Rupert sat, nodding vaguely at the others, then subsided into fixed stares at the doctor but not at each other. The room was warm.

'Who are you, monsieur, if you please?' the doctor asked the Burberry man in French.

'I am Jacques Delamer, from Saint-Gond – Monsieur Venn's man of business – do you say "business manager"? I direct the vineyard and his affairs generally. I consider him a close friend as well. I read the news in the *journal* this morning, and called here immediately, I was given the grim details, and I leapt into my car. V*oilà.* We are only two hours south of here.'

The doctor nodded and without preamble began in English. 'I must repeat to you what you know already, that we are not happy with Monsieur Venn's condition,

Monsieur Venn has not revived.' He said this again in French, perhaps for the benefit of the stranger. 'He has warmed up to normal body temperature, but he still needs powerful medicaments to support his blood pressure and heartbeat. These have not returned by themselves as is necessary, and worst of all, he has not regained any brain function. None at all. In fact things have worsened as his body warms. His brain shows no signs of returning as it should have by now – frankly we are afraid he will not revive. That is a possibility you must prepare yourself for.' His tone was direct, though he had tried to infuse it with sympathy.

'Not revive?' cried Posy and Rupert. Posy mistrusted the doctor's tone of sympathy, the concern, her own ignorance of medical details. What were they hearing?

'We have considerable experience with this sort of injury, but to be absolutely certain, we will wait another twenty-four hours before we make any predictions.'

'But he's breathing perfectly!' Posy persisted.

'As you know, he is being kept alive on a *respirateur*. He seems to be breathing because the respirating machine is forcing air in and out of his lungs. His heart cannot by itself create a blood pressure, and so he has no ability for it to beat or for his lungs to breathe without assistance. In such a case, eventually the only thing to do is to detach the patient from the artificial machines. We always make that decision heavy-heartedly, when we are sure it is the medically correct decision. But it is important that you prepare yourself, and, more important, that you understand and accept if we come to the conclusion that there is no hope.'

In some way, Posy thought, she had been prepared for the doctor's pronouncement, but she was also prepared to resist it. The world of medicine was full of reports of miracle and surprise. She looked at Rupert. She could see that he, too, wanted to protest the doctor's pessimistic conclusions, but probably felt that nuances of language eluded him for expressing mistrust of finalities.

'He is alive only technically?' asked the strange man with the Burberry, in French.

'That is what appears to be the case. But we need to wait another twenty-four hours.'

'But isn't there always a chance? How can you be sure?' asked Rupert.

'I'm afraid there is little chance,' said Dr Lamm, 'but we have to wait. Of course, miracles do occur, and we are doing everything we can.'

'It only happened last night!' Posy protested. 'It seems premature to talk like this, we should have another opinion, you hear of people in comas waking up after ever so long . . .'

Kip was relieved at her combative tone. It didn't seem okay to him, either, to just say, Well, okay then, unplug the machine. If they would do that to Adrian they would do it to Kerry. 'What about my sister . . . ?' he began.

'Yes, what about Mrs Venn?' asked Rupert.

'She is not worse, perhaps a tiny bit better,' said the doctor.

'She's not . . .'

'No, she is completely alive, if we preserve certain distinctions. Your sister's chances are very much better,' the doctor said, with a kind smile for Kip. 'Monsieur

Venn, though he is on life support, is in a deep vegetative state. He shows no signs of essential activity. With her there is much more hope. It is not always possible to tell. When someone is hypothermic, sometimes it is only a matter of restoring the body temperature. Her brain is working and so we expect her to wake up, though it may be several days, even weeks, before she fully recovers,' the doctor said.

Now the man in Burberry half rose to his feet, as at a public meeting, looked over the back of his chair at the others, and said, 'I have some questions, if you don't mind.' Now speaking in accented English, his French accent leaving no doubt of his nationality. 'Is this all of the family?'

'I believe these are all the family, except for the little boy,' said the doctor. 'And of course Madame Venn is present, but not present.'

'Harry's here but he's at the hotel,' Kip said.

'So – not Harry and not – Monsieur Venn's wife,' conceded the newcomer. 'Only half the family, in fact. I feel sure he would want – would want the whole family to agree . . . to be with him perhaps . . .'

'Family accord is not a medical concern, monsieur,' said the doctor. 'Of course we want all the family to be informed and in agreement about the medical situation here, but the caprices of individual members cannot stand in the way of what is best for the patient. Perhaps I do not understand your standing in the matter . . .'

'Legally, morally, none, none, I am his business manager, but his friend also,' said Monsieur Delamer.

'I understand that you may wish to assemble all the

family,' said the doctor. 'That is perfectly reasonable, but not strictly speaking within our purview, and obviously Madame Venn and the baby cannot participate in any decisions. It is for you, or other members of the family, to contact whoever else is involved . . .'

'It is the matter of the *coffre*,' said Mr Delamer.

'Oh, really,' cried Posy. 'That's a bit premature, isn't it? Father is not going to die.'

'Not a coffin, a *coffre*,' said Mr Delamer after a blank second. Rupert, who had been better than Posy at French, whispered, 'I think it's the safe-deposit box.'

'It is infinitely easier, especially in France, if the *coffre* were to be opened while Mr Venn is still alive. I'm sorry, I hardly expected we would need to be discussing this. We could take this up later, if we were agreed to – delay any, um – major decisions until perhaps tomorrow. I would like to explain this technicality to Mr Venn's family.'

The doctor opened and closed his mouth. What could be the difficulty really? 'Yes, certainly, I was not proposing anything precipitate. We fully understand people must make their peace, they must say their *adieux*. I only wanted to prepare you.' In his tone the slight irritation one feels when the agenda, weighty as it was, has been wrested away. 'I simply wanted you all to know where matters stand. Till tomorrow then, when we will discuss this again and see where we are.'

Father's business manager, Monsieur Delamer, rang Rupert's room a bit before the dinner hour and proposed having a word with him and his sister. Delamer explained that he was installed in another hotel nearby, but would be coming to dine in the famous restaurant of the Hôtel Croix St Bernard, and would gladly meet them wherever suitable, perhaps in one of the rooms, his or Miss Venn's. The bar would probably not be quite the place.

Rupert agreed, suggesting his own room. Posy was famously messy and threw her clothes about. He needed to find out about the relation of Father to this Frenchman. In London, Father had Mr Osworthy, his solicitor for thirty years, but since Father had spent more and more time at his French château, where the Icarus Press was, it stood to reason he might have some local French person to deal with French matters. Had Pam indeed called Mr Osworthy? If so, which of the two – Osworthy or this man, Mr Delamer – should they listen to in the case of conflicting advice? Rupert felt a little wary, but acknowledged to himself that Delamer, being in France, was probably more up to date in Father's confidence.

Posy appeared beforehand, dressed rather too glamorously for dinner, with a plunging neckline, and sat on Rupert's bed. 'I suppose it's all right to smoke?'

'I wish you wouldn't,' said Rupert.

Posy sniffed at Rupert's prissy ways – it was one of their quarrels. He scowled at her neckline.

Mr Delamer tapped discreetly on the door and slipped inside like someone carrying contraband. He was wearing a sport jacket and furry après-ski boots in which he had walked from his nearby hotel. They gave him the chair and Rupert sat next to Posy on the bed.

'It is said,' Delamer began, 'that Chef Jaffe's concoction of *ris de veau* and *homard* is something extraordinary. He is reputed for his original ideas – his gnocci of courgette is something else splendid I have tasted. Are you *en pension* or ordering *à la carte*?

'We're taking the meals that come with the rooms,' said Posy. 'Is that *pension*?'

'*Demi-pension,* actually, unless you stipulate full board, but then you are obliged to come in for lunch and, frankly, I cannot myself manage three such meals a day, though my wife ... We stayed at this hotel for several years, but had not planned it this year. Of course, and here I am, most unexpected and sad.'

'You wanted to discuss ... ?'

'Yes. I wanted to continue what we discussed this afternoon. The *coffre*. You say "safety-deposit box"?'

'Safe-deposit box, safe-deposit box.'

'Ah. Well, I wished to advise you that whatever may happen, frankly, I would advise opening the safety-deposit box at the bank while Monsieur Venn is alive. As soon as possible. The point is, you will not be able to do it when he is gone. At a death, the state seals it up, and then appraises the contents for you to pay taxes on. There are several valuable things in it that could be – disposed of more easily if they weren't part of his estate. I myself have a power to dispose of – certain things, but I have only a half power, that is, with someone else, to open the box, and am not sure who actually has the key. We have most certainly noted this in our records, but I came away so rapidly when I heard the news.'

At the further mention of valuable things in the coffre, his listeners appeared to focus more closely.

'I have the impression that it is Madame Hyack, his secretary, but it may be Madame Venn, of course, who has the key and the second half-power of attorney for opening it.'

'What's in Father's coffer, then?' Rupert asked.

'Mostly first editions, fine editions, some very valuable in fact. I'm thinking of the very high value the state will place on them for the purposes of death duties. Let me assure you, it is altogether legal to think of such matters before – the event. Otherwise I would not be advising you this way. Let me call Madame Hyack.'

'By all means,' said Rupert, looking for an expression of dissent in Posy's face and seeing none.

'Perhaps some gold as well, and Madame Venn's jewelry,' added Monsieur Delamer. 'Perhaps his small Bonnard. He was advised to put it away whenever they left home, and from time to time he remembered to do so.'

'What about his will?' Rupert ventured.

'I don't think his *testament* is there,' Delamer said. Hope now rose again in them. They had supposed his will would be in England with Mr Osworthy, and though they had been sure he had meant to cut them out, in his anger

87

at their mother, who had been obstinate about divorce, if there was no will in France, maybe, as he had expected to live forever, he hadn't actually got around to a new one mentioning Harry; or there might be other quirks. It still seemed possible that though their father could have cut them out altogether and left everything to his new wife, or the baby, maybe he hadn't got around to it.

'You can see,' said Monsieur Delamer, 'whatever happens, we must hope it will not happen tomorrow. I will leave first thing in the morning and tend to the *coffre* tomorrow afternoon. It would be best, of course, if you, or one of you, came with me.'

Off the lounge bar at the lower level, beyond the billiard room, was a large meeting room, and an event being held there was announced on the discreet standard at the front desk, for six o'clock, when people would have come in from the slopes but before dinner. Dr Franz Hoffmannstuck, an eminent curator from Zurich, Switzerland, would present 'The Art of the Drap,' which Amy had to look up: tablecloth. She also received a private invitation slipped under the door of her room, where, also, were messages from her ski instructor and Géraldine Chastine, call them, and the usual business calls from Palo Alto.

She went along to the lounge bar at six. Why not? Linen had been part of her agenda from the beginning. 'They don't know how to iron a tablecloth,' the woman in the antique shop had said.

The meeting room had been prepared with a blackboard, a stack of leaflets, and several immense, elaborate tablecloths, immaculately starched and monogrammed, which were draped over easels, the floor beneath covered in muslin so their folds would not touch the common carpet.

Twenty or so people came in – one man and the rest mothers and daughters or, like Amy, women by themselves, some familiar with each other from the ski room or the cooking lesson, smiling at one and all at having discovered this community of interest. Dr Hoffmann-stuck himself hovered nearby, plainly keeping an eye on his linen treasures, but with an air of welcome and detachment, until ten minutes past six, when he stepped up to his blackboard and began to explain, in a mysterious Continental accent, his lifelong interest, passion, expertise in linen as the keeper of the collections at Schloss – Amy missed the name of the Schloss.

There was the history of table linen from the time of the Coptic Christians, possibly the ancient Greeks. Renaissance linen, eighteenth-century linen, nineteenth-century linen, modern linen. There was the remedy for stains, a section of study all its own, which he would demonstrate some details of presently. There was the preparation, ironing, and storage of linen. There was the prevention of yellowing, the necessity of bleaching, the dangers of bleaching, the correct method of folding after *repassage*. There were differences in modern and antique linens to consider, the qualities of ancient fibers. There was the mending of antique linens. There were modern facilities devoted to this, also to the correct methods of laundering of fine works too large or difficult to be dealt with in the private house.

After outlining the content of the lecture to follow, he began with stains, creating a sympathetic stir by holding up a small tablecloth and dumping red wine on it. Amy took notes on the removal of this stain. Her attention wandered a little during the historical section, though she took the general point that linen was an art form, revered down the centuries, specially conserved in furniture designed for it, the centerpiece of trousseaus and dowries, inheritable, to be cherished like any patrimony; and that women were generally its guardians. This conjured up guilty memories of whole sections of museums she had skipped over, filled with vitrines of faded doilies and ugly tatting. She now regretted disdaining this field of female endeavor, and the fact that in her condo in Palo Alto she didn't have so much as a cloth napkin, exactly as the wry woman in the Seattle antique shop would have predicted.

Amy was from a family careful of things handed down. She had been instructed in their origins – this cup belonged to Aunt Fan, this belonged to Ben Armstrong, Cousin Dandy Churchill. All these things were waiting for her at her mother's, but she had always refused to take them, saying, 'When I get a place.' Though she had a condo, it was nearly empty, and had not really interested her. Eventually she would have a beautiful house and would take the tureen, the pink candy bowl, the collection of Watseka spoons. She would need tablecloths, undoubtedly.

'In the eighteenth century, the common practice was to bleach the linen by moonlight,' said the doctor, returning Amy's attention to him with a snap. Moonlight?

'They believed the sun too destructive. In the great houses, special racks were constructed upon which to extend the sheets. In modest homes, the women would spread the linen on bushes at night after the dew had fallen and when the moon came up. Then they would take it in just before the morning dew, lustrously pale under the magical effect of the moon's rays.

'These historic pieces from the most important castles of Bavaria' – he indicated the tablecloths present – 'have been treated in this fashion, as you can see from the perfection of their preservation. The earliest is late eighteenth century, thought to have been in the collection of the empress, though without the imperial monogram – apparently marked with her maiden monogram. The other two are nineteenth century, the one from the English royal household, the other from an important bourgeois Swiss household. The Statler Collection, of which I have the honor to be the curator, has the bulk of surviving imperial linen in Austria today, and an important collection of European linens from foreign royal households, for instance Siamese and Nepalese linens imported originally from Holland in the early sixteenth century.'

Amy, despite herself, was struck by the romantic image in her imagination of wide-gowned women spreading sheets by moonlight. Nowhere to do that in her Palo Alto condo, but she'd be buying a house eventually. Her mind pictured a vast armoire and folded linen in it. No doubt there was some essential significance to linen she had never been aware of, connecting you to human and especially female history.

After an agonizing debate with herself, involving a stern interior lecture about money in general, her own ample supply of it, and her plan to devote herself to cultivating such graceful virtues as hospitality, she bought three tablecloths, one an immense sea of snowy damask, eighteenth century; another vast embroidered blue with a scalloped border; the third an historic cloth of hem-stitched ecru, formerly in the possession of a minor Bavarian nobleman, and dozens of napkins for each, at a total cost of nine thousand dollars, this sum itself reassuring as to the perfection of her choices, the eventual success of her dinner parties, though the price was plenty shocking to her practical side. The combined weight of these cloths was such that Mr Hoffmanstuck himself bore them to her room for her. She told herself she ought to be thrilled, but really she had a feeling of dismay at her temerity, especially when elsewhere, though not in Valméri, people were starving. She knew she would have to get over these paradoxical compunctions and learn to spend money casually.

At dinner, heart still beating with the rashness of her purchases, she had sat as she had promised at the table with young Kip and his little charge, Harry. Though she had no experience with children, she seemed to have a better instinct than Kip for straightening the child's bib and dabbing at the smears of spinach on his cheeks. Rather grandly, the distinguished kitchen had concocted purees and other baby dishes for Harry. Yet the evening was long for Kip and Amy both.

Dinner was okay, Kip thought, helping Harry eat took up some time, but then getting him to bed and all – that was no easier than it had been last night. He was never going to become a parent, for sure. Amy had found herself wishing there were at least another grown-up at the table. She had learned that Kip was from Oregon, and that, having no real home after the death of his parents, he had been sent to a boarding school in Squaw Valley, California, dedicated to ski and snowboard competitions, and getting you through the SATs eventually. This school was being paid for by Adrian, his sister's husband, a very nice guy, in Kip's view. Adrian had also paid for this trip, at the semester break. Amy assured him she was familiar with Squaw Valley, had skied there herself years ago.

Their conversation, after it had surveyed his school, his hopes, the fate of his parents, and the medical situation, had faltered. 'Tomorrow, if it's nice, and Harry's baby-sitter works out, you and I can make a few runs,' she proposed. Kip politely agreed, though he knew there were few adults at the hotel, from what he had seen, who were at his level, and he'd be obliged to modify his speed and go on skis, not snowboard. But he didn't really mind, and he was glad to have Amy to talk to, someone concerned for his situation.

'Harry doesn't know what's happening,' Kip confided. Of course not, Amy started to say, but she saw that it was because Kip was young himself that this surprised him. Children must attribute sentience to fellow children in a way adults don't. She was touched at her own perception that this tall male being was still a kid, as close to Harry's age as to hers, or, as she was nearly thirty, closer.

'The hotel guy wanted me to go through Adrian's stuff, before the people from England came. I didn't like to do it, but what if I need something, like for Harry?'

'Did you?'

'I took some money,' he confided. She could see it was on his mind. 'I'm keeping track, though.'

'Yes, it's okay, you have to have a way of paying for things,' Amy agreed. 'Does he seem to miss his mom?'

'He cries a lot at night. He wakes up.'

Later, Amy had a couple of drinks in the village with Paul-Louis, her new ski instructor. Amy had signed up with the handsomest ski instructor, because it was not strictly true that she didn't intend to meet men, she just intended not to get seriously involved with one. This didn't rule out having some fun, and she had decided beforehand that a ski instructor, with whom she would enroll for the two-week session, would likely be her choice of companion. To be an après-ski escort was an accepted role for a ski instructor, one he would have had experience with and therefore be uncomplicated about. She hoped for someone good looking and also French, which, keeping in mind her wish for cultural breadth, would put any relationship into the realm of research. By now she had also the poet Robin Crumley ('well known in England,' the *princesse* had whispered); she ruled out Joe Daggart, who was attractive but American – he had rather vaguely described his job in Geneva as 'extradition negotiator.' She also reserved the Baron Otto option, though he was somewhat older, probably in his forties, and Austrian, which was not far from being a German.

In the long run, men weren't in her plan. When Amy's good fortune had become known in her family (why did they think of it as 'good fortune' instead of 'Amy's brilliant coup'?), after suggestions about how she might help out her needy sister Nan, and a few of her cousins, came the cautionary tales about the notorious bad judgment of rich women when it came to men; and there was also that dreaded hazard for female heiresses, the gigolo, and the fortune hunter.

Her aunt Sarah pressed on her biographies of forlorn Doris Duke, pathetic Barbara Hutton, Peggy Guggenheim, and there were Vanderbilts and Rockefellers. There were elderly maidens taken in by scoundrelly young male factotums – gardeners and secretaries who schemed eventually to inherit. There were the much married who squandered their fortunes in alimony and payoffs for a succession of handsome but sleazy Eurotrash racing-boat husbands. (Did they never meet some nice doctor or accountant?) There were smoking, alcoholism, suicide, and deaths under suspicious circumstances. There were nice American heiresses married off to English lords who betrayed them and took their money, girls stranded in Europe bereft of their fortunes by sexist, retrograde European marriage laws. There were fragile, vulnerable actresses and tense women CEOs. There seemed to be no examples of ordinary happiness.

'Here, honey, I picked this up somewhere, I thought you might find it interesting,' her mother and aunts were always saying. Amy didn't read these books, but she glanced at the jacket copy and more than once leafed through to the ending, or far enough to get the idea. Paradoxically, such tales had not induced a mistrust of men – she got along with men – but only scorn for the women who had let themselves get so messed up. She understood the historical reasons for this – they were mostly women without professions or interesting work, socialized in a day when being married defined you; even geniuses like Georgia O'Keeffe had been born under the influence of the universal belief that a woman must be married. And the rich ones probably had hideous over-protected childhoods. Everyone knew you couldn't be born rich and be well adjusted.

But in her case, as she didn't plan to marry just yet,

there was no need to forgo male company in the meantime. She hoped she would recognize insincerity when she met it, but it was important to preserve wonder and joy, and not become suspicious and paranoid. She knew all this, and was not suspicious or paranoid by nature, so was not apt, she hoped, to fall prey to one of the unlovely fates. And her heart, she knew, was impervious.

This was not in her view a good thing. At some level, she wished for her heart to be broken, or in some other way to indulge the potentiality for emotion and passion that she knew must lie somewhere beneath her practical commonsense surface. At least she hoped it did, and from time to time wondered if, maybe, it didn't, and she really was just a stable, contented, commonsensical person with no depths at all. It was her greatest fear.

She couldn't remember whether she or Paul-Louis had proposed the drink. He explained the village of Valméri like a tour guide: it had kept its timbered, indigenous structures, two-storied dwellings with stalls on the lower floors to winter cows in, their warmth and odors rising to comfort a shivering family during the freezing months. Most of these barn levels had now been converted to mother-in-law apartments or for lodging skiers during the winter. There were small hotels, galleries for art, and expensive retail objects – watches, furs, elaborate ski costumes, boots. A post office, meteorology station, railroad ticket agent, ski rentals, the cinema, concert hall and skating rink, a dozen restaurants, and the vast building that housed the ski gondolas which nested at night like spoons. A mood of frivolity in every bar reigned amid the faint odor of what smelled like grass to Amy – but could have been the local tobacco, or even linament. Otherwise it didn't seem a very wild scene – there was probably more cocaine in Silicon Valley, by far – but this was restful and here she felt less square than she felt, or used to feel, in the high-tech, high-stakes world at home.

Paul-Louis had a regular hangout where they went, drank a couple of beers, and shouted over the lame European hip-hop. He walked Amy back fairly early, they had another beer in the bar of the Croix St Bernard, and then Amy said good-night and went off to do her French lesson and go to bed, tired and bemused. All was working out as she had hoped, almost. Here were interesting people enough, knowledge in the abstract, and experience. Culture, as she had imagined it – a rich concoction of art and music discussed in old languages with assured taste – wasn't here exactly unless you counted the refinements of the dining room, but culture could wait for Paris.

The tablecloths, she decided, were on track, but Paul-Louis had been a little disappointing. In their nightly talks, her financial manager, Sigrid, had laughed, and elaborated on her advice to go have affairs in the no-fault climate of a European ski resort. 'Why else go there?' Sigrid tended to think men were good for one thing only, but Amy often liked them for themselves. Not that he wasn't attractive – he was, very, with his deep tan and prominent European nose. But, flattered by her evident interest in him, he had spent the evening telling her of the procedures necessary for getting into pharmacy school, how many of the exams he had passed, or flunked the first time, how shaky his future if he weren't to pass the next one, the difficulties of living in Aix if you were used to the Savoie, how many of his friends had just opted to stay in the Alps at ski-related jobs, in his view relatively dead end, plus many ended up dead eventually, in avalanches and other accidents, as had happened to the brother of a friend. She did manage to pin him down on a couple of her issues, such as the new parabolics, or her problem unweighting into the left turn, but things were far from moving toward the romantic. However, she told herself, the ice was broken, and things could develop slowly if they were meant to.

She was impressed by Europeans, definitely – their education, the breadth of their culture. Even Paul-Louis had more general information than she did. But she was also disoriented. So much to do, so little time, as Winston Churchill said, of something or other. Despite herself, she knew about corporate buyouts. What did she know about poetry, about meter and stanza form, music, tradition, masterpieces? About world religion, Hinduism, Buddhism? The white-wine glass, the red-wine glass? What was a *godet*? What was the line between despair and cynicism, between taste and vulgarity – a word she had often heard used about the houses her friends were build-ing? How to make a soufflé such as the remarkable soufflé of cheese and anchovy they had been served at dinner? She recognized that it was not going to be easy to be rich, it was a project and a job, and she knew she must now be wary of the capricious frivolity that often overtook people in her situation. She had seen her friends suddenly take up hot-air ballooning and expensive incunabula. How much more virtuous her own aims, how much less attainable.

13

After a dinner of *omble* in wine, *pommes dauphine,* eaten in a depressed, inattentive mood, Posy and Rupert Venn went to sit in the lounge bar, where people congregated for coffee and drinks, and a pianist and a bass player took requests for old American show tunes and more Russian folk music. They chose a banquette against the end wall away from the bar, around which merry guests circled on their drinks missions, and away from the musicians, who were improvising the Russian songs. She recognized 'The Volga Boatman.' The people singing tearfully in deep Boris Gudenov voices must be Russians. Rupert drank a beer and then suddenly said he was going to bed. He had to get up early for the unwanted excursion to Father's coffer. He had a put-upon air that irritated Posy.

'I hate to go. I have the feeling Father will die if I don't watch him,' he said.

'I'll be watching for the two of us,' Posy assured him.

'Yes, but what if he dies when I'm not there?' They agreed that could happen, but didn't believe it would. In his heart, Rupert believed that Posy would somehow mess up the job of sitting by Father's bedside; on the other hand, it was only he who could speak French to Mr Delamer.

*

When Posy sat alone in the bar, people spoke pleasantly to her, she to them, but nothing ripened into a conversation, nor did she care. She saw Kip come in, order a Coke, and sit at one end of the bar. Posy might have talked to him but didn't – she knew she wasn't being very nice to Kip, but she supposed she was angry about Harry's existence, and the wife's, neither thing Kip's fault. She couldn't bring herself to get involved with him or to go down to the hospital one more time tonight, which she supposed she ought to. Now the American blonde with the long braid who had sat with Kip at dinner entered with a tan chap who looked like a ski instructor. Posy admired the poise and confidence of American girls – sometimes verging on the brash – admired their boyish clothes. This one was talking to Kip and motioned him over to sit with them. Posy wondered what their connection was, Americanness, no doubt.

Her mood, between grief and a passive, rather comfortable acceptance of waiting at this hotel, suited her. There was nothing she could do but sit smoking in an agreeable Alpine refuge, and she had the feeling of anonymity and freedom that vacationers experience, despite this not being vacation but a painful family trauma. Making an effort to stop thinking about her own situation, she directed her attention outward, and couldn't help noticing the handsome man who sat down near her reading a newspaper from the rack of newspapers on sticks.

Posy, looking at him, experienced a strange visceral turmoil, out of the blue having the irrational image of herself putting her lips to his brown throat, where his collar was open, where a pulse must beat, feeling his life at her lips. She shivered; it was the image of herself as a vampire. Had she been staring? His dark eyes met her blue stare; she looked at her shoes, her breath taken away by the horrible inappropriateness of her thoughts at this time, but it must have something to do with Father, mustn't it, these thoughts of life beating, life force? Death and – this – were related; it was all in Thomas Mann, it was in nature.

Despite these compunctions, Posy smiled. He nodded civilly and looked again at his paper, evidently considering whether conversation was inevitable, then looked up again, acknowledging her empty glass.

'Would you like something? I'm just getting myself a cognac,' he said in French. He was amazingly good looking, she thought.

'*Non, merci,*' she said.

'A brandy?' he repeated in English. 'Please, allow me.'

'Oh, well, thanks,' she reconsidered, recognizing that this simple exchange, the essence of a classical pickup, would commit her to conversation and to staying up awhile longer, though she was actually dead tired after driving through the night last night. He went over to the little bar and came back with two cognacs in big snifters.

'I'm Emile Abboud,' smiled the handsome man, his face somehow harmonizing a manly square jaw with graceful curves of eyebrow, lashes, cleft chin shadowed with beard, upcurving lips displaying a smile of astounding whiteness. She heard his name as Abbot, or maybe Booth, and he had pronounced it with a certain flourish, as if she ought to have heard it before.

'I'm Posy,' she said.

'*Anglaise ou américaine?*'

'English.' And she certainly wasn't going to struggle on in French. His English was fine, she saw, even his accent was not too pronounced.

'So I thought. I was just now reading the words of your prime minister, so sycophantic in his pro-American effusions. Do you find him so? Sycophantic and pro-American? A lackey to the American president, a bully and a liar?'

'I suppose he is,' Posy admitted. 'I've given up thinking about politics. Politicians are so dreadfully boring.' Though she was not in the habit of picking up men in bars, it came to her as almost primal knowledge that since they were required to expend so many words, and get through so many minutes of conversation, before reaching the right stage of alcohol-abetted friendliness, the right feeling of camaraderie, attraction, and accord that could then run to further things, or not – this was only an incubation period, and they might as well talk about politics while coming down with the full-blown thing. But politics wasn't her strongest subject. For instance, who was the prime minister of France? She was suddenly blank on that.

'Did you just get here today?' she asked.

'Yes, just a half an hour ago.'

'Are you skiing tomorrow?'

'No. Are you?'

'Probably not. I'm actually not much of a skier,' Posy admitted. 'The last time I skied was a few years ago, in Val d'Isère, and I savaged my knee on the first day. No, I'm here on business. With my brother,' she added in case he had seen Rupert.

'Yes, that is my situation too. "Unforeseen business." Luckily I got here in time for dinner, which did much to reconcile me to passing a few days in the Alps. The table here is very good.'

'Well, you must be a true Frenchman, we're already having a food discussion,' Posy said. His English was so good, so unaccented, she thought maybe he wasn't French at all but some sort of sheik. Sheiks were always well educated, and had gone to Oxford or Cambridge or Harvard, not that she had ever met one.

'We could turn to other subjects. You are easily the most beautiful girl in the room.'

'You don't expect me to discuss my looks.'

'No, I suppose not. Female beauty is another French interest, though.'

'We – English girls – are all very touchy about French girls, they are all so pretty and chic.'

'You don't find them rather thin and calculating and pulled together?'

'Well, an Englishman would have no way of describing someone's look, pulled together or the contrary. They don't notice what women wear.'

'That is a national difference, then,' said Emile.

Posy could feel her mood lifting, like clouds drifting away and a big heavenly beacon beginning to break through, singling her out with its ray as if to warm a patch of fun and forgetfulness just for her. Things will be bad again in the morning, but for now all is permitted. That's what ski resorts are like.

He had put his newspaper aside with the air of a man who is not going to resist the change of program.

'We could dance,' he suggested. 'Less dangerous than skiing.' Posy was not so sure about that, but agreed. They stood and moved a few feet toward the small chairless space in front of the musicians where a few couples had been dancing, but just as they stepped up, the musicians stopped the Tyrolean polka they'd been playing and went off on a break. He took her arm and they sat back down. Even his light touch on her shoulder made her feel short of breath.

'Are you – what, a soccer player?' she guessed. She had noticed his strength and lithe bearing in the instant he had led her to dance. It appeared that she could not have said anything that could have pleased him more. For an instant his handsome face wore the unmistakable expression of complimented vanity, then of modest denial.

'I'm a teacher,' he said, 'and a sort of journalist.' She would never tell him she was the credit manager of a chain of underwear stores. She wouldn't even tell him her last name.

'What kind of teacher?'

'I teach at a university in Paris called Sciences Po.'

'I just came down from university last year.' He seemed charmed by her account of Cambridge, her studies in literature. She warmed to a man who appreciated women who had studied seriously, so not the case on the London job market at the moment, or the marriage market, for that matter. It was astonishing how a French person could have absorbed so much of Oxbridge lore – he wondered if she had ever been punting, and whether each student had a servant, as it appeared from books, and was it true there were no bathrooms, and no edible food, and did the cheese really come after the dessert? He was nice even if he had some negative ideas about England. As she told him about the traditions of Cambridge, she couldn't forbear mentioning that she'd done well there, and people were bloody surprised too.

'You know a lot about England, you must read a lot of English books,' she said. She was a little dizzy. She knew absolutely that this was going to end in bed, it was almost just a question of how to pass a decent interval before they could go to it. She indulged this fine idea of sleeping with an unfamiliar sheik on her first night away from England – it would be to exact a sort of revenge for the cruel disruptions of fate. Quite apart from the stirring in her lower belly and the feeling of warmth between her legs, the prospect had a sort of abstract charm, a philosophical appeal, not that she had read philosophy (Rupert had, though). The idea of an *acte gratuit*, without motive (well, pleasure), something between people uncommitted, unconnected to each other, an act with no past and no future, an exercise of pure will and pure self-indulgence, came from Gide. Or was it Sartre?

Emile – or something similar, whatever he had told her his name was – waved for another pair of drinks. They carried on with the banal, arch sort of conversation that both knew was just killing time.

'Oh, we cannot resist beautiful English girls,' he said presently. 'It is even a feature of our pornography, a perverse dream of sullying the pale, delicious, puddings with our dark passion.' Posy believed him, and didn't say aloud, but thought, that the opposite was also true, she was drawn to the idea of sheiks and pashas, though the only ones she had actually seen, in Harrods, say, or accompanying a bevy of black-covered women in Marks and Spencer, were seldom attractive, and usually fat. It was more the idea of sheiks that was sexually exciting. Though perhaps by 'our' he had meant Frenchmen? Frenchmen or sheiks, the attraction of opposites was another law of life, perhaps even a physical principle – it was all in D. H. Lawrence.

Thinking of D. H. Lawrence gave her courage, for people were always having impulsive sexual encounters in Lawrence. It was easier to think of doing so outside London, though she had done some fairly crazy things there, too, though never with an absolute stranger and mostly when she was a teenager and sort of miserable. There was a connection to misery now – poor Father – but lust was a better description of her present mood, a delightful feeling, and urgent in its promptings, above all signifying that you were your own person and not a pawn of fate, and no one knew her in distant Valméri anyhow. You were supposed to screw around at a ski resort. Then there was the idea of affirmation. Faced with death – that of a parent symbolizing and prefiguring your own – what was more defiant and positive than making love, even though, logically, it ought to include the making of a new life, but never mind that. You read of people in prison making love, and during the plague.

He answered her question: the idea of the *acte gratuit* came from Gide. He seemed to be thinking in a similar vein, for he now made some remark about the awkward moment between desire and the *passage à l'acte*.

Neither he nor she had any condoms, the search for

which might have shaken their exhilarated mood; but some were to be had from the little store of sundries kept in the manager's office for emergencies. That the youthful Jaffe had learned his hotel-school lessons well was attested to by the complete impassivity with which he responded to Emile's inquiry, as Posy lingered out of sight in the corridor.

Once in his room, Posy experienced some embarrassment and some apprehensiveness, feeling a bit disheveled, though she had washed up before dinner, and wishing she had on better things underneath. There was also the thing she had heard about Arabs and depilation, though this was a Frenchman not a sheik, and some French girls she had seen on a beach when she was younger had gobs of hair under their arms though going topless. But she consoled herself by remembering that even if you were going to be an international adventuress on a global scale, you couldn't possibly anticipate the erotic predilections of every nationality.

He, however, was clearly a man at home in his own territory, and she needn't have worried. It was all smoothly, even brilliantly, performed, though with no complicated positions out of *The Arab Art of Love*, which was anyway maybe not a real book but a title invented by Anthony Powell, her own countryman, in the one of his novels she had read. She crept back to her own room at almost two, burning with the excitement of her clandestine adventure, glad not to run into anyone who could have spotted instantly 'the lineaments of satisfied desire.' (Blake)

PART 2

Hospital

*L'hypocrisie est un hommage que le vice
rend à la vertu.*

– *La Rochefoucauld* (Maximes)

14

The printed program placed on each breakfast table each morning, after giving the weather report, gave the movie schedule for the two cinemas in the village, and then a brief reprise of the morning's news. This morning, Wednesday, the guests were told, to general disapproval, that the American embassy in Paris had dismissed out of hand charges of American warplanes being responsible for the avalanches. There was even a hint that the embassy spokesman had laughed at the idea, just as Amy had. Journalists attending a press conference in Washington had met with the same response when asking the same question. When asked whether there would at least be an investigation, the American officials had derided the notion.

This American indifference to the feelings of Valméri was ill received by the skiers at the hotel. In the ski room in the morning, people discussed the typical Yankee arrogance. Joe Daggart, the only American besides Amy, sent her a commiserating glance. Amy bent to the work of putting on her boots, burning to protest to the Europeans that she was sure, whatever the facts, that the pilots could not have realized what had happened. She also knew her protests would fail to convince, and anyhow, in law, intention has little weight; but her blood speeded up throughout the morning whenever she thought of these unfair assumptions. Luckily the intense joys of the slopes prevented her thoughts from wandering too often. Resentment would recur when she was on the lifts, though never on the descent, when she felt only freedom and exhilaration. *'Très, très bien,'* Paul-Louis encouraged her, and several times led her down black-marked pistes!

Posy woke in the morning feeling free of the oppression, guilt, and anger that had weighed on her since they had first heard the news of Father's accident. No question but that the transient pleasures of love translate into some abiding chemical alteration of the brain and bloodstream. Sex was absolutely good for you and necessary, even as previously practiced in a British version with sweating, slightly overweight former classmates; but now a quantum-leap improvement, a revelation. She relished the advantages of her new lover – his handsome looks, staying power, enthusiasm, and above all tactful way of treating it all with just the right tone of affection, admiration, and slight detachment, as in a French film. What relief and happiness. A minor setback to her morale when on the way to the hospital she stopped in the village and tried to buy some lacy red underwear, only to be told that her size was not 'local.' But even this, even the prospect of the morning with Father, even the gray sky, could not mar her happy anticipation of a second rendezvous with the handsome Frenchman that afternoon.

Posy had set out to the hospital early. Once there, the reality of Father's condition consumed her emotions again. She was slightly resentful that she would have to sit there all day while Rupert went off with Monsieur Delamer to wherever it was Father kept his safe deposit box. But they had agreed that both of them being at the hospital would not help Father. Even one of them could not help Father, as he lay there, his chest moving slightly with the wheeze of the machine, purple streaks developing on the one arm that lay outside the covers, pierced with needles attached to tubes attached to standing cranes with bottles hanging from them, the revolting bottle collecting yellow fluid that hung below the coverlet at the side of the bed, an appalling smell of stuffiness, medicine, and flesh.

She had a book, *Joseph and His Brothers,* by Thomas Mann, which she plunged into, to distract from stirring thoughts of her new French friend, but other concerns reeled through her brain too. She raised her head from time to time and spoke to Father. She would ask the doctor again if everything was being done. It didn't seem right to be riffling in his safe-deposit box, but of course they weren't taking anything, they were just taking things out of the box, in the event that – in the event. It would be looked after by his reputable man of business, whatever that role was called in France, Monsieur Delamer.

At times she glanced over at Father's wife, Kerry, purplish and inert under the blue-white overhead light. Kerry lay as still as Father, but some quality of her condition animated the nurses to hover over her with more active concern, poking, shifting, clucking to her. Posy was able to feel, little by little, some pity for Kerry. It wasn't her fault she'd been taken in by the homely old seducer, she wasn't the first, mysterious though it seemed to Posy, thinking of his craggy face, his froggy, Rumpelstiltskin form. It was Father's energy that drew people to him, her mother had always said.

Spending the long hours at Father's side, punctuated, though, with lots of walking around and crossing the street for coffee and to smoke and notice things. French dogs are so small, she thought. Snow up to their bellies, freezing their little whatnots, they should keep the poor things inside. Little dogs, the wonderful smells of baking everywhere, no books in English. She had more than enough time to review the situation from all points of view. She couldn't but admit she wasn't sorry not to be in London at her job-hunting, it looked as if she was doomed to go back to her dumb job as credit manager for the Rahni Boutiques, tights and knickers for the rest of her life.

In a tangle of thoughts and erotic reveries, among hopes that Father wouldn't die, another hope, glittering like a coin in a thicket, that if he did, he would have remembered her – and Rupert, of course – as he probably had, but it wasn't impossible in his infatuation with his new wife, in his rejuvenated, no doubt Viagra-driven life – it was too possible that the American would get everything. He might have left her and Rupert a token sum, but he had been angry at them both for their support of their mother. Father and Pam had been married for twenty-five years, and their children naturally expected coming into something eventually, in the normal way. Posy had undoubtedly jeopardized their chances – she had even told him he was behaving like a swine, said it flatly to his face, 'swine.' How she wished she hadn't. Plus at the time he had been criticizing everything about her – haircut (okay, somewhat punk, looking back on it, for one winter only), weight, about a stone greater than now, green nails. It had been a low moment for her; nonetheless, she got a good Cambridge degree, which he wasn't even interested in. Rage, hope, greed, concern, and other turbulent emotions prodded her, her eyes fixed on *Joseph and His Brothers* – she was reading all Mann's books. The theme of fraternal rivalry depressed her, though.

Kerry's little brother came in once in the morning to stand gawkily for a few minutes talking to Kerry. At first he had seemed to feel shy to be speaking out loud with Posy sitting there, but little by little he had lost this inhibition, urging his sister to consciousness like a teammate. He was a well-mannered boy, for an American, and Posy wondered if he had some new Yankee medical information about talking to the comatose. Somehow she didn't trust herself to speak to Father without giving him a piece of her mind.

At about eleven, the doctor and another man came into the intensive care ward. This second man was handsome, brown, compact, in an open shirt and a bomber jacket, too lightly dressed for the snow. She stared in stupefaction. It was her last night's lover. For the first instant he was not sure he had recognized her. He glanced at her uncomprehendingly, then at the two beds, then spoke in French to the doctor. The doctor with him was the regular one, and whatever he whispered to Emile, Emile looked over again at her with a frankly shocked expression, then smiled politely, even warmly, and looked down at Father again. His suprise, perhaps stupefaction, was evident to Posy, if not to the doctor. But – how bizarre – she realized she had not told him about Father. Some other connection entirely must have brought him here. He had said he was a sort of journalist – was he here a journalist with an interest in Father? Was Father so well known in France that journalists would concern themselves? Now she saw that his face had reddened slightly as he glanced at her again.

Each had now recognized the amazing, unfortunate fact that the practically anonymous partner of the night before, with whom there was some expectation and hope of renewed transports later on this afternoon, had some connection to the comatose Venn, and that therefore they had some connection to each other. Knowing what she knew now, her responses of the night before, of visceral desire, became if anything more powerful. Still, she couldn't imagine what his interest in Father could be.

For his part, Emile quickly divined from her dutiful station by Venn's bed that Posy was a relative, probably a daughter, and therefore the half-sister of his wife. And therefore a potential wellspring of trouble and complication, which if anything increased his desire for her and heightened the discomfort of renunciation. For of course things must end here.

'You know Monsieur Abboud, of course,' said the doctor to Posy. This struck Posy in its guilty, carnal sense, chilling her with the idea that the doctor somehow knew what had happened last night and that it somehow compromised Father's treatment.

'Miss Venn and I have met at the hotel.'

Posy returned his polite smile as neutrally as she could,

none the wiser as to why he was there. Rattled, they were unable quite to look at each other. Abboud continued staring down at Father, Posy back at her shoes.

'Probably there is a special limbo for souls who have met with sporting disasters,' said Abboud eventually, of Father. 'It's a far from heroic, but also not quite futile, not quite despicable fate. But, excuse me – Miss Venn – it's not for me to be speaking of your parent's fate.'

'It's kind of you to take an interest,' she said.

'In effect, he is "dead"?' Monsieur Abboud asked the doctor.

'Yes.'

'In a dream of death? Does he hear? See?'

'A futile dream,' said the doctor. 'Some believe they hear, but I have never seen anything to suggest it.'

'Reveillez-vous, monsieur,' said Abboud sternly to Father.

'Miss Venn, we will want to speak again at five this afternoon,' said the doctor, taking Abboud's arm in the proprietary manner of a tour guide.

'Is Miss Venn returning to her hotel?' Abboud asked Posy.

'No – I guess I should stay here,' she said, longing to go with him. He nodded.

'Until this afternoon, then,' he said, and went out with the doctor, leaving Posy completely ignorant of his connection to medicine or to Father.

She immediately felt her mistake. Out of some sort of dread of what would happen to Father if she didn't sit there every minute, she had not gone back to the hotel, despite her intense wish to talk to Mr Abbot. Now, for lack of a certain name, she found herself thinking of him as Monsieur Abbot. Mr Abbot had violated the perfect anonymity of their encounter by turning up in her actual life. She also felt she deserved the personal suffering attendant upon sitting there in ignorance and confusion.

The afternoon passed with stupefying slowness, but the identity of Emile gave Posy something to brood about beside Father's condition. She tried out every possible explanation for his presence in Father's life, and none was plausible. This didn't mean that her heart didn't pound when thinking of being in his arms. Had she made a minor error – it was nothing irreversible, after all – or really embarked on a serious complication? Why was she sitting here like a stone, poisoning Father with her complicated vibes, when she ought to go back to the hotel, find Monsieur Abbot, and have a talk?

Posy also didn't like it that there were so few other people there when they assembled yet again to talk about Father at five. Rupert and Monsieur Delamer, who had gone to the Luberon to open Father's coffer, had not returned, and she – to her everlasting ignominy, she felt – was still somewhat resentful of Rupert's trek to the south of France on an apparently dutiful mission. He had always had a talent for evading the unpleasantest chores. She knew she ought not to think of sitting by Father's bedside as an unpleasant chore. Irritation rose in her, as it was wont to do since childhood when Rupert had compelled her with pinches to pick things up or dry the dishes when these tasks had been allotted to him. It was just a reflex now to feel a knot of temper swell at the least infraction by Rupert of the rules of sibling fairness. Her rational self could overrule these feelings, but, sitting here by Father, she had no access to her rational self.

She tried to get Rupert on his cell phone, but couldn't. She herself had called Mr Osworthy, Father's solicitor, and learned from his office that he was hurrying to Valméri, but he hadn't yet arrived. Here in the doctor's office were only Kip and Monsieur Abboud. She had corrected her understanding of his name, but his connection to Father was still unknown. Undoubtedly decisions would fall upon her, but she was still in the dark, and the idea of illness or accident had always made her sick, and brought out her anger at anyone who could make her suffer like this. Father and – it was her sudden intuition – Mr Abboud. It was hopeless.

They sat in a row of chairs. 'Miss Venn,' Emile began, with heavy emphasis, as if she had lied about her identity, and he looked unhappy, even angry at her. He was about to say more when the doctor came in with an air of brisk normalcy, took off his white coat, and reached for his suit coat from the back of his chair. He nodded to them as he put it on. '*Bonjour.*'

'*Bonjour,*' they said. Without prologue, the doctor plunged into a recitation of what they had seen for themselves, that there were no changes in Monsieur Venn's condition. Madame Venn was somewhat improved, but Monsieur still required medicine to support his blood pressure and showed no neurological signs of recovery, not the slightest. Dr Lamm was sorry to tell them that the medical staff and the family were likely facing a decision about when to end the futile treatment.

"Pulling the plug' on Father, then?' Posy asked, using the bitter, shocking phrase she imagined that callous doctors used. 'Even though it isn't always possible to tell what will happen?'

'The plug?' The doctor didn't seem familiar with the expression. 'If you could notify anyone else who may be concerned, family consensus is important.'

'Is it necessary that the whole family be here?' asked Emile. 'My wife is not here.'

'No, no. Yet people often wish it, to accompany, to witness. Others do not wish this.'

'What about my sister . . .' Kip began.

'Somewhat better.'

'I mean, shouldn't she be the one to decide, if there's anything to decide about Adrian?'

The doctor said that it might ultimately be kinder for Madame Venn to awaken to the finality of her husband dead, 'not to be put through the wracking – is that the English word – process of decision.'

'We couldn't decide such a thing, it should be his wife.' Posy agreed with Kip.

'When Kerry wakes up she could, you know, say what *she* would want,' Kip agreed, grateful to Posy for understanding what was in his mind too. It would be awful for her to wake up and find out they'd decided to let Adrian die. 'If we waited, then Adrian would still be alive when she wakes up, and she could say what she wants to do,' he tried to explain more completely to the doctor.

'Perhaps Father has told her what he would wish – "Do everything," or else "Do not let me linger,"' Posy agreed.

'I think she would want to know,' said Kip, but now

the others fixed him with looks that said, You are only a boy.

'We might easily wait another twenty-four hours, even longer, if that would give you the reassurance that there is really no more hope,' conceded the doctor. To Emile, 'Monsieur Abboud, your wife would have time to arrive.'

'Excuse me, but may I ask,' said Posy to Emile, 'who is your wife?'

'My wife? She is Victoire, Mr Venn's' – here he looked at Posy, his more intimate recollections visible to her behind his eyes, and she hoped not to the doctor – 'eldest daughter? She can't be here, so – I am here.'

Posy stared at him. She had never heard a syllable about anyone called Victoire. Victoire, an eldest daughter? That is, a sister to herself? The doctor looked slightly baffled at this ignorance on the part of one Venn of the existence of another.

'Oh, yes,' she said, inwardly reeling and wishing that Rupert were there.

'Till tomorrow, then,' said the doctor, dismissing them. They stood, obedient.

'Would you like a ride to the hotel?' she asked Emile.

'Please,' he agreed. She knew she ought to offer Kip a ride, too, but that would foreclose a candid conversation with Emile, so she decided not to. But when the boy stuck close to them anyway, she couldn't very well not take him along. Kip got in the backseat, and she drove them to the hotel, talking generally of Father and the doctor's grim prognosis. Her heart was already hardening with resolution to put this little potential drama behind them and concentrate on Father's welfare, as she ought to have done all along.

As they walked across the icy sidewalk outside the hospital, Emile took her elbow, but so far he had said nothing. When they were a few steps ahead of Kip he said, in a low voice, 'A pity. *Gênant*. An unwelcome complication.'

'I was really hoping for another go,' Posy admitted.

'So was I.'

'Oh, it's the story of my life,' cried Posy, with passionate resentment. 'Something always happens to spoil things.'

'Really? You are the dark sister, then?'

'Victoire. Victory,' said Posy. 'Nothing could spoil her life, I imagine.'

'Yes, my wife is a child of light,' Emile agreed.

They said very little after this. Posy's thoughts kept slipping away from Father and into thoughts about the unknown sister. About the significance of names. Two sisters, one called Posy, i.e., an insignificant, humble, and transient bloom, as in *The Flower Beneath the Foot,* by Ronald Firbank, the other called Victoire, mighty marble statue, headless but triumphantly winged.

Thoughts about how unlucky she was. About how things she got involved in were apt to get spoiled. Her heart apt to be broken. Her little dash with Emile had begun to assume a preciousness out of proportion to its duration or intensity.

When they reached the door of the hotel she was able to say in the lightest tone she could manage, 'Now you see, there is a black sheep in every family.'

'*Lequel?* Which of us do you mean?' said Emile. They waited until Kip thanked Posy and walked into the hotel. Emile stood for a moment. 'In some societies, men are expected to marry their wives' sisters,' he remarked cheerfully. 'It is not everywhere disapproved, though, of course, alas, we are not in one of those societies.'

'Well . . .' They stood awkwardly. 'Perhaps a drink after dinner?' he said.

'Right,' Posy agreed.

This Wednesday afternoon, Géraldine Chastine went for
tea, as she often did, with her friends Wendi Le Vert and
Tammy de Bretteville, two American women married to
Frenchmen, and loyal friends as well as part of her professional world. Today, at Wendi's, they began as usual
by catching up on their children. Géraldine, Wendi, and
Tammy could fill each other in on the children almost
in the manner of the old story where people told jokes
by merely mentioning an assigned number. 'Victoire had a
doctor's appointment' would be the shorthand, the mere
phrase was enough to imply a whole constellation of bad
gynecological news, low back pain, some indignity at the
Hôpital des Femmes Malades.

The problems of their respective children were
acknowledged among them – Wendi's married daughter,
Laure, had had somewhat too many children too rapidly;
Vincent, Tammy's son, was still out of work, her daughter, Corinne, was almost comically tactless and married
to a spendthrift; and Géraldine's daughter, Victoire –
Victoire a girl universally beloved for her charm and
energy and the poetic desperation of her situation – was
a concern to them all, standing as she did for everything
French and right-thinking, while being, paradoxically,
a living example of how it would get you nowhere.
Or worse than nowhere, which in Victoire's case was

the eighteenth arrondissement in subsidized housing, with a troublesome Tunisian husband, two dusky babies, endless child-care problems, a tipped uterus, and a low-paying job.

Géraldine especially was an object of sympathy because her friends were aware of the secret taint in Victoire's blood, the permanent strike against the poor young woman that she was three quarters an Anglo-Saxon, Géraldine's mother having been Australian. Then, she was the result of Géraldine's liaison with an Englishman, a brief relationship whimsically resulting in a baby, who was then adopted by Eric Chastine, whom Géraldine had met and married soon after Victoire's birth, thirty years ago. Since Victoire was born in France, been raised as French, had always lived in France, and had a French passport, she had never in her own mind thought of herself as anything but French. Wendi and Tammy, knowing the story, had long silently ascribed some of Victoire's difficulties to the facts of her conception. Being American, they didn't really understand why Géraldine let all this bug her, but they accepted her maternal concern.

Today the talk was of death. Madame Arias, the concierge, had lost her husband, to their eyes a short, sullen, lazy man who let his wife do all the heavy work, except for taking out the garbage containers, and always refused to meet the eyes of the building's occupants. But Madame Arias was devastated, and they could all understand emotional devastation, especially Wendi, who was a widow, but Géraldine and Tammy could, too, now that the apprehensions normal to their phase of life had begun to creep in on them: all was going to end badly for everyone. Eventually something would happen to Eric, to Tammy's husband, Marc, to the three of them, though they were women – yes, all would end badly, as it must.

'Is there anything anyone can do for Madame Arias?'

'We'll go to the service, of course. She'll appreciate that.'

'I feel ashamed of all my hard thoughts about him,' Géraldine said. 'I didn't know he had a heart problem.'

'The *obsèques* will be in Ivry. I hope Ivry is all right with her. Sometimes they prefer to be buried in Portugal,' said Tammy.

The teacups were refilled – *thé vert,* recently found to have anticancer properties. They found a few good things to say of Monsieur Arias – his celerity with the bins, his willingness, before his hernia operation, to help with heavy deliveries. But the universal nature of death itself oppressed them, like cold drops down the neck. She could not help thinking of Adrian Venn.

They passed to the subject of their meeting: an apartment for Géraldine's friend from California. Tammy had quickly found an exquisite small place – two bedrooms on the Quai Malaquais – that might suit, but Amy would have to take it immediately, before it was listed publicly. Géraldine had now seen the space and had called Amy in her room one night before dinner, to speak with enthusiasm of its beautiful view of the Seine, twelve-foot ceilings and nice panelling, two small bedrooms and perfect kitchen recently redone, the rent rather high: forty-two thousand francs a month, seven thousand euros, but then she wouldn't be wanting it forever. Unfurnished, but that was usually better, and Amy could see to the furnishings when she got to Paris, or, if more convenient, Géraldine could ask one of her friends to do some of the basics.

This was Tammy, passionate about the progress she had already made. 'I've found some wonderful chairs, Jean-Marie Fred, signed, but how does she feel about Art Deco? And I wish I had a sense of her budget. These are a bargain but they're still five thousand euros apiece, and we'd need a pair, to merge convincingly with the general Louis Seize *tendance.*'

'She hasn't raised a peep about money,' Géraldine said significantly. Only people who knew her as well as Wendi and Tammy did could have heard in her voice that note of maternal pride, the rich Amy so much the ideal daughter that Victoire, poor girl, did not have any interest in being stylish, *maquillée,* a hostess.

'I've also discovered a wonderful curtain lady,' said her friend Wendi. 'From the Antilles, works for nothing and does the most exquisite shirring. Nobody really understands curtains anymore. I see heavy yellow silk brocade with peach silk linings . . .'

Each nightfall, in the hours before dinner, the switchboard at the Hôtel Croix St Bernard hummed with reprises of the day, verifications, entreaties, reproaches, conversations with stockbrokers living in parts of the planet where the markets were still open, consultations from California not feasible before seven P.M. in France.

Leaving Emile, Posy rushed to her room and called her mother, but didn't succeed in reaching her. She was maddened with frustration at not being able to tell Pam about the unknown sister, and was unable to guess whether her mother had ever heard of this infant. Was it her father's dark secret or known to them both? She couldn't stop saying the name to herself: Victoire. Victoire. Emile and Victoire.

Rupert Venn called Posy from Saint-Gond to say they would not be back tonight; Father's secretary, Madame Hyack, proved to have the second safe-deposit key, and was away until tomorrow. He sighed, feeling sorry for himself. He was invited to dinner chez Monsieur Delamer and regarded it as a heavy prospect. Having just come back to her room, Posy scolded him for not welcoming this chance, so rarely afforded to English people, to eat in a real French home. Rupert was still mellow from a rather nice lunch with Delamer, though he didn't say so to Posy, who he knew had the harder role, staying with Father. He had always, at least when he himself was old enough to understand, worried about Posy's tendency to make herself miserable and lose her temper.

'We have a sister,' Posy said, and told him the news. Rupert was amazed and strangely excited that life could suddenly present something surprising along with the inevitable bad news.

Emile Abboud called his mother-in-law, Géraldine, to say that the prospects for Venn were grim and that he himself could do little and might as well come back to Paris – in a day or two. In the meantime she should try to convince Victoire to come have a look at her comatose parent, though he knew she probably wouldn't.

'He is going to die, then? Stay another few days, dear, for me. I think Victoire might yet come join you.'

'She's not too angry with me for being here instead of her?'

'Of course. She says, "The only man in France to pay more attention to his mother-in-law than to his wife."'

'She will come to see I "have her welfare at heart."' Emile laughed.

'Are there other children? What are they like?'

'He's stifled in progeny – there are an English brother and sister, a baby called Harry with an American mother – she's in a coma too – some kid of fourteen or so – who can say others will not appear?'

'The wife's in a coma? I'm sorry for Vee's sake there aren't fewer children.' Géraldine laughed, realizing that this sounded rather callous. 'We must hope he's awfully rich.'

'There seems to be little concern for his "soul,"' Emile observed. 'No one has called a priest. But no doubt the souls of Englishmen are disposed differently from the rest of us?'

It occurred to Géraldine that here was an argument that might weigh with the somewhat pious Victoire: concern for the rascal Venn's soul. Victoire liked to think of a world in spiritual balance. Her mother was not sure where this tendency came from, as the family was secular in its views.

'You must certainly introduce yourself to my young friend Amy Hawkins. She's skiing there alone,' Géraldine had told him. She ordinarily would hesitate to introduce him to attractive single women, but Amy would meet him

129

eventually, and it would seem odd not to make them aware of each other, staying in the same hotel. Victoire would be there soon enough.

Then Géraldine called Amy to see if she was still having a good time, and to review some details of the apartment Tammy had found for her. With some misgiving, she mentioned that her son-in-law also happened to be there at the Croix St Bernard. 'Quite well known, on television sometimes, he's gaining a name . . .' Amy thought she already had noticed him.

16

After dinner, Posy, like everyone else, headed for the lounge bar, and sat thinking both of Emile and, enviously, of Rupert dining with the provincial business manager, surely not as well as the guests at the Hôtel Croix St Bernard had dined, but blissfully removed from her turbulent discoveries. Her pulse quickened when she was joined (as she had hoped) by Emile, husband of her supposed sister, another alluring mystery. She welcomed a chance at last to understand more about it, though the relationship was now clouded with renunciation and awkwardness. He, however, appeared perfectly at ease, had conquered his earlier air of embarrassment and passed into the easy familiarity of a brother-in-law.

'*Bonsoir*. Hello,' he said. '*Copains de la tempête,*' and instantly picked up her lack of comprehension. 'Companions in the storm. Don't you say that in English? Would you like something? A cognac?' He disappeared for a few moments and came back to sit beside her with two snifters of brandy. He lit her cigarette. She told him about Rupert and the safe-deposit box journey, hoping to signal Rupert's absence.

'And what "treasures" were unearthed in the fabled *coffre*? Have they reported?'

'They can't get into it till tomorrow.'

'Ah. The poor fellow has another day of life, then.'

'Father's life does not depend on that,' she said, indignation stirring at the detachment of his tone, its vague accusation of callousness and pragmatism.

'No? Lucky for him, *alors*. My wife refuses to come, you know – that's why it is I who am here.'

'I wondered about that,' Posy said. 'We had never heard of your wife. It was quite a surprise. What's her name?'

'Victoire.'

'I meant, who is her mother?'

'Ah – the redoubtable – is that the word I mean? – Géraldine Chastine.' He told her what little he knew about the early marriage, or nonmarriage, or one-night stand, of Géraldine and Venn.

'Did my father know about Victoire?'

'I believe so . . . Actually, I have no idea.'

'Does she look like me?'

'Not much. Maybe something about the fair coloring – we dark fellows are like moths to flames. She is older than you, thinner perhaps. I should say has not your voluptuous beauty.' His eyes met hers. Again she had an almost unpleasant visceral stirring.

'Perhaps Father will have left her something,' Posy said.

'In France, you know, Father has no say in the matter. Of course he has left her something, if there's anything to leave. Do you know anything about how your father was fixed?'

'Not really. I was surprised to hear about gold coins and a Bonnard.'

'Though it may be that the illegitimate children don't get quite as large a share as the legitimate ones.'

'There are Rupert and me, and of course the baby,

Harry. But we think he may have left it all to his new wife. He would have done, wouldn't he?' She couldn't bring herself to say 'Kerry.' This man was her ally, after all, and would understand. 'He was very stuck on her . . .' Her mind reviewed the unpleasant scenes she had happened to witness between her mother and father on the subject of Kerry.

'Madame Venn was better today,' he said. 'But no, she cannot inherit it all, we are in France. Through the "majesty" of Napoleon's vision, successions are mostly secured to the children.'

'Well, anyway, Father isn't dead,' she guiltily said. A pause.

'He is dead, you know, Posy.'

Posy stared into her drink, heart pounding, but it was not the idea of father's death, it was the presence of Emile. She had a sudden intimation of where proximity, conversation, and the brandy could lead them again, and she was saying to herself, why not? What did she care about some hypothetical half-sister who wasn't here? If you couldn't be totally bad at a stressful, unnatural time like this, when could you? Tonight was perfect, with Rupert not here . . . Her mind trailed on, trying to think of something to say in the present moment.

'I loved going to bed with you,' she suddenly said, surprised at the elegaic, plaintive tone of her own voice. 'Don't you think we could, one last time . . . I mean . . . ?'

She would afterward think about his expression. Was he about to say no or yes? With her rotten luck, she was never to know, for here was Christian Jaffe coming toward her, and bending to whisper that Mr Osworthy had arrived, and had asked him to let her know and would she follow him?

'Right, thanks,' sighed Posy. She got up. 'Mr Osworthy is my father's solicitor, and I guess I have to go speak to him.'

Emile nodded, rose as she rose. He might have indicated that he would wait till she had finished with Mr Osworthy, but instead he said, 'Good night. I'm sure we'll meet tomorrow,' his expression now seeming quite indifferent to this revision of her erotic hopes, whatever he had been going to say. As Posy left the bar, she immediately began to see the moment in a more sensible way – what had she been thinking of? – but she forgave herself, in view of the stress they were all under, for having these inclinations toward her exotic stepbrother-in-law, whatever that made them as relatives.

Mr Osworthy stood by the front desk, bending over his valise. His white hair and city clothes marked him immediately as British, out of place and damp with snow, and he wore a cross, punitive expression, like a bailiff. When he saw Posy he shook her hand, but with a frown, and said, 'Where's Rupert, then?'

'Hullo, Mr Osworthy. He's with Father's French man of business, taking some things out of Father's safety-deposit box while he's still alive.'

'Really? The French amaze me.' He frowned more severely. 'I'll have a whiskey and turn in, I suppose. Rupert can tell me about it tomorrow. What time will he be back?'

'Sometime tomorrow afternoon, I guess.' She gave him such details as she knew, not failing to notice that

Rupert seemed to be, in Mr Osworthy's mind, the only responsible person in the family.

Mr Osworthy handed his valise to Mademoiselle Jaffe. '*Poovez voo déposer ma valise?*' he said in clear British French. '*Je vais au bar.* Well, Posy, I won't keep you up. I know how hard this is on you.' Posy felt herself sent to bed, but she obeyed. She supposed she ought to tell Mr Osworthy about the existence of the sister, or maybe he knew. It was clear Mr Osworthy could see into her heart and would know that she had been thinking about going to bed with Mr Abboud, and would impede all her other desires too. She lay awake a long time, half hoping for Emile's tap at her door, though of course she knew he didn't know which was her room, but she could think of ways he could find out if motivated.

Amy, sitting with Kip and Joe Daggart in the bar, noticed Posy and the dark, handsome man. Did Kip know who he was?

'He was at the hospital,' Kip said.

'Emile someone – I've seen him on television,' Joe Daggart said. Emile someone was a newcomer. At dinner tonight, Amy had sat at table with a prince, even if Romanian, and princess, even if American, a nationality distant and submerged in this individual. The prince and *princesse*, though aristocrats, were little wizened people in their seventies, with hair dyed black and speaking an English of incredible vivacity. Joe Daggart had eaten with them too. Amy felt pleased with the number of her new acquaintances. By now she could meet the eyes of several other of the hotel guests with a friendly nod and smiles, and it all gave her a pleasant sense of being familiar and worldly. She knew better than to be impressed – this friendliness was owing to no quality of her own except that she could afford to stay at this hotel; but she marvelled at the ease with which you could enter an alternative and fabled reality. Whether you could stay there or would want to was another matter.

She could happily stay awhile longer in the world of skiing, for certain. Today the slight anxiety that had hung over the entire valley since the avalanches had eased further, and she had had the intermittent sense of exhilaration and power skiers are meant to have. At one period in college she had lived for skiing. It was the same period when her friends – so fortuitously, it would prove – had been the geeky physics and math majors who would later make her fortune, and they had been skiers too. Many was the night she had slept over at their computer dump of an apartment littered with hard drives and smelling of solder, so they could get up at three and be at Tahoe and on the slopes by nine. But since then she hadn't had time for it, and now wanted to have again the thrilling sense of speed and freedom it brought.

She thought about the dinner conversation. 'We heard about your good deed,' the *princesse* had said in a perfectly American accent. For a millisecond, Amy couldn't place her good deed: paying for Kip's baby-sitter apparently was meant. She wondered how they could have heard of it.

'What a handsome thing!' exclaimed the prince.

'It was very thoughtful,' said the *princesse*. Amy, grateful for a subject, told them what Kip had told her of his sister's condition.

'It's so terrible for him,' she said. 'His sister in a coma, and they have no relatives or anyone.' The others turned their faces to where Kip sat at his table, jamming food into the tot.

'The eyelids fluttering is apparently a very good sign,' Amy went on. 'They expect her eventually to be okay.'

'And you, dear, are from California, Robin says.' All in all, it made Amy uneasy to have the light of their interest directed on her. She knew what people really thought of Californians and people from Silicon Valley.

'Have you been there?' she asked, to change the course of the conversation. They had been to Carmel and Monterey, where the prince had played the course at Pebble Beach.

It had come up at this dinner that there is something the French call *l'esprit de l'escalier*, stairway wit. It refers to the things you think up later that you should have said. She had been suffering from it her whole life long without knowing it had a name, and it was what kept her awake now. Whole passages from the dinner conversation ran through her mind now, in which she had been inevitably really lame.

'How many languages does the educated person speak?' she had asked at one point, meaning to launch a spritely debate (a group team leadership technique promulgated widely in Silicon Valley, which, in the main, she scorned but could not be unaware of.)

'Ah. Speak or read?' asked Robin Crumley.

'Well, isn't it the same?' (Definitely not, she now saw. Dumb.)

'Not at all,' said the *princesse* Mawlesky.

'I haven't really begun my French lessons, I'm planning to do that in Paris, but I'm starting to read,' Amy had said. (Two errors: non sequitur, talking about self.)

'Four, I think,' said Robin Crumley. 'Speak two fluently, have a reading knowledge of two more, that's a minimum, but we Anglo-Saxons are at a disadvantage, we're so bad at languages.'

'What languages do you speak? "Have," I should say,' asked Amy. 'What languages do you have?'

'English, and French, a little Italian. I'd always been planning to read Dante in the original, but I'm ashamed to say I've never done it. Of course I do have a little Welsh, but I don't count it. People say that Catalan . . . it's a funny story about how I came to learn Catalan . . .'

Oh, God, thought Amy, doubting she would ever learn even two.

Then, to her chagrin now, she had gone on to tell them about the Crakes method, a technique where you learn four languages at once, for which she was hoping to find a teacher.

'Good God, whatever for?' said Robin Crumley.

'Yes, four at once. While you're learning the French word for tree, say, you might as well learn the German and the Italian and the Greek at the same time.' Or was the fourth one Latin?

'*Albero? Baum?*' said the prince wonderingly, as if these words had been in his brain from birth, and he couldn't remember a time he didn't know them, or envision a being so low she would have to struggle to acquire these simple basic nouns.

And, worst of all, at another moment she had mentioned Darwin. 'Do Europeans believe in Darwin?' She had thought she had an opening for a discussion of mutual aid.

They had looked at her, as if to say, Believe in? In the religious sense?

'I'm not aware that the ideas of Darwin are an issue of faith,' said Robin Crumley. 'Are they not agreed upon? Natural selection, the survival of the fittest?'

'Not in America,' said Amy. 'Of course, with our tradition of dissent, nothing is agreed upon. Many people are challenging Darwin, both from the left and the right – the latter the fundamentalists, but that's another thing. The point is, the survival of the fittest is what stuck in your mind. I expect you regard that as the abiding principle of social organization.'

'Undoubtedly. Darwin seemed to be a master psychologist, whatever he lacked as a biologist.'

'No, no,' she had cried, 'the other way round! He was a masterly biologist, but not much of a student of human behavior. He never noticed that the fittest species survived because of strategies of cooperation.'

'As we see among the tribes of Africa, or in Kosovo,' laughed the *princesse*.

'A good example. The people who are going to survive there are the NATO powers who are cooperating against all those factions and nationalities who are destroying each other instead of cooperating . . .' How she regretted now her earnest tone, the flush she had felt rising to her cheeks.

At the same time, now, she despised herself for feeling

the least chagrin. Why should she feel concern for the opinions of a bunch of seedy Europeans whom she could buy and sell, probably, not that that was a criterion. What she hated was confirming by her own example their notions of the naive and unlettered American. She was not a crass rube, she was an intelligent and hardworking person, immensely successful by her own efforts, whose experiences with cultural subjects had been limited until now by circumstance. She had to keep reminding herself of this.

17

Mr Trevor Osworthy had been unsettled and shocked by Posy's news that Rupert Venn had been asked to lend himself to an unsavory scheme to open Venn's safe-deposit box without express instructions from its owner, or even the owner's wife, and was even more alarmed to hear of the interference of a shady French businessman. It was worrying to hear that this person had authorization to open the box, and it unsettled the whole foundation of the orderly processes that could be expected to ensue when a person died, if Venn were to die. Even three whiskies in the bar of the Hôtel Croix St Bernard didn't prevent him from lying awake, brooding, and, eventually, forming a resolution.

His first move, after breakfast, was to go directly to the hospital, without Posy and before Rupert's return, to see for himself the medical situation. He thus arrived early, during the ward rounds. 'Don't mind me, *ne me regardez pas*,' he assured the surprised doctors. The covers were unmounded, and Mrs Venn's form lay in its yellow hospital gown tied with strings, so short Mr Osworthy was obliged to avert his eyes, before being shooed out of the room anyway. He had never met the new Mrs Venn, and had to say that her reputed freshness and charm were far from apparent. Bluish stalk legs sticking from under a smelly, crinkled garment, hair of an indeterminate color clotted to a damp head, tubes. Through the oval window of the door, from the hall Osworthy could see the doctors tickling her foot while another pair, like a team of torturers, shone a light in her eye. When the doctors moved on to another bed, Osworthy charged in again and moved to the bedside of a thing that must be Venn, poor devil, a being of a terrible color, plastic tubes coming out of his nose and mouth, and a great many more attached to his wrists, ankles, and, from its location, to his genitals, painful thought.

'Venn, good Lord,' Osworthy murmured. Pam Venn had been right to ask him to come, even though she wasn't directly interested. Osworthy knew how Venn had left things, and it wasn't to Pam. A lovely woman, Pam Venn, he had always thought, and he hadn't been fully in sympathy with some of the harsh measures Adrian had been capable of suggesting to overcome her disinclination to divorce.

Now, however, it was plain that the first thing to be done was to get the man to England, in the hope of saving his life.

When Posy, with some disgust when she thought about Rupert's having now got out of two days of bedside sitting (reproaching herself for such thoughts), arrived at the hospital armed with her book and packet of cigarettes, she found a fracas in progress. The doctor was wildly addressing and, it seemed, denouncing, Mr Osworthy, in the presence of Father's inert form, shouting over the wheezing din of the machines. Osworthy drew Posy into the discussion without delay.

'I'm telling the man we want to transfer him immediately. I've spoken to London and the medical evacuation people. It's a tricky business, but luckily his insurance will pay; it seems he took the ski insurance, I'm damned suprised.'

'London?' Posy stared at Father's apparatus, the imposing size of the life-giving machines.

'I must say, Posy, it should have been obvious to Rupert – to you, for that matter – that he should have been evacuated two days ago. This hospital – look around you! It can hardly be equipped with all that's needed, there's been no consultant – the French could have proposed a consultant, it's unimaginable they didn't . . .' He ranted on in this style. The doctor, appearing to find in Posy the hope of someone who would listen to reason, turned to her and switched from excited French into English, explaining the reasons why it would be dangerous folly to move her father, all was being done that could possibly be done, the facilities didn't exist on any known plane to transport someone on life support.

'This is not Saudi Arabia, mademoiselle, we do not have intensive care units on planes.'

'We want to do the right thing,' she said uncertainly.

'The man will never survive the trip, we are doing everything humanly possible right here. It is not rocket science, the man is nearly dead, we can only –'

'You must try to arrange it. Whatever happens –' said Osworthy.

'But the danger, the expense . . . ?'

'Whatever happens, he would want to be in England,' said Osworthy, and Posy didn't actually see that she could argue with that.

'I have said, there is no plane with an intensive unit, no one would take a patient in this condition –'

'Or an equipped ambulance,' Osworthy insisted. 'I will look into it. If we can get him to the Brompton Hospital. I know the consultants there.'

'And what about Madame Venn? And will all the children agree?' said the doctor.

'Agree? Why should they object?'

'Well, to die in England and to die in France – it is two different things, evidently,' said the doctor.

This was not evident to Posy nor, at first, to Mr Osworthy. They were stopped, they reflected.

'The point is, he should not die,' said Osworthy with great assurance. 'I'll go the hotel. When do we expect Rupert, Posy?'

Posy sat a little while longer with Father, half persuaded by Mr Osworthy that maybe English medicine would have an answer, and shocked at herself for not having looked into it, she who was usually able to see the practical side of things. How she wished for Rupert, if only to berate him for leaving her to deal with all this. She wondered if Father weren't a little worse today, a bluish cast to his skin, dark blotches under his eyes that hadn't been there yesterday.

She had found a photograph of him, stuck in her book; she had clipped it from a newspaper a few months ago. Father is attending a publishers' meeting with a member of a trade commission representing book manufacturers in Brussels, to oppose a projected tariff on books in stock, in the warehouse, or on publishers' shelves. While others in the photo seem animated, or are simulating animated discussion, Father stares blankly at the photographer, not seeking the approval of the camera but uninvolved in what is going on around him, distanced or shadowed by something in the future or distracted by some memory. Posy had seen other photographs like this, of other people, who would die soon after. If it were in color, it might show the aura of death, if you believed in auras. At the time, they had said with some malice, 'Looks like his life with Kerry isn't a bed of roses.'

She was shaken, and as she sat throughout the morning her dismay worsened, thinking that their easy acquiescence to the decision to probably pull the plug one of these days, their acceptance of the doctor's dictum, made this bedside vigil a kind of act of bad faith, of hypocrisy. Here she was hoping for him to get better and at the same time planning his death instead of actively soliciting his recovery. She tried to force her mind around to a hope he could recover, this emotion in turn warring with her real vengeful feeling that he had brought all this on himself, silly bloke, with his girl-wife and a dozen other birds before, giving all that trouble to them all and especially to Mother.

From time to time during these boring vigils, Posy allowed herself to dream of a vast inheritance. She knew Father wasn't rich like that, of course, this was just a reverie. With the vast inheritence she could say sod the bras and knickers boutique and could open something of her own, dealing in old paisley shawls and steamer trunks, say, or get a job as a researcher at the BBC, which would pay nothing, but you met everybody and it led to something. Or just do nothing and buy a house to fix up. Of course she knew that her share of whatever Father had would not, ever, add up to an independent income, but she would invest wisely . . .

Eventually she went back to the hotel. Dr Lamm had approached her one more time before she left, saying with Gallic certitude, 'It is futile to move your father, it is wrong, and it is impossible.'

The day was snowing and dark, so most of the skiers had come in or had stayed in, and were taking lunch at the hotel. Rupert got back from Saint-Gond as it was being served, and joined Posy and Osworthy at their table. Posy had just been pointing out Kip and baby Harry sitting nearby, with the American heiress, or such was the rumor about her that Posy had heard in the bar. Osworthy turned from his study of Kip and Harry to greet Rupert, delighted to see Rupert, a responsible male Venn.

'I feel I must speak frankly, now that you're here, Rupert. I was quite surprised to hear what you were off doing. It could have the appearance of crime. You wouldn't want it to look like you were helping yourself.'

'I suppose not,' said Rupert, 'but it seems to be commonly done here.'

'Important to avoid getting implicated in something like that. I think you should know, too, if your father dies, you don't come in for much – something, of course. You, too, Posy. The bulk of his estate goes to his wife, naturally enough. Nothing abnormal in that.'

'We know that, or we expected it, anyhow.'

'What did you actually find in the safe-deposit box?'

'Pretty much what we'd been told: some gold coins, a small painting signed by Bonnard, old books, some jewelry. The *notaire* took everything out and we locked it in his office safe. He wrote out a receipt for me. I couldn't tell if any of it had any value, but he seemed relieved the French tax people wouldn't get their hands on it.'

'I am sure there is a penalty for hiding things from the fiscal authorities. How long the arms of the French fiscal authorities are I couldn't say,' said Osworthy, his sniff suggesting his contempt for the sleazy local practices, opening private safe-deposit boxes, secreting funds. He rose.

'I'll just go over and have a look at young Harry, present myself, it looks like he's in charge, the older boy I mean. He's the brother of Mrs Venn? Who are the women? He may need some help with a baby that young. Posy, did you offer to help?'

'God, no,' mouthed Posy to Mr Osworthy's back.

'To tell the truth,' Rupert told Posy, 'when I saw Father's stuff, it wrenched me in a way his situation hadn't yet. There was a sort of presence to his things – you sensed the person who had chosen them, cared for them, loved these old books – or I guess he loved them. He valued them, anyhow, paid for them, put them away. He had thoughts and hopes – do you know what I mean? Suddenly in the midst of having thoughts, he's lying like a vegetable. It was like looking at his diary or his clothes. It made me hope all the more that he'll live. I hope he does, and I hope he won't be too frosted that we got into his box.'

Approaching their table, Mr Osworthy presented himself to Kip and Amy. 'Adrian Venn's solicitor. Came in last night. I take it this is Harry? What a fine fellow. I'd heard a lot about him from Adrian – apple of his eye, you know.'

Kip started politely to rise, but was pushed back into his chair by the friendly paw of Osworthy.

'This is Kip Canby, Harry's uncle,' Amy said. 'I'm Amy Hawkins, a friend of Kip's, and this is Miss, I mean Mademoiselle Walther, who helps with Harry.' The Jaffes had found a teenager from the village, to be supervised by the hotel's own chambermaid Tamara, and Kip would only have to look after the baby at night. Amy had told Christian Jaffe she would pay for it, it was little enough that she could do, though it occurred to her that it was really this man's obligation, if he was the family lawyer.

'Hello, Harry,' said Osworthy, patting the baby's head. 'You've got Harry organized, I see, Kip. I just wanted to tell you how things stand. We think Harry's father has a greater chance if we get him to England. I've decided to remove him to the Brompton Hospital in London if all goes well. They have expert teams for these things. Well known – all the sheiks and mullahs come right to England. Apparently it's complicated, aerial transport with respirators and so on, but it can be done. I'll be working on it this afternoon.'

Kip heard this in amazement and with relief, followed immediately by a new fear. It was probably good they were planning to take Adrian to a bigger hospital, but what about Kerry, and what about him, and Harry?

'What about Kerry?' he asked.

'They say she's doing a bit better, so we'll concentrate on Venn for the moment. I think the doctor would say there was no point in taking the risks involved in trans-

148

port where the situation is not desperate.' Osworthy's voice had the falsely soothing tones of a school psychologist. Kip didn't buy it. Despite what the doctors said, he couldn't see that Kerry was any better at all, didn't she need saving by the Brompton Hospital too? He glanced at Amy. She was the only person he had talked about all this to, plus she seemed to know about the law. He liked the idea of them all going to England where he could talk to people in English.

Osworthy invited Kip to come to his suite before dinner tonight. 'You too, madam, if you like. I should have some news by then. Bring everyone involved,' he added in the authoritative voice of someone who is finally getting the bunglers organized. He nodded and went back to his table.

Kip looked across the room at Emile Abboud. Though he came to the hospital meetings, Kip didn't know how Mr Abboud was involved exactly, or whether he should be told about Mr Osworthy's meeting. Abboud was reading the paper by the windows, apparently waiting for his soup. Kip didn't really think he himself should go to Mr Osworthy's meeting, either, it was more about Adrian. As usual, no one talked about Kerry.

'As long as your sister's doing okay, it might be better to leave her as she is,' Amy said, agreeing with Osworthy. 'It's probably complicated to arrange moving someone in intensive care.'

'They say she's doing okay, but she hasn't changed at all that I can see,' Kip said. 'She just lies there.' He heard his voice quaver.

On the other hand, Amy thought, with her practical

concerns, it was possible these English people were trying to run out on Kip's sister's care, or planning to abandon her in some way, leaving Kip to make decisions and pay the bills. She promised Kip to have a frank talk with Mr Osworthy about some of these issues.

Mr Osworthy's voice almost shook with his outrage as he sat down again at his table. 'You didn't tell me, Posy, that the American boy had hired counsel, surely that wasn't necessary? I'm certainly acting in the interests of everyone concerned, especially the baby; after all, he's Adrian's principle heir, with his mother, so I hardly think . . .'

'I don't think she's his lawyer, but I don't know anything about it, Mr Osworthy,' said Posy in as docile a voice as possible. 'How would I?'

'American lawyers are notorious ambulance-chasers, probably she got wind of it,' said Rupert.

'I mean, why is it my bloody fault?' Posy went on in a stronger voice.

'I will advise her that she should move her client to a more up-to-date facility if they are not satisfied with her progress in Moutiers. But I had understood they expect Mrs Venn to wake up soon,' went on Mr Osworthy in a tone that suggested he felt a deep sense of injury at Amy's involvement.

'It seems to me Kerry is *your* client,' Posy pointed out. 'I've never heard that the American is a lawyer.'

'Time will tell,' said Mr Osworthy.

18

In her room before dressing for Osworthy's meeting and dinner, Amy did her CD-ROM French lesson, called her financial person, Sigrid, then turned on the radio and lay in the bathtub listening to music punctuated with announcements in the unfamiliar language. After the stormy morning, the afternoon had started out with a wintry glint of sun, and she'd gone out, but hadn't worn a sweater under her ski jumpsuit *(combinaison)*, so that when the skies clouded over again at the end of the day she had got cold but had been too far from the hotel to go in. Now, as she was chilled to the bone, the hot water felt wonderful. It's nice being cold, then warm, being tired, being exhilarated, she thought. She had made progress under the eyes of Paul-Louis, the delightful French ski instructor who drove her up and down pistes that she had thought were too hard for her in a language she could not understand.

It's sort of nice not understanding what people on the radio were saying – something about Haydn, she thought. Any familiar word leapt out at her. It was soothing not to understand the rest and not be asked to understand. The mind seeks blankness from time to time, the way you have to run down the battery of your computer from time to time. An emptiness to fill with a headier, more concentrated program of new ingredients. Haydn, French literature, antiques correctly patinated, geopolitics. Once you've decided to jettison the old knowledge – both the baby and the bathwater – the possibilities are ripe for a new soup of limitless savor.

Kip was getting help from Miss Walther, so he could go skiing and spend some time, without Harry, at Kerry's bedside – he was conscientious about this. Yet he had Harry with him an awful lot, it seemed to him, especially all night. He found that if he kept Harry up watching TV he slept later. It was remarkable that a baby could watch TV. Kip remembered seeing on television an account of a school where girls in his same grade, though in another school, had to carry ten pound sacks of flour around all the time to make them conscious of what it would be like to have a baby. He wasn't even a girl and he was conscious of it for sure. He had bought some blocks and other stuff at a shop in the village and had charged it on Adrian's credit card. That made him feel sort of criminal though he knew it was all right. He thought as he went to Mr Osworthy's room that he should explain this to Mr Osworthy.

Osworthy, finding himself in a distant Alpine village with a decent allocation for expenses, had ordered several *plateaux* of oysters from room service and two bottles of champagne, to soothe his clients' spirits and, not incidentally, since he found himself in a fine hotel, to sample its amenities himself. Though French, therefore transported here God knew in what conditions, the oysters should be all right, it being winter. The waitress had spread towels on the bureau to protect it, and arranged along it the platters of heaped crushed ice and the opened creatures on their icy beds. The two bottles in buckets on teetery stands were placed at the end with five glasses poised to be filled. Did it look too festive in view of the circumstances? He hoped not. Six dozen oysters divided among five people, five into seventy-two ... maybe the American boy wouldn't eat any, or Posy. Women often didn't like oysters.

He took this assembly most seriously. Having set his staff, in prospect, to looking into some of Adrian's affairs, he had been surprised to find them in solid, even astounding, affluence. Even his vineyard, from a brief review of his French tax returns, appeared to have made money. His press, for years a losing self-indulgence, had recently sometimes made money, his investments, in the long boom of the eighties, had boomed. Osworthy was gratified but challenged. He would of course have given the humblest tinker all his advice and expertise if the fellow was his client, but the aura of money suddenly haloing the raffish Venn lent a certain sacred importance to the trust Venn had placed in him, and lent a certain bracing interest to the whole thing too.

The heirs – he thought of them as the heirs though Adrian was not dead – arrived, a little somber. The American youth, still in ski clothes and après-ski boots, came in exuding a brisk boyish fragrance of outdoors and cold. He had brought with him the woman who had been sitting with him at lunch, the attractive Californian who was, or wasn't, his lawyer. This person, Miss Hawkins, was dressed for dinner in a simple black dress, as though in mourning already. She was pretty, in his opinion, with a polished simplicity that made poor Posy seem all the more blowsy. Osworthy had noticed that Posy's clothes were always quite inappropriate – rather low necked and tight. Some women couldn't help looking like tarts no matter what they wore, and poor Posy was evidently one of them, though she had a good Cambridge degree. Doubtless, too, styles had changed. Both Miss Hawkins and the boy declined oysters, and took on panicked expressions when these were offered a second time. *Tant mieux,* as they say here, thought Osworthy, the more for the rest of us.

He explained that he hadn't made much progress that afternoon in organizing the transport of the patient, doubly difficult over the objections of the French doctors and with the absolute nonexistence of a vehicle of any kind capable of transporting a patient on life support. Fortunately, Adrian was holding his own, had not got worse, so there was still tomorrow. 'I've been on the telephone the whole afternoon. I expect my efforts to bear fruit by tomorrow, but we may have underestimated the difficulties here. Mind you, I find the French doctors absurdly territorial. It wounds their vanity to imply they haven't been doing all that can be done. It would help if they would cooperate. We must, we must, get him home,' said Osworthy fervently.

Osworthy wondered if the American boy understood the importance of transporting Venn. Of course, the boy's interests were directly counter to those of Rupert and Posy, in that his sister would get virtually nothing if Adrian died here in France, with its Napoleonic prejudices against wives, and everything if (when?) he died in London, with things left according to his will. Was that why he had brought the American lawyer? He looked a young boy for such calculation, so it must be the woman who had thought it through. Osworthy asked if there were any questions, in part to learn what they did understand. He tried to clarify further.

'I asked you all here, because I think everyone should understand the situation. There is no mystery, and I want no one to harbor false expectations. In the case of his death, Mr Venn's will leaves his estate to his wife, Kerry Canby, with a small sum for his children Rupert and Posy, a few thousand pounds apiece as I remember. Young Harry is not mentioned in particular, but I think, without doubt, that the law would hold him to be included, because he was not excluded. There is no comma after the word *children*, and I don't doubt that will be a matter of dispute, but –'

'Can we talk about expenses for one minute,' interrupted the American, Miss Hawkins, and her demure, appealing face had suddenly a rather set expression. 'Kip and Harry are dependent on Mr Venn, or his estate, to defray their current living expenses, and I have some concerns about Harry's future, both the expenses and custody.'

'Harry's mother is expected to recover,' said Osworthy severely.

'A. Will she be liable for her husband's medical expenses if in French law she doesn't inherit? B. For the hotel bill?' said Amy, looking at her notes.

'Ah, Miss Hawkins, that is my point,' said Mr Osworthy, seeing a way to enlist her support, for they were, after all, on the same side as to where poor Venn should die. 'That's why, whatever happens, it's essential it happen in England, where Kerry Venn has the natural widow's rights and obligations according to Mr Venn's clear intentions. Here – I'm not clear, but it appears to be otherwise. I cannot speak for France, and I cannot off the top of my head resolve the question of which national law would prevail in the case of an Englishman dying in France or vice versa. God alone knows who the French would think should pay the hotel bill.'

'Kip is in no position to take care of financial matters himself,' Amy said. 'Mr Venn has been supporting him and paying his school fees.'

'Unfortunately, no one dies without effect. We cannot help what we cannot help,' sighed Osworthy.

'But the French doctors think he's certain to die no matter where,' Posy said in her quarrelsome way. 'If that's true, I don't know that I want Father to die in England. Why would I? From what I'm hearing, if he dies in England, Rupert and I get two beans, and if he dies here, we get our full share of his money.'

'It's hardly a time to privilege your personal motives, Posy,' Osworthy said, deeply shocked. 'There may be a chance of saving him. Surely you want that?'

Posy's defiant outburst could not prevail against such a reproach. 'Of course,' she said meekly. 'But our other sister may not be so compliant.'

'For God's sake, what other sister?' Osworthy snapped.

'You mean nobody's told you?' said Posy with great

enjoyment at seeing the stunned expression that momentarily froze Osworthy's jowly face.

Posy and Rupert, having thanked Mr Osworthy for his efforts in behalf of their father, said they would see him at dinner and took themselves off to the bar for something stronger than champagne.

'I'm going skiing tomorrow,' Rupert announced, somewhat defiantly. 'I'll look in at the hospital early and come in again at the end of the day.'

He had been cheered at the addition to the gloomy conference orchestrated by Osworthy of the unexpected American lawyer, or whatever she was, who had seemed both lovely and reasonable, and not as if she would make trouble. She was here to take cooking lessons and skiing lessons, she had said, and had invited him to join a skiing party with them in the morning – the boy Kip, some other people she'd met, and Robin Crumley, the famous poet, not that he had read much poetry since leaving school, but Crumley was often on the telly, writing about country life, the roses blowing in the hedges and so on, and then a thorn. There was always a thorn, or a worm. 'I *thought* that was Robin Crumley,' he had said to Posy. Crumley didn't ski but would come by car to meet them at lunch in some village their monitor would take them to. He stole a glance at Posy to see if she would utterly resent his defection, and saw from her scowl that she would.

'You could come in the car with Robin Crumley,' he said, and she brightened. 'I'll see to it.'

'Do you secretly think Father's wife is going to die too?' said Posy, who had evidently been thinking about this.

'Supposedly not.'

'I would hope they would tell us the truth, because if they're both going to die, it would be better if she died first,' Posy said. Rupert, to his chagrin, instantly saw what she meant. If Father died first, his money went to his wife, and then when she died the baby would get it all; but if she died first, they were directly in line. That's if they were both going to die.

'That's just in England,' he said.

'I cannot believe we're saying these things, but anyway, it's plain that Father must die in France. It's going to turn out that way anyhow,' Posy said. 'We aren't causing it by saying it. Mr Osworthy will never find an airplane willing to transport him.'

They made their way to where Emile was sitting. They all nodded cordially and Rupert and Posy slid in next to him.

'I looked in at the hospital at about five,' he told them. 'They were quite encouraged about something to do with Madame Venn's condition. No change in that of your father.'

'Could we speak frankly?' Posy asked, fooling with a cigarette to master the confusion that seized her whenever she met this man. 'Have you heard that Father's lawyer wants to move him to England, in hopes he can be saved there? That would be marvelous, but who can believe he can be saved? Not the doctor, that's clear. We think it's more that Mr Osworthy wants Father to die under the British flag because it makes a difference to what happens to – well, everything, his château and money.'

Emile considered this. 'I suppose it would. The laws of succession are probably very different in the two countries, though I don't know what they are. England, I'm sure, is very capricious.'

'Why capricious?' They bridled alertly.

'The English indulge the caprices of the dying, I gather. France disregards them for good reason, to avoid the stupid or inappropriate things people do at the last minute to seal themselves to life.'

'You don't think people should be able to do what they want with their money?'

'Certainly not,' said Emile.

Rupert intervened smoothly. 'The point is that you – that is, your wife – and Posy and I are sort of on the same side in this. It's better for us all, if Father were to die, that he did it in France. It was you who told me that in France you can't disinherit your children.'

'Which has been held by many to be a great pity,' said Emile.

Emile was a natural troublemaker in part because he was intelligent, and delighted in the complications a moment of obstinacy or a noncompliant gesture or impulsive action could bring on. He had always enjoyed observing these complications, and submitted to the deepening cynicism they inspired in him with a sense of his own perfectability. In time he could become a perfect cynic. But first he would have to master his own inclinations to give in to joy, love, and the like, emotions that got in the way of calculation. Now he wavered between having a laugh with these attractive but apparently perfidious English people, whose interests were the same as Victoire's, and suggesting that they just pull the plug on their father, who was effectively dead anyhow, as no one seemed able to admit.

'I think Victoire needs to come down here,' he told Géraldine later on the telephone. 'Just remind her that it's the *patrimoine* of Nike and Salome that's at stake.' He explained to her what he suspected the motives were behind the effort of his attorney to move the moribund Venn to England.

'Vee would never go anywhere just for money,' Géraldine said. 'I'll have to give her a better reason. Perhaps to please you, Emile, if you told her you'd like a few days together.'

'Why not?' said Emile. *Pourquoi pas?*

Emile, now that he had been here awhile, had begun to feel less impatient to be back in Paris, though he would be forced to go back on Monday at the latest for his weekly appearance on a Tuesday television roundtable. Meantime, at the Hôtel Croix St Bernard, there was a quiet cardroom where he could work, there was the exotic company of skiers, English people, an assortment of pretty women – though the little dash with Miss Venn was not to be continued – and the very good food, which interested him as it would any Frenchman, however intellectual. The rhythm of life in a gracious hotel had its soothing effect on him, as it did those of most of the hotel guests who weren't partying in the village discos or soaking in their tubs in the spa room after a day outside.

The Venn affair and the numbers of people who kept

showing up because of it made Emile wonder if the money involved weren't more substantial than he had supposed. He hadn't asked Géraldine about the sums – he himself was not venal. Géraldine was, however, so he should have guessed from her concern that some money came into it. Still, Venn was English, and the English were all poor as grasshoppers, judging from the frayed cuffs and hole-riddled sweater of the noted English poet Robin Crumley, like himself a nonskier, so also to be found writing in the mornings in the cardroom. They had become acquainted when they exchanged a few words on the book Emile was reading, by P. G. Wodehouse. Emile had found it on the hotel shelves, and it amazed him. Emile had heard of Crumley, and Crumley, the latter seemed to imply, had heard of Emile.

It was from this poet that Emile had gleaned some bits of hotel gossip, for instance that there were uncrowned heads of European royalty and an unattached, very rich American girl, something about an electronics fortune or anyway some commodity more ephemeral than the classical sources of American fortunes like timber, rail-roads or oil. Emile had doubted the extent of this fortune much as he did that of Venn, for he saw no bodyguards or duennas, though he had no doubt the girl in question was Géraldine's friend, and he could easily find out the true story. He agreed that she was beautiful.

'But it seems unlikely that immensely rich girls just walk around,' he objected.

'And she's very sprightly and sweet,' said Robin Crumley. 'I don't know when I've been so struck by someone's freshness, sweetness – a rose, veritably.'

'You're married, I expect,' said Robin during one of their conversations. Emile agreed he was.

'I've never married. Not inclined to. To tell the truth, I've never much related to the female body.' There was a certain practised smoothness to this confession that told Emile he had made it before, was used to making it. For his part, Emile was used to sexual overtures from men as well as women and usually just pretended not to have heard them, if this was one.

'Perhaps you guessed that. So I've never really explored my heterosexual side – I do believe that everyone is bisexual, don't you? And now to have fallen in love at last – I speak of the delectable Amy.'

'I agree that she is very pretty. But she's an American,' said Emile sternly.

'I like Americans. Their simplicity and sense of entitlement enchant me. Especially their simplicity.'

'Doesn't that describe women in general?' said Emile.

'In fact, I think less and less about the physical.' His concerned expression suggested to Emile that, *au contraire,* he was thinking more about it, and finding it troubling.

'I would agree there is a certain theoretical or arbitrary aspect to sexuality,' said Emile cautiously, 'but the body must be willing to go along with whatever is decided.' He was thinking of Foucault, *pauvre type.*

'For some the body rules, but that was never my case,' sighed Robin Crumley.

Emile had ignored Géraldine's suggestion that he meet Amy Hawkins. He had no wish to meet Americans. He had devoted considerable thought, ink, and airwaves to the subject of cultural difference, and as a certified French intellectual, he had one especially dogmatic, unwavering, and largely unexamined belief, clung to with almost religious fervor: the unregenerate wickedness of America. This naturally extended to Americans themselves, though he knew only his mother-in-law's appalling *décoratrice* friends. (Géraldine herself he liked as well as men ever like their mothers-in-law, ambivalently, in that they incarnate the eventual metamorphosis of their wives.) She seemed to understand very well the ways Victoire, with her goodness and political correctness, could be impossible. It was paradoxical: though he liked Géraldine – he appreciated her reluctance to comment on the situation between him and Victoire, for instance – he mistrusted her mixture of good taste and commercial instinct.

He everywhere found examples of the detestability of Americans – brash, arrogant, loud-talking, and loud-dressing bullies with no understanding of other cultures, a complete lack of interest in things beyond themselves, and concerned only with American hegemony. He would not voluntarily make the acquaintance of one, and didn't anticipate that he'd have to.

He had noticed Géraldine's little friend Amy, in fact of above medium height, in the bar after the lifts had closed, or at meals, often being monopolized by Crumley and an elderly Polish prince, and increasingly by others too. An heiress? He deplored the crass materialism of the Englishman and the others who fawned over her, something that didn't escape him, though he had no doubt that Crumley's infatuation had other grounds too. She, for her part, from afar seemed natural and full of smiles –

Americans with their smiling masks and the rather impervious beauty of their bland features, perhaps the reflex of their inner emptiness.

He was a little disconcerted to notice, in the bar before dinner, Kip, the boy in charge of Victoire's baby half-brother, in the company of this same American friend. Despite Géraldine's urging, he made no attempt to introduce himself to her, and his greatest dread was that something in his present situation would require him to.

Amy and Kip both somehow felt his, or someone's, gaze on them, which made them both turn. Having been caught staring, Emile made a little bow of his head. Amy felt an almost unpleasant crawl of apprehension. This man seemed to have the same effect on others too.

19

The hotel had now formalized Amy's habit of sitting at meals with Kip or someone else by giving away her former single table and showing her directly to Kip and Harry when she came to the dining room. She and Kip had installed Mademoiselle Walther, the baby-sitter, there, too, for lunches, but after one dinner, because she was running out of things to talk about with Kip, Amy invited someone else to join them, tonight the American from Geneva, Joe Daggart, whose hotel room, she discovered, was actually right next to hers. She especially wanted to ask him what he might know about the available rescue services in Switzerland.

He didn't know much. 'I'm an extradition consultant,' he had explained. 'Or call it facilitator. I represent various American state governments, and the feds, in negotiating extraditions. European governments often won't extradite an American criminal when the death penalty is involved, so my job is to negotiate the concessions we are able to make – new trials, reduced sentences, life instead of death penalty, and so on – to accommodate their notions. I find out what assurances we are able to make to the Europeans, and what compromises they'll take. I'm working on a horrible case at the moment, the guy who strangled the four ten-year-olds behind the ice rink, he's holed up in Deauville.'

'Goodness, I hope you aren't trying to get him off,' she said.

'Not exactly. It's a problem in the capital cases,' he said. 'We try to get the American prosecutors to ask for life with no parole instead, but it's often tough because they face political pressure in the States. Everybody wants to fry this bastard. Sometimes an impasse can last for years.'

Amy, who knew little about criminal law, found this fascinating. She liked Daggart. She would ask him more generally how he found living in Europe, whether he missed America and so on, though it might be well to stay away from politics, as she sensed that his were not hers.

For now, she knew enough to steer clear of the inheritance issues too, even though they would affect Kip, and she sure wasn't going to meddle in issues of European medical ethics; all the same, she didn't see how it could hurt to get Daggart's help in arranging a medical ambulance of some sort that might save Kip's sister and her husband.

'You must know the Red Cross, Médecins Sans Frontières, people like that,' she implored. Daggart did know some agencies. The insurance would eventually repay the cost of this expensive venture, she wasn't worried about that, but she had seen immediately that as in America, when insurance claims were involved, rescue agencies would be wary. At home, the plane would be faster in coming if she could offer the money up front – how different could it be in Europe? She set a mental cost limit – how could you put a price on human life, though? She had made her suggestion to Mr Osworthy as she had left his meeting, and he gratefully considered it.

'You mean you have some means of advancing the funds?' he asked warily, it occurring to him that maybe there were financial implications he hadn't been aware of, big money somewhere behind Kerry Venn, perhaps. 'The people here are only used to organizing the transport of uncomplicated fractures or the odd woman in labor, or getting a stroke victim to Lyon. People are flown to England all the time, but evidently not on life support and not if they're not stable. Venn looks stable enough to me, he hasn't so much as twitched since I've been here.'

'I expect the money in advance will help. It's an expensive trip, insurance companies are slow to repay, nobody likes to deal with them.'

'Money does seem to overcome many a scruple. Thank you, Miss Hawkins, this is most understanding. Of course it's also in your client's interest.'

'I'm not sure what you mean. I'm just concerned about Mrs Venn.'

She put the matter now to Joe Daggart. 'If they need the money up front, I could advance it. I'd like to help.'

'I have no idea who would do it. I do know something about the cost, on account of another situation I was in; it would be about twenty thousand dollars.' He looked at her alertly.

'It's okay, lives are at stake. After all, I'll be getting it back eventually.'

'Victoire,' Géraldine said, 'I'm going to keep Nike and Salome for a few days for you, and you are going down to Valméri to help Emile. It isn't fair for you to make him go through it all, stuck among perfect strangers in the middle of a family drama. He ought to have his wife with him.'

'I doubt he said that, Maman,' said Vee. 'That doesn't sound at all like Emile.'

'That is my understanding of his simple remark "I wish Victoire were here." Interpret it however you will. Anyhow, a few days alone together in a nice hotel is good for any couple.' It was the closest she had ever come to mentioning Victoire's marital problems.

With it put this way, Vee could have few objections, and Géraldine met each of them: she could cancel the play group for one session, could go down after the performance of her trio at the opening of a department store Saturday afternoon. Now some subtle mental revisions set in, and Vee began to ask herself if maybe she hadn't been flippant and unfilial on the matter of her dying father. Probably it was just injured vanity, and disappointment that he had never cared to see her that had made her refuse to go to him. Now she almost regretted her, hasty reaction, and she had begun to see that it had been selfish of her to deny a dying man the satisfaction, if such it would be, of seeing his long-lost daughter.

Perhaps his other children had been a disappointment to him, and it would make him happy to see a child of his who was blooming and productive, with lovely children of her own. Perhaps she should take Nike and Salome? Perhaps the glimmer of happiness and hope from seeing them could actually make a difference to his chances of living? She had heard it could. How could she not go if she had a chance of saving him, whatever her personal feelings? When Géraldine urged her yet again, she was on the point of having decided anyway, and the idea that

Emile would like it made her duty even clearer. She'd go. She organized a substitute flautist, collected Nike and Salome from school on Friday afternoon, took them to Géraldine's, and set off by metro for the Gare de Lyon.

Getting Emile into bed again proved easier than Posy had dared to hope. It was not the matter of a conscious plan, she told herself, but more like destiny guiding both their impulses. Opportunity: after dinner, Rupert had gone up early, bearing in mind the ski expedition for the following day. There was the natural geniality prompted in all of them by the wine at dinner – Emile had eaten with Robin Crumley and a stylish couple from Munich who were mad Francophiles and had seen both Crumley and Emile on the Arte book program *A Lire*. Then, a couple of drinks at the bar afterward, and a discussion of their mutual concerns about the nationality of poor Venn's death, put them in a mood of accord that soon moved beyond this depressing subject back into the more life-affirming realms of attraction and desire.

For Emile, at heart a romantic like all left-inclined intellectuals, Posy appeared to be his wife Vee perfected – rounder, more impulsive, absolutely throbbing with possibility and sexiness, and with the added charm of epitomizing that frosty race the British, whose conquest gave a certain political satisfaction as well. Here was the sister fate had actually intended for him.

For Posy, whose own responses were less theoretical, there was no complication she would have to brood warily on, apart from the possible one of his relation to her hypothetical half-sister. In the main, her relationship to the unknown Vee was forgotten entirely in the hot mood of determination to be penetrated by this gorgeous sheik/Frenchman. They went to Emile's room. They deserved a little last fling, they said, for all they were enduring – the distress, the sadness, the boredom. It was a tremendous success, a sensual feast, as sticky and energetic as Posy had ever had, leaving her wondering if there might not be huge national differences no one ever spoke of. The subject certainly deserved some research. They enthusiastically agreed to meet again tomorrow, maybe after lunch, or just before dinner, when it would be supposed they were up changing and their deathbed duties were over for the day.

20

This was Friday, the day they had planned their expedition to Saint-Jean-de-Belleville, but snow was falling so heavily they would have to postpone it. The sky was thick and gray-yellow, with snowflakes hurling themselves in swirling flurries against the roofs, and a howling wind had shut down the lifts. The sound of snowplows already gearing into action to groom the pistes was muffled by the thick storm, and the breakfast bulletin informed the guests that the upper runs were impassable, the temperature minus twelve. Even though she had no feeling for centigrade, Amy knew that was cold.

Despite this, Rupert got himself outfitted with skis and proceeded up and down several slopes with the stately pace of someone who goes skiing once a year for a week, competent but cautious, correct, resolving to hit the moguls with more attack tomorrow when the visibility was better. Kip Canby, recognizable in hindsight by his khaki suit and blue helmet, went flashing by him on a snowboard before he registered who it was.

Amy was somewhat relieved there would be no skiing for her today, so she could feel no ambivalence if she stayed in to work on the issue of transporting Mr Venn to England. That done, at eleven she could take one of the cooking classes she so far had not had time for. She had breakfast, alone – Kip and Harry weren't down yet – and waited till nine, when she presumed Swiss offices would open, then went back to her room to make a few phone calls, and had no problem at all making herself understood; everyone spoke English.

Amy was good at challenges, and had no thought of failing even though Mr Osworthy had failed. Paying for Venn's plane was also a karmic gesture in the service of mutual aid. Good fortune can only pull you along with it for so long before you start to feel you should keep making little deposits, to keep up a minimum balance of deserving, so she was happy at the chance to make this effort.

She saw Osworthy's error, had grasped immediately that to invoke insurance at this stage was counterproductive. Even though transporting Venn was ultimately an insurance matter, she knew that everyone from the Red Cross to Doctors Without Borders would respond better to being paid for the flight with money up front, and this she could easily guarantee with her platinum card. How expensive could it be? Insurance claims would be settled eventually – she had no concerns about that, but meantime, following the general instructions of Joe Daggart, she called the numbers on her list of agencies compiled from the Minitel in Christian Jaffe's office, and it was not long before she was able to give Mr Osworthy the news that a medevac plane, supplied by the Swiss Alpine Aerial Rescue Mission, SAARM, could be in Albertville by tomorrow morning, weather permitting, and assuming it wasn't needed for some more urgent humanitarian task. Transferring Venn to the plane in Albertville would take an hour, the flight an hour and a half, and they could be in Stansted by tomorrow noon. She loved the drama of this – the ambulances, the heroic haste, white-coated paramedics waiting at the airport in London.

'Thank God, brilliantly done, Miss Hawkins, I couldn't budge those fellows. You Yanks!' said Mr Osworthy.

She also liked the idea that it was she putting up the money for it. She was not indifferent to her money. She loved the idea of how truly amazed people would be if they knew how really rich she was. It amazed her whenever she thought of it, which she did surprisingly seldom – once a day, more or less, when she checked her brokerage accounts or spoke to Sigrid. But her money didn't control her, it freed her, and the little reminders, like this, from time to time, of what having access to a large sum of cash could actually accomplish for others startled her like sweetness or cold on a tooth.

She also spoke to Géraldine on the telephone. That morning, Géraldine, Tammy, and Wendi Le Vert had met to discuss Amy's apartment, but before getting down to business they heard each other's news of husbands and children. They were loyal mothers and loyal friends, intimate up to a point – the point of intrusiveness or criticism. They laughed ruefully at the things that befell Victoire or Laure or Corinne, and often were able to help each other out if someone's husband knew a consultant at Hôpital Salpetrière, or was looking for a bookkeeper, or had found a reliable painter. (Madame d'Argel, on the third floor – Estelle – to whom they spoke cordially, was not included in the closer friendship, in part perhaps because of her busy career as a novelist, but more because of her tendency to crow about the successes of her perfect children, especially the recently married Anne-Sophie.) The objection Géraldine, Wendi, and Tammy felt to this transgression was too delicate to articulate even to themselves: the possession by another of too-perfect offspring jeopardized the mood of supportive loyalty each woman liked to feel in herself toward her friends. But of course, Géraldine had Victoire, who was perfect in her own way.

'I have Salome and Nike this weekend. Victoire is going down to Valméri to be with Emile. Her father's still in intensive care.' Géraldine described the situation. They all agreed that Emile had behaved with unusual complaisance and that Victoire was right, and also prudent, to go sit by the bedside of her father.

Passing to decor, 'I see the salon in that same darkish turquoise they have at Sceaux. Have you seen the château at Sceaux?' Tammy asked. 'It's in the park there. The main salon is painted this lovely dark turquoise with the woodwork in paler green, white ceiling, and then a chandelier. Amy's room screams for a real downright unabashed crystal chandelier. I tell people, if you can afford it, go for it.'

'A lot of people get Wendi Le Vert to help them. It's tricky getting things done if you don't speak French,' Géraldine assured Amy. Amy had mixed feelings about using someone like a decorator, believing she would profit from making her own mistakes. On the other hand, the idea of going into a French store and buying something like a mattress seemed to call for more effort and expense of spirit than it could be worth. She would prefer to go along with Wendi for the decorative items. While Wendi spotted things and negotiated, she, Amy, could indicate her feelings by imperceptible nods, slowly gaining confidence and experience. But meanwhile Wendi could handle the bed and bath towels and stuff like that alone. She gave the go-ahead.

When she and Géraldine hung up, Amy had had a moment of forlornness, not exactly homesickness, but she felt far away from home, a bit as if she had been standing on an iceberg that had broken off and was bearing her on a cold, dark ocean of mystery and incertitude toward elusive and slightly unfriendly new civilizations, where she would be required to change all of her ways. She thought for some reason of the large form of Baron Otto, and of how she was skiing much better than before, and of how each day brought challenge and improvement, and with that she went down to the cooking lesson in a better frame of mind.

The subject of the cooking lesson was announced on the bulletin board posted by the front desk in the lobby: *bisque d'homard* and *timbale de saumon*. Amy reported at the appointed hour of eleven at the door of the spotless and elegant kitchen – stainless steel tables, racks of shining copper pans, and vats of steaming soups. She was given an apron, along with two Japanese women, a German couple, the handsome television celebrity she had now figured out to be Géraldine's son-in-law, the poet Robin Crumley, a man from Luxembourg, a pudgy Russian woman and one of her daughters. Chef Jaffe entered with an air of majesty. He would be speaking French, he told them affably, and his daughter Christine would translate into English. He hoped they could all get along in just the two languages. All assented. Behind Chef Jaffe, two huge lobsters glared balefully from the counter where they were upended, waving their rubber-banded claws.

Chef Jaffe explained that the class would observe each step of the preparation, then, assembled into two teams of five, they would duplicate the maneuver the chef had just performed. Thus Amy found herself rolling flour and butter into a ball, not a hard thing to do, and chopping a shallot, also decidedly within her powers.

'A roux – a roux,' Robin Crumley chanted, poetically entranced by the music of these syllables as he worked awkwardly beside her. The two Russians, also on her team, seemed not to want to perform these hands-on tasks, but smiled encouragingly as Amy relinquished the knife to Crumley, and he to the other man, an investment councilor from Luxembourg. Smiling and deferring to each other, they sautéed their shallots, browned their roux, and began to add a fishy liquid that Chef Jaffe explained had been made beforehand but which they would be duplicating from scratch with the shells of the lobsters.

'Now we prepare Monsieur Homard,' Chef Jaffe said, picking up the first of his victims and displaying the living creature to the admiring students, its claws and antennae waving at them resentfully. All at once, the chef viciously dismembered it before their eyes. Rip, crack. He tore the head off, then the claws, then divided its spine. Amy thought she heard it scream. Shaken, she looked away. Even the Japanese, supposedly a cruel race, what with their samurai tradition and Bataan, gasped with shock.

When the first lobster had been hacked into lumps, the chef handed the second lobster to the television personality, Mr Abboud. This man took the thing and stared at it, holding it well away from his body. After a few seconds, he handed it back.

'I don't think I can do it,' he said. 'I know, how can I call myself a "Frenchman"? Still – I cannot.' He smiled. He was incredibly handsome, Amy thought, if you liked that type, and she certainly honored the man's reluctance to kill. All the other class members appeared to shrink with the fear that they'd be chosen next. Briskly, half apologetically, with a contemptuous smile for her companions, the Russian lady took the lobster and tore it, claws from body, head, tail, with her strong hands, and put it on the counter in front of the chef, who proceeded to extract the meat from claws and tail, and pulverize the shells with the back of his implement. In seconds, what had been alive – though, Amy hoped, unreflective – was now an inert soup ingredient. This, at any rate, had a certain Darwinian finality. Thus was life fleeting and harsh, thus were the French hard pragmatists, lacking empathy for lesser members of the food chain, especially when it was a question of the honor of their famous cuisine.

Or so remarked Robin Crumley afterward as they sat over their tiny cups of lobster bisque and nibbled at their timbales of salmon. The two teams sat at separate tables in the kitchen itself, and while they ate, Chef Jaffe lectured them on what they should be tasting. Amy noticed that

Robin was apparently friendly with Mr Abboud. Though each sat with his own team, the two men commented to each other on the lesson.

'Of course, in England we have the Royal Humane Society. I don't know if it covers lobsters,' whispered Robin seditiously. 'To say nothing of PETA, the people that liberate lab rats. I believe it originated in England, but perhaps you have it in the States too?'

'Maybe there isn't a humane way to kill lobsters,' said Amy, who had always thought that boiling water seemed awfully cruel too.

They went back to their workstations. Amy filled her notebook. Each phrase from Christine's lips had brought new evidence of Amy's complete ignorance of the basic essentials of cooking. Every Frenchman knew more than she did. *Roux. Relever* – brown a little. Who could have dreamed of bashing lobster shells and then boiling them? Pleasure coursed through her veins to think of the hours of discovery ahead of her, and to discover that such hands as hers could create a pastry case. It was no more than diligence. What a revelation! She saw that she could become a brilliant cook.

At the end of the session, their minds and notebooks stuffed, Chef Jaffe released them.

'You've met Miss Hawkins?' said Robin to Emile on their way up the stairs. 'Amy, let me present Emile Abboud.' Not in position to shake hands, they murmured acknowledgments of each other and the Géraldine connection, Emile somewhat abstractedly, having begun to think of his rendezvous with Posy. Up to then, Amy had thought the man she was personally most attracted to in the hotel, in terms of sleeping with, was either her ski instructor, Paul-Louis, or, weird to say, the baron Otto. This she ascribed to the mesmerizing effect of the Nazi villains in movies she and her friends had watched as children, sinister blond men in jodhpurs with riding crops, though of course they rooted for the American prisoners and valiant British spies. Now here was Emile Abboud. Never mind, men were far from being her concern at the moment. She did wonder if Baron Otto would have killed the lobster, and felt sure he would.

Despite her favorable impression of Emile, he was looking at her with undisguised dislike, not something she was used to. 'I heard about your unwelcome intrusion into the Venn *affaire*,' he said. 'I should not have been surprised. You people are not known for minding your own business.'

'You mean the plane or the baby-sitter?' Amy asked, quite surprised by his quarrelsome, critical remark, and not immediately sure how Géraldine's son-in-law was involved with the Venns.

'The plane. Maître Osworthy tells me you have arranged to transport Mr Venn to London,' he said. 'May I ask what your interest is, or is it just typical arrogant American meddling?' His tone was as cold as his expression.

'Dear me!' commented Robin Crumley.

'They hope they might save him in London – in the hope that . . .' said Amy uncertainly, taken aback. Who could challenge a mission of mercy?

'The man is dead, mademoiselle, it is a kidnapping of a

corpse. I believe the idea is to have him formally declared dead in England to avoid French taxes, and I am surprised that an ethical medical transport company would agree to do it.' Or that an ethical person would organize it, said his tone.

The idea that the plane was simply a tax-evasion maneuver shocked Amy. No one had told her anything about Venn's actual condition, and from what Kip had said, she had imagined him hovering between life and death. Was it all a big waste of money and time, a futile effort? She didn't want to be a part of something so controversial.

'I'm trying to help the young brother, Kip – the brother of Mrs Venn. He seems to feel the rest of the family isn't too concerned about his sister's welfare,' she said.

'Ah. Well, yes, of course you are. If the man is declared dead in England, it will be better for him – for his sister, rather.'

Amy at once realized that there were issues she hadn't fully understood, and had better find out more about. Osworthy had alluded to them, but they hadn't seemed important. 'Perhaps I'm not well informed. Let's have a drink later, could we?' she suggested. 'I'd be grateful if you would explain all that.' Meantime, she thought, she would have a word with Mr Osworthy.

'All right. Before dinner,' he said, looking at his watch. 'Let us say eight o'clock in the bar.'

'I think I have time to walk into the village,' she said suddenly. 'It's nice, walking in the snow.' She had been seized with a feeling of confusion she couldn't explain.

'I'll come with you,' Robin Crumley said. 'I need to get some postcards. Do come along, old fellow.'

'I can't just now,' Emile said, with another look at his watch. 'I have a rendezvous,' and he hurried off.

While others were taking the cookery lesson, Kip had
gone to the hospital, still in his ski clothes. Despite the
storm, he had made a few runs in the morning. Not being
able to see didn't bother him, but when conditions
grew too miserable even for him, he took the Biovil lift
and skied down to the village, left his snowboard in the
garde-ski, and caught a shuttle down to Moutiers to look in
at Kerry. He had many more things to worry about than
just her recovery: What was the hospital going to cost?
Was Amy right that he might be made to pay? Was the
baby-sitter, Mademoiselle Walther – a formal name for
someone with a vague teen manner who was not much
older than he – really being okay with Harry? What did it
mean that the English people wanted to take Adrian to
London but not Kerry? What would he do if she died,
where would he live?

One worry overshadowed the others. He was thinking
about how everyone believed that American planes had
set off the avalanches, and he had realized that if the
vibration of a plane could have done it, so, too, could
he himself. The memory was acute. He'd been snowboarding on a slope above Adrian and Kerry, and had
been almost alone on the snowboard course, with its
jumps and dips. Ebullient with the pleasures of exercise
and solitude, he had joyfully let out an enormous shout

that had come back in echoes from the sides of the chute. Now he was thinking the unthinkable: probably he had set the avalanche off himself. People would eventually figure this out. Even if he didn't go to prison, everyone would know he had killed his sister and her husband, and they wouldn't give him any money, or let him have anything to do with Harry, or want him around.

'*Bonjour, Keep,*' said one of the nurses, the one that seemed to like him and be glad when he came in. He had perfected his '*Bonjour*' and '*À bientôt.*' So had his friend, Amy, and they said these words to each other when meeting at the hotel or on the slopes. Now he sat in the chair near the head of Kerry's bed and began as usual to talk to her.

'Hi, Kerry, it's me, Kip. I'm here. Just came to tell you that Harry is fine. He's a great little kid. He didn't cry so much last night either. He ate some mashed carrots by himself. He feeds himself really well.' He said all the things he could think of in this vein.

Posy Venn was sitting there as usual with her book, watching over her father. Kip thought Posy was incredibly foxy, as much of a fox as Amy though different, and had longed for her to seem to see him. Today she gave him a slight smile, some improvement from the usual. Today she looked softer and friendlier where she often looked fierce.

'Uh – how's Adrian today?' Kip asked.

'The same.' Posy sighed. 'There's a chance of the plane late this afternoon, if the snow stops, or tomorrow morning. I don't know why it matters if it snows. I thought they had instruments in planes.'

This seemed to Kip a subject to talk to Kerry about. 'They might take Adrian to London,' he said. 'Would you like to go, Kerry? Want to go to London?'

Suddenly, it seemed to him Kerry was listening. There was a different quality to her comatose inertia, perhaps she had made a slight stir and blinked her eyes. She had understood and responded, he was sure. 'Hey,' he cried. 'She answered me.'

Posy looked up from her book. 'Really?'

'Look. Hey, Kerry, want to go to London?' But this time there was no response from Kerry.

'Kerry! Kerry? Want to see Harry?' Again it seemed that he saw a tiny acknowledgment, a flutter of response, as though her eyeballs moved beneath her closed lids. Excited, he ran to tell the nurse, who came and prodded her, and pulled open her eyelids. She saw nothing changed.

'Rien. Desolée.' But she began to hook up another instrument to Kerry's arm.

But he'd seen it, he knew he had, and would tell Dr Lamm.

'Posy, tell them. I saw it,' Kip pleaded.

'Yes, of course, but – oh, dear,' Posy said, 'I have to run, I'm late, I can't believe the time.' She had a stricken expression and fled without looking back. Kip knew she wasn't really interested in whether Kerry came back to life. Kip pleaded with the nurses to call the doctor, and to try again to rouse Kerry. She had come back to life for an instant, he knew it, and he wanted to share his joy and relief.

*

184

Posy was late for her assignation with Emile – they had fixed upon a stolen hour before dinner when neither would be missed. She tapped discreetly on his door, he was there, embraced her, led her directly to bed, and with his ardor and expertise, the hour passed quickly. Up from the dreamy heat and carnal scents of the bedclothes, Posy rose, dressed, kissed Emile long, passionately, and cracked open his door to see if the corridor was clear.

'I'll get up eventually, and meet you in the bar before dinner,' Emile said, stirring and propping himself up in bed, shaking off the agreeable postcoital torpor, admiring Posy's full form and well-chosen pink sweater, for the moment forgetting about his upcoming rendezvous in the bar with the mistrusted American woman. He supposed Vee would not have worn that flowered skirt, but it looked nice on Posy. She laid her finger across her lips and slipped out the door.

As she walked with studied nonchalance across the lobby toward the staircase, she saw standing at the desk a woman who could only be Victoire. Dressed in dark jeans and a white turtleneck, she was a slightly smaller, more delicate, lighter-haired, thinner, and more ineffably French version of Posy herself – it was *herself* Posy recognized. Her first feeling was of happiness, but a chill of panic stopped her. The wife was going to throw open the bedroom door to find her husband concupiscently lolling in midafternoon in a waft of perfume and sex. Should she dart back and warn Emile? But it was too late – Christian Jaffe was coming around the desk and picking up Vee's little suitcase, and Vee was preparing to follow him as he led the way past Posy toward the Abboud chamber.

Options reeled through Posy's mind: hide, stare straight ahead, stop and greet. She instinctively did the latter.

'Excuse me, but could you possibly be Victoire?' Victoire, looking startled, said she was. '*Oui.*' Carefully remaining in French.

'I'm Posy Venn. I'd be your half-sister. I'd been hoping we would meet.'

Vee looked at the tousled, flame-cheeked stranger. Yes, she could see something of herself, a more rounded, chestnut-haired, higher-colored version. She warmed, she laughed delightedly, and enfolded Posy with sisterly enthusiasm.

'I didn't want to come,' she said, 'but I am already glad. We must talk and talk. You must tell me everything about my father, about everything. Well, I will put my valise in the room and come right back.' Christian Jaffe, carrying the suitcase, took a step toward the room. Posy could stall them no more. With luck, Emile was out of bed by now, maybe in the shower, or changing for dinner, though luck was something Posy never considered herself likely to have.

'You and, um, your husband should join us before dinner and we'll have dinner together. With Rupert and me. I'll tell the dining room,' suggested Posy. Their hands remained enlaced. Victoire gave her beautiful, musical laugh and agreed to all that.

Oh, bloody hell, thought the desperate Posy as she ran to her room, already smitten with Victoire as well as with Emile. Though her little brother, Harry, hadn't inspired her interest, the idea of a sister did, and the real sister was thrillingly a sort of idealized self; they were both cast-off girl children, and Victoire had endearing defects – her nose was somewhat red from the cold, for instance, and she ought to wear more makeup.

At the hospital, the evening rituals were beginning. Almost unremarked, Kerry Venn became aware that she was in a bed somewhere. She knew she was Kerry, and registered the footfalls of people in the room, their voices ... she liked hearing the voices. They kept her from falling. It would be easy to slide off into the thing that lurked beneath her, but each footfall brought her back, not to her body, she had no sense of that, but to certain words that trailed across her brain, women's voices, warm room. She was comfortable, she lacked for nothing, she was glad not to be part of the whispers and anxious laughter, the footsteps she was aware of beyond her. She was aware of someone quite near her saying 'I think the boy was right!' *Le garçon avait raison.*

Amy and Robin Crumley set their faces against the blowing snow and stamped across the ski slope between the hotel and the road, a shortcut to the village now rendered drifted and deep by the day's snowfall. The Englishman had very inadequate boots and a thin-looking parka, more of a raincoat. Amy very nearly put out her hand to steady his progress but supposed he would not like being treated like an elderly gentleman. He had a sort of forced gaiety she respected, as she always respected people who set their faces to things and overcame difficulty. What his difficulty was she had no idea – money, probably. No doubt poets were underpaid. She would read his poems.

But just as she was enjoying the feeling of being the lone American in the Alps, she was surprised to see an American military vehicle – if she wasn't mistaken – pulled up in front of the Produits Savoyard store, and two men in American uniforms coming out, carrying paper bags, followed by Joe Daggart. She waved at him, but he seemed not to recognize her, which was not surprising, since she was wearing parka, hat, muffler, and goggles against the blowing snow, and was indistinguishable from everybody else walking carefully along the icy sidewalks in the unabating storm. From closer up, the insignia on the jeep door could be seen to read USAF. The men dived into it, and the driver pulled away. She glimpsed them in the backseat, pulling sausages out of their bags. Joe Daggart didn't get in. He hailed Amy and Robin as he came closer and recognized them, perhaps especially Crumley's storky figure in its old green anorak.

'Amy, Crumley. Did you ski in all this muck?'

'We took the cooking lesson,' Amy explained. 'Is there an air base near here?'

'What? Oh, some liaison people in Geneva, up here checking out this avalanche thing. Damage control.'

At the newsagent they were greeted by blazoned headlines about American denials of responsibility for the avalanche deaths. The infuriated European press gave all the details, especially the laughter of the press attaché. Amy bought the *International Herald Tribune* and the *Financial Times*, and tried to decipher the French and Italian papers arrayed on the racks, surrounded by people reading and shaking their heads. YANKS DENY VIBRATION DEATHS. Even the British papers went on about the regrettable American tendency to bluster and bully before the truth came out, as it always did. French government ministers were quoted as saying they would bring the matter up in The Hague, in Brussels, in Strasbourg. Amy thought this was most unfair, since she had seen for herself that Americans were investigating the claims. She was sure a good-faith effort was being made to find out whether the noise of an airplane could indeed set off a slide. Newspapers always rushed to judgment, she thought indignantly, and never apologized when they were proved wrong.

Robin Crumley browsed along the shelves of a section of books in English.

'I thought I might find something of mine, to present to you,' he said. 'But no. The French are not keen on English poetry. We English, on the other hand, are very admiring of French poetry – Verlaine, Baudelaire, Villon. We have in all a more catholic approach to literature. They are so preoccupied by their language, limited as it is.'

'Limited?' said Amy, thinking that this presented a ray of hope, a finite end to her labors.

'A relatively small vocabulary, so they have to use the same word for a number of things, another sort of problem.'

Standing in the long line of damp, bundled-up newspaper buyers, they reached the checkout stand.

'What do you think you'll do?' asked the cashier, a woman, seeing their papers.

About what? Amy didn't know. 'Do?'

'The people should be compensated at least,' she remonstrated, shaking her head at the idea of human perfidy, Amy's in particular. 'You can't just act like nothing happened.'

As at other times, Amy felt she was being made to stand for all Americans, and she hardly knew how to contain her outrage at this personal criticism. She had nothing to do with the avalanche, yet she was being made to take moral responsibility for it, for a whole category, a whole nation of people who also didn't have anything to do with it. It was stereotyping, it was profiling. They said 'you Americans' as if a Californian were like someone from Mississippi. Didn't they know how big America was, how disparate? Anyway, as if Americans had something to do with the snow conditions in the Alps! Not that she wasn't an American, but she was she, herself, not just a representative specimen of her countrymen. She hadn't even voted for the present president, certainly not.

At the same time, she knew she should rise above mere private resentments; since European criticisms were generic, they were not directed at her personally. They blamed all Americans.

And now she must face Mr Abboud and, no doubt, more criticism.

'Won't you come with me?' she proposed to Crumley as they walked back to the hotel, their newspapers tucked under their parkas to protect them from the still-falling snow. 'You seem to get along with Mr Abboud better than I do.'

22

Mr Abboud, waiting at the bar, had a changed air from their encounter on the stair after the cooking lesson. Now he seemed relaxed and subdued, and had an eye on the door. But he rose cordially enough when Amy came into the bar with Robin. Would they have a kir? A whiskey?

'What exactly is your interest in sending the dying Mr Venn to England?' he asked Amy, returning to this subject as soon as they were served. 'Since it is counter to my own advantage, I still find myself wondering.'

'Amy is just an angel, she does things out of goodness,' cried Robin. 'And of course the Brompton Hospital is world famous.'

'Do I have to have an interest?' asked Amy. 'What a cynical view of life! Perhaps that's very French.' She was not sure why this provoking man was goading her to make insulting ethnic slurs, which was not like her.

'People usually have an interest. Mine is in part selfish, in part an unselfish wish to see the rational laws of France prevail over English chaos,' he said.

'Now, really,' said Robin Crumley. 'What's the legal difference, by the way?'

Abboud now assumed a rapt camera-ready expression and a certain preacherly tone as he launched into an explanation. 'It's a telling difference. When it comes to his will, an Englishman, having earned his fortune, can indulge any whim of his doddering mind – reward the housemaid, leave it all to a home for cats. He can punish any ungrateful or unsuccessful child of his by leaving it nothing.'

'Quite right,' said Crumley.

'In France, who gets what is spelled out, children getting equal shares, a spouse only a small percentage – even parents inherit, rather than spouses, if there are no children. France has in view that property should remain in the family, children getting fair shares, no one generation impoverishing the next, ensuring the orderly progress of society. Which is the best system? The French, undoubtedly. More people are better off under a system of forced equity than when things are left to caprice.'

'It sounds stifling,' Amy objected. 'Why does anyone bother to behave well to their parents if they'll get the money anyway?'

'I call *that* a cynical view of life. It's a horrible view. People behave well to their parents out of natural good feeling, they love them.' Though he loved his parents, at one stage Emile had been ashamed of them, brown, unfashionable Maghrebites, his mother barely able to control her inclination to put on a headscarf.

'Often they hate them, never see them, refuse to speak to them,' Amy pointed out.

'Not if they expect to get any money. In England – people jump through hoops. In France, we naturally revere our parents. When you can't control your children by threatening to change your will, you can be assured their feelings are of spontaneous, natural affection when they are nice to you.'

These were matters Amy had never considered. Her parents were in good health and lived two hours from her, in Ukiah. She knew she should go and see them more often.

'The triumph of French law is that it protects French people,' Emile continued. 'That is not true of all bodies of law. Some have been designed to oppress, some to enrich a small constituency –' Suddenly Emile looked beyond them and abruptly stood up. 'May I present my wife, Victoire,' he said, as they were joined by a pretty, ethereal-looking blonde, presumably, if Amy had it figured out right, yet another offspring of the mysterious Venn.

'*Mais oui,* you are a friend of Maman,' said Victoire to Amy. 'She said I must say hello to you. She tells me she has found you a wonderful apartment.' This allowed Amy a few seconds finally to put the situation in place: Géraldine Chastine was Victoire's mother, Victoire was something – half-sister – to the Venns. The man was married to Victoire. The world at that moment seemed deliciously small to Amy, to have, even, the reassuring dimensions of Silicon Valley. But how sad that Géraldine's nice daughter was married to this most disagreeable, if handsome, man.

After the Abbouds went in to dinner, Amy had stayed in the bar a minute to glance through the *Herald Tribune*, noting further a curious item pertaining to the avalanches, that there had been a small demonstration outside the American State Department by a group – it didn't quite say of scruffy ideologues – demanding accountability and transparency when it came to American airplanes in foreign places, possibly inflicting damage again, this time on valued allies. A spokesman had told the paper that the government was exposing innocent American tourists to risk by not telling them of developing enmity in formerly friendly places where America had caused damage and death. Amy wondered, but not seriously, if that could include Valméri?

At dinner, the guests at the Hôtel Croix St Bernard had the novelty of two American military officers in uniform dining at one of the tables. Some said army, some said air force, it was hard to tell from across the room.

'I think army,' said Marie-France Chatigny-Dové. 'I think the air force wears blue.' The prince and *princesse* agreed. In the bar after dinner, some guests were heard to criticize the management for admitting such people to the dining room. 'Those are the same chaps we saw in the village questioning local merchants,' Robin Crumley was able to inform them. All agreed that their presence must have something to do with the avalanches. That morning's bulletin was still lying on the tables:

Americans deny presence of American overflights. Pentagon spokesman says no American planes were near the Alps at all, let alone in the area of Valméri where the destructive avalanches of last week had caused, finally, nine dead.

Posy and Rupert's dinner with their new sister Victoire and her attractive husband had not seemed awkward, although, as Posy had spent the afternoon in bed with the husband, it might have, and Emile treated both her and his wife with impassive politeness, his lovely smile and rather cynical discourses delivered without regard to who received them, in the manner of other public performers. It was all Posy could do to refrain from pressing Emile with her foot or allowing her hand to brush his.

Both Rupert and Posy had loved Victoire at once. Rupert felt a true affinity, and he could tell that Posy did, too, with their newfound sister. There must be something magnetic, some pull of the DNA, that accounted for their recognition of Victoire, transcending mere acquaintance, so powerfully connected did they feel. There was the family resemblance, but it was more than that. It was as if some Platonic ideal of a sister was now his in the form of the (evidently) good Victoire, in place of the (bad) Posy. Not that Posy was very bad, but even during this dinner she exhibited some of her worst qualities – restlessness, lack of ease, even acquisitiveness. He caught her looking at Emile, just intercepted the tiniest glance of a kind that warned him that some outburst was preparing. Perhaps she wanted Emile to leave so they could talk to Victoire, or maybe she didn't like Frenchmen.

They were recounting to Victoire their family life with Father, emphasizing his brilliance as a publisher and foibles as a parent, and had arrived at the divorce and the character and present life of their mother. In turn, Victoire told them about her mother, Géraldine, but said she was unable to imagine Géraldine separately from her stepfather, Eric, who, she emphasized, was her 'real' papa, let alone imagine her mother as a teenaged girl briefly involved with a Venn in his twenties.

'It's *trop dommage* that I should only learn about him now.' She sighed. 'Now that it's too late.'

'Oh, no,' Posy protested. 'The Brompton Hospital is world famous, we haven't given up hope.'

'Well,' said Victoire, 'tell me some more. Have he and your mother remained on good terms?'

'Not really. They hate each other, actually. But I should think it was quite a happy marriage until Kerry,' Rupert said.

'Oh, poor Kerry,' cried Victoire. 'I must embrace her. She will revive? Oh, and the poor little baby, the little orphan boy.'

Yes, thought Rupert, it's Victoire who has all the good instincts, and Posy is just a bitch. Strange to say, tears had sprung to Posy's eyes just then.

They discussed tomorrow's outing to Saint-Jean-de-Belleville. Posy knew that joy was never unalloyed. The happy prospect of driving somewhere with Emile was now marred by the arrival of Victoire. Luckily, Victoire declined to go with them to lunch; she would instead go to the hospital to see her unknown father, she said. Posy wondered if Victoire fully understood Father's condition. Deep, deep coma, practically a vegetable, they emphasized, but perhaps Victoire didn't recognize such absolutes as coma; perhaps she could shine through comas. She was evidently a person of unusual serenity, or maybe it was that since she didn't yet have a personal feeling for Father – how could she? – she didn't really care.

Posy was also thinking that Victoire didn't have the air of a woman who watched her husband closely, though Posy could see her adoration and desire for him, and took pains to show none of that herself. Of course she wouldn't want Victoire to know, but still more, she wouldn't want Rupert to know, he disapproved of her so much already. She knew there was no chance of a furtive embrace from Emile in the corridor later. Would this incestuous adultery, she was wondering, bring a tragic curse down upon the house of Venn? Was she enacting a destiny set in motion by her father's adulteries? Were they all under a curse, as in a Greek drama? Which one? Aeschylus? For some reason, her eyes had again filled with tears.

Amy, feeling a sudden lapse in her capacity for sociability, went to her room after dinner and turned on the TV. She had missed the very beginning of the program that came up, but it was evidently some fable or costume drama. An aristocratic-looking man was talking to a governessy-looking woman in a mannish suit, with a beautiful château in the background, all soothing and European enough to bear watching for a few minutes. The aristocrat wore riding boots and reminded her of her mental picture of the baron. Together the man and woman look downhill to where a group of five pretty young women in girlish frocks are being handed by a chauffeur out of a large car, taking their suitcases out, laughing to one another. Cut to the aristocrat's deeply absorbed stare at the pretty young women, the governess giving him a knowing smile. He smiles at her and shakes her hand. The girls carry their suitcases into the château.

Cut to a scene on the lawn. The girls are assembled on little canvas folding stools with their paintboxes and brushes. One girl is posing for the others in a white dress trimmed with a blue sash. The governess is holding a postcard of a painting by Gainsborough, which the model is emulating. The governess shuffles her postcards and directs them to assume new positions, *après* Watteau. So much was clear without understanding the French, though Amy thought she had begun to improve her auditory skills and could discern *merci, à bientôt,* and several other phrases.

The governess shows the girls a picture from the classical nude to imitate. Laughing, the girls begin taking off their clothes. Now they are naked. Two of the girls stand on their heads, their crotches eye-level with the other girls and the camera. The right-side-up girls begin to trim the pubic hair of the upended ones. The governess, with the picture in hand, demands to know what they are doing, a very good question that Amy wonders about too. '*Pas de poil,*' they say. Amy looks up *poil* in her dictionary: coat, mane, pubic hair. The girls indicate the picture of marble nymphs who have no pubic hair. From his window, the baron watches lustfully as the naked girls assume the postcard tableau.

Amazed, Amy looked at the time, the channel: main channel, not some in-house rental channel. Porn! Children all over France could be watching this! All at once she felt shocked, even embarrassed, and abruptly turned off the television. She didn't think of herself as a prude, but what if Kip was in his room watching at this moment? Completely disturbing to an adolescent boy. Also, how horrible if some porn charge would be added to her bill. How bizarre that the French would allow such programs in prime time. But of course, they are French. What was one to conclude?

PART 3
Snow

Être ou ne pas être. Telle est la question.

– William Shakespeare, *Hamlet*

*Je suis ici envoyée de par Dieu . . . pour
vous bouter hors de toute la France.*

– Jeanne d'Arc, letter to the
Duke of Bedford

23

Americans are often astonished when they find that the European Alps are more cragged, looming, beautiful, alien, and insurmountable than their majestic North American mountain range, the Rockies. Americans have popularly believed the Alps to be soft, rounded, and old. Amy had believed that until she saw them. In fact, the hotel brochure had explained, the only way they do not surpass the Rockies is that the Alps are not higher. It is as if the whole continent of Europe somehow starts at a lower point, sunk under the weight of millennia. The Alpine mountain ranges were thrown up, however, more recently than those of the Rockies or the Sierra Nevada, hence the unworn and challenging summits, the durable glaciers and rivers of ice the Rockies don't have.

From the promotional material, Amy had learned that the Valley of Valméri is one of a system of four valleys etched between the imposing peaks along the border of Switzerland and France; the mountains are covered with snow from November to May or June, with streams running through the crevasses in summer, and with wildflowers and small animals adding to an impression of Alpine idyll. In summer, cows, sometimes belled in the Swiss fashion, are brought up from the charming villages to graze. Humans have been here for millennia. Recently, the remains of a Stone Age climber, with cloak and touching, frayed sandals, were found embedded in the ice of prehistory only now risen to the surface.

It was these vastnesses that the skiing party would now traverse. Rupert went down to breakfast in his ski clothes, reassuring himself that if all went according to medical plan, Father would be flown back to London later today. Because only medical personnel would be allowed to fly with him in the small ambulance plane, Mr Osworthy, at his own insistence, would go back in a scheduled commercial plane from Geneva in time to meet the medical plane in London, and Posy and Rupert would drive home to England later tonight or even tomorrow morning. Meantime, as they would not be permitted to hover around the paramedics and pilots to impede them in their work, Rupert felt no sense of guilt about going off to spend the last day on skis instead. Their own role here was over. 'Yet,' he remarked, 'odd to feel a pang about leaving.'

'Yes, our last day here,' Posy lamented, thinking about how blessings are always mixed, enjoyments are always shadowed with the premonition of their transience. She could not confide her reason for feeling the sadness of this, but Rupert caught her tone. He ate his toast and gazed out the windows of the dining room at the gaining light on the top of Mount Benoît, and the slip of cloud. Was the cloud arriving to herald a gray day, or departing to leave a sky clear and bright for the projected outing to Saint-Jean-de-Belleville?

'You'll stop at the hospital?' he asked Posy, wanting there to be some representative there, even if it wasn't he. 'You can see Father off and come back here. Then when

I get off the slopes, five-ish, we'll set out for London.' But his presumption of Posy's dutifulness was wrong. She, Emile, and Robin Crumley were planning to meet him and the other skiers for lunch. She had volunteered to drive them. 'I can't let them down.' She smiled.

The family would be represented at the hospital by Victoire. 'I so look forward to spending the morning at the hospital with my newfound father, until he should be loaded onto the plane.' At the moment she was playing with her new little brother Harry, while the baby-sitter looked on. 'I will talk to him,' she promised them. 'At some level he will hear. I will tell him about his first grandchildren, and I will play the flute for him. Just think, his grandchildren are older than his youngest child! They say that music can penetrate the mind in its darkest caves of retreat.'

At nine-thirty, Kip, Amy, Rupert, and Madame Marie-France Chatigny-Dové met at the foot of the Equeriel lift and waited for Paul-Louis, who was to guide them. The prince had woken with a headache and was not coming. Joe Daggart, who also had been going to ski with them, came up to beg off too – he had to go with the American investigators, he said. The two military men Amy had seen the night before, now dressed in white jumpsuits, waited for Daggart by a snowmobile, but didn't themselves come forward in greeting.

'They really shouldn't allow snowmobiles,' Amy observed. 'I believe that in our national parks, they're forbidden.'

'These count as emergency vehicles, I think,' Daggart

assured her. 'Regular snowmobiles would not be allowed, no. I'm not so sure about in American national parks.'

'Europeans are not very sensitive to noise,' said Amy. 'All those horns and scooters and Vespas.' As soon as she said this, she realized it was a little tactless. The others forebore to mention noisy things they had witnessed in the U.S., but from Marie-France's expression, Amy could see that she herself had been insensitive. And she hardly wanted the day to deteriorate into chauvinist arguments. 'Almost as bad as America,' she said, hastily trying to repair the situation. It came to her that this was the first time in her life that she would be the only American in a group of others – well, with Kip. At the same time, she felt at ease, as if she belonged here. At least on a ski slope she could fit in, quite unlike during cookery lessons or at the dinner table, not that she cared.

She attributed her enjoyment of the Hôtel Croix St Bernard to A. the high proportion of people who could speak English, even though they chose not to much of the time, and it wasn't conducive to her learning French. And, B. the general level of friendliness and good manners of people here, even the French, unlike what you were often told to expect. And C. the good luck to have fallen among really nice, interesting people. Even the English brother, up till now so much that British combination of reserved and hearty, was getting to seem like an attractive, regular guy and a pretty good skier. She thought of extending the ski part of her little sabbatical before going on the Paris adventures ahead of her.

They had high hopes for a perfect day. The first blue traces of sky had extended into a full cloudlessness, the sun promised to appear, the snow was perfect after the addition of the powder layer in the night. In their brightly colored suits they all had the look of space travelers newly landed on a white planet, or athletes ready for the Olympics, especially Kip, whose parka had windows for showing passes and loops with bits of equipment hanging off, whose gloves were stout and worn, whose boots were venerably scuffed.

The pretty American, Amy, was especially calm and confident. Rupert was a little wary of her after the meeting in Mr Osworthy's room, where she had raised some pointed questions. Her voice, also, though by no means as awful as the voices of some American women, was distinctly American in its intonation. He was wary of businesswomen in general, as you were always warned to be, though in her private capacity of skier, he thought her perfectly nice and feminine, and Madame Chevigny-Dové was calmly competent too. As to how well they skied – that's the kind of thing you can't know till you begin, like playing tennis with somebody for the first time. Paul-Louis was a reassuring presence, a handsome, deeply bronzed Frenchman with a cheerful, silent manner, who touched his gloved hand to Rupert's when they were introduced, in the fashion of a boxer saluting his opponent.

'Thanks for thinking of me for this outing.' Rupert smiled at Amy. 'I wouldn't have missed it.'

'Oh, don't thank me,' she said.

When they were all assembled, they started, paired off, and were hoisted into the sky by the lift chairs, and into their individual reveries. To get to Saint-Jean-de-Belleville required a promenade, as it was euphemistically called, of some thirty or forty kilometers, beginning from the top of the glacier three thousand feet above them, following a complex route of chair lifts and *télécabines* up, and thrilling descents over the ridges toward the farthest of the valleys. Rupert had been shown the route on the map, but now, seeing the reality of the heights and expanse, he felt a moment of compunction, wondering if his skiing would be solid enough to keep him up with the others, and if the terrain would prove to be too difficult after all.

'*Ooh-la-la, que c'est beau,*' said Marie-France to Rupert, with whom she was sharing a chair, looking at the shimmering mountain peaks laid out below them like beaten egg whites in a bowl. 'Yes,' he said, 'absolute beauty, man's insignificance, that sort of thing.' From her expression, she was quite astonished and very impressed to find such sentiments in an Englishman, and gaily tapped his knee.

'*Oui, c'est super-beau,*' said Paul-Louis to Amy, who, as his main client, was never out of his gaze, though he kept them all in view like an anxious shepherd. Amy shouted back at them, as they swung through space, that she had never seen anything to equal the expanse of the white peaks covered with clouds and snow, untracked, indifferent to human incursion. This was the point of skiing, to share in this exhilarating beauty and be reminded of man's insignificance. She wished she could have a more original, a more daring, response than that. How limited she felt herself, how tragic it was not to have been born a poet or some other creative, expressive person, someone who would know what to do with the emotions that moved her. She momentarily admired Robin Crumley for trying to express the inexpressable, and vowed again to read his poetry.

Kip was distracted and withdrawn. His thoughts were fastened on what he had seen yesterday, Kerry's moment of consciousness. No one else had seen it or believed him, as if just because you were younger, you didn't know what you had seen. He was still oppressed with the idea that he himself had sent the snow down on her, and he was worried because he hadn't gone to see her this morning. He probably ought to turn back and ski down to the hospital. Maybe he'd take Harry to see her again. Maybe by now she could hear her baby, now that some of the cold had lifted from her brain. When would they realize it had been he who started the avalanche?

The others were puzzled that from time to time, Kip, strangely, would go off piste and utter loud shouts and yips into canyons, no one knew why. Boyish exuberance didn't seem quite to explain it. He was trying to see if he could dislodge snow with noise alone.

'This is where the Valméri avalanche caught the skiers, look there, the litter of broken twigs and bent trees.' Paul-Louis pointed across the slope. Amy wondered where the unfortunate people had been standing, and how they had been found in the huge, deep deposit of snow that filled a gulley to their right: Had she herself skied right here? Something about the sight frightened her unduly.

Skiing is the most solitary of occupations, the skier alone with his knees and ankles, the feel of his boots, thoughts only of the next mogul or angle of the hill, until he reaches the bottom, when, in the lift line, rejoining his companions, observations are exchanged, joy expressed. On the chair lift, swinging out into chilly space, brief conversation was possible, but it was also the moment to reapply sunscreen or struggle with a boot. The next kilometers were accomplished without difficulty in companionable solitude, and everyone was reassured, especially when Kip seemed content to stay with them, which must mean that their levels of skill didn't appall him. There were some glassy patches on north-facing slopes, but in general they found themselves making good progress, enjoying the beautiful scenery, the sting of the frozen, glittering air, the sound of their skis. The light remained good except for momentary streams of fragile veil across the morning sun, quickly pushed away by a little rising wind. Little troops of French children, like tiny forest trolls, whizzed by them with their Snow White *monitrices*.

'The school vacations have started,' Marie-France said.

To her chagrin, Amy fell twice, Paul-Louis cheerfully sidestepping up the slope to help her to her feet. Marie-France fell, too, but Rupert's stolid weekend style bore him along without mishap. He was enjoying the feel of his edges in the turns, their increasing authority, the action of his knees. In fact, he was well pleased with his returning prowess. Another week here and he'd be in form, maybe even improve. This evidence of his powers raised entire questions about the rest of his life. Did he want to spend it in the City, in the direction in which he'd embarked, bonds? Shouldn't he at least switch to commodities futures? Shouldn't he return to philosophy, and lead a life that gave him time to ski and other things like skiing, a life glorious and active, filled with poets and pretty girls like Amy or glamorous Frenchwomen like Madame Chatigny-Dové, both of whom seemed so much brighter and more useful than the rather Sloaney girls he took out in London or indeed than the Sloanes here in Valméri? He had discovered a whole nest of English chalet girls in the village, where he had taken to going after dinner. They were all named Henrietta or Lavinia, were mostly already paired off with ski instructors, but were jolly and welcoming, and there was something of a scene, people his own age at least, and unlike the people at the hotel, easy to fall in with. He'd drink a few beers, maybe dance, maybe chat someone up promisingly, and then remember Father and go on back to the hotel sorrowing.

The beauty of skiing is that you cannot dwell on your hopes and life decisions while doing it: while skiing you must think about your skis, the slope, the shift of the weight of your body, the knees, the release of the ankles. He was skiing faster than before, almost as fast as Kip. For a couple of hours they worked their way eastward through the mountain valleys, up on trams and chair lifts, down, on- and sometimes off-piste. Finally, Paul-Louis stopped them at the top of a run and pointed ahead. They could see below them the jaunty little spire of the church of Saint-Jean-de-Belleville and the smoke of the chimneys of the village houses, small stone structures barely set off from the rocky boulders among which they nestled, all dusted with snow. A well-regarded bistro, L'Edelweiss, had been recommended, and the hotel had phoned ahead to book their table.

As they had skied with enthusiastic and slightly

competitive speed all morning, the sight and promise of lunch, and the apparent ease of the long run before them to the restaurant, brought a cheer from the whole party. Now Rupert was skiing much faster than Amy, who, with the village in sight, moderated her speed as if fearing that something might endanger her safe arrival for the well-deserved repast. They flew on down toward the village, leaving graceful, symmetrical tracery arcs behind them in the snow, testimony to their smooth rhythmic turns and strengthening thighs.

24

Posy's party left the hotel in her car at about eleven, planning to stop in Moutiers at the hospital, which was on the way out of the valley toward Saint-Jean-de-Belleville, to see Father and drop Victoire. The plane was not expected until the afternoon, so they were surprised to find a group of men in green coveralls already standing at Venn's bed discussing in German the problems involved in transporting a patient on life support.

'The man is only alive because he's being breathed,' the doctor was ranting to them for the hundredth time. 'It is a most shameless plot so that he may breathe his last artificial sigh in England.' Perhaps he hoped that Anglophobic feelings would cause the Swiss paramedics to resist this wily English maneuver. Now that transport was a reality, a not quite disinterested indignation had arisen in Emile in Victoire's behalf, to think of her losing her inheritance, and he expressed his support for the doctor's position: the man should not be taken to England. Posy agreed, and the paramedics, accustomed to praise and urgent encouragement from the people they were helping, were confused and dismayed by these contradictory objections from members of a victim's family.

'You should confront the English lawyer, or the American woman, let them know you are wise to their cynical and hypocritical plot,' said Dr Lamm to Emile and Posy in a tone so bitter that Emile dismissed it as owing to wounded professional pride. Emile in truth felt ambivalent about how to spend the morning, both looking forward to an outing in the mountains and inclined to stay and meddle in Victoire's behalf, for she was, after all, his wife.

A respite provided itself. A special piece of equipment the medics had not thought of would be needed for the electric generator in the ambulance that was to transport Venn to the nearby town of Albertville, to the only airport. This article was being driven up from Geneva during the morning, but it didn't appear that departure would be ready before late afternoon. Posy and Emile each felt relieved, not to have to forgo the pleasant prospect of lunch together outside the valley, and there was still time for another impediment to develop. Perhaps Venn would miraculously wake up in the meantime. 'Do you think he looks better? It's as if he knows he's going home,' said Posy.

Somewhat uneasily they took their leave just as Mr Osworthy was arriving, and set off on the snowy road for Saint-Jean-de-Belleville and their lunch rendezvous with the skiers – Amy, Rupert, Paul-Louis, and Madame Chatigny-Dové. Posy, wracked with premonitions, took a long look of farewell at her father just in case, but no one wanted to articulate the gloomy forebodings they all felt.

Victoire sat down next to Venn. After studying the face of this stranger and finding no resemblance to herself, she nonetheless tried to feel regret for having missed the chance to become acquainted with him. Bringing out her flute, she seated herself at her father's bedside. She was able to feel the tender concern one felt for anyone who was ill, but she was disappointed that she didn't feel anything more than that for this inert person to whom she owed her biological existence. She accepted the fact of his paternity. She had to. If her father had been someone else, she herself would be someone else.

She thought about this wonderingly, knowing these were thoughts appropriate to childhood – it was just that she hadn't had them before; the feeling of narrow escape from being someone else impressed her with the luck of being herself, though it didn't do to dwell on the ways one might have been better. The inevitability of her fragile spine and straight nose. These thoughts didn't intensify her feeling for Mr Venn, though. She would do whatever she could to help. As the paramedics checked him, discussed, and waited for their missing piece of hardware, she performed the adagio from Lully's *Andromache*.

To an American and city dweller like Kerry Venn, who had grown up in Portland, Oregon, background music, omnipresent in American stores and elevators, was an integral part of consciousness itself, so that a few hours later when she began to recover consciousness, it was not as a fresh sensation that she heard music, knew it, even – 'Sheep May Safely Graze.' She heard it as the reflex of her own mind. The melody, played on a flute, replaced actual thoughts, was her whole consciousness for some moments until the components of the experience of hearing it gathered in her consciousness. She supposed she was dreaming, then separated herself from the dream and came to feel the bed under her and the light covers over her. She recognized that she was in bed, that real sounds were being addressed to her.

She opened her eyes. Ceiling. Some constraints, something attached to her arm pulling painfully at the skin on the back of both hands. Tube or something between her legs. A hospital, then, but why the beautiful music, suitable to being on the other side of some immense blank, somewhere she felt she had just been? The music stopped and a beautiful face smiled over her.

'*Superbe,*' said the voice, 'she's waking.' Other faces peered down at her. Kerry floated back to wherever she'd been, then back here again. Someone wrapped something around her arm. Kerry squeezed a hand when asked to.

'*Oui, oui, oui,*' said a nurse. '*Elle serre la main.*' She obeyed the instruction to open her eyes. The nurses smiled at each other, and Sister Bénédicte went to call the doctor, for it was he who would decide when to remove the apparatus of coma, for her coma was lifting, and soon she would not need the breathing tube, the heart monitor, and the rest, and could speak and reward their patience. This gratifying moment communicated itself even to the paramedics concerned with transferring the comatose husband and his complicated tubes and cumbersome machines onto a stretcher for transport. They left this business for a moment to take turns staring into the eyes, opening and shutting on command, of the tractable, increasingly sentient wife.

'*Bienvenue, madame,*' someone said, moved, and other voices were saying '*Bon,* Kerry, *bon.*' She tried to find the first face again, so lovely had it been, so welcoming. Now jubilant flute strains again, and someone stroked her hair, and men's voices now rose. She tried to lift her head but couldn't. She became aware that something was blocking her throat, hard impediments like sticks stuck down her throat, hurting her, and she tried to reach for them, to pull them out.

'Sedative,' someone said. 'We cannot take out the tubes until tomorrow, until we are sure. Or perhaps late this afternoon. Light sedation until then. She does not need to speak.'

'She'll come back rapidly now,' said another.

'Poor woman,' said the nurses to each other as the complicated removal of Venn proceeded, after her *calvaire* to wake up and find her husband taken off to London.

'Think how happy the others will be,' said Victoire, laying aside her flute. 'Now I almost think I should have gone to London with Mr Osworthy. I see that my father had the more need of music – it seems his wife was about to wake up on her own.'

Other voices discussed this. Kerry heard part, slipping in and out of consciousness, in and out of dream. Someone did something to the IV fluids and then she slept deeply.

It was already after one o'clock. The village of Saint-Jean-de-Belleville was made up of mossy gray stone houses, sturdy, avalanche proof, planted self-satisfiedly in the narrow gorge of a little ice-covered river. Amy thought she had never seen anything so pretty. Bistro Edelweiss was visible across the flat field at the bottom of the run, and they made toward it, walking in or carrying their skis and placing them in a rack outside the stone building. The proprietor was waiting for them, remarking that their companions had already arrived. Inside, a table for eight had been set in a window alcove, where Posy, Emile, and Robin were pouring from a pitcher of the local white wine. They had left Victoire at the hospital, and, in answer to Rupert's anxious inquiries, said things appeared to be going well with the airlift.

The automobile party greeted the skiers with admiration and congratulations slightly tinged, perhaps, with envy. Amy was waved into a place next to Robin Crumley and across from Emile and Posy, who were sitting side by side with an air Amy recognized but couldn't put a name to – of acquaintance, or ease. Paul-Louis sat next to her on her other side and poured her a glass of wine. 'I give you not too much,' he warned, 'my skiers 'ave to return safely.'

Monsieur le propriétaire proposed several local specialities – *tartelette*, fondue, raclette, and a liqueur made from a local bush; they were shown one of them growing in a tub by the window. Amy left her choice up to Paul-Louis, who decreed they all have raclette, green salad, and more wine.

'What was it like? What did you do?' the others demanded, but there is a sameness to the events of a good morning of skiing that baffled their powers of description. They, or rather Rupert, recounted what he could of their exploits in the dazzling chutes, on the expanse of glacier. Soon there was more delight as the raclette machine, an imposing sort of broiler, was set up, under which they would melt lumps of cheese onto boiled potatoes, as the waiter demonstrated.

Amy was still entranced by the national diversity of her companions. In Palo Alto, though everyone was of course an individual, there was a sameness to her friends and colleagues, all Americans except for three Indians from India. English Mr Crumley she thought especially gallant in the way he braved the elements. Though he didn't ski, and seemed so spidery of frame, he probably had the blood of polar explorers in his veins. French Marie-France was elegantly thin and fearless, though she should be counseled about sunscreen, the wonderfully athletic Paul-Louis, too, though tan was in the nature of an occupational hazard in his case. Nothing seemed to be happening with Paul-Louis, but he had given her many really helpful pointers about visualization on moguls. He, Marie-France, and Emile, French though from different worlds, appeared to have bonded, attested to by their in-jokes about the French, their slight apprehensiveness about what the English people might say or do, and their uniform reaction to what happened next. Amy also noticed that Posy was uneasy with the Frenchman, even though he was her brother-in-law, but she could understand it, he somehow made Amy uneasy too.

As the process of setting up the raclette got under way, all at once the quiet of the mountain village was ruptured by the aggressive intrusion of violent sound, unmistakably of internal combustion engines, vrooming and choking beneath the windows of the restaurant, men's voices, and even, Amy thought, the smell of gasoline seeping into the woodsy calm of the cozy room. The door banged open, and a party of eight coveralled and helmeted men came in, all too clearly Americans, the ones they had seen setting out on snowmobiles, among them Joe Daggart.

'*Mon Dieu,*' said Emile. '*Quel ennui.* What a bore.'

'At least if they're in here, they're not outside running their machines,' remarked Posy.

'They are very noisy,' agreed Marie-France, nodding her head toward the men, who were talking loudly.

'Male, at least. What's tough is a restaurant with noisy American women, they are so ... uh, not you, Amy, of course,' said Robin Crumley.

'At least there's only one of me,' said Amy, rather tartly, but she, too, was disappointed to have her countrymen throng in, diminishing the quaint foreign Alpine charm of the occasion and her feeling of distance and adventure, though she would never say this to the others.

'Good heavens, I didn't mean you,' Robin insisted.

'They're trying to figure out what caused the avalanche,' Amy said. 'Shouldn't they be allowed to have lunch?'

'They're trying to figure out how they didn't cause the avalanche,' said Emile.

'What exactly is the matter with that?' Amy asked.

'Oh, nothing really. But do they need to be here? America is "often in our thoughts," but better in our thoughts than in our restaurants or, needless to say, our skies.'

'What objection specifically?' Amy persisted, but received no answer.

The arrival of the newcomers also strained the resources of the little restaurant. The men were out of scale. Tables had to be pushed together to form a surface big enough for their party, chairs brought up. The new table of Americans was placed so close to Amy's group that all were obliged to nod to each other with an appearance of civility. The exception to this friendliness seemed to be Joe Daggart, who sat at the opposite side of their table and seemed anxious not to acknowledge any of them.

All the Americans were military handsome, with their close-cut hair and freckled faces. One of them, to Amy's chagrin and the delight of the others, said, 'Howdy.'

'Howdy,' said the Europeans, their faces perfect masks of cordiality. Emile said something in French to amuse the others and didn't try to explain. Amy resolved to work harder at her French, maybe private lessons when she got to Paris, but she also thought again how odious the man Emile was, sarcastic and hostile, though it could be he didn't realize she didn't speak French. Rupert's sister was looking sort of blank too.

'Damned if they look into it, damned if they don't,' Amy went on about the avalanche inquiry. 'According to you.'

Emile explained his objections. 'It's only that their presence diminishes the "grandeur" of our idea of them. Up close, the Great Power loses its imputed malevolence, so we lose our fear of it. In general, Great Powers are more effective as an absence. Personified, a powerful institution is just some . . . individuals and a snowmobile, or a set of libidinous priests.' Amy couldn't tell what he was getting at really.

'As with God, I imagine,' agreed Robin. 'Awe and absence go together.'

'When it comes to holding on to power, being present is an unwise strategy, as God has divined,' agreed Emile.

'Well, it seems to me they're just trying to cooperate in an effort to get to the bottom of the avalanche,' Amy persisted. 'Cooperation is a useful social ideal.' She recognized from their smiles that she was being earnest and literal-minded.

'Few social ideals survive their translation from the abstract to useful application,' Emile said. 'In their abstract form they are useful, in their practical application they amount to meddling.'

'So you think we shouldn't apply social ideals for fear of damaging them?' said Amy, taking a certain legalistic interest in the point.

'Apply them by all means, forgivingly. Be aware of the practical difficulties.'

'Why wouldn't that apply to absence and presence? In your argument, you should be forgiving of their snowmobiles, or my airlift.'

Emile looked at her sharply and said, 'I suppose so.'

Just now, great platters of beef jerky, potatoes, and slices of cheese were brought, and they turned to the business of sticking little panfuls of cheese under the grill to melt, and scraping it over the other stuff, engrossed in the gooey, fatty, and delicious result. This process was admired by the Americans at the next table, who leaned over with friendly smiles.

'Say, what is the name of that, that you're having?' asked one. Paul-Louis told them, and the Americans ordered it for themselves.

'I think they are *charmants* in their white *combinaisons*,' said Marie-France, sliding her glance toward the Americans. 'In any case, it wouldn't be these men who set off the avalanche.'

'Tomorrow we'll be in England,' said Posy suddenly, over a mouthful of cheese and grison. 'All of this a dream.' It seemed to Amy a banal observation; she was surprised at the gloom of the young woman's tone. Despite the legalities, shouldn't they be happy to have their father safely installed in England, with specialists, royally appointed consultants, and modern expertise?

Paul-Louis refilled their glasses with wine, skipping Emile, who was obliged to advance his glass.

'Oh, *excusez-moi, monsieur.* I thought that, well – I thought in your religion . . .'

Emile gave a sardonic smile, which seemed to say, What do you think my religion is?

Paul-Louis looked mortified, and reddened as if he had been struck.

'I'll always think of this lunch,' Posy persevered on the socially neutral topic, but wondering what Emile's religion was, actually.

'So will I,' said Robin Crumley, with what seemed a rather inappropriate romantic smile at Amy, or perhaps she was the only person to notice it. She was at pains not to react, beyond her usual, to some minds rather general, smile, so American.

Rupert understood Posy's sadness, not unlike his own, after this taste they were having of unmediated freedom and hotel luxury – enjoyable except for the bedside duties to do with Father. His boring job in the City and Posy's boutique would henceforward seem even more confining and low. A taste of pleasure ruins you for sacrifice, he had to admit.

Raclette ingredients were prepared for the Americans, the long forks distributed, two other machines plugged in at their table. At the insertion of the second plug, all the grills on both tables sputtered and died as one, the lights went out, and the music went off. The distant fuses had blown. Those at Amy's table, in their satiated state, merely blinked with regret, but a great cry of dismay rose from the hungry Americans. The proprietor rushed off somewhere; bustle and alarm ruled for rather longer, it seemed to Amy, than would have happened in the U.S., where you could just reset the circuit breakers.

'Father must be in the sky by now,' continued Posy in the dimness. 'Mr Osworthy too. They could be in London right now, and we are here.' There seemed no necessary reply. The waiter appeared with a pitcher of a clear liquor, the local *gennepi*, he explained, to ease them through this unexpected hiatus, as the cheese hardened on their plates. The hungry Americans remonstrated good-naturedly, and one, standing up, offered to help with the situation.

'Go, Mr Fuse,' said his companions.

'Yes, Mr Venn is in the air, thanks to Miss Hawkins,' said Emile. 'Beyond the reach of the quirky laws of France.' Posy and Rupert didn't need reminding of this aspect of the airplane rescue.

'I must say, we weren't entirely convinced that Father needed to go . . . in his condition,' Rupert said to Amy. By *convinced*, said his tone, he meant 'happy.' Weren't entirely happy that Father should go, had mixed feelings perhaps.

'Another example of unilateral American meddling,

with no regard for the consequences to others,' Emile went on.

'Why didn't you just come out and say you didn't want him to go?' said Amy, beginning again to feel put upon, tired of this subject the man seemed unable to let go of. 'I don't understand all this terminal reticence. I was only trying to help. Your lawyer, Mr Osworthy, seems to feel he can be saved.' It was only now getting through to her that maybe they didn't want their father saved, even. How naive she was, not to have seen that. Of course! They had explained to her that there was some detail of international law, and now she finally grasped that the noble Mr Osworthy was having to override a rebellious group of disappointed would-be heirs. Amy respected even more their polite reluctance to have said anything, a reticence, after all, known as a national characteristic they probably couldn't even help having.

'Americans are generally good natured, they try to be helpful,' said Robin, whether speaking of the American fuse-mender or trying to repair his remark about the female voice.

'No one cares about my sister,' said Kip suddenly. Receiving their startled looks, he stammered on. 'She was awake yesterday. No one talks about her at all, she might as well be a big lump of cheese . . . she might as well be dead.'

Startled, they protested. 'But she is doing so well, we are all so concerned . . .'

'Harry too. Harry is a person, you know – he's a little kid, he doesn't know what's happening . . .'

Amy, despite her affection for him, had consigned Kip

to the category of adolescent boy, that is to say, an un-known and unknowable being. Now she looked at him more closely. He had expressed these feelings before, but she hadn't considered she could do anything about them, and so had paid little attention. Now she could see the passionate expression of his eyes, the depth of his uncertainty and resentment. The others muttered reassuringly that they thought of Kerry all the time, she was doing so well, it wouldn't do to uproot her and so on.

'If Kerry has a chance, it should have been her that went to London. That's what they do on *M*A*S*H*, they airlift the people that have the best chance,' said Kip.

Amy saw she was at fault about that, absolutely, hadn't paid enough attention to Kerry's situation, had believed what Kip had told her about the reassuring things the doctors were saying about his sister.

'I'm sure we all deserve these salutary rebukes,' Emile said, but his was the only mea culpa, and of questionable sincerity.

As the interval without electricity extended, others of the Americans got up and left the table, apparently to help Mr Fuse in the troubleshooting effort. Since no one in Amy's party knew anything about electricity, they all sat passively, glumly regarding their lumpy blobs of congealing cheese. Despite Emile, a measure of camaraderie was developing between the two tables, especially between the Americans and Madame Chatigny-Dové, who was seated closest to them, and passed them over some potatoes and cornichons. 'To keep you alive.' She laughed flirtatiously.

Eventually the lights came back on and the grills began

to reheat. The Americans came back to their table, shaking their heads at what they had seen of a Byzantine wiring system completely outside their experience. The gratified proprietor attended them with excessive friendliness, and poured large vials of his fiery pine-bush liqueur for them, their cheese melted, talk rose. Marie-France and Rupert fell into more conversation with them; they confirmed that they were there to look into the snow conditions and avalanche control programs in the area.

'Damage control,' said one. Amy didn't think they made it clear enough that they'd had nothing to do with the avalanches. She noticed that Kip hung on their words.

When they had finished and the machines were taken away, the waiter, with that special smirk waiters use to discuss dessert, proposed *sorbets* and *tartes au pommes*. Amy was relieved that they weren't expected, after all that cheese, to eat another cheese course, too, though she had already learned to like it, and to distinguish Bries from Camemberts. They followed with coffee and more of the local *gennepi*. She had begun to be worried that the hour was getting late, but the others seemed content to linger at the table, and now Paul-Louis had stopped glancing out of the window. Perhaps in his mind they had already gone past the time they had to leave if they were returning on skis. The Americans called for their check, paid, and clattered down the wooden stairs to the toilets in their heavy snowmobile boots, then up them and out to start up their noisy vehicles again. Kip said he wanted to look at these machines and went outside with them. Paul-Louis made no effort to move his party.

The noise of snowmobile engines again split the Alpine peace: Emile rolled his eyes at Posy and Rupert. Now Paul-Louis had signalled for the check. This brought to them all the usual moment of check anxiety. They were seven, not all of them Paul-Louis's clients, so Amy hoped he wasn't going to think of paying for everybody from his low wage. If it were just Paul-Louis and she, she would pay, the established protocol for client and instructor, but the authority with which he waved at the waiter made her fear that some impulse of proprietary French hospitality had carried him away. With luck, the other men would intervene and slap down their credit cards the way Americans would have known to do.

However, this didn't happen. The others stirred and buttoned their sweaters. Only Rupert said, 'Let me . . .' in a concerned voice unmatched by any gesture toward his pocket. Everyone seemed under a spell, including Paul-Louis, who, as the waiter placed the big bill before him, had the numb look of someone who has just put his life savings on a horse to win. Such a moment of unspoken struggle, both interior and social, lasts only a split second but seems much longer, eons, until Amy got out her card and placed it on the tray. This brought on a flurry of movements and murmurs, 'Oh, no, let me, let's split it, thanks,' as if they had all been released from the evil force that had paralyzed them. Posy pulled on her red sweater and went off to the bathroom. Amy just hoped her card wasn't maxed out after the big expense of the airplane to London. But no.

Amy certainly didn't mind paying for lunch, but one detail troubled her a little: why had the others let her do it

226

with such docility? It must mean they knew she could afford it, not that it was a secret, but them knowing made her uneasy in a way she couldn't identify, which was strange, because she was totally happy to pay, it was nothing. She hoped she wasn't getting complicated and paranoid about this issue of money, or stingy, the way rich people often got.

The waiter brought the mound of parkas. Though from inside the restaurant the weather had only been perceptible as a darkening sky, when they stepped outside they could see that it was snowing heavily. 'Eet ees too late now to ski,' Paul-Louis said. Perhaps he had allowed them to sit there so long because he'd known all along they wouldn't be able to ski back. Perhaps he had planned it like this, thought them too feeble to make it back, or figured he'd done enough. 'It's better if you go in the shuttle,' the little mountain bus that travelled a circuit of villages returning skiers and hotel workers to where they had started. Amy had to admit she felt a certain relief. Like the others, she was full of juniper liqueur and wine.

There was another problem. Kip had vanished. So had his snowboard, indicating that he had set off alone, or with the Americans, to return by the pistes the way they had come. Paul-Louis frowned, his expression concerned, though he only shook his head as if in despair at youth, recklessness, Americans. He seemed to hesitate about what to do. In only a couple of hours, the snow had made more progress than they could have imagined, a cold wind had mounted as it had done every afternoon all week, and the road was already glassy with ice.

Paul-Louis did decide that Posy should not drive her

car. 'Not without chains. You can get your car tomorrow.'

'We have to go to London tonight,' Posy protested.

Paul-Louis was still weighing whether he should go after Kip or stay to help the others. 'I will drive your car back, mademoiselle,' he decided. 'I cannot let you do it. This is my fault for letting you eat for so long. You will not be able to leave Valméri tonight, either, mademoiselle.' Posy gratefully handed over her keys, but mentally reserved the option to leave if she felt like it. Paul-Louis called the ski patrol to alert them that the boy was skiing alone on the way back to Valméri, and showed the others where to wait for their bus. 'I'll go with Paul-Louis,' Rupert said, 'in case of a problem with the car.'

25

The little van with its load of skiers and hotel workers was on time despite the weather, and, though feeling full and relaxed, they put their skis onto its rack and climbed aboard with a mild sense of anticlimax at missing the ski home. The bus was already crowded with skiers and chambermaids in printed housedresses and serviceable boots and parkas, chattering away among themselves in the rather harsh-sounding local dialect. Posy and Marie-France were given seats by men who stood up, but Emile, Robin, and Amy had to stand in front by the driver, swaying and clinging, beginning to catch some of the hilarity that seemed already to be infecting the van. It was clear that the driver was hurrying on his rounds, perhaps fearing that people could be stranded in a worsening storm. No road conditions served to abate his speed as they swayed and swerved, people laughing louder with every skid.

It was only minutes until, with a dreamlike deliberation, the van seemed to sway its rear end to and fro like a dog shaking off water, and then began to slide sidewise as if carried on a moving sidewalk. The passengers felt themselves hurtle around inside, banging into one another, and then they found themselves buried in a bank of snow, blueish darkness against the windows, all this enacted in a strange, elongated, silent instant. Immediately cries rose up. The driver shouted '*Ça va?*' – a phrase Amy had learned means 'Is everything okay?' '*Ça va, ça va,*' everyone shouted back, though a child had begun to cry. The driver got out of his seat and pushed past those who were lying against the entrance to try the sliding door, which opened. Snow tumbled in.

They had gone off the road and come to rest in a gully already filled with soft snow, which had saved them but now engulfed them. They lay only a few feet below the roadbed, but would have to be dug out before they could move, and in the end would probably have to be towed. The relative calm with which the passengers reacted suggested that such events were commonplace. The first step seemed to be to dig a means of escape for themselves, but in the meantime it bothered Amy that the driver restarted and kept the motor running so that the mufflers were undoubtedly blocked by snow. Didn't they know about carbon monoxide? She couldn't begin to explain, and she comforted herself that as she had never heard of whole parties of Alpine bus passengers dying together of carbon monoxide poisoning, perhaps she was being overanxious.

'*Restez-là restez là,*' the driver enjoined them. The men hoisted themselves out through windows and counseled the lightly dressed maids and the children to stay inside. Amy followed Marie-France when their turn came to clamber out, but got right back in again, feeling herself in the way of the digging as the men, including Emile and Robin, these two with their hands bare, began to flail away the snow from the sides of the vehicle. To Amy's relief, the engine had died and the driver didn't get back inside to start it again. The cold grew intense.

Tribal forms of cooperation are sometimes quite exotic, including those practiced by Alpine tribes, to Amy's admiring analysis. The digging lasted for forty minutes before the men declared a path to be cleared, the engine was started again, and the men came back into the van, voices raised in laughter and satisfaction at the teamwork and manly duties manfully performed. The French maids praised them, and, amazing to Amy, took the icy hands of the men and guided them up inside their anoraks, and even inside their blouses to warm them. The men gleefully thanked the ladies, with a great deal of leering laughter, the women laughing too, despite cold hands on their breasts. '*Ici, pauvres hommes,*' they said, crossing their arms across their chests the better to enfold the hands.

To Amy's further surprise, Robin Crumley had fallen into the collective mood of jubilation and made a move to put his hands inside her jacket. She jumped back, startled, and eluded him; the instant passed, almost simultaneous with her regret and feeling of shame at being so uptight and prudish, so unequal to the French mood, so American not to be able to fall in with this odd event. Crumley's face took on an expression of injured innocence, as if to say she had misunderstood his gesture. She felt her face grow as red as his ears.

It became clear that the bus could not move by itself, and the driver called for assistance, urging his passengers up to the highway where rescuers with cars would be picking them up. Why this had not been arranged before wasn't clear – perhaps some local code would have prevented the women passengers from deserting the male passengers at their snow-shovelling labors. As they waited on the highway in the swirling snow, Amy, clutching her skis and stomping her feet in their heavy ski boots, was now worrying both about Kip and about how she had behaved just now to Robin Crumley. His impulse had been strange – it was more as if he meant to emulate, without really understanding, the hearty show of lust, or form of gallantry, as he perceived it being practised by others. Perhaps she had shrunk less from puritanism (specifically an American flaw?) than from injured vanity (a universal tendency?), hurt and shocked that someone so elderly and stringy would think himself qualified, or think her so needy, that she would let someone like him feel her up, even though this supposedly wasn't feeling up, it was handwarming, and he had been as stalwart as any of the other diggers, and just as much in need of warm hands. Looking at the episode as a flaw in herself made her action seemed uncalled for, a defeat of her principles, a failure to live up to the spirit of community she saw the local people so joyfully embodying. Never mind, personal flaws can be remedied; she'd be nicer to him in the future.

Baron Otto had welcomed the call soliciting volunteers in private autos with chains to rescue stranded bus passengers and hotel guests. He had just weathered a scene with his peppery wife, Fennie, who was American by passport, though raised in Germany in a military family, and had an American directness. He had always believed that cultural disconnection accounted for her chronic discontent and jealousy. Feeling slightly mystified by both the American and the German sensibilities, she tended to misconstrue almost everything he did, and now had misunderstood his list of Paris errands, beginning with 'Géraldine C, 10:00,' taking it as a record of his assignations, an unreasonable interpretation given that it would have taken the stamina of a bisexual stallion, as he thought resentfully ('Antoine de Persand, 14:00') to work through the whole register of names. But Fennie had held to the belief that Paris was iniquity and men were wanderers.

Amy was conscious and rather gratified that the baron Otto made a point of attending to her, though also to two chambermaids whom they deposited quite soon at a hotel down the road. He took considerable time affixing her skis to the roof rack of his Mercedes station wagon, and installed her in the front seat next to him.

'Miss Hawkins, you must be tired. Your ordeal –'

'Not really. We only skied to Saint-Jean-de-Belleville. Then we had a long lunch.'

'The accident not too stressful?' He thought her dimples adorable.

Oh, Baron Otto, I'm not that fragile, she wanted to protest. He always thought the worst of her, perhaps of Americans in general – people who ignore warning signs, cause avalanches, speak only English, and are easily tired. She couldn't explain to herself why she wanted the good opinion of this slightly portly Austrian with the pale Alpine eyes of a husky. 'No, no,' she said. 'No one was hurt.'

'It would be possible – we are just near – I would very much like to show you our chalet – a real mountain chalet, if you would consent to a small detour?'

Amy, in the spirit of adventure that had borne her along thus far through the day, suspended any theory about what this could portend. 'I'd love to see a chalet,' she said.

The baron drove a few more minutes, then parked by a towering snowbank, alongside which a path was just visible in the late afternoon darkness. 'We'll have to walk up the drive, it isn't yet plowed.'

Getting out, Amy slipped in her ski boots. He took her arm, and she stumped clumsily alongside him toward a distant light shining on the stone porch of a chalet whose architectural charm could only be inferred – steep-pitched roof, gingerbread eaves, barrels on the porch to be planted in geraniums in summer, a modern expanse of glass updating the classic details, a massive door, opened with one of the keys on his massive key ring. What about the size of a man's key ring? Amy saw she must be tired after all: Her thoughts were getting silly.

'My wife must be at her class.'

This development, no wife around, was classic enough to alert Amy but not to alarm. She hadn't been especially expecting a wife.

'Here we are,' said the baron, touching light switches that silently illuminated the room. Rustic sofas, a mezzanine across one end, bright wall hangings, gave a luxurious, if routinely mountainlike, atmosphere, rather like a condo in Aspen or Vail. An ancient butter churn had been made into a lamp, and a sled into a coffee table. Antlers. Was this Americanization of the Alps or had Americans borrowed this kitschy but authentic decor? She was learning that she didn't have to judge.

'Of course you can get no idea of the view at this time of day,' he said, touching another button that drew back the curtains from across the massive windows. 'This is one of the larger units, but even the smallest have all the luxury features. Sit down, sit down!'

'Oh, I'm kind of wet,' she said, but sat down anyway.

'Drink? We can have our apéritif here. I expect you would like to see the kitchen and so on.'

Amy had little interest in kitchens, but knew them to be part of her program and that she had better develop an interest in learning what you would need to cook, say, a lobster, or things au gratin. 'Yes, indeed!' she said, getting up again. The baron led the way through a door at the back beneath the mezannine.

'What will you drink?'

'Do you have any *gennepi*?' she said, remembering the name of the delightful local liqueur they had drunk in Saint-Jean-de-Belleville. She saw at once from the baron's expression this was not something in his cupboard, or maybe you didn't drink it at this time of day? The more you knew, the more the possibilities for social miscalculations extended themselves, still, it shouldn't be a serious faux pas to have asked for the wrong liqueur.

'Campari, or perhaps martini? Gin?'

'Gin, please,' accepting the most familiar.

'All units have the American Amana refrigator, the Miele stovetop and dishwasher, German, all state of the art,' said the baron, opening the refrigerator.

Amy was about to frame a perceptive question on stovetops when they both became aware of someone coming into the kitchen. They turned. A woman of the baron's age in trousers and turtleneck stood there, a pretty woman if she hadn't been scowling.

'Oh, my God, Otto, isn't this a bit blatant? I see I shouldn't have opened my mouth, I've goaded you into bringing them home.' An American accent with the slightly foreign intonations Amy had heard in the speech of other Americans long resident in Europe, like Princesse Mawlesky.

'Yes, you have,' agreed Otto, grimly. 'But I don't think we have to continue our conversation in front of Miss Hawkins.'

'Miss Hawkins. Where did you find Miss Hawkins?' as if Amy weren't there. 'Never mind, I definitely don't want to know.'

'Miss Hawkins, my wife Fennie.'

Amy, embarrassed by the discomfort of the baron and the anger of his wife, gave him a sympathetic glance and smiled placatingly at Fennie.

'My class was cancelled, which you didn't bargain on,' went on Fennie.

'I was bringing Miss Hawkins to meet you. She's your countrywoman, from . . .'

'You thought I wouldn't be home till eight o'clock.'

'. . . Excitement around here, Fennie, today – people stranded, accidents. Miss Hawkins was in an accident in the St Croix van.'

'Luckily she's come through fine, it looks to me.'

'Probably I should be getting back,' said Amy. 'Thank you for showing me the lovely unit.'

The angry Fennie now turned a strained smile on Amy. The baron, looking uncomfortable, said that they must finish their drink. 'Fennie, what will you have?'

Amy had imagined the baron in Palo Alto, or more like

Woodside, where it was horsier, in boots and jodhpurs, which he would look good in, a burly, strong-looking man. Summer in Woodside, winter here in his chalet, with lots of skiing and European company. This was a more promising fantasy than any involving the serious, responsible Paul-Louis. Too bad about this wife. Her eyes met the baron's. As he read her thoughts, she read his: embarrassment and desire, and she realized it was in her power to cheer him up a lot. Fennie perched tensely on a chair and accepted a gin and ice. She seemed all too intuitive and continued her needling as they drank.

Embarrassed by his outburst at lunch, Kip had left the others and taken the gondola, which was still optimistically sending its little eggs up into the face of the blizzard; but at the top he judged the visibility too bad, and wended his way down the most visible pistes toward Méribel. Here the intervalley jitneys and buses assembled for the skiers coming off the slopes, and he took the one that went direct to Moutiers. He came into the hospital upon the scene of excitement surrounding Kerry's awakening. Kerry had been on his mind all day, and now he saw that it had been ESP, because there must have been a further change in her condition. At first he feared it was a change for the worst, and he drew nearer with a sick feeling. But the expressions on the faces of the nurses and the doctor reassured him.

'Is she waking up?'

'Yes, indeed!'

'Is she okay now?'

'She is doing so well!' agreed one of the nurses.

Much to his embarrassment, Kip burst into tears. He couldn't control these babyish sobs, he could be Harry. He stood at Kerry's bed sobbing and laughing at the same time.

'Right on, Kerry. Hey, hey, Kerry,' sobbing and laughing. Victoire was there, and smiled at him.

'Someone was protecting her, *elle avait une protectrice,*' remarked the nurse, embracing Kip.

'I think so too,' said the lovely Victoire.

'When can she talk? When can I talk to her?' He dried his eyes and got his breath.

'You can talk to her now. She cannot talk back.'

'Can she understand?'

'Yes, they say so,' Victoire told him, pleased to see the boy's happiness. 'They will have to take out the tubes before she can talk to you. In a day or two.'

Kip plunked himself down on one of the chairs, his ski boots dripping with melting snow, suddenly tired. He ought to talk to Kerry, even if she couldn't talk to him, and tell her Harry was okay. He began the monologue so familiar to him, the things he'd been saying all week, Harry okay, everything okay.

'Poor woman,' whispered the nurses. 'She doesn't know her husband has been taken away to Angleterre.'

'How long before she will be able to sit up and talk?' asked Victoire of the nurse, Nurse Bénédicte. 'How interesting it is to see someone come back to life, but music has that effect, as we know from the story of Orpheus, Apollo *aussi* and his connection to Aesculapius.' She pulled up a chair and sat down beside Kerry. Kerry tried to turn her head slightly to watch Victoire, as if she wanted to see things and hear words spoken, grounding her in the here, wherever they were.

'She might never remember, people don't ever remember the blow that stuns them, only the moments before it, leading up to it, or sometimes the memory is gone about everything that happened for much longer before. Depends on the severity of the blow,' said the nurse.

26

Robin Crumley was relieved to be back at the hotel, after an afternoon that had in every way reinforced his mistrust of snow. His emotions were in turmoil. To find himself entranced with the beautiful, rich American young woman! How regrettable that this had come so late in his life. People normally felt this in their teens. He was at such a disadvantage! How he regretted his rather asexual, donnish, even narcissistic single life until now, with its consequent relative lack of experience, not much happening with either sex, only an odd dash from time to time . . . And it was even worse that the infatuation had struck while he was in France, a land ignorant of his poetry and in general dismissive of the mighty literature of his nation – a people content to hear Shakespeare in translation, Mark Antony saying to Julius Caesar, '*Bonjour, monsieur,*' instead of 'Hail, Caesar,' and other such absurdities. A people who bestowed their Légion d'Honneur on English romance novelists, a people for whom Barbara Cartland was as good as Elizabeth Bowen, or Jerry Lewis as good as Olivier.

The American, Amy, however, showed such a fresh intelligence, she would surely profit from a more comprehensive exposure to literature. She was woefully ignorant. The young English girl, Posy, knew much more about literature – a commentary on American education.

On hotel stationery he wrote down from memory, hesitating over a line or so, two of his poems, intending to present them to Amy later in the bar. She would read them tonight and they would furnish a conversation tomorrow, when he would explain some of the poetical principles involved, the tradition of terza rima – he wasn't sure where American education stopped vis-à-vis poetry, some of the ideas might lead naturally into the erotic or anyway romantic. As an afterthought he decided to ask the desk to make another copy and he would give one to the intelligent Frenchman Emile, who appeared to be interested in poetry and might value a fair copy in the poet's own hand.

He went to the window to close the shutters where the cold leaked through the wooden window frames and icy glass. Outside, the lights glittered in the village and the falling snow was pink in the neon glow of the ice rink sign. He noticed Amy herself, only now back, getting out of a car driven by the German real-estate agent – it must have been he who had picked her up earlier at the scene of the bus accident. The man was lifting her skis off the roof of his car. Amy, watching him, stamped her feet in the cold. They were laughing. Then, strange beyond belief, as Robin watched, the man rested her skis against the fender of his car and began to kiss her. Her hat fell off. She retrieved it and turned again to him. They resumed a brief kiss. Quickly, heart beating, Robin banged his shutters closed. He looked at his watch. She was only now getting home, an hour and a half after him, could have been doing anything in the meantime.

*

When Rupert reached the hotel, there was the little red light blinking on his phone. News from London, or maybe something on the whereabouts of Kip. He had been reassuring himself that the ski patrol had been told to look for the boy. He deliberately waited until he had got out of his wet ski clothes before dialing the operator as instructed. Christian Jaffe at the desk answered.

'You have *un message*,' said Christian Jaffe. 'You are to call Mr Osworthy in London at this number.' Eagerly and in dread, Rupert wrote down the number and asked Jaffe to dial it.

'Oh, Rupert,' said Osworthy immediately, 'I have bad news, I'm afraid.'

'He didn't make it,' Rupert said.

'I'm sorry to tell you. He made it to London, for that matter,' Osworthy said, 'but he died soon after we arrived at the Brompton. His brain – I'm sorry, this is rather shocking – his brain began to swell, and there is apparently no remedy for that, all is over.'

'I see,' said Rupert, shocked even though he had been more than prepared, these last few days, for the probability of this outcome. 'I'll tell Posy. Will you speak to my mother?'

'I have spoken to her. I have asked her what she wants to do.'

'Hardly up to her, is it?'

'The present Mrs Venn is not in a condition to make decisions. I believe, in fact, you children must decide, and your mother has said she has no views.'

'Yes, well, let me take this in, Mr Osworthy. Where is he now?'

'I assume that is a practical and not a metaphysical question. In the morgue at the Brompton awaiting removal to the mortuary.'

'There's a storm at the moment, we can't start for London tonight. We'll hope to get a start tomorrow morning and be back in London tomorrow afternoon,' Rupert said, part of him feeling tears beginning, part of him relieved not to be setting out into the snowy darkness, it not mattering now.

'Notify the French chap, you have his number, I assume?' suggested Osworthy.

'Monsieur Delamer, yes.'

'I'll call you later, Rupert, with some other matters, I know you want to be alone now,' said Osworthy, and rang off.

Rupert sat in the chair in his room for a while, then went off to find Posy. He passed Emile Abboud in the hall – a right chap after all, had dug snow valiantly along with everyone else and talked wittily about it at the same time. He supposed he should tell Abboud about Father, so he could himself tell his wife; but for Victoire to know before Posy did seemed disloyal to Posy somehow.

Posy was in her room, eyes teary, face streaked with eye gunk, as if she had heard the news already. Maybe Osworthy had called her. It was strange when she seemed not to have heard.

'What?' she said crossly at finding it was Rupert at the door.

'You've heard?'

'No, what?'

'Father died.'

Posy's face cleared, assumed an expression of skepticism. 'How could he die, hooked up to all those machines? What do you mean?'

'Osworthy called. He said his brain swelled. Can I come in?'

'Oh, no, yes, sorry. Gosh.' Posy's tears were starting again. What had she been crying about if not Father? 'Gosh, I didn't expect that. Did you? After all this time. I mean I guess it was only a week, but it seemed – I thought he was going to make it.' She wedged her fist into her eyes. 'Didn't you?'

'I don't know. I guess I wasn't surprised. I guess the longer it went on the less I thought he was going to survive.'

'Does Mother know?'

'Yes, but I haven't talked to her.'

'Oh, what can one say? Bloody hell. Poor Father.'

'I know,' said Rupert. They sat awhile sighing desultory sighs and exchanging an occasional word, waiting for the full force of grief to declare itself, as it surely would.

'We'll go in the morning. Does Mother want us tonight?'

'I haven't talked to her.'

'Right.'

'I suppose we should tell Victoire.'

'I don't know if I can face having dinner with them,' Posy said. 'If I can't, I'll just have something in my room.'

'Be there,' said Rupert firmly.

Posy had been crying in her room because she had been unexpectedly embraced by Emile, animating all the

244

emotion she had kept at cheerful arm's length all afternoon. When they had returned to the hotel, wet and wool-smelling from their bus accident, he had come down the hall with her, stepped inside her bedroom door, and kissed her ardently. Kissed her ardently, looked long and regretfully into her eyes, covered her breasts with his hands as if memorizing them. She pushed his hands away and began to cry. At this, his manner became one of gentlemanly concern – what was the matter? How could he help?

'It's just that I'm sorry to leave,' she apologized, pulling herself together, not wishing to repel him with her drippy tears. 'It's better not to have good experiences, this hotel, our little times together – everything seems so much worse now, not even counting poor Father. What's happening to Father just symbolizes the disappointments of my life.' Aware that this sounded selfish and melodramatic, she could not keep from saying it.

'How old are you, Posy?' asked Emile. 'Twenty-one or two?'

'Twenty-two,' she admitted. 'But old for my age, and gifted with foresight, and I foresee I am never to have anything I want. Is it even worth it being alive?' This stuck her as such a bitter question, her tears flowed again.

'How do we know what we want? Remember the old caution, I believe it was an Englishman – Oscar Wilde? – who said there are two tragedies in life – not to get what you want, and to get it, of which getting it is worse.'

'I don't want much, I only want something interesting to do – nothing more than anyone would want. And love, I guess.'

'Love and interest are so much more than anyone has, probably.' Emile now seemed interested less in her state of mind than in the philosophical question, old as it was. 'Of course I love you, Posy. One must always love to make love, lovemaking must *mean* something.'

Posy sensed a translation problem, *love* as in '*J'aime Coca-Cola,*' or '*J'aime ma VW . . . ,*' a word having a mysteriously different weight in French, lighter. 'I know we don't know each other well enough for love. I know I can't say I want you without scaring you.' She sighed, regretting the gloppy feel of her heavy English words. There was indeed a trace of inquietude in his expression as Emile kissed her again and left, saying they would see each other at dinner. Making no response to her sad little confession.

Baron Otto went with Amy to her room, walking in plain view through the lobby and into the elevator. Perhaps, as a person well known in the hotel, no one noticed his movements; or perhaps he was hoping to be reported to Fennie. He took the key from her, opened the door, and came inside.

Amy, who had skied forty kilometers, sweating inside her ski suit, and was soaked to her pores in the tobacco smoke that clung even to nonsmokers after being in a French restaurant or bar, said she'd have a shower.

'No, no,' the baron protested. '"*Ne te lave pas.*"'

'What?'

'As Napoleon wrote to Josephine. His most famous phrase.' He moved to embrace her.

'I guess you'll have to explain,' Amy said.

'He wrote her, when he was away campaigning, when

he was coming home, not to bathe. He must have liked –
have liked . . .'

'Oh,' agreed Amy, supposing generally whatever was
suggested by old Anna Magnani movies, sweat-soaked
women going into Italian barns with farmhands, earthi-
ness generally not appreciated in Palo Alto, nor, would
she have thought, in Germany, also not a Latin culture.

The baron himself smelled delightfully of some
cologne, and had a large pink body, with an enthusiastic
member springing from a nest of golden hair. Amy's own
enthusiasms were stirred by the sight. Things foreign and
unsettling could be reduced to cheering familiarity by
taking off your clothes. It made her realize she had been
homesick or something, and that this was more than just
being nice to the baron.

He was a man in the grip of passion, whether inspired
by Amy's naked form or the resolve to affront his wife,
Amy was not sure. Probably both. How reassuring to find
that she could understand a few things about international
human nature after all. She undid her braid and let her
hair fall down.

If there was disappointment about actually doing it with
the baron, it was only that there was nothing specifically baronial or Austrian about it. The ingredients were
familiar – disrobing, kisses, foreplay, contraceptive reassurance, the act, the climax (her, then him, as if they'd
had years of practice), the whole rather short lived but
satisfactory. It was even sort of extra exciting to find
herself under such a large, that is to say almost heavy, man,
something solid and Mitteleuropean about that. He would
look great in a black leather raincoat, or the ruffled shirt

247

worn by the lordly aristocrat in the porn film. These mental pictures had made her come sooner than she might have. She was comfortable with the fact that people didn't have to apologize for or disclose their sexual fantasies.

Afterward, they showered and had champagne from the minibar. It was already almost nine. This had been a long day. 'We could get some room service,' Amy said. 'But I suppose you are expected home?'

'*Nein*. No, no. The room-service menu is rather limited, and besides, they are having a special carp from Lac Leman in the dining room tonight. I will stay to dinner and woo you as I would a client. No one will think it odd.' To her surprise, Amy felt some disappointment in this, would have liked just a sandwich in the room, but gamely brushed her hair and prepared to go down to dinner, watched at her toilette by the admiring baron.

Victoire had spent the day at the hospital, but came back to the hotel in time for dinner, which she and Emile had arranged that morning to eat with her Venn siblings at eight-thirty. She was elated, and trod as lightly as a sprite, despite a day in the depressing precincts of needles and serums. Her tendencies to happiness had been animated by Kerry coming to life, despite the sad condition of her new papa. In their room, speaking through the bathroom door to Emile in the shower, she gave him a glowing account of Kerry's miraculous awakening, Kip's joy, the prospects for a good recovery.

'Surely not miraculous, in that she has all along been expected to wake. "Fortuitous" better say.' Emile's tone critical, as usual, of her hyperbole.

'Though she will be sad to find her husband has been sent off to Londres. Tomorrow she will speak to us. She cannot yet speak, she has those hoses down her throat.'

Only to be cast into sadness to hear from Rupert and Posy, in the lounge before dinner, the triste news from London about her papa.

'We have some bad news, Victoire.' Of course she could read their faces.

'Oh, no.'

'"Didn't make it" was how Mr Osworthy put it,' Rupert told them. The opposite of hyperbole. Didn't make it. It had begun to sound like a moral failing of Venn's own.

Victoire's impulse was to go find little Harry – now, like her he would never know his father. But Harry would be in bed by now. The four sat in a corner of the bar, waiting for dinner and drinking whiskey, a little at cross-purposes, with Posy and Rupert not wanting to talk about Father, sunk in their sadness and regrets, Victoire wanting to hear all about him, Emile somewhat bored with the subject of Father, although not saying so, and hardly surprised at his death.

'He never actually spoke a word to me in my life,' sighed Victoire, bemused by this mischance. 'He never saw me, really.' It was a blessing that she had come down to Valméri at all, according to some grand design, she was sure – perhaps the greater meaning had been all along to put her in touch with her two new half-siblings, who were reminiscing about her papa; she listened attentively.

'Father was all right when we were little,' Posy was saying, 'but he was very self-centered. He had his toys, and he wanted all his toys and wanted to play with them all the time. Boats, horses, new cars all the time, and Pam just had this Morris Minor with us jammed in the backseat. She had that car for fifteen years.'

'Many, many pretty young women working in his office, high turnover,' said Rupert.

'We're not to speak ill of him,' Posy said. 'But it's hard.'

'He was never mean about money, even with Pam after the divorce, if something came up.'

'I am told he was a publishing genius. My mother says that, she has followed his activities in publishing,' said Victoire.

'He was interested in cooking. He was a wonderful cook,' said Posy. 'He was a wonderful eater, and he knew everything about wine.'

'I never even knew he could ski,' said Rupert. 'Our family never went on skiing holidays. It may have been something to do with Kerry. Her brother is a fine skier.'

'Who is going to tell her, poor woman?' said Victoire. 'Do you know, she woke up today.' Here was one piece of good news at least.

'They probably haven't heard about Father at the hospital, unless Mr Osworthy called them, but why would he?'

'Let her get a little stronger,' Rupert advised. 'The doctor should decide what to tell her.' They all agreed with that. They themselves would stop in to say goodbye to Kerry and tell the doctor about Father's death, tomorrow morning as they left for England, though perhaps by then Mr Osworthy would have already telephoned Dr Lamm.

'Oh, no, London tomorrow, horrible Mr Osworthy, horrible aftermath, funeral, horrible everything,' cried Posy, not caring if she seemed to Emile a discontented, bad person, what difference did it make, they would never see each other again. She knew she shouldn't be thinking about Emile when she should be thinking about Father. She couldn't help looking at him, either, and once caught him looking at her. He was sitting next to Victoire with a particular expression of uxorious detachment or resignation.

Posy could imagine being married to Emile, who she knew would be a whole lot of trouble, between infidelity and expensive hobbies – could he be a bit like Father? But it wouldn't matter, because instead of being a credit manager for a chain of boutiques, she would be the wife of a French intellectual and live in Paris. To occupy that enviable position, she would put up with a lot, but as Victoire (her own sister!) occupied the role of Emile's wife already, it seemed that all possible paths for her imagination to travel were blocked by some irrefutable reality. Even her mind couldn't meander without impediment. She knew self-pity was a base emotion, especially unseemly in light of poor Father, but it engulfed her all the same.

And now her personal misery was compounded by remorse at having gone with the others to lunch instead of waiting at the hospital to see Father off in the plane, at least to have looked in his face one more time. Instead, he'd been bundled off like so much cargo, trustfully confided to others, out of mind. It was true that she had been gazing into his gray, vacant face for days, but that didn't compensate for her inattention at the crucial moment of his final departure. They ought not to have sent him; perhaps it was being airborne that brought on the swelling. She and Rupert should have defied Mr Osworthy and his avatar, the meddlesome American Amy. How credulous of them to believe that the Brompton held out hope. The French doctor had been right all along . . . they shouldn't have accepted the American's offer of help.

Thus her emotions raged. How inconsequential is love beside death. Father dead! Had he known he was dying, had a last moment of awareness, had he been aware all along? If so, perhaps he was comforted that she, Posy, had sat all week by his bedside. She grasped at the hope that he had somehow been aware of her devotion.

27

Finding some solace in each other, Posy and Rupert sat together at the table awhile over dessert. Emile excused himself, saying he would leave them to their private grief. Victoire stayed with her two new siblings, perfectly tactful, not pretending she had known Father, but saddened in the appropriate degree.

'At least he has brought us together. He would have wanted that, I am sure. I am sure he was a man who would have wanted to die in an active, manly way, as has happened. He would not have wanted to linger, comatose, perhaps his brain damaged – the doctor said they could not rule out brain damage.' She thought of other consolations.

Rupert had skied and was tired, but he stayed, partly out of consideration for Posy, partly because he didn't want to be alone. It was understandable that Posy's grief was stronger than his, in proportion to her anger, which had been greater and more painful than his own. His own grief was milder, personal, hard to explain even to himself. He had a sense of loss, sorrow for the past few years when they hadn't been close. At least they hadn't been estranged the way the more explosive Posy had been, after one particular scene.

But Posy's sadness now seemed all encompassing.

She seemed to mourn some basic disorder in the world, some cosmic misalignment affecting her personally.

There was another subject of worry. They were all conscious of but had not brought up the dreaded subject of the will, or spoken of the fact that, as he had died in London, Father's fortune, whatever it proved, would go to Kerry and Harry according to his will instead of to any of them according to Napolean's notion of social order.

They noticed Amy Hawkins and a stout pink man come in, later than was her habit, to eat dinner, seeming untroubled, even happy, unknowing of their own pain.

In itself they thought the late dining hour would not be remarked. Amy had begun eating at nine or even nine-thirty some nights, in part because Harry would by then be in bed, but mostly because people in California, getting to their offices at nine or ten A.M. in California, tended to call her at seven P.M. in the Alps. Therefore, sometimes until Alpine nine *(vingt-et-une heures)* she was on the phone discussing the affairs of their late company, which was leaving more loose ends than anyone had imagined, managing her personal financial affairs, talking to her parents, touching base with the realtor who was supposed to be selling her condo, or catching up on the local news.

Half the dining room had finished when they came in. Amy didn't see Kip, which continued to worry her. Perhaps he had come into dinner early? Another strange thing – Rupert and Posy, so friendly all day and at lunch, now seemed surly and glum, and barely nodded to her as she and the baron came in.

Though she had noticed that sexual intercourse usually

had the opposite effect on men, it had driven the baron into a pitch of vivacity; he fed her a snail from his fork with a show of intimacy that flooded her cheeks with an embarrassed flush to think that everyone could notice. She had already begun to feel she had made a dreadful mistake.

Rupert had just reached his room after dinner, dreading the solitude and the thoughts of Father that were bound to crowd in, so he leapt up eagerly at the tap on his door. It was Kip, safe and sound. This was a huge relief, even though Victoire had mentioned seeing him at the hospital.

'I hope it's not too late,' Kip said. 'I just wanted to tell you that my sister woke up today. I skied down there this afternoon, and they were all excited. Her eyes were open, she could squeeze my hand and everything.'

'Victoire told us,' Rupert said. 'Great news, of course. Does Mr Osworthy know?

'I don't know.'

'Is she out of the woods?'

'I guess so. Everybody seems really happy, but she can't talk yet, she has a tube in her throat.'

'You heard that my father died on the way to London?'

Kip blinked. 'Nobody said that,' he said. 'At the hospital, nobody knew.'

'Maybe nobody told them,' Rupert said.

'That's tough,' Kip said, thinking what bad luck that was for old Adrian, who had been pretty nice. Poor Kerry. Somebody would have to tell her. He thought about how horrible it would be for her to wake up to news like that.

'I'll call Mr Osworthy in the morning and give him the good news about your sister.'

'Did you get back from that village okay? I looked for Amy but she wasn't in her room.'

'We were obliged to ride home in a van,' admitted Rupert.

'Does Amy know about Adrian?'

'I don't suppose she does.'

'Maybe she's back now, I'll tell her,' Kip said. He hoped she wouldn't chew him out, but the whole lunch had pissed him off, everyone ignoring Amy or being rude to her, and then letting her pay for the whole thing, and Paul-Louis, who was a good skier but not that great a monitor as far as he could see, and no one mentioning Kerry or Adrian hardly at all.

Amy finally bade Otto good-night in the lobby and saw him off, his expression grimly settling into one of determination to work on innocent explanations for his lateness that would satisfy his wife. For her part, Amy strove for an uncomplicated way of saying good-night that would imply that she would make no claim on his further attentions, a friendly and worldly parting, as in French movies. As they were in full view of everyone in the lobby, they shook hands. Once in her room, she sank, frankly tired, which was unusual for her, but she could forgive it in that she had skied for some hours, been in a bus accident, beheld a family quarrel, made love to a baron, and eaten a rich dinner. Tomorrow she would weigh whether these activities, mostly frivolous, could constitute a Life, as she had always understood people to be responsible for making for themselves – making their beds and lying on them, finding ways to be useful and involved, constructing a meaningful and satisfying existence from the raw materials one was handed. Her tablecloths, an imposing pile folded on the luggage rack, invited reflection.

Tonight, however, she would get a good sleep. When she crawled into the bed, which had been remade while she was at dinner, little chocolates laid on the pillow, only then did she notice the red light on her telephone pulsing imperatively. Given the time of day, it was probably a call from California. Briefly she imagined it was Sigrid calling to say the markets had collapsed and she had no more money, a sort of retribution for having so enjoyed the day. But it was Mr Osworthy calling from London to tell her that the heroic rescue effort today had been to no avail, and that Mr Venn, once in London, had irreversibly died.

Amy was not given to gratuitous self-reproach, but she did regret her part in the matter and even wondered if it weren't her punishment for being here in self-indulgent luxury, or for stepping into the Venns' affairs. She would have to master this tendency to feel guilty about pleasure and indolence. Of course Mr Venn's death was not her punishment! She had acted out of trustful good nature to help Kip and his sister. How sad for them all, also the English brother and sister and the French daughter married to the odious Emile. She would tell them of her regrets tomorrow.

'I suppose it was a long chance,' she said to Mr Osworthy.

'Yes, probably. A pity he wasn't taken to the Brompton

at once.' Did Amy detect a faint note of criticism, or only self-criticism?

'You did the best you could,' she assured him. 'The man was buried in an avalanche, after all.'

As she was sinking once again into exhausted sleep, someone knocked on her door, with towels maybe, or something about the minibar, though until now the Croix St Bernard had been free of these hotel nuisances.

'Not now,' she said in a loud, dismissive voice.

'Amy?'

It was Kip's voice, so she got out of bed. She put on the terry-cloth thing from the bathroom and peered out at Kip. When she saw him, she lost her temper, seized him by the shoulders, and shook him.

'Where were you? Don't you ever do anything like that again,' she heard herself screech. 'We were all frantic. Poor Paul-Louis! What on earth were you thinking of, you little jerk, that was so thoughtless . . .' Until she heard herself say all this, she didn't even realize how much Kip's vanishing after lunch had been on her mind. Now she felt like such a mean hag – the poor kid was close to tears, and at the same time he was grinning. 'I wanted to tell you about Kerry,' he said. 'She woke up.' So it was Amy who said she was sorry, and hugged him, and told him what a great job he was doing. At this, he looked so pleased, it crossed her mind for the first time that he might have a kind of crush on her.

Eventually he left, and she once again went to bed. She wasn't sleepy; she had the impulse to call Sigrid or Forrest or her parents. She wanted someone to talk to. Self improvement was a solitary business. The whole time she had been here, she had been feeling like a spy, or someone in disguise, unable to talk about her real situation in life, her conversations limited to empty social exchanges and one sexual interlude. Of course, wasn't that the situation of any hotel guest? In a hotel, all were devoid of pasts, of contexts, everybody interacting in the present, putting forward only as much of themselves as necessary. Being a hotel guest was somewhat lonely, was the truth of it.

In the night she woke up thinking about how in the morning she would tell the Venns she was sorry their father had died, and sorry for her part in it. But something else had woken her. It began to seep back into her mind that she had slept with the baron, what an idiotic thing to do! What could she have been thinking of? She forced herself to go back to sleep and stop remembering it until tomorrow.

28

Though it seemed to her that she slept no more the rest of the night, nonetheless, she woke thinking at first that her dreams had been troubled by a bizarre fantasy. It was the feeling that something lay on her bosom, heavy and impish, smirking. What it was came back immediately – she had slept with a German real estate developer she barely knew, and had the deepest intuition that the after-math would be troublesome. For one thing, his poor wife – he was obviously an incorrigible philanderer.

She stumbled to the bathroom trying to think what had made her do it, and remembered the explanation that had seemed plausible, and even exculpatory, in the night. She'd been stirred by, drawn to, the handsome television personality Emile at lunch, obviously had fallen a little in love with him before that, maybe at the moment that he had refused to kill the lobster. Put frankly, she had been aroused, wanting to get laid, and had displaced this feeling of erotic restlessness onto the baron. And of course she'd been sorry for the poor man with that wife. She would definitely put this behind her. Once frailty is identified, it can be slain. Otherwise a lovely day yesterday, the Alps laid out before them, a domain of impregnable beauty, the company of Europeans, mysterious and yet familiar.

At breakfast, she went straight to their table to tell the Venns of her regrets about their father. They were sitting in silence, Rupert in ski clothes, Posy looking tousled and cross, the French sister composed and courteous. There was a strong family resemblance, a similar sort of certitude of expression on their handsome faces. He – Emile – was not there, so she had no way of testing her theory that she had slept with Otto because she had been attracted to the Frenchman.

'Yes, very sad,' Rupert said, rising at her approach. 'Won't you sit down?' Amy hesitated and sat down, and moved her cup for the waiter who wandered with the coffeepot.

'We knew it was probably inevitable,' he added. Posy looked up from the gloom through which she'd been staring at her plate and gave a little nod. Victoire smiled sweetly. 'The doctors had never been optimistic.'

'Maybe he shouldn't have been moved,' Amy brought herself to say. 'I just assumed – I'm sorry for my part in it.' She didn't find it easy to apologize for a well-intentioned action, and she doubted it had actually brought on Mr Venn's death, but how did one know? This is what Posy and Rupert murmured politely, reassuring her: How could anyone know? She appreciated their chilly British politeness where she might have expected reproaches.

'It is so American to help,' said Victoire in a friendly voice. 'Your long tradition of saving Europeans!'

Yet Amy had the distinct impression they believed that moving their father had killed him – had jolted or unplugged him, had exposed him to glitch and jostle, and that she was responsible, for without her he wouldn't have gone. Plus they hadn't asked for her help.

She stayed a few minutes longer and then rose, not

wishing to intrude any longer on their grief. As she was crossing the lobby, on her way to put on her ski stuff, a man carrying a giant bouquet approached the desk. Roses and poinsettias, the latter an allusion to the season and the roses, perhaps, to an eventual spring, or to some attitude of the heart. Her own heart sank. The Jaffe daughter at the desk accepted the flowers with an appropriate expression of approval that one of their guests was receiving such a conspicuous, expensive tribute. Was having an affair. Amy's fears were justified; after reading the card, the girl glanced at her with a significant smile. A chambermaid appeared, together the two read the card again, the maid bore the flowers off.

As Amy dressed, the tap came at the door, and the chambermaid came in with the flowers, in a vase Miss Jaffe had found, and the card, from Otto. Amy saw what the Jaffes must have seen: a baron's crest, or whatever it was, a little gold circle with a star in it, and the initals *OS* marking the envelope, for those who knew it, as being unmistakably from him. The chambermaid gave her a warm grin. Not that Amy cared really, maybe they'd think she'd bought a chalet. Yet she felt her face getting warm from embarrassment and apprehensiveness. Oh, woe, why had she done it? Of course, it hadn't seemed so bad at the time.

In the morning the nurses had helped Kerry to sit up. 'That is better. They have taken out those tubes, poor Madame Venn.' She didn't remember when they had taken the tubes out of her throat, but it must have been during the night, or while she was sedated. Now her mind felt remarkably clear, as if activated by an off/on switch now switched on. The immediate past was a black trough, then going backward beyond it, clear memories on the other side, of being in Valméri, the hotel, Harry and Kip, Adrian in his khaki ski coverall and boots of midnight-blue. The hotel, then the trough of blackness, during which something must have happened, then this hospital. Where were Adrian and Harry? It seemed odd that no one was here except the beaming nurse telling her she would be all right and they would move her to a room for a few days.

'Where is my baby? My husband?' she cried. Words you would expect as a first utterance from a wife and mother, nodded the satisfied nurses.

'Safe, safe. Harry will be in to see you. Your husband is in another hospital, madame. He has been taken to London to specialists.'

Kerry concentrated on remembering, and, the way a paralyzed person might be urged to try to move his limbs – to try, to try – the nurse urged her to try to remember what had happened. Some of it would come back eventually on its own, the doctor told her, but trying to remember can set in motion the repair of those neurons, those frozen cells ... and she did remember they'd been skiing. At first that seemed enough of a memory. 'We were skiing!' and the nurses cheered her on, yes, yes, then what?

After breakfast, Rupert telephoned Mr Osworthy to tell him about Kerry's regaining consciousness. Osworthy received this news with relief. 'Frankly, the problems if she hadn't, the custodial arrangements, the guardianship issues . . .'

'I'll be seeing her later. We're setting out for London this morning but we'll stop at the hospital to introduce ourselves to her. We should be in London by tonight.'

'I would be much obliged if you could talk to her, Rupert. If she is able to say, I would very much like to know what she would wish for – for the formalities. And if she is going to be well enough to travel soon, I would be grateful if you'd stay there long enough to help her with coming back here,' Osworthy said. 'She should have someone with her, and as for the service, we would wish to wait till she can be there . . . I recognize – to stay would be an act of human kindness – you are under no obligation to see to her. But the estate would cover the expense of the hotel for another day or so if you could bring yourself to stay on. Otherwise I'll have to come myself, and there is quite a bit to be done here. I'll call Dr Lamm, I want to tell him about Adrian. Of course he will crow.'

'I'll talk to Posy,' Rupert said. 'I think she will feel we should be with Mother. For myself, I'm by no means averse to another day here, there's nothing to do for Father now.'

'Perhaps Posy could come back to be with your mother, you stay. A word to the wise, Rupert. I have seen such situations before. You and Posy can live in friendship and harmony with your father's widow, or set off a bevy of conflicts. If you all get along, she may see the justice of doing the right thing with Adrian's estate vis-à-vis mementos and things your father meant you to have.

Alternatively, she may take care of her own child, period. So much is often a matter of diplomacy and goodwill.'

'Are you saying we should be nice to her because she'll stiff us otherwise?'

'I don't know that that would be my phrase. Of course friendship and harmony are their own reward,' said Osworthy.

'I'll see what the situation is with Kerry and ring you,' Rupert said.

Posy felt they ought to be with their mother, who was bound to be feeling sad at the death of Father, a natural emotion, though illicit, trespassing on the sorrow of the present wife. She didn't add that she didn't want to be near Emile and Victoire.

'If we were in England, things would be easier, we would have to bake, feed people, give drinks. Here there is nothing to do besides think about Father,' she said to Rupert in the car, driving to the hospital to check on Kerry.

Once there, Father's death was brought home to them by the empty space in the intensive care ward where he had been, a vacancy they could not help noticing from the corridor. His bed had been wheeled away altogether. Now the nurses were gathered around the heroine Kerry, who had been moved from intensive care to a regular hospital room and was propped up in a tilted bed, wearing a yellow hospital gown, smiling, thanking people for their kindness in a hoarse whisper. It was the first time Posy and Rupert had ever seen her, if you didn't count her inert form this past week.

The swelling of her face had diminished, and despite bruises she must have had something close to her normal appearance. Rupert found something very American about her looks, with nothing of his mother's elegance, but perhaps it was unfair to judge her in this condition. She was young, but otherwise seemed an unlikely femme fatale to have seduced Father, an actually rather average-looking young woman, with light brown hair and freckled skin and strapping size even after her ordeal, five nine or ten, taller than Father. Now she was pale, her cheeks sunken and eyes dull, but when she came back to strength, she would still not be much of a beauty, just more of a force for a healthy lifestyle, it seemed to Rupert. There was something beyond the hospital smell in the air, as if she were exuding the sweetish poisons they had pumped into her.

Everyone took an interest in someone newly awakened from a coma, newly returned from the beyond she is imagined to have glimpsed. Perhaps, as with the first moments after waking from a dream, in the first moments of consciousness she can harden the memory of what she saw there. Perhaps there is a fixative that will prevent the images from disappearing in the blot of light that blinds the eyes opening on the real room, real noises impinging. Perhaps the fixative is speech, questions and answers: Where were you? What did you see? Did you happen to see God or at least the tunnel?

A memory, an image, gathered itself forcibly in Kerry's memory, as if being fortified directly by the fluids dripping into her arm. It swelled, grew in clarity and brilliance, reconstituting itself. She and Adrian had been skiing. For some reason, they had turned and, up the slope above them, had seen a figure – a woman, she was pretty sure – wearing something metal or behind something metal, whose glint had caught them. She began falteringly to tell of it.

'A light or a beam; it was maybe that which had caused us to turn. She wore a helmet, and had something like a spear or sword upraised.'

'Man or woman?' asked the nurse.

'A woman, because her long hair blew around her face.' The picture was all suddenly vivid, she could almost feel the wind she saw whipping the hair across the face of the woman above them. Pointing, gesturing, carrying a spear. It seemed important to keep on with this remembering, more important than ascertaining the whereabouts of Adrian and Harry; the faces of people around her wore joyful, supportive expressions, so that she knew nothing bad had happened to them.

Nurse Bénédicte, in a whisper as they approached, informed Posy and Rupert of what was happening: Madame Venn had been able to remember something of what had happened before the avalanche; she had seen a vision or warning, or had seen the actual cause of the avalanche. When she could speak more, they would have the explanation.

'May we talk to her?'

'Not too long, she is still weak,' said the nurse. 'Madame Venn, your relatives are here.'

They stepped forward. 'It's Posy and Rupert. We haven't met . . .' Rupert began. 'Adrian's children. We just

came to tell you we're happy to see you feeling better.'
He could already see that the doctor would have to be
the one to tell her the bad news about Father, he couldn't
face doing it.

'Oh,' said Kerry weakly. 'Did you see Harry? Your little
brother, you know, your little half-brother.'

'We did, a charming boy,' said Rupert. 'He was at the
hotel with us.'

'Well, not with us, being looked after, though,' Posy
amended.

'Yes, my brother, Kip,' said Kerry.

'Yes, of course we met Kip too. I think they are coming
to see you this morning.'

Kerry turned her head away from Rupert to speak to
the nurse. 'There was someone, I think she was pointing
to Adrian,' she said. 'He is dead, isn't he?'

'We haven't heard so, madame,' said the nurse.

'Oh, thank God ... She had this sword or spear in
her hand and she pointed it at Adrian. At the time, we
didn't understand, but looking back, I see that she was
warning Adrian.'

Nurse Bénédicte touched Rupert's shoulder and
motioned them back a few paces. 'She has told us a little.
Just before the slide, she looked behind them to see a
woman wearing armor or a shield, and a weapon she
pointed at them. She is quite clear about it,' she whispered.

'How odd.'

'Yes, it is. Anyone else who was there must also have
perished, but no one else is reported missing.'

'Does she think this mysterious figure caused the
avalanche?'

'It seems she believes it was warning them. We will learn more as her mind becomes clearer. Mrs Venn, tell us again about what you saw just before the avalanche.'

'Yes, I turned, and a woman was here, a ways away, with a spear or lance, pointed at Adrian. She glittered all silvery in a beam of light, as though she was wearing armor. It was very clear. Oh, and she had a shield. There was something written on it, but I don't remember what.'

Just then, Harry ran in, followed by Kip, and seized Kerry's attention. Kip was beaming with anticipation of Kerry's joy. Harry threw himself toward his mother so violently that the nurses had to catch him and lift him carefully onto Kerry's bed. Tears ran down Kerry's face along with her smiles. The assembled hospital personnel, and even Posy and Rupert, felt their eyes fill.

Nurse Bénédicte, walking Rupert and Posy toward the waiting room, said, 'It sounds to us like Jeanne d'Arc. She doesn't say so herself. It is not the Virgin, apparently.' Seeing their incomprehension, she added, 'Madame Venn's vision. It seems to us it might have been Jeanne d'Arc.'

Nurse Bénédicte, who had had a vocation as a *réligeuse* but not gone on with it, was in general disapproving of local rumors of apparitions and miracles – these cropped up all the time in the Alps and were never serious – but there was something intriguing about Kerry Venn's experience, especially as she, Bénédicte, had with her own eyes seen the patient lying in a coma for almost a week, a woman who was probably not even a Catholic, so Bénédicte was sure there was no possibility of her having been manipulated by, or made a victim of, religious super-stititon. Though rational explanations were the most likely, there were mysteries one should not discount; the mind didn't have to understand everything.

'Of course we are not sure. She describes the scene as it came to her, and it sounds to us more like an apparition, though it could have been a person, of course.' Posy and Rupert, wearing the expressions to be expected of English skeptics, began to grasp that it really appeared to Nurse Bénédicte that Kerry had had a vision of, or received a visitation from, Joan of Arc. Kerry's eyes did have an otherworldly expression, a glow of having seen super-natural things, but this was no doubt the effect of medicine or coma.

They had half hoped that Kerry would have already heard about Father's death, but as the nurses had denied it, it seemed harder to tell her, disturbing her happy embraces of her little son and her brother, and her attempt to remember what she had seen. Drawing Nurse Bénédicte farther into the hall, Rupert whispered the news of Father's death. The nurse did not seem greatly surprised, expressing only the most conventional sympathy and looking conspiratorially in at Kerry. It seemed to Rupert she might even feel some satisfaction at so dire a result because Father had been removed from their care.

'She knows, at some level she understands,' Nurse Bénédicte said.

'But still she must be told,' Rupert insisted.

'Of course. Maybe a bit later, when she is stronger. Will you do it? Or the doctor, perhaps?'

'We don't really know her . . .'

'The doctor, *bien sûr*. But you know, this is very interesting, what she saw just before the accident.'

They agreed that it was most important that Kerry recover the memory fully, for her own psychic peace, so that an amnesic trough or chasm didn't frighten her forever, and she could deal with it and move on, truly accepting that Adrian was gone.

Dr Lamm approached as they spoke.

'Did you hear, Doctor, that Mr Venn didn't survive the trip to London?' Nurse Bénédicte whispered to him, the satisfaction in her voice plain to the ear of one who was inclined to hear it.

Dr Lamm sniffed irascibly. 'How could he have survived? He was dead before he left France. The man had not had so much as a brain blip in three days.' They somberly contemplated this fact, the folly of the rescue plane, the fragile human emotions that had driven the situation, the decisive role of money in claiming victory for one point of view over the other – for someone had paid for that plane.

Posy and Rupert noted, without thinking much of it then, that the doctor had said that Father was dead in France. In their grief, Posy and Rupert had still not allowed themselves to discuss what each had perhaps thought of, that Father's dying in England made all the difference to Harry and the newly resurrected Kerry, who would inherit, and of course, in a negative sense, to themselves, who wouldn't.

'How very sad for the little boy – he'll never remember his father,' Dr Lamm said to Rupert. 'Do you want me to tell her? I would prefer to leave it to you.'

'If you would tell her, Doctor . . .' said Rupert.

'She knows it anyway,' said Nurse Bénédicte. *'Elle l'a senti.'* Dr Lamm, looking displeased at his role, stepped gravely into the room and approached Kerry's bed.

Kerry received the news with serenity. 'Yes, I understood that,' she said. 'That was the meaning of what I saw.' Rupert, stepping forward, emboldened, explained that Mr Osworthy was handling funeral arrangements in London, and that he and Posy would wait in Valméri to travel with her when she was able. How sad they all were . . .

At this, Dr Lamm had another word with Rupert. Rupert needed to know that Kerry would require a long convalescence. Several ribs and an arm were fractured, the lack of reflexes that had worried them when she was unconscious came from an injury to her spine, the deep bruises would take weeks to heal. 'The two victims were tumbled like shoes in a dryer,' said the doctor, though this didn't seem to Rupert like a helpful metaphor.

Welcoming anything that took their minds off death, the three older Venn offspring stood in the hall and laughed a little about Kerry's vision. Still, it was puzzling. 'What could a woman with a shield have been doing there?' Victoire wondered.

'Those snow saucers look like shields,' Posy said. 'It was probably someone with a snow saucer.'

'Or a snow machine,' said Rupert. 'Or a silver lamé skiing costume? Someone might still be buried up there?'

'Yes, if someone really was there, she was probably caught in the same slide,' Posy said, thinking of the icy death, the recklessness of going out into nature. Uncertain about what to do, instead of starting for London they returned to the Hôtel Croix St Bernard.

In the late afternoon, Rupert, with instructions from Mr Osworthy to ask Kerry about the funeral arrangements, if she were well enough, went back to the hospital alone and again gained access to her room through a throng of people – not medical-looking people but people with notebooks. Kerry was about the same, wan but propped up. The nurse whispered that she had slept after lunch and was making brilliant gains in strength and morale, though there were the concerns about her spine. They also thought perhaps she had been distracted by people peeking in to hear her speak of Ste. Jeanne and had not quite absorbed the fact of her husband's death.

'I'm so sorry to have to bring this up,' said Rupert to Kerry, 'but did he ever say what he would want? About being buried? Cremation? Did he leave any instructions?'

Kerry looked vague, apathetic.

'We have made some tentative arrangements, Mr Osworthy has, I mean. Cremation in London when you can travel, then you can decide about the disposition of, of the ashes,' Rupert went on.

'Who is Mr Osworthy?' asked Kerry.

'Father's lawyer in London.'

'England! No way,' said Kerry. 'We live in France! Our whole life is here. Harry will want to visit his father's grave when he gets older, he shouldn't have to go to England.'

'Well, ashes, you could bring them back here,' Rupert said.

'I couldn't stand the idea of Adrian being burned,' Kerry said, her eyes filling with tears. 'I think he ought to be buried in Saint-Gond, in the proper way, in the churchyard. I'll have to think about it.' She began to cry, which everyone could understand, and the nurses shooed the visitors out.

'If she is peremptory now, think of how she'll be when she realizes she is a rich woman, comparatively speaking. That is my experience with Americans, peremptory – they have no cultural norms to guide their behavior,' said Osworthy.

'Rich?'

'I think it's fair to tell you that your father's French estate comes to more than I myself had anticipated. Some investments, some abundant harvests, some inspired speculation. I'd rather not go into specifics of the bequests until I've had a chance to look at them more closely, in a day or two. There are one or two details I had not appreciated before. Not that it affects you, really. Kerry inherits, as I told you, but be reassured your bequests are still there.' Though they had learned resignation, they could not prevent their hopes from soaring a little, if only because a bequest would sweeten the bitter loss of Father. Without something to hope for, they had nothing to do, in the boredom that follows a death, but mourn and wait for the claims of their unsatisfactory daily lives to reassert themselves.

29

Monday morning in Maida Vale, W9. Pamela Venn puts in a phone call to Géraldine Chastine in Paris.

Over the weekend, she had talked to Mr Osworthy more than once, even though she was not the concerned widow, and he had told her how Adrian's will had left things. Pam was deeply unhappy, not on her own behalf, for she hadn't expected anything, but for Rupert and Posy, especially Posy. Kerry and Harry would inherit everything, as expected; luckily, however, Adrian had left Rupert a fair legacy. He could not tell her how much before he told Rupert, but in the low five figures.

'But there is something awkward, Pam,' said Osworthy. 'I'm afraid he has left Posy quite a bit less.'

'Less?' repeated Pam.

'I'm afraid so.'

Pamela was disappointed. But of course she should not have been surprised. It was Posy who had quarreled with and defied him and derided his marriage plans. The vengeful man had punished her! She minded the insult to Posy more than the whole unfairness to both of her children, that after more than twenty years during which they were more or less dutiful offspring, they were to be treated in such a fashion at the end. She would have liked to blame this unfairness entirely on the influence of the new wife, a calculating American, but she knew deep down that it was Adrian's own nature to punish and torment people who didn't agree with him, quintessentially the quarrelsome Posy, who needed the money. Rupert, hardworking and phlegmatic, would earn his own tens of thousands of pounds, while Posy's prospects weren't much, and she was the more vulnerable in all ways. Pam's heart burned for her restive daughter. 'What about the press, the vineyards?' she had asked Osworthy. 'The wife gets those, I suppose.'

'Yes, according to his wishes. I've turned the French end of it over to our branch in Paris, because there are procedures to be followed over there.'

Procedures. Dim memories of procedures in the novels of Balzac, notaries and unscrupulous, scheming relatives, daunted her spirit even more. It would be merciful if Posy could be kept from finding out what her father had done, for it would wound her so; she, Pam, would like to make up the difference if she could, but she had no money.

It stayed on her mind, and finally she asked Posy, still at the Hôtel Croix, to ask Victoire (a hidden daughter, that in itself an astounding development!) for her mother's phone number. Perhaps that unknown woman would be even more displeased than Pam at the way her own daughter had been treated, had always been treated – unless the devious Venn had secretly all along known of Victoire, pampered her, sent presents on her birthdays and the rest, indulging Victoire to the disadvantage of Posy. Nothing was beyond Pam's imagination, but her instinct told her she had an ally in another woman whose offspring by Adrian was being slighted.

Géraldine Chastine fortunately proved to speak perfect

English, and was cordial, even warm, to Pam on the phone. The two discarded women quickly forged a bond on the coals of resentments smoldering for more than thirty years – since the resentments weren't against each other. Géraldine, for her part, even found that her indignation was mitigated slightly by the small possibility that Venn had never heard about Victoire's existence, as far as Pam knew.

'I sent him word, but perhaps he didn't get it. The mails thirty years ago were by no means as reliable as now, and he had gone back to England by the time I realized . . . At least he didn't oppose the designation of his name on the birth registration.' Pam didn't observe aloud, but her rapid calculation confirmed, that she herself had just been married to Adrian when Victoire was conceived. Luckily she was beyond being wounded by this.

She was glad she had called Géraldine for another, much more important reason. She learned that Géraldine was not convinced that Venn could just give away to his new young wife a château, vineyards and the rest of his French property, whatever the wishes expressed in his English will.

'There are laws! A man cannot own property in this country and leave his children with nothing.'

'Really?' Pam asked her to explain, hope stirring that his unjust neglect of Posy and Rupert in England would be redressed in France.

'I've already telephoned someone who is more or less our family lawyer, who is going to involve himself in the matter. At least, he will telephone the English lawyer,' Géraldine explained. 'The two will discuss the situation.'

'But he died here in England.' That was the fact.

'Nonetheless. Monsieur de Persand is on his way to Valméri as we speak. He said he was in no way averse to a day or two in the snow, and he will discuss the situation with your children and Victoire,' Géraldine told Pam.

'This is wonderful,' said Pam enthusiastically. 'I believe I will come to Paris one of these days, Géraldine, if I may call you that.'

'I so hope you will! You'd be welcome to stay with us, or I can find a hotel nearby. Perhaps you should come rather soon,' said Géraldine.

'Do not budge,' Pamela told Posy and Rupert on the phone. 'There is nothing to do here, for him or for me, and I want you to stay and talk to Victoire's French lawyer, a Mr Antoine de Persand.'

That afternoon, Emile went down to the hospital, wanting to see for himself the woman whose remarkable vision was already being spoken of at the hotel. In her room, a crowd of strangers and hospital staff stood around Kerry, who was saying, as if addressing her own question, 'This was not a vision, it was an actual woman. There was nothing supernatural about it. It was a woman in armor, I'm not saying who it was, it's you who are calling her Joan of Arc. I have my ideas, of course. But it was real, she was really there . . .'

'Jeanne d'Arc – "the bulb is burned out in the bathroom," get it?' said Kip to Victoire, who had been there since morning. She laughed politely, frowned.

'No,' she admitted. Neither did Emile.

'Might it also have been Marianne?' Victoire suggested

after a moment. 'Symbol of France? Or any of several local saints? But she must tell us about this herself.'

Dr Lamm had appeared, and the nurses shooed the reporters, and the mayor, out into the hall. It had struck Emile, in his role as television commentator, that this all had considerable news value, and he stepped backward into the midst of the people who crowded the hall outside the room to talk to the locals who had come to listen to Kerry. The first person he spoke to identified herself as a representative of the Maid of Orléans Society, which interested itself generally with sightings, legends, and memorabilia concerning the warlike saint.

'Until now, she has never been associated with this area, but her appearances have been increasingly far afield and no longer confined to the area around Orléans,' she said.

'*Sans doute, madame,* the saint was defending the whole of France, whether against the English – that is to say, poor Mr Venn – or against the American airplanes is hard to know,' smiled Emile, who was realizing that there was much to enjoy in the St Joan furor.

A reporter for the local paper agreed with the saint's probable motives. He had come to write up the incident, and been chatting with Dr Lamm for some time in the corridor outside Kerry's room. The reporter's own view was that the saint had appeared at this time because, with her military connections, she was responding to the presence of foreign military planes and NATO, entities that had exerted their effect on the local collective unconscious, especially at this moment of international turmoil. Emile kept to himself the objection that Kerry had been in a coma and unaware of the military presence, and also, as a foreigner, perhaps didn't have access to the collective unconscious of the French, itself sensing however sub-liminally the troubled gathering of war clouds in the world.

He was not surprised to see CNN arrive by dinnertime.

Sitting with Joe Daggart and Paul-Louis in front of the television in the lounge after a bracing day on the slopes, Amy was amazed to see it was Emile Abboud being interviewed on CNN, standing with another man against a backdrop of Alpine peaks of blazing white and a sky of gentian blue, a springlike conjunction she had not personally observed during this somber week of January weather. A close-up focused on a simple wooden cross emerging from drifted snow. The two men were talking about the local mountain traditions – saintly apparitions, and certain historic ghosts who emerged at holidays. Amy tested her responses for signs of frisson at the sight of the man who had driven her into the arms of the baron, but she didn't feel anything except interest, and admiration of his telegenic demeanor.

'Professor Emile Abboud, Ecole Supérieur des – uh, that translates to "Science and Politics." It is the first time, Professor, is it not, that St Joan has been seen around here?' His tone was the jocular one reserved by CNN reporters for lighter news features about odd tribal customs, pagan fetes, cute animals.

'Yes, she is not generally associated with this region,' said Emile. 'She confines herself to the area around Orléans where she lived, fought, and died. The fact that she now turns up here – I suppose it is globalization.' On television, his harmonious features were even more compelling, his smile the smile of a film actor, his French accent more pronounced than in person. Now Amy felt the familiar stirring, but suppressed it sternly.

'Is it significant that she has appeared to an American?'

Emile thought about it. 'That her victim was English is perfectly consistent with tradition, at least. The devil is known to take the form of the godly. What could be more suitable for Jeanne to do to the English and their avatars, the Americans, than to remove them?'

'Could it be a hoax?'

'Or a form of mass hysteria. The vision raises some questions: Is there a collective unconscious? Does a young Mrs Venn from America have access to our French one? What is the mechanism by which we see something that is not there? Is it suggestion, or something material visible only to some eyes? An intuitive sense only? These have always been the questions asked during, say, the séances held by the mediums in the nineteenth century, and the explanation has always been: fraud, delusion, the collaboration of someone desperate to believe with someone desperate to have them believe for some ulterior reason. Here, however, we have a declaration by someone who has no reason to believe or disbelieve, it is a disinterested testimony, an apparently true account.'

'Will the Vatican attempt to verify this event?' asked CNN.

'The Vatican? No, I seriously doubt it. Especially as Mrs Venn is not Catholic.'

'And what about the allegations that American planes were behind the recent lethal avalanches?'

'I believe that is being investigated,' said Emile.

'Thank you, Professor Abboud, for giving us your time,' said CNN.

'Abboud knows that if there were planes, they were French planes. That's our conclusion. I told him myself, French or British, the joint-venture SST people who built the Concorde,' Daggart said.

'Why don't they come out and say so, then? It's easier to let Americans take the rap, as usual,' said Amy.

'The problem is, we're not so sure an airplane can cause an avalanche. It's far from clear,' cautioned Joe. 'It's actually far from clear that there were airplanes there at all, though there are some witnesses to say so. We haven't been able to study the flight plans yet, French or American.'

Tonight was, again, the weekly welcome cocktail in the upper lobby, and for those staying longer than a week, it gave almost the feeling of blasé belonging Amy could remember having as an Old Camper, to watch the un-instructed newcomers in their clean clothes, with their earnest, cooperative expressions. As she had done at the last party, Amy began by talking to the American, Joe Daggart, but now that she was more widely acquainted, she also had a few subjects in common with others of the cheerful Eurotrash skiers, like Marie-France Chatigny-Dové or the prince Mawlesky. It would not have occurred to her to bring up Silicon Valley with anyone. It had stopped amazing her how unconcerned everyone here was with software, a world apart. But now she could discuss outrageous rulings in Brussels, and war crime trials in The Hague.

'Amy, my dearest dear,' said Robin Crumley, taking both her hands. 'To think we are leaving, the Mawleskys and I, first thing in the morning. Back to London for me. But tell me when you'll be in Paris – I'll come see you. With the Eurostar it's a matter of three hours, and we mustn't let our friendship die.'

Amy could not but be gratified to be designated the friend of a well-known British poet, and smiled despite the slight uneasiness his enthusiasm made her feel, at remembering her rudeness to him in the hotel van. She gave him Madame Chastine's phone as a way of getting in touch with her, for she had no idea where she'd be.

Baron Otto, too, made his way to her side, pronouncing cheerful banalities – 'the Boucle Noire was entirely *glacée* by this afternoon' – remarks that she was not able to discover any double meaning in, if any were intended – along with special emphatic looks for her alone. She fervently hoped that he would not single her out for too much attention that others might understand. Despite herself, she found that she had a feeling of intimacy with Otto, which she was afraid must show, and she was glad the quarrelsome Frau Otto hadn't come to the party.

To her discomfort, he had joined her and Paul-Louis at lunch on the pistes that afternoon, at one of the little mountain restaurants that dotted the vast slopes. In he came, in his Tyrolean kit of woolen knickers and green socks, looking for her. He used cross-country skis, telemarking impressively down the slope they could see outside the picture window of the restaurant, and bursting inside with a great deal of heartiness. Amy was wary, but his manner had been perfect. Even so, thinking of the attractive younger guys like Paul-Louis, or even Rupert Venn, whom she had seen in a new light when she noticed Marie-France looking at him at lunch, it had embarrassed her again to think of what had happened with the baron. Still, no regrets, as a matter of principle.

Now, at the party, however, she found his portly glow almost endearing. To her chagrin, Amy had found herself thinking about the baron all day, wondering, for instance, if he often slept with clients, and how old he was, and whether he had been good at school. Apart from the vague erotic yearning probably triggered by Emile, she was still at a loss to explain how she had found herself going to bed with Otto – was it his sudden, ardent declaration, his air of worldliness, his terrible wife, that had animated her sympathy? Or all of these? Yet there was nothing to regret – and no regrets was a rule for living if there ever was one. It crossed her mind that she might indeed like a little chalet in the Alps, but of course that was ridiculous. Still, she could come for a month or so each winter and rent it out the rest of the time, she and Otto would ... But, no, she didn't even like him. And to his credit, Otto had not brought up the subject of real estate again.

In truth, Amy had another more insistent worry. People at the cocktail were talking about the vision of Joan of Arc that Kip's sister Mrs Venn had experienced before the avalanche. She had seen the short CNN sequence starring Emile, and then the TV in the bar before this party had been switched to Euronews, which ran twice through an avalanche sequence and then had shown statues and old engravings of Joan of Arc, the meaning clear enough to her without her understanding French. For the first time, it crossed her mind to wonder where she herself had been that afternoon of the slide.

This was because of something that had struck her that morning. After breakfast, as she put on her ski stuff and was leaving her room, a ray of light from the window, striking her reflection in the mirror, had startled her. What she saw was an image of glittering silver, now seeming, to her mind looking back, almost like a suit of armor, as if she herself could have been mistaken for Joan of Arc. Of course it was preposterous that it could have been her; yet she thought of it.

'It is an alternative theory to the theory of American warplanes,' she heard someone saying.

'It is an American plot, exploiting local superstitions to divert attention from the warplanes,' said someone else.

'If someone saw a person uphill, that person would almost certainly have been killed in the slide,' said someone else, a comfort for Amy in that as she wasn't dead, it couldn't have been her.

Emile Abboud was now here in this room, surrounded by admirers – people were such fools for anyone on TV – and it was said that he would be making other appearances on CNN, besides his normal round table on Antenne Deux, both channels interested in the mounting public attention to the Maid of Orléans so strangely transported to the Alps.

'The U.S. has no female icon,' Emile was in the course of saying to his admirers. Amy edged nearer.

'The Statue of Liberty,' said the *princesse* Mawlesky. 'The Statue of Liberty is a woman.'

'Yes, true, but sent them by France. Liberté, Egalité – the virtues are always feminine, in Latin languages if not in life, because the words are feminine. America has an icon in Uncle Sam, though whether he is a potent emotional symbol the way St Joan or the Virgin Mary are, I am unable to say, not being American.'

Amy thought about the skinny figure in striped pants, with his tall hat and rather scraggly beard – who was he? Definitely not a compelling personification of patriotic emotions, except perhaps feelings of guilt and duty: Uncle Sam wants you. But she had never felt he had wanted her, particularly.

'We don't need a rallying symbol,' she could not forbear remarking, though it was intruding into the general conversation.

'You rally around your presidents, even when they're rascals. Of course, none have been such rascals as French presidents, I'll admit.' Emile and the others laughed indulgently, and someone said, 'Félix Faure.'

'Mitterrand.'

'And they are Protestants,' put in Madame Chatigny-Dové. 'Americans, I mean.'

'What has that got to do with it?' Amy wondered.

'The Catholic tradition of praying to the Virgin has accustomed them to matriarchal figures of reverence. The Anglo-Saxon countries are more macho,' said Robin Crumley. 'John Bull, Uncle Sam.'

'We don't rally around our presidents,' Amy protested. 'Only half the people do, at any one time. In France, people forget this, they think we are all alike.'

'Honestly, one hears such very silly things about

America, that French people believe, I mean,' said Victoire. 'Misconceptions, for instance that the dogs don't bark there. I have actually heard that.'

She looked at Amy, as if waiting for assurance that this was not true. With patriotic indignation, Amy withheld it; let her think dogs don't bark in America.

'Buffon thought the dogs didn't bark and the people were stunted on account of the climate,' Emile said. 'Is that not true then?'

'He is joking. Of course we know that is very silly,' said Victoire.

'Poor Amy, the French are so savage on the subject of Americans,' said Baron Otto. 'Don't pay attenion to them at all.' He had an urbane smile for his French friends and gave Amy a sort of Teutonic bow.

'We are also hard on ourselves,' said Emile.

'France began by swearing eternal friendship to us,' Amy reminded them. 'Lafayette named his child after George Washington even. He was helping our revolution.'

'If you like, the French helped out the American revolutionaries in order to inconvenience the British, not from fellow feeling. Oh, I don't deny the friendship between Washington and Lafayette, but by all accounts, Washington was a remarkable man. France has been unfaithful recently, perhaps, but there are always reasons, as in a marriage. Misunderstandings, collisions of temperament,' said Emile. 'Who is to say which of the couple is at fault? We blame you, of course, for your banalities, your vulgarities, your successful movies . . .'

To be reproached for vulgarity was more than Amy could bear. 'We saved you twice!'

'There is the fault,' smiled Emile. 'That is what we cannot forgive.'

'Do you think there's something between them?' Robin Crumley whispered to Emile when the guests had moved on.

'Who?'

'The Teutonic fellow and Amy.'

'I don't see anything special. Why?'

'A sort of intimacy?'

'Do you care?'

'Intensely. Girls like that should not be allowed out for people to feed on. She arouses all my chivalrous impulses. He is a fortune-hunting lout.'

'I think you must be wrong about her money, Crumley. There is no aura of that. Look at Madame Renan, there, or the Croatian beauty over there, their jewelry, the afternoons spent at the coiffeur. Those are the *poules de luxe*. *L'Américaine* has none of that. She's a single girl on the lookout for men is all.'

'Millions, my dear, look again.'

Emile, looking again, shrugged. 'I'm no expert,' he said. But perhaps he was suggestible, he admitted to himself, for he did begin to detect something in her indifference to fashion or adornment that could mean money – or it could be the hopeless American lack of chic. Either way, it mattered not at all to him. Yet he kept thinking about her. He tried to brush aside these stirrings of interest.

He looked around for Victoire, ready to go in to

dinner. She had been standing at his elbow during the conversation, and now had fled.

Victoire looked pale. She had received a bolt of understanding. Somehow she had intercepted Emile's glance at, or with, Posy, and knew unmistakably in her blood that something had happened between them. Since she first arrived, Victoire had observed that Posy was always gazing at Emile, but she was used to people gazing at Emile, men and women both. His beauty was a part of the reason for her own adoration, not the essential, of course, but a part, and just a little bit because it is nice to have something that others desire. She had learned there was a price – nobody could resist the constant blandishments the world seemed to offer Emile, not just sexual but in all kinds of things, posts, contacts, and she was proud of the fact that he never connived and never exerted himself for money, wasn't mercenary or corrupt. He didn't have to be. But now the price was too high. The look he had exchanged with Posy was Emile's look for someone he had been to bed with, where he had put his fingers, his *sexe* – oh, she couldn't think of it.

The first effect of this intuition was physical, a chill that swept across her skin and clutched at her throat, her gorge rose. She drew her scarf around her shoulders, icy as a person in shock. Luckily the constriction in her throat prevented her from crying out in some indignant protest, so that the desire to scream and throw herself at Posy was replaced by a silent hot flare on her cheeks. No one seemed to notice the change in her.

It was unbearable that fate should trick her affections in the space of a few days, should bring her a new sister while giving her as a husband a man who would betray her with her own sister. No, that was thinking backward: she'd been given a sister, but a sister who would prey on her husband. All that she had ever thought and known, including that Emile, like all men, she supposed, was not always faithful, was now stood on end. Bitter to think that fortune had sent her an unknown parent, money even, and two siblings she had been prepared to love, and with it the poison gift of a heart broken, and a future entwined with them.

Her heart raced. Perfidious Albion. This was what the English were like, the horrible English with their poor personal hygiene, slippery morals, sleazy business practices, hopeless engineering ... To find herself half-sister to a monster, conspiring against her and discussing her. Rage boiled up like steam in a kettle, whistled in her ears, and escaped, replaced by heartbreak. Certain that everyone could read on her face what she had seen, she murmured something and stumbled off to the ladies' lounge, telling herself that maybe it had been her imagination. Maybe Emile, after all an only child, had a brotherly feeling for the buxom bright-cheeked Posy. But she knew better. It was the look he had had for her, and now for Posy, affectionate to his women, like some Mormon patriarch or African chieftain – though maybe there was some cultural influence from his parents living all that time in Senegal, something not entirely his fault.

Vicious imaginings seeped into her mind. How horrible Posy must look naked, big blubbery breasts, great purple nipples, probably strong English smell of – of sheep, fish and chips, soot, trains, the vomit she had once smelled in the British Museum as a child taken to Londres, hating the cold rooms, the flannel sheets, the unstrained tea, the greasy chops, the too sweet chocolate, the brown teeth, the tooting voices ... what did they have, really, *les Anglais*, besides Shakespeare?

She sat on the dressing stool and gasped for breath. She saw the other woman there look at her in alarm – it was the American, Amy, dressed for cocktails, who had come in for a Kleenex. She looked concerned, saying 'Is everything okay?' Victoire leapt up and smiled brightly and rummaged for her lip gloss.

Amy, who had been inclined to like Posy better than Victoire, now included the so obviously upset Victoire in the range of her sympathy. She had liked Posy because she was English and endearingly ramshackle, had admired her mop of tousled curls, while Victoire's perfection was slightly daunting, with her blond hair, good English, and radiance bespeaking some level of spiritual attainment. Now she saw that Victoire was suffering too – it was the death of their father, she was sure, and she was moved to touch her arm reassuringly, and murmur sympathy.

'Oh, yes, it's so sad about poor Papa. I never knew him,' Victoire said. 'That is so sad. It just came over me – never mind. I didn't want Rupert and Posy to see me like this, it makes it harder for them.' We will leave the hotel, of course, tomorrow morning, she thought. Emile would come with her, of that she was determined. She would not speak of this horrible intimation, would say they had to get back to the children, period. She need not decide now whether she would ever mention it, ever.

Amy hugged her, thinking how sad it was, truly, and how brave all these survivors were. Now she watched Victoire, she who seemed so natural looking, having mastered her tears, reapply a slight gloss to her lips, smooth her brows and lashes with a little brush, fluff up her hair, fold and refold her scarf, and dab perfume on her temples, earlobes, wrists, and between her last and fourth fingers on each hand, all this while turning brightly to the subject of the excellent local carp the dining room had served last night. Amy carefully noted each detail of the Frenchwoman's toilette.

Kip was waiting with Harry at their table when Amy came in to dine. Harry had grown to enjoy Amy's arrivals and count on them, and signalled approval by beating his spoon on his high-chair tray. Amy rather dreaded telling Kip that she had decided to leave Valméri a little early, for a variety of reasons, none of which she could exactly name. Madame Chastine had said that though her apartment was far from ready, it was habitable, and part of her sudden need to get to Paris, she told herself, was a wish to be in on the process of furnishing and choosing for it. Each day had brought a phone call, sometimes two, from Géraldine or the decorators, the Americans named Tammy and Wendi, with questions: Did she have strong aversions to any color, for instance robin's-egg blue, in the version found in the Grand Trianon? How resolutely faithful did she want to be to the style of the seventeenth century? Transitional to Louis XVI? Some people found Louis XIV a little somber – what were her views?

She didn't have answers for these questions, but she didn't want other people to decide for her either. She wanted to examine the alternatives and discuss them. Nor had she said, 'Spare no expense,' though they seemed to have inferred something of the sort. Expenses were being run up with a confidence that she would agree that made her uneasy. She didn't exactly know how to communicate this to Madame Chastine without seeming mistrustful or quibbling. Without indulging her uneasiness, she had gone so far as to read the real estate ads in the *International Herald Tribune* to get an idea of what things should cost, and had been interested to see that these employed expressions that would be thought politically incorrect in America. 'Close to churches,' or 'walk to shopping' (or even 'dumb waiter'). The local consciousness was obviously not raised about the fact that not all people attend church, not everyone can walk, and that working in a restaurant is not to be sneered at. Perhaps their historical disruptions had rendered them less sensitive.

Another reason she thought she ought to leave was the tenderness with which the baron had said, in a low voice, as she left the cocktail party, 'Unfortunately I am expected at a dinner tonight,' as if she would be wanting him to account for his movements. She feared entanglement. She remembered the bouquet. So she must tell Kip she was going. He would be disappointed, she knew, but at least his sister was on the mend and things would soon be back to normal. He didn't respond to this bracing view of it; he looked horrified.

*

293

Any of the guests passing through the lobby at the end of dinner would have noticed the tall, balding, imposing Frenchman registering. With him was a very beautiful, extremely pregnant woman, something not often seen in ski resorts. The man filled out little message forms for the Jaffe daughter to stuff in several mailboxes. Posy, coming by, noticed that her box now contained a message, which she hoped would be from Emile, who was set to leave in the morning, as they were themselves. Instead it said succinctly:

M. Antoine de Persand, de la part de Madame Chastine and Madame Crawford Venn, voudrait parler avec Mlle. Posy Venn. Téléphonez ch. 40, s'il vous plaît.

Posy went straight to look for Rupert, to discuss what this new person could want. The newcomers had gone directly to the dining room, apparently quite delighted with the snowy Alpine ambience and the prospect of a delicious dinner, and their eyes never left each other.

A candlelight memorial service for the victims of the avalanches was to be held tonight after dinner, in the village church, and Amy, who hadn't planned to go, changed her mind and duly went along to it, as a co-operative gesture, out of loyalty to Kip and because of her acquaintance with the Venns. The little church with its picturesque steeple had been remodelled inside in a modern style at the time of the building of the tourist center, with a gaunt Christ on a cross of blond wood against a brick wall behind the altar, tasteful pews the color of ash, and abstract stained-glass windows influenced by someone like Mondrian. People tiptoeing in and ranging along both sides of the center aisle were each given a candle. Amy gathered that there would be a signal, she hoped internationally comprehensible, to light them at a given moment. She supposed this was a Catholic church, the first she had ever been in.

Many hotel guests were recognizable among the crowd thronging in, all in après-ski boots and warm coats, bringing the smell of wool and damp. There were Otto and his wife. She carefully sat well behind them. The Venn siblings filed in and sat in the second and third rows behind what appeared to be the entitled mourners of others lost in the slides, Victoire sitting with Harry, Kip, and Mr Abboud, behind Posy and Rupert. Amy was pleased to see that they had included Harry and Kip, a sign of accord among the Venn family, yet it was somewhat strange they didn't sit all together.

It seemed a long wait and it was rather chilly in the church. You were apparently meant to keep your coat on, though Amy saw Posy Venn throw hers off. Eventually, a priest in his robes entered, nodded, and began to speak in a grave voice. She could imagine what he was saying: prayers for the souls of the lost, thanks for preserving the rest of us. There were responses from the people, but only the name of Adrian Venn leapt out for Amy from among the names of the people in behalf of whom they had gathered. Despite her general disapproval of religion (following Prince Kropotkin) and incomprehension of the language, she was seized with the general reverence, and meditated sincerely on the issues of danger and death, and felt gratitude for having personally escaped the self-invited perils of the mountains. She knew she had made the right decision to leave before tempting fate any further. When the moment came to light the candles, she, like other nonsmokers (all Americans?), was obliged to turn to others for a light. It was Paul-Louis who reached over her shoulder with a lighter.

'Pay, pay, pay,' people said all around her, a stark litany, but not an unrealistic analysis, of life's guilty feelings of obligation.

'Peace,' said Paul-Louis to Amy. Oh. *Paix, paix, paix.* How embarrassing to have heard their word for 'peace' as 'pay.'

'You haven't seen my place,' he said to her as they shuffled out of the church. 'If you aren't doing anything now?' Amy sighed. She felt a little frisson of temptation, but it was too late. Why had he waited so long?

'Tonight I have to get back,' she said. 'My office is calling me at ten. But I have time for a drink. My treat!' Then, not wanting to foreclose any options, she touched his arm and said, 'I'll be coming back a lot to Valméri.'

As they stepped into the lighted vestibule, Amy, wearing the jacket of her ski suit, felt herself to be bathed in silvery guilt. Everyone must notice that she shone in the *lumière* like an armored apparition. Looking around to see whether Baron Otto noticed her walking with Paul-Louis, she saw an expression of surprise on his face, surely remembering – he was the only one to know – that she had been out skiing the afternoon of the avalanche.

Then Madame Chatigny-Dové said it out loud. 'My word, mademoiselle, you could be Jeanne herself.' And instantly, Amy was sure that it was true, she was. She felt everyone's gaze, heard the murmur of voices she took to be expressing shock and even – was she imagining this – condemnation. She heard the European anger at her, Amy Hawkins, singing in her ears, and clinging to Paul-Louis, she fled.

Outside, she tried to think more calmly. She was clear about her decision to leave Valméri, though her appointed sojourn was not up, and go to Paris a bit early. She had already grasped, in this short time, that you have to learn to be idle, it was a skill, and skiing constituted a kind of idleness she hadn't mastered yet. In Paris she would try to do more reading.

Of course she wouldn't be idle eventually – would have her foundation and the work of mutual aid. But in the interstices of her time here in Europe learning one thing and another, she could be learning more. French and German for sure, by the Crakes method; with a teacher, as she could already see that by yourself you tended to let your lessons slide. And perhaps diction or voice lessons, for she had noticed the several references to American female voices, and now that these had been brought to her attention, she could begin to hear what people meant when other American women were in the room. She had no idea whether she herself had this sharp, overloud voice. Not that the Europeans sounded so great, speaking in high, unnatural, singsong voices she found irritating, though Madame Chatigny-Dové had a sexy growl that sounded good.

In Paul-Louis's favorite bar, Les Neiges, she told him she would have to cancel her *abonnement* for the coming week. '*Mais,* Amy, you have just found your form,' he said, dismayed. She assured him she would come back often, she would e-mail in advance, he had been wonderful. She was firm. She could not resist asking him why he had only now proposed she go up to his rooms?

'I like you a lot, Amy . . .' he said.

'Too bad you didn't – um – give a sign.' Amy smiled regretfully. 'Why didn't you?'

'Can I tell you truly?'

'I'd like to know, actually. No one ever turned down my most blatant overtures before. Almost never.'

'I didn't know you were leaving so soon.'

'Yes, but?'

'Well, we talk – the other ski instructors, we all tell each other things, and they all say it is just better not to fuck the American girls, because they think you are going to get married to them.'

Amy laughed. Could that be true? It sounded like an international misunderstanding, but how had it arisen?

In her nightly chat with Sigrid, Amy told her about the Joan of Arc excitement, and the shiny silverness of her own expensive gray Boegner *combinaison*. 'Do you think it could have been me? How horrible if I thought that! But it can't be. I think I'd know it if there'd been a slide right there, avalanches are unbelievably loud – they've been replaying them endlessly on TV. I didn't hear anything that day, it was as silent as a tomb.'

'Amy,' said Sigrid in a voice suddenly somber, 'say nothing to anyone. Promise me. This is very important. Do you understand what I'm saying? Not a word.'

Amy did see. She tended to forget how drastically her personal liability situation had changed.

30

This morning the Alpine rescue people were at the hospital interviewing Kerry, encouraging her to explore her memory more deeply, minutely, so they could judge whether someone else might not be buried in the path of the avalanche, either the woman Kerry had seen or something that could explain her vision. They had tentatively concluded that the slide had developed between the Venns and the figure above them, and they were planning to take dogs and some sort of sonar into the area to search for another possible victim.

Finding the whole phenomenon fascinating, Emile had begun interviewing local citizens, clergy, and psychiatrists, and dragging them before the cameras. He was now discussing the fruits of his interviews, and their implications, with other media representatives, who turned up their tape recorders whenever Kerry spoke.

'She pointed her spear at us, specifically at my husband, and then we heard a low rumbling and something began to move toward us.' Kerry's tale had become more detailed as she was pressed to remember more and more of it. Emile was particularly fascinated by the elaborations, both with the form they were taking and the extent to which they appeared to incorporate the questions she was asked. Setting aside the possibility that she was manipulating the situation in a state of clear-minded purposefulness, it was as if the coma had left her brain in a condition where anything could be suggested to her and become transformed into memory. Thus, both *Paris Match* and *L'Express* were able today to find new aspects of her account that were convincingly Joan of Arc, in particular details of the armor. When they asked her if she was close enough to see any signs of the saint's recorded wounds on the armor, she said, 'I was fairly far away, but it seems to me there was something, a mark, over the breast.'

Triumphant glances from the media: Joan famously suffered a chest wound. Sportwear logo, thought Emile.

'Yes, I do believe that in the near-death experience one might have access to perceptions that are valid even if you never can find them again. The vision itself fades when you return to consciousness, but the memory of having seen something remains very clear. That accounts for the desperation people feel trying to recover or recapture that moment of clear vision ...' Kerry was telling *L'Express*.

Kerry had let Rupert know first thing this morning that she had rethought and relented about Father's burial. She was still adamant that he not remain in England, but now that her mind was stronger, she admitted that something must be done, though she herself was in no condition to do it. She asked Rupert to let Mr Osworthy know that she would not oppose cremation in England, with the ashes to be brought back to her for burial, or storage, or scattering, in France.

'After all, St Joan was cremated too,' she remarked, mysteriously and, to Rupert, rather inappropriately. 'It's not as if Harry is old enough to remember anything,' she added.

With this final issue settled, Posy and Rupert could at last leave for England to represent Kerry, and of course themselves, at the event – was cremation a ritual? A ceremony? Posy didn't know how to describe it; and one of them would bring the ashes back to Kerry. From London, Mr Osworthy, sounding relieved, and evidently under some pressure to remove Father's body from the Brompton Hospital Morgue, urged them to make haste.

It was just as well she was leaving, Posy thought. As well as with mindless longing and grief, she was struggling with remorse – struggling not to feel it whenever she was with Victoire, when it took the form of shame for her betrayal of her beautiful new sister, or with Emile, when it took the form of desire and her sense of its hopelessness, her feeling that only to see him would be enough, in the long future of, if she was lucky, buying trips to Paris on behalf of the Rahni Boutique. She had never felt such longing as she felt for Emile; it kept at her like a rash.

Before leaving this afternoon, they were to have a word with Monsieur de Persand, whom Victoire knew as a friend of her parents, and who at her mother's request would presumably be counseling them on their rights – hers, Harry's, Posy's, and Rupert's, now that Papa had died in England where things were so different. He had suggested an eleven o'clock meeting in the dining room.

Rupert decided to go out for a few runs first. It was certainly his last day of skiing for God knew how long. As he was putting his skis on at the edge of the run from the hotel to the uphill lift, he could watch Robin Crumley and his friends the prince Whatevers piling into a taxi. The doorman was heaping suitcases into the trunk. Then Amy came out of the hotel with Kip, and as they were laying out their skis, Crumley saw her and waved violently.

'Amy, Amy, *à bientôt à Paris! A bientôt!*' he cried. She fastened him with her dimpled smile and waved her mittened hand. He continued to wave through the back window of the taxi as it pulled away. Rupert waved too.

He came in at ten-thirty and turned in his skis for good. Persand was sitting at a table for four in the deserted dining room. Oddly, his companion at last night's dinner – they had presumed she was Madame de Persand – sat at another table reading the *International Herald Tribune* and didn't greet them. Perhaps her pregnancy made her dislike strangers before lunch, or perhaps it was a discretion issue, to do with the privacy of Father's will. Kip and Harry weren't there, and needless to say, not Kerry.

After the formalities of ordering them coffee and croissants, Monsieur de Persand gave a little peroration. 'Madame Chastine and Madame Crawford Venn – the latter I have not met – have suggested I explain to you a little of the process following the death of someone who owns property in France. Mr Venn's *notaire* in the village of Saint-Gond has requested sealing the château while an inventory is made of the contents. This is being done. As Madame Venn is not in residence, it is a normal precaution – there is danger of burglary or pilfering in these remote areas.' He didn't need to say, 'So none of you can go help yourselves,' but Posy and Rupert both took this sense of his explanation, and saw Victoire rustle and draw herself up with her Gallic pout.

Since they had no intention of looting the château, and not seeing what this had to do with them, they nodded with puzzlement. It seemed a hardship for Kerry, if she planned to go home, to have her house sealed up. Rupert pointed this out. Persand shrugged.

'With the *notaire,* Maître Lepage, I have already written the Tribunal of the Conseil d'Etat to begin the necessary process of the disposition of the estate. There will be taxes, that is the most serious concern for you.'

Only Victoire frowned in alarm. Posy and Rupert, believing themselves out of it, took some little satisfaction that it would be Kerry, at least, who would pay the taxes.

'Then, when it comes to a large property – some might say a cumbersome property – and with several heirs in common, you will need to discuss whether you will be selling it, or if not, how to maintain it and to whom assign responsibilities. I have not yet heard whether Madame Venn – the present Madame Venn – has the *usufruit*, that is, whether she has a right to stay in it for her lifetime. Unless a French will is found, that would not be automatically the case. Of course, the infant will have his share in it, along with you, and no court would deny her the right to stay there to care for her child. Nor would you, I'm sure, but in case of a sale ... you can see there are issues to be settled. There is a commercial press, I'm told? Who is to run it?'

'Wait a minute,' Rupert said. 'I don't understand.'

'What can happen is that some heirs will wish to sell, others wish to keep a property, some to buy out the others, et cetera. The worst thing that can happen is acrimony; I do advise you to keep things as cooperative and *amicales* as possible.'

'But Father didn't leave us his château,' said Posy. 'Naturally.'

'The château is in France and therefore subject to the laws in France, mademoiselle, that much is clear. French law will govern property in France.' He went on to explain some of the conditions of French law, delicately noting that there was also an issue covered by French law, originally the 'Loi de 12 Brumaire, An II,' 1793, though subsequently amended, wherein even an illegitimate daughter was to get a share.

That is, Father's French property would go to his children. They gaped. His children, themselves. They asked him to repeat this, to explain it. This startling reversal of fortune, or poison gift, whichever it was to be, so caught them unaware that they at first fell silent.

'My God, my God,' Posy moaned deliriously. 'It's true, then? We're rich?'

'Rich?' Monsieur de Persand cautioned. 'I wouldn't say so. The taxes alone will be immense – but we will know more after our consultations with the English tax people.'

Sad as he was about Father, Rupert, hearing Monsieur de Persand's words, suddenly saw what a gift he was to receive. Beyond the château, he would receive a vocation. He would take over Father's press! This filial act would solve all the problems of his life. He had always had a taste for books, and now his experience of the world of finance, though not extensive, had given him a certain familiarity with business, and at least the conviction that he could learn publishing. He'd established rapport with Mr Delamer, who ran other aspects of the modest empire Father was being discovered to have had. It all made perfect sense. His heart overflowed with relief and love for Father.

The more Rupert thought about it, the more he was drawn to the life of a publisher. In fact, the idea was thrilling. He relished a publisher's independence, and a life in the south of France, a terrain practically reserved for English people. The only obstacle was Kerry, who might possibly hope to run the press herself and naturally had a superior claim to it, if she wanted it. He had no idea about Kerry, what her hopes and tastes might be, if any – he didn't think that Americans were often drawn to such chancy, humanistic enterprises. But it was clear that whatever the moral thing to do, it was they, not Kerry, who were inheriting and would decide, a remarkable reversal of fortunes that put him in an entirely admiring frame of mind about France. Victoire said, '*Bien sûr!* It is wisely done, and I for my part have no doubt we will all be models of cooperation.' Then she moved off so rapidly after the interview, barely telling them goodbye, so cold in manner that cooperation seemed unlikely.

'Sealed? She cannot even stay in her home?' said Osworthy on the telephone later, worrying about Kerry. 'The French treat widows appallingly – it's practically suttee.' If he was at all pleased for Posy and Rupert, he didn't say so.

*

305

Rupert was elated, but after the interview with Monsieur de Persand, Posy went to her room to cry, in a mixture of sadness and relief. Tears had crowded against her nose during the conversation and made her head hurt. She felt that a week of tears was waiting to flow, but when she got into her room, she couldn't make them come. The crushing hopelessness of everything, Father's tragedy, the stupidity of living, the complete ruin of her own life, the sudden gift of a château – mortal and worldly, these things were all impacted in her sinuses and behind her ears, making an intolerable ache that would not dissolve into tears.

How odd for an English girl to be saved by the wisdom of Napoleon, if Napoleon it had been, second only to Hitler in the list of tyrants who had attempted to conquer their sacred isle. She lay on her bed, she stood up and got a wet cloth, which trickled uncomfortably into her ears, she took a bath, and there, as if by suggestion, her tears blending with the rush of the faucet, she wept, sadness and joy intermingled. She decided to stay here in her room until it was time to go, to avoid seeing anyone, especially Emile, and when Rupert called her at four, she said she was ill and was lying down. She was not ill, she was just gobsmacked.

'Ill? We have to go.'

'I know.'

'When will you be ready?'

'I'll go on the train.'

'No, no. I'll wait till you feel better.'

She saw it was useless to delay what was inevitable. 'I'll be ready by five.'

'Let me know if you need help,' he said. 'We can talk in the car. What's the matter, anyway?'

'I don't know,' she said. But she did know, it was the hopelessness of life, poor Father gone to his grave in a state of spiritual imbalance because estranged from his daughter, and poor Emile never to know the passionate devotion she might have given him, and poor Posy herself, faced with an entire future of tormenting sibling visits in which she would have to see him, his children, his wife . . . Certain other scenarios were enacted in her mind. The death of Emile was one, in a spectacular snowslide or road accident, with sweet, French Victoire claiming his corpse. Such harsh fantasies kept coming into her head unbidden, though she tried not to give in and enjoy them.

He expected Posy and Rupert would be back late tonight. In London, poor Osworthy was brooding about the coming explosion. Posy Venn would have to be told, by himself, alas, of the manner in which her father had treated her in his will, a codicil he had not personally supervised the drafting of, and would certainly have advised against. He was strictly against vengeance from beyond the grave, and had seen too many situations where impulsive codicils had been regretted even by those who made them. It was bad of Venn. Here the capricious father's consideration was not primogeniture but revenge, or, rather, resentment, petulant resentment, not something that should be indulged. It was not as if there was a name to be handed down, these weren't lords. And he had personally seen several instances where the girl in a family was the more intelligent and deserving – not necessarily the case here, but sometimes the case. Luckily, English girls must be used to getting less than their brothers. Though not strictly fair, it was perfectly natural.

Amy and Kip made a quick trajet to Méribel and back, Amy on skis, Kip slithering ahead or around her on his board, discussing recent developments during their pauses or on the lift. The decision to leave Valméri seemed to lighten Amy's skis and ignite her turns with rapturous ease, but she knew she had to inform Kip about her plans to leave, a less happy prospect. Receiving this news, after the first shock Kip seemed to recover his equanimity. He didn't know what was going to happen to himself, but he thought things were going to be okay now that Kerry was better.

As Amy listened, little by little his fears came out. At first so relieved by Kerry's awakening, he was plunged again into a wash of uncertainty. He was expected back at his school in California, but nothing had been said about his airplane tickets, or when he could go, and no one had stepped in to take charge of Harry's future. It was plain that Kerry wasn't ready to go home, she couldn't even walk yet, and every hour they seemed to find something smashed in her, or a new nonworking part. Anyway, she was locked out of her house. Kip told Amy that the new plan, suggested by the doctor this morning, was to take her to Paris, to a convalescent clinic, but no one said what was supposed to happen to him. He hated how he was always whining to Amy, but she always had good ideas.

She would think about it, she said. She asked him what

he thought of the bizarre French thing of people believing in Joan of Arc, whom Kerry had never claimed to have seen, exactly, but the claim that was now being imputed to her. They discussed the possibilities.

'Anyway I think I started the avalanche,' Kip said with sudden vehemence. 'I could have started it. I was right up there above them on my snowboard. That's probably what Kerry saw, it's sort of shiny green on the bottom if you pick it up. I had just been with them, and they said they were going to have lunch in the Arbre de Pin, so I said I'd go in and take over Harry and they said great. So I took the lift up so I could ski down to the hotel, and then I went through the snowboard chute right there.'

'It couldn't have been you. What about the spear?' Amy asked. 'It was someone with ski poles.'

'But I made a lot of noise. I whooped and hollered. That could cause a slide.'

Amy hated herself for feeling at least a little glad that there were other possibilities besides herself. And there remained the possibility that Joan of Arc, whoever she really was, had been buried in the slide and lay frozen up there beneath the snow.

'It could have been me for that matter, in my silver-gray ski thing, waving a pole,' she reassured him.

Coming down to the hotel for lunch, they had run into the French lawyer who Kip had told her was coming on a mission that concerned Harry. He was just stepping outside with a pretty pregnant woman and Emile Abboud, all three of them carrying snowshoes. Amy quickly explained her role as Kip's friend, counselor in effect, and mentioned her concerns about Kip, his school, decisions needing to be made. She and Kip were both baffled to gather from Monsieur de Persand's taciturn responses that fortunes had changed from what they had understood only yesterday, when Kerry and Harry had been heirs to a fortune. Today it was Kerry who had no right to be in the château, and little orphan Harry was of small concern to anyone, though he would inherit with his half-sisters and half-brother. This new man didn't seem prepared to help organize a baby-sitter in Paris or say what Kip should do; he seemed to regard Kip as outside his sphere of concerns.

'If Harry has a share in the estate, shouldn't there be a means of advancing some money for his lodging?' she persisted.

'These are matters to discuss with the *notaire*,' he said. 'It is he who will be charged with the practical dispensations.'

'Who is he?'

'I really don't understand your interest in all this, madame.'

Amy was exasperated. 'Kip is a fourteen-year-old boy entirely dependent on his sister. I think it's appalling the way people are treating him.'

'These practical details are outside my purview, I'm afraid,' said Monsieur de Persand. 'I understand that Kip's sister is better and will be able to decide what she will do. I do not represent the family except informally, as a friend of Madame Abboud's mother.'

Amy did wonder what role Géraldine was playing in all this, but recognized a stonewall tone. It seemed clear to her that Kip should stay in Europe as long as Kerry was ill, so maybe there was some school he could go to in Paris, near the convalescent place where Kerry would be. This was not a negative – some exposure to French education would be good for him. Maybe she would get a tutor for herself and Kip at the same time. She didn't understand why everyone was so unhelpful and mean about Harry and poor, virtuous Kip.

The ungrateful Kip did not seemed pleased at her conversation with Monsieur de Persand. 'You just think of me as a fourteen-year-old boy, don't you?' he asked as they went inside.

'Okay, you're almost fifteen, and a much better skier than I'll ever be. You've got respect, okay?' Her tone tried to be jocular, but she suddenly realized how charged with emotion his words had been. When Amy spoke to Mr Osworthy on the telephone and reported on the service, she raised the question of Kerry not being allowed to go home. Osworthy confirmed it, was furious.

'Sealed up, people doing inventories. It's the two mothers, Pam Venn and a Madame Chastine, who are insisting, protecting the interests of their children, as they see it.'

'Oh, yes, I know Madame Chastine,' said Amy, still bemused by the connectedness of all things in an old society, so different from the abrupt disjunctions of California.

Amy supposed it was in the interests of connectedness that she had suggested that the Abbouds join her for dinner. Posy and Rupert were gone back to London, the rest of them would be off in the morning. This last night would be her only chance to encourage some contact between the Abbouds and Kip and Harry, in the hope that the Abbouds would feel some responsibility or interest in Kip, perhaps invite him in Paris, or at least acknowledge the sibling bond between Victoire and Harry. She was doing this for Kip's sake, otherwise she would surely not have wished to associate with Mr Abboud, such an unpleasant person, though she had decided the wife was lovely. How could she for a moment have blamed her ill-considered dash with the baron on an attraction to this conceited television personality?

They accepted, and joined her in the bar at eight-thirty, spruce in city clothes. She had not seen the couple together, but together they were more than picturesque – she so fair and angelic, he so dark in contrast; they almost made Amy uncomfortable. You couldn't help thinking of them in bed together. Kip and Harry sat for a while on a stool near them, Kip eating pretzels and olives; then Mademoiselle Walther came for Harry, and the others went into dinner.

Joe Daggart was joining them, too, and was waiting at the table. Amy had already begun to feel it was an unlikely conjunction of dinner companions, these stiffish Parisians with an American teenager, the mysterious Joe, and herself; but she persevered in the name of her project of bringing them together. Poor Kip would need to know people in Paris, if her plans went well. Across the room, she could see the unhelpful Paris lawyer and his expectant wife, probably their last fling before parenthood weighed them down.

Joe Daggart rose when the others joined him. He seemed to know Emile.

'May I present my wife Victoire? Joe Daggart,' Emile said. 'This afternoon Daggart was telling us about the avalanche inquiry.'

'Warplanes after all?' said Amy, hoping it was so.

'Not American planes,' said Daggart. 'We think the planes people claimed to hear were French or English, from the joint SST project, but the French won't confirm this. The SSTs are not supposed to fly over land. Remains to be seen if a plane can cause an avalanche anyhow. A sonic boom certainly could, but no one heard an actual sonic boom, and skiers declench more avalanches than airplanes. I think the airplane theory is a red herring, frankly.'

'Just another convenient way to blame the U.S.,' agreed Amy, trying to remember if she had seen or heard planes that fateful afternoon. It had been snowing. How could people have seen anything?

'I think the best theory so far is that put forward by the French ski patrol – that the Venns caused the avalanche themselves. They were just under the crest of a convex slope, traversing rather than in the fall line, just asking for an avalanche, in fact.'

'I am so *désolée*, we have to go back to Paris in the morning, to leave all this,' Victoire said suddenly. 'Mama says we must . . . the children . . .'

Emile looked at her with an air of surprise, as if this was the first he had heard of these plans. Other memorable exchanges at dinner, as Amy thought about it later, included the inevitable clash with this same quarrelsome man. Why had she thought him attractive? Turning to her, he asked, 'Have you ever read a French book?'

'Of course.' What did he take her for?

'A book in French, I mean to say.'

'Well, in translation.'

'Which?'

Les Misérables.

'Oh? Before or after you saw the play?'

'I haven't seen the play.'

'And that's the only book?'

Amy had to think. *'The Three Musketeers.'*

'Any more?'

'I don't think so,' she apologized. 'But I don't read much fiction.'

Le Comte de Monte Cristo?

'I saw the movie,' she sighed, adding, *'Tale of Two Cities,'* before remembering that was not a French novel. But she had one triumphant title in reserve. 'I've read de Tocqueville! Well, in English.' For she had. His eyes widened in astonishment, or perhaps doubt. She wanted to know why he wanted to know all this. Only later did she think she should have asked him what books he had read in English, if any.

After dinner, Abboud excused himself to have a word with Monsieur de Persand, who had recently been appointed to a position in the government, underminister of finance or something, and from whom he wanted, wearing his journalist hat, to elicit an opinion about some world event. Amy walked with Victoire and Joe back to the bar. The pianist, who had been playing show tunes, now launched into some classical piece for his own amusement, drawing Amy's attention to the music. It gave her a kind of hopeless feeling. Not only French literature but the whole subject of music lay before her. Oh, God, it was vast. Something about this piece brought the name of Chopin to her mind; was it some emphatic chords in the left hand? Maybe she wasn't hopeless. In Paris, she would go to concerts relentlessly and improve her ability to discern at least the works of Chopin from among the tumult of all the music pulsing through the world.

'The English are very fond of Berlioz,' said Victoire, nodding at the pianist. 'He suits the primitive, wild natures they conceal behind their polite facades. I did not think he composed for the piano – perhaps this is someone else's arrangement.'

The baron and his wife came in, in the company of the wealthy German couple from Bremen. Amy could hear them at the end of the bar, conversing in German. Once or twice Otto sent her an affectionate, knowing, but discreet glance, and the silver buttons on his loden jacket glittered in the firelight. Her face felt hot with the wish it all had not happened.

'Did you learn your English here? How old were you when you learned it?' she asked Victoire.

'I learned as a child in school, but also Maman insisted we were sent to England in the summers. I stayed with an English family, such experiences as that.'

Yes, you have to learn other languages as a child, Amy consoled herself. 'Your English is perfect,' she said.

'Oh, thank you, no, I make *beaucoup de* faults.'

Strangely they heard Emile Abboud's voice doing

another guest spot on CNN, evidently on tape, since the speaker himself was right here in the bar. His words had an uncanny appropriateness: 'That is the beauty of a powerful symbol, it is mutable and can signify for the times, any times. Joan has a meaning for our era different, no doubt, than for her own. She might now stand for, say, resistance to Anglophonia, or for the rising power of the female sex.' Amy glanced up to see that the actual Emile, coming back into the bar, was listening to himself, rating his own performance.

'Have you read Max Weber?' she found a moment to ask him. 'He says that religion is an invention of the unconscious, expressing our anxieties and fears. But what fear does St Joan of Arc express?'

'Fear of the alien invader,' Emile said.

It occurred to her she had one thing to do before she left Valméri. As she packed that night, she rolled up her silver Boegner *combinaison*, stuffed it in the laundry bag, and put it in the wastebasket, where it didn't quite fit. Feeling like a criminal, she took it out again, and went downstairs and outside to leave it in one of the giant bins the village provided for the many local chalet guests who did their own cooking and generated mountains of trash.

Amy would have preferred to take the four-hour train trip to Paris by herself, reading a book or working on her laptop. She had neglected letters to write, business concerns, and she was not making much progress with *The Red and the Black*. But she found herself agreeing, in her role as Kip's friend, to accompany him, Harry, and Mademoiselle Walther, Kerry, and a nurse for Kerry. They would be met at the Gare de Lyon by some sort of ambulance for Kerry, who would be taken directly to the private clinic outside Paris that had been selected by Dr Lamm. Géraldine Chastine would meet Amy and the others. A hotel had been organized for Kip, Miss Walther, and Harry at a level of comfort thought suitable by the lawyers, i.e., rather basic. Géraldine had hesitated over what would be suitable for Amy, and decided to put her in the Bristol for the few days until her apartment was finished being equipped with basic bed, chairs, kitchen gear – though the process of adding elegant details would be ongoing. Despite the early-morning hour in general darkness, Amy felt optimistic, even eager to be turning another page in her life.

They settled into their seats with all the calm of a train journey – so different from the misery of a plane trip, Amy thought. Kerry was tired and silent – perhaps it was too soon for her to move. Her large, rather strangely luminous eyes were closed, her head resting back with an air of being in pain. Amy had introduced herself, but Kerry seemed uninterested in who she was, or in talking, even to Kip. She made no responses to Amy's overtures. How was she feeling? Her baleful silence seemed to say, How do you think I'm feeling? Did she look forward to Paris? 'Not really' was the only thing she said. Kip, sitting next to Amy, was excited and talkative. Amy put down her book. She would have liked to read, and to think about the possible significance of her time in Valméri. Had she gained? Lost? Learned? But she listened patiently, affectionately, to Kip's conclusions about European skiing, extreme events for snowboarders, what Paris would be like.

But they had just left Moutiers when silently the train glided and lurched to a stop, and with a few convulsive jerks settled into inertia and blackness. A voice spoke in the darkness of the rapid restoration of lights, which came back on, and heat, which didn't. Though the compartment had been hot, now it began almost immediately to be cold. Amy, next to the window, pressed her forehead against the icy glass to peer into the dark, but could make out only an impression of a siding, and people with male voices banging around in the snow.

Miss Walther took Harry to walk in the corridor. Amy tried to master a certain irritation she felt as she sat there. Even stuck, she reminded herself, a train was a wonderful invention, collective and efficient, a fine example of mutual aid. It was the automobile, an aspect of selfish individualism, that had ruined America. Who had invented the train? The steam engine, for that matter? She could almost remember. Robert Fulton? Or was that the steamboat? Watt? Other inventors came to mind. Eli

Whitney: cotton gin. What good had school done if you were doomed to forget the simple facts you learned there? She hoped the familiar names had simply retreated to another storage area of her brain, blocked by French words, and phrases like *Défense de fumer*, that no one paid attention to and smoked anyway.

In the growing cold, her mind reviewed the past days. Besides the Otto mistake, she understood that she had made a mistake meddling in the affair of Mr Venn: life's lessons must be assimilated, not just received. The lesson was that having the money to solve a problem does not absolve you from examining the problem personally to be sure you do the right thing. She should have informed herself about Mr Venn's condition and not accepted at face value wishful opinions flavored by hope, venality, or nationalism. Had she talked to the doctor herself, for instance, she might have appreciated the true situation as she now saw it: Osworthy spiriting away the moribund Venn for reasons of his own. Okay, she'd assimilated that.

Her reflection in the dark window showed someone who looked exactly as she had ten days ago, yet concealed, already, some experiences, some conclusions, unavailable then. Some things remained to be understood, but they eluded her. Were they intellectual or to do with the heart? Were they specific to Europe, or could she learn them anywhere? Was there something about California that impeded these hoped-for discoveries? Maybe Paris would provide whatever they were. Despite her self-reproach, her spirit lifted at this reminder that her adventure was to continue.

PART 4
Paris

*When it comes to happiness, it has only one use,
to make unhappiness possible.*

– Albert Camus

*Personal salvation is granted to those
who seek the salvation of all.*

– Nikolai Berdaeyev

32

'Makeaballbouncy, makeaballbouncy, makeaballbouncy . . .'
Amy sang this phrase at various pitches until it satisfied
April Stanton, her teacher, another member of what Amy
had come to think of as Géraldine Chastine's American
Paris Mafia. Her homework was a series of ohms and
eehms, which, though April had assured her that her
speaking voice didn't have the timbre Europeans seemed
to detest, was designed to cure it anyway. Amy had hoped
for a French teacher, a little professor – someone in a
garret; but April lived in an Haussmanian apartment in the
sixteenth arrondissement and her husband did investment
banking.

Amy walked home, across the Pont d'Alma and along
the Left Bank. Paris seemed warm compared to Valméri.
There was no snow, and steam rose invitingly out of the
vents and manholes from an immense underworld beneath the city. You would have expected the homeless to
congregate at these points of warmth, but, as Géraldine
had explained, 'There aren't any homeless in Paris, oh,
except the few clochards who resolutely cling to their way
of life on metro platforms and never bother anyone.'
Now that she had been here some weeks, it was these out-
casts Amy had the most fellow feeling for, as lonesome
and without direction as herself.

A lot of minor things had gone wrong, and these had

begun to produce doubts, and undermine the normal cheerfulness she had thought she would recover once she got here. Not that everyone hadn't been nice. Of course they had been as nice as anyone could be, or nicer, making her wonder whether her money might be playing a role. She could not bring herself to really believe this. Apart from the uncertainties of the cooking school, the language school, the voice lessons, and the French dinner parties, three more important things, at least, were seriously worrying her, maybe four.

First, a ripple of unease from California. Her computer and fax machines offended Tammy with their utilitarian ugliness because they were obliged to be in the living room – '*salon*' – where the phone plug was, and hence had to sit on the beautiful Louis XIV–style bureau, a good eighteenth-century copy. (*Bureau* = desk.) Amy didn't understand why the phone company couldn't put the plug in another room, but so it was.

When the fax was plugged in for the first time, it had almost immediately produced clippings from *The New York Times* sent by Sigrid regarding impending war plans, and one from the *San Jose Mercury News* about herself, with an old photo and the story of Joan of Arc, emphasizing the stubborn persistence of Alpine superstitions, now being invoked to conceal military buildups, and accidentally involving innocent Bay Area dotcom entrepreneur Amy Hawkins, accused for mysterious geopolitical purposes yet to be revealed. As Amy so far as she knew had not been accused of anything, this odd news item had something like the effect of a projection of some inner vibration of her own secret worries, mysteriously telegraphed to a California newspaper editor. She tried not to think about this menacing item, but couldn't quite put it out of her mind.

Then, a growing, vague confusion about having money. Her apartment was extremely pretty and comfortable – she was pleased. It was two floors up, with no elevator, though of course she didn't need an elevator.

'It's just that for this much money, you'd expect one,' she had observed meekly to Tammy. 'Really, Amy, you can't have all the American comforts if you want seventeenth century,' Tammy had said, as if Amy were a Beverly Hillbilly.

The curtains of gray silk, hugely voluminous, matched the sky. All the time Amy was at Valméri, Tammy or Wendi had been calling with such questions as what did she think of gray, or of silk? Fine, great, Amy had said, and now just slightly permitted herself the observation that a more cheerful color in this cheerless weather might have been prettier.

'That's a really Californian idea,' Tammy had said. 'Blue and yellow don't actually look that great in Paris. It's a question of the light.'

So far, any friction with this unfamiliar culture had been smoothed by Géraldine Chastine or this battery of American women who seemed so attentive and friendly, at first Amy had thought out of fellow feeling. But then she'd had a bill from Tammy for fourteen thousand euros, for some chairs, 'service,' and ten percent. This didn't seem unfair, of course, it just made Amy aware of an element she hadn't been aware of before, of commerce, reminding her that no one takes you shopping for the fun of it.

Still, Amy knew she would never herself have had the wisdom and experience to choose these particular chairs, which looked somewhat plain, not what you thought of as French-looking chairs with gilded legs and flowery upholstery; these had backs upholstered in black leather, with blond wood arms, and were 'signed.' She didn't completely like them. Tammy's bill had prepared Amy to expect a number of bills from people who had been helpful this week.

She was worried about Kip too. It had taken a few days to deal with Kip's situation, a school outside Paris, not very convenient to Kerry's clinic but only a short trip on the RER, which was a thing they had here in addition to trains, buses, and the metro. Amy missed having a car, would have liked to get into her Audi and whiz around Paris some midnight when all the other cars would be holed up, God knew where they went.

Yet, wandering around on foot was quite thrilling – the beauty of each street, the way the buildings leaned into each other or out over the cobblestones like disapproving elders, the serene Louvre right across the bridge, 'St Germain,' the 'Deux Magots' – names familiar to her by some mysterious process of osmosis even though she had never for one second instructed herself in the geography of Paris. But she had to work at keeping her level of attention, of being thrilled, up to pitch. She would find herself lapsing into her own thoughts about what was happening in Palo Alto, or the market, or even about her brother's expected baby. She hoped she wasn't going to morph into one of those sad, professional aunts with no lives of their own.

Maybe she and Kip would go to the château at Fontainebleau some Saturday and look at what color the curtains were. Poor Kip had been rather ruthlessly installed in the Ecole Bilingue de Versailles, a day school with a small number of boarders, which had consented to take him for a few weeks while his fate was decided or the term ended. Though she had informed herself about all this, Amy had no further hand in making decisions about Kip's future; but she spoke to him often, almost every night, and knew he was hoping to go back to his regular school in California. Amy admired Kip, he was a brave boy to have done his job by little Harry and now to find himself in a strange land in a strange language – she tried to remember what she herself had been like at age fourteen, and couldn't remember at all, except to be sure she had been restless and unhappy, and determined to get out of Ukiah.

What happened to Kip next term depended on Kerry's fate – how the unforeseen death of her husband had left her fixed, whether she could afford his school fees in America, or even whether it might not be better to send him to England, where there were more boarding schools and he would be closer by. Then there were the Swiss schools, though these tended to be depositories for the attention-deficit children of American corporate employees abroad, divorced Eurotrash, or the generally wayward who had gone through all the American schools who would have them.

It was on Amy's mind that she still had not been to see Kerry. Her ostensible reason had been Kerry's reserve on the train, giving the strong impression Kerry didn't want to see her, and perhaps anyone, but she knew this was only a weak excuse. Maybe she was afraid Kerry would realize she had seen Amy on that slope.

She had had more than a few moments of wondering if she should have come to Paris at all. It was going to be a little difficult, unlike at the Hôtel Croix St Bernard, which had been easy, with pleasant people, food and amusement to hand. Here she was on her own alone, despite the charm of her apartment that this pack of nice women had organized in a miraculous period of time, and the list of phone numbers – friends of Géraldine, friends of friends, Tammy, Kerry's clinic, her doctor, the French teacher, the Etoile Cooking School that everyone said was great, and in English besides. In truth she was a little forlorn. Yet inner resource was a goal in itself; solitude led to it. She reminded herself she had not experienced solitude since – well, she had never experienced solitude, until now, and she didn't like it. For the first time, and this was her main worry, she felt that her enterprise of self-improvement might fail.

33

Posy had uneasily been able to tell that something was wrong when they first got back to London and Mr Osworthy still hemmed and hawed about the legal situation in England. Finally, Posy and Rupert had been convened to the offices of Osworthy, Park, and George, a straightforward legal firm in Mayfair, to hear about the legacy that Father had left her as his final expression of her value and place in his heart.

Mr Osworthy began by saying, 'It would seem that England takes the position that the last will and testament of its citizen the late Adrian Venn is in order, leaving everything to his wife, this to include his property in France, a small painting by the artist Bonnard, a house in Randolph Avenue – this latter perhaps the object of some litigation, as it had not been properly rerecorded after his divorce from Mrs Pamela Venn, to whom it had been legally awarded – and a portfolio of shares. If England had its way, Mrs Kerry Venn could expect to have, at the end of the day, more than a million pounds, assuming that the nation of France would allow the death duties on property in France, which was, alas, the main part of Venn's estate, to be paid in England.' There would be negotiations; there were tax treaties.

Kerry was getting everything, as expected. Posy had been prepared for this. Rahni boutique, Rahni boutique, forever. Obviously, her and Rupert's prospects here were dim. All the way back from France she had been telling herself that, and was used to the idea of getting little or nothing, telling herself that her suffering for Father must be a disinterested, even ennobling sort of suffering, a harmonizing emotion with no end but some sort of spiritual idea of being at peace with herself and with her idea of Father, and for him, too, if he could at some level hear her.

But Mr Osworthy had much more to tell them, his jowly face long with concern. Much was to do with the France/England situation, but finally he got to the delicate subject of Posy's inheritance.

'Of course he has mentioned you both in his will, as I had told you. Rupert will have ten thousand pounds. Posy – I'm afraid here you have not fared so well.'

'Just tell me, Mr Osworthy,' said Posy, with foreboding despite herself.

'Well, your father was an old-style Englishman, he evidently believed in leaving things to the oldest son, but he did remember you, to the sum of ten pounds, which is a testamentary way of acknowledging you and your position as his daughter ... He doesn't have a large fortune in England, just some shares, things like that ...'

'He left me ten pounds?'

Posy could see that Rupert and Mr Osworthy were watching her for signs of tantrum or breakdown. Though she wanted to say Sod Father and Sod you, Mr Osworthy, she thanked him in a dignified way. She didn't just then feel how crushing the blow was, maybe had expected it. The capricious unfairness of life in general had been weighing on her so much that this was only confirmation of it. She felt unbodied, a person without weight or power in the world, like a feeble breeze, to have had no effect or such a negative one on her own father, on Emile, no effect on anyone anywhere, as if she had never been born. So she was beyond being wounded by his ten pound legacy, though bitterness was a harder feeling to control. She would have to struggle against bitterness, as she knew it was a soul-destroying emotion, let loose in her like cancer. Such was Father's wicked power from beyond the grave that he had managed to tarnish all of them with distrust and exasperation.

Rupert for his part was tarnished in his own eyes because he had reacted badly, or felt that he had, to a proposal put to him earlier by his mother, who had by now been forewarned by Mr Osworthy about the unequal treatment Posy and Rupert would receive. He blamed the soulless boredom of bond trading, an activity his colleagues seemed to find wildly exciting, for having affected his character. Before Posy found out about Father's will, Pamela had floated the idea to him, behind Posy's back, of splitting his own legacy, the ten thousand pounds, with Posy, without telling her what Father's will really said, thereby sparing her the sadness of knowing what Father had intended.

She explained her reasoning. 'We would just say he left you each five thousand. She wouldn't have to know what the will actually said. I'd pay you back the five thousand, over time – I don't have the money now, I'm afraid, Rupe. In the long run, you'd come out the same. Could you do this? I'm afraid for Posy. She'll mind so much.' She saw Rupert's startled and disappointed expression.

Rupert was ashamed of himself for hesitating and at the same time felt resentment of his mother for making this request. He couldn't help thinking that Posy should have anticipated some sort of effect before she pissed Father off. Of course, no one expected Father to die.

'I could sell the house,' said Pam. 'It's too big anyhow.'

'God, Pam, can't you think of something else to make me feel really like a shit?' But even with his mother's promise to pay him back, he couldn't bring himself to split the money with Posy. He thought he might need it right away to get the publishing business. He dithered and temporized, and finally refused.

After the meeting with Mr Osworthy, over tea, Rupert had told Posy about their mother's handsome concern, and of his own moral failure. He left dangling there for Posy a sort of half offer to loan her the money if she ever needed it. Anyway, it would be months before they actually saw any cash, whether ten or ten thousand, and in the meantime, Rupert was plainly troubled by the feeling that he'd behaved badly, and so had Pam, in putting him in the position of doing so. Pam, for her part, felt that both of the children blamed her for some unstated failing, perhaps in the bedroom, or as a cook, to account for their father's leaving them in the first place, eventually to find Kerry and perish.

Inheriting part of a château in France went some way to cheer Posy, enough that she'd behaved well to Rupert about the English legacy. 'I'd rather die than take the bloody money anyway.'

'Well, five thousand, I don't know what you'd plan to do with it, but . . . if you want it, I . . .'

But the château, too, portended problems, just as the suave Monsieur de Persand had predicted. If she was ever to have any money for her own plans (antiquities store, shop dealing in Cashmere shawls, little house in Chelsea . . .) she would need to sell her share. A piece of crumbling real estate was no use to her. Rupert, on the other hand, was hoping to keep the château and direct Father's publishing business, the perfect escape from Bondage, as he'd come to call his job in the City. He assumed that their stepmother, Kerry, would welcome some effort like that, though no one had yet discussed it with her. He therefore would prefer to use his English ten thousand pounds toward the death duties owed in France so they would not have to sell the château, a view directly opposed to Posy's.

In the weeks since then, Posy had languished, less boisterous and combative than Rupert had ever seen her. He spoke of it to Pam. At first they had been thinking that Posy was overreacting to Father's death, as if she were the sole bereaved. Hadn't Rupert, too, lost his father? As everyone must eventually lose his father – she wasn't singled out. Still, she seemed to mourn Father as if his loss was meant to symbolize all the disasters of her life – even though, from what Rupert could see, her life had been relatively disaster free: she was good looking, had a responsible job, a Cambridge degree. Once he was moved to lean across the table and put his arm around her; from the stiffness of her body he came to think that she was worried about more than just Father. Perhaps she was sick, or nearing a breakdown.

Maybe she was, she herself thought. In limbo in England, going every day to the Rahni Boutique on the Kings Road, to an airless little room on the second floor where the accounting was done, sometimes taking a turn at the shop level, where the clientele reacted quizzically to her Oxbridge accent. The power over her imagination of the château money grew, came more and more to symbolize freedom – a freedom never to be hers without money. She knew she should be happy as part owner of a château and of the things found in Father's safe-deposit box, but even this change in fortune could not dislodge the dull despair, the leaden pall, events had cast over her life.

The more she came to see that death and disappointment were life's realities, the more important to her future did the money seem, and the more rightfully hers it came to seem. Paradoxically, at the same time, the possibility of some money, even the designated ten pounds, forced her to confront the real conditions of her life, presently pointed toward this dull job and no love life to speak of except what she'd have to work too hard at lining up, and just a general depressing flatness as she plodded on to middle age. Self-pity overcame her whenever she began to think like this, and hardened her resolve to get her share of the money and with it take her life in charge, even though this meant thwarting Rupert.

Today Posy was taking the underground from her apartment off the Portobello Road to the Eurostar terminal at Waterloo Station, struggling to carry her rolling suitcase up the stairs at the connection in the Picadilly Station. She had called her mother to be sure Pam had not changed her mind about her making this journey, had no regrets that it was she making this sacred (word used with irony) trip to France with Father's ashes. It was Posy carrying the ashes today because Rupert couldn't get any more time off work, and they all thought it would be inappropriate for Pam to be the one to deliver them to Father's widow. Posy had sensed in Pam and Rupert a little mistrust, as if she might intend to desecrate Father's ashes – flush them, maybe.

She bought *Vogue* and a *Pariscope* in the Eurostar waiting room, and began to feel mildly excited, apart from her difficult errand, by the idea of Paris. She'd be away from the Rahni Boutique, revelling in adventure, French food, absence from England, perhaps a glimpse of Emile. The train was called. As she rolled her case toward the escalators, she saw in front of her a familiar-looking back – tall, thin shoulders and neck, white hair with a curious pinkishness, rumpled coat – unquestionably Robin Crumley the poet, headed like her for Paris, with the *Financial Times* under his arm.

'Hullo, there,' she said, rolling up abreast of him. 'I guess they can't keep us away from those croissants and snails.'

'Hullo! How nice! Miss Venn! Posy!' he replied, with extreme cordiality, reassuring her that she was not intruding, he would be delighted if they sat together – she had acted diffidently for what did she know about poets on train journeys – would they be gregarious or deep in thought?

On the way, she told him about the things she hoped to do in Paris, not mentioning her grisly parcel. He said he was spending the weekend with the Desmarais, some delightful French people he sometimes visited in the summer in the Dordogne. Now they were all going to attend the performances of some Pinter plays in French in Paris. He also hoped while in Paris to see the American, Amy Hawkins, whom they had all met in Valméri – did Posy remember her? He and Posy reminisced about their lunch at Saint-Jean-de-Belleville and its aftermath of snowdrifts and rescue – to think it was so short a time ago, yet seemed so long when you had gone back to England, where everything was so unlike. They bought some small bottles of red wine, Badoît, and sandwiches from the bar car, and chatted over lunch.

'What do you think of Wordsworth?' she asked, and other such things. 'Does a celebrated poet of today owe him anything? I seem to hear Wordworthian echoes in some of your work, though it's very much in your own voice of course.'

'Oh, everything, my greatest inspiration. The *Preludes,* intensely,' said Crumley, thinking what a delightful young woman Posy was, much nicer and more relaxed here, out of the snow and relieved of the tension of her poor father's condition. 'It was Wordsworth who freed us, in some ways.'

'The language?'

'The simple diction, the meditative line . . .'

He agreed that the way she had been treated in her father's will was outrageous, though she tried to present it with some jocularity, and he was happy to hear about her share in the property in the south of France, which must after all come to something – a half a million even, before taxes.

'There is nothing that becomes a woman like property,' he said in his most Wildean way, or was it Shaw, only half joking. He'd looked at the prices of French real estate. Posy thought him incredibly sympathetic – his niceness had not struck her before. She could see he had been through harrowing things himself – he didn't say what. She found his frayed cuffs sympathetic, too, a famous, distinguished, but impecunious person, sort of like D. H. Lawrence; there was even a resemblance – the stalky neck and badly cut hair.

Pamela Venn and Trevor Osworthy were also coming to Paris, the next day. Osworthy had arranged rooms for all of them at the Hôtel de Lille, a small hotel suggested by Géraldine, not far from her own apartment and, for that matter, Amy's, where they expected Posy would already be installed. Pamela had no Paris plans but to visit museums and go shopping, apart from meeting her homologue Géraldine, and, she supposed, being present at whatever sort of ritual the children and the widow intended for Adrian. In London they had had a simple cremation, but had hesitated to organize the memorial service, out of a feeling that Kerry would want to be there. Still, there had been an appreciative obituary in the *Times* and *Guardian* both, the latter with photo. Pam had clipped extra copies for, eventually, Kerry.

It had been years since she had been in Paris – the Louvre had been remodelled since the last time she had been here, with the glass pyramid perched in its courtyard, now a fixture of Paris scenery, that was how long it had been! She marvelled at how most things had stayed unchanged, and looked forward to cassoulet and *confit de canard* and decent *camembert*.

'Yes, the cheese is very good,' Osworthy allowed.

On the train, he confided to Pamela his problems with settling the estate. He was faced with meetings with the French tax officials in an attempt to reconcile the English and French testamentary discrepancies. He was fairly sure things would boil down to paying taxes on the French property in France, on the English estate in England, each nation agreeing to ignore Venn's possessions in the other country; but at the moment, each nation seemed disposed to regard Adrian's entire estate, whether in France or England, as taxable by itself. He was baffled by some French ideas, but luckily there were tax treaties, and it would be sorted out. Luckily, Adrian had kept his legal domicile in England, otherwise France would be sure to tax the English estate as well. As it was, they might avoid this.

One especially strange tax provision was that Victoire, an illegitimate child, was going to inherit in France equally, or almost equally, with Posy and Rupert, though Venn had not even mentioned her in his will, nor indeed had he ever acknowledged her. Mr Osworthy was indignant. 'This would never happen in England unless the deceased had intended it, and Adrian certainly had not intended any such thing – may not even have known of this woman's existence. Some bizarre French Revolutionary logic which rewards people for being love children. Only the French!' Though he acknowledged the sentimental charm of the idea of privileging love children, Osworthy was deeply outraged at the total violation, imposed by French laws, of Adrian's testamentary intentions, clearly expressed, that his wife and youngest child inherit his goods and chattels, with ten thousand pounds for his older son and ten pounds for Posy. What could be clearer, or for that matter more sensibly organized? There was the upbringing and education of baby Harry yet to be paid for. Kerry had been living in the château, it was her home. Rupert didn't need the money, he was grown, employed, set on his path.

'No, it was badly done by Adrian,' Pamela disagreed.

Osworthy felt a moral obligation to Kerry Venn to see that she was not done out of what Adrian had so plainly intended for his beloved wife. Even if he could not compel Posy and Rupert to comply, he could make them aware of the ethics of the situation. 'In decency, Posy and Rupert should refuse their shares in behalf of Kerry and Harry.'

'What an idea!' cried Pamela.

'But even if they did, there is no controlling that wild card, the French daughter,' she who had never set eyes on Venn and now was to claim his property.

Meantime, he knew that Rupert was worried that Posy, now that she knew of Father's vindictive ten-pound legacy, would insist on the château being sold. This was another issue provoked by French laws addressing the problem of dividing property among four heirs. Instead of the sensible English custom of keeping an estate intact by giving it all to the eldest son, the French law, as he understood it, provided that in the case of disagreement about whether to keep a château, say, property will be sold and the money divided up. What a shame! Rupert and Harry, being males, could be counted on to behave sensibly; Rupert dreamed of stepping into his father's shoes as director of the press, not that he knew anything about presses. Kerry would stay in the château and raise Harry. But the future rested with Posy and Victoire, neither of whom seemed the least interested in châteaux or publishing, and as it was in their power, in the power of any one of them, to call in her share, and given that none of them had the money to buy the others out, this would probably happen.

Osworthy had weighed whether, were Rupert to give Posy half – or even all – of his English ten thousand pounds, she would still want to sell her share of the château, and predicted she would. Ten thousand was not enough to keep her or change her life. A pity. If the place were sold, Harry and Kerry would be out of a home, and the press would have to close or move, an enterprise of huge, probably fatal, proportions. If Rupert had to pay rent somewhere else, he probably could not run it profitably, whereas he had a chance of success if it could stay where it was. There was every reason to hold on to the château, whatever sort of dinosaur it might be, while its loss would disrupt almost all of them. A slim hope lay in the possibility that there would be enough money for Kerry in England, after death duties paid there, to enable her to buy out Posy and Victoire. But on the whole he didn't think there would be enough money for that.

34

Amy had had a week of her cooking school, enough to reassure her that this skill was not beyond her, and even to suggest that she might have a feel for pâtisserie and purees – her *gougère* (first lesson) had turned out delicious, and so, too, her *velouté de chou-fleur*. She had been given an understanding of *crème* soups, pureed legumes, and the principles of *rôtisserie*, by which was not meant a turning spit, as she had always thought, but simple roasting, which was no more than a matter of an oven thermometer and a meat thermometer, well within her level of competence. Could it be that French cultural superiority was based on an intimidating air of mystery that would prove to have little behind it? She actually looked forward to the unimaginably elaborate skills she would have by the end of the five-week course, and to the surprise of her parents and friends when she got home.

French was another matter. Here she felt retarded, though the teacher assured her she was better than many Americans, and not nearly as backward as Chinese and Japanese people, who seemed unable to learn it at all, or even if they understood its principles, were unable to pronounce it. At least Amy had a clear American accent people could understand. The French teacher, Mademoiselle Godrion, didn't grasp that Amy found this praise completely wounding, quite apart from the insult to her Asian friends. She had really wanted to sound French, not American, wanted to be indistinguishable from a French person, and wanted to assimilate mysteriously the core of cultural assumptions that went with the language but which seemed, alas, still opaque to her.

Now, little by little, she understood that none of this was going to happen. She would always sound like an American. Pronunciation aside, the grammar was slow going, too, and speaking aloud in a market or social setting was still utterly beyond her, cheerful, gregarious person though she knew herself to be. Mademoiselle Godrion and she managed well enough. *(Bonjour, mademoiselle. Comment-allez vous?)* Her reading skills surged forward with the daily stint with the *Figaro* and the *Pariscope*, but she could not rid herself of the feeling, the whole time, that the effort might not be worth it, because no revelations lay before her, and even if there were some, she was not prepared for them.

Robin Crumley and Posy Venn had spent the afternoon in the little hotel on the rue de Lille, in bed, Posy teaching Robin certain things she had learned, from Emile in fact, though she didn't mention that. What a surprise that Robin was not gay, though he was veiled about the nature of his past experiences. She was naked, astride him, his expression was dreamily rapt, his erection very sturdy. She had actually read a number of his poems, even before they had met, and some of the most beautiful lines streamed through her mind now.

He had been quite compliant on the train, even eager,

given that she had thought him rather above or beyond sex, for instance hadn't seemed interested at all in the glamorous Frenchwomen at the Hôtel Croix, sticking to his friends the desiccated little Eurotrash couple, despite being much younger than they. He proved to be forty-eight, though she had thought older. The first time had come about on the train, with the inspiration of the red wine, and involved them locking themselves, with many giggles, in the toilet – fortunately, it being the Eurostar, a larger and cleaner place than train toilets in general; with rather unsatisfactory results, but technically a success, in that they had completed the act, even if it was a bit inconvenient and hasty, with people trying the door and so on – and confirmed a promising relationship.

For his part, Robin was perfectly thrilled that Posy had proposed this way of passing the afternoon. He saw with almost painful clarity that he had left too many aspects of his life untended. Yesterday, arriving in the Gare du Nord, he had rung Madame Desmarais, who had expected him to lunch, made his excuses, and they had come to the hotel where Mr Osworthy had made reservations for Posy, the Lille. They had been here ever since, his spirits almost hysterically rising. Really, the vagina has something!

Posy's presence in his life seemed to raise a storm of vital questions in his mind, especially concerning the need of the human heart to attach itself. Of course it needed to, and here she was, as beautiful as a handmaiden of the Round Table as she stooped to sweep his shirt into the hotel laundry sack, and now filling out the laundry slip like the most organized amanuensis; how thrilling that she desired him, and in her role of lover was as passionate as a cat – a woman of infinite variety.

A certain boredom he had been feeling lately with life in general, he could sense was beginning to lift, or a corner of it, at least. He had the sense it might lift entirely, eventually. It was a question of gravity. His mind toyed with the pun. Gravity: seriousness and the pull of the earth. The earth itself a metaphor for the dark pull of the sexual self. He had truly not given enough weight to his Dionysian self, had too privileged the Olympian.

He would see the Desmarais later, when he went to stay with them. Tonight, Robin Crumley reminded Posy, he had been invited to a cocktail party being given in Amy Hawkins's honor by Géraldine Chastine, Posy's half-sister's mother. Surely Posy had been invited?

'Yes, but I'm not going. You go, I don't want to. I don't want to see any of them ever again,' Posy said, and instead lay back on the bed, brooding on the nature of her next move. 'I'll go and find us another hotel. My mother and Mr Osworthy are staying at this one, which I think is rather off-putting.'

Victoire and the children arrived at Géraldine's at four, Nike and Salome in matching Scottish-plaid party dresses and ballerina shoes. They embraced their grandmother. Géraldine could see at once that Victoire wore a pained, damp look quite unlike her normal self; her usual halo of hair was flat, her eyes narrow with resolve. She carried a suitcase. She withheld any explanation of her mood, as if waiting for a better moment, but took her little case into her old bedroom, now used by Géraldine for her business records, present wrapping, and storing out-of-season clothes. More trouble with Emile, thought Géraldine.

'*Allez, les enfants, regardez la télé dans le bureau de Grand-papa.*' The little girls, of almost the same age, looked at each other and alertly dawdled off, ears straining.

'Maman, I have left Emile,' whispered Victoire. 'I see now that things will never change. Some women endure what – what I have had to endure, but not I. I don't want the girls to see their mother as an abject victim, I want – I want out!'

What had brought this on now, after their apparently harmonious trip to Valméri, with its brilliant *suite* for Emile? Since they returned from Valméri, Emile had seen his star rise. His visibility in the matter of Joan of Arc, and his already large following for his roundtable appearances on TV, had led Antoine de Persand, who himself had recently joined the cabinet as an underminister, to contact Emile about a new role as press secretary to the minister, a position, once he was inside the government, that would yield fascinating prospects of influence, preference, and even a salary. The news of his new appointment had been announced.

Géraldine saw that it was probably the prospect of inheriting money that had made Victoire suddenly feel independent – though it was not to be that much money, either, if Géraldine had guessed correctly. Certainly not enough to live on forever, with no other income. She tried to think how to explain this to the impractical Victoire. If only Victoire were more like Amy, she could not help but think.

'I know. Emile will have to help. Men must support

345

their children. Of course they must. I will insist on every-thing, everything will be correct. It has been hard, Maman, but I know I am right . . .' And much more in this vein. Géraldine found herself rather irritated to find such willful wrongheadedness in her formerly sweet-natured, long-suffering daughter. What was the eloquent but inscrutable American phrase? The worm, something about the worm turning.

The doorbell. It would be the guest of honor, Amy Hawkins, who had said she'd come early to help. Géraldine looked at the clock, and postponed further discussion with Victoire.

'Nothing hasty, *ma chérie,* it is complicated – men, marriage. We will talk about this.'

Amy had heard that it was rare for French people to invite Americans and others to their private dwellings, so she was touched by the gesture of a party. She had insisted on contributing something, but Géraldine had refused so firmly that it was quite an impasse until Amy was finally allowed to pay for the champagne, which Géraldine ordered and had sent.

Amy looked forward to seeing her various new friends from Valméri – the sweet Victoire, undoubtedly, maybe the irritating Emile, even Robin Crumley, who was to be in town and had telephoned from London. It would be nice to meet old friends, welcome presences among the strangers Géraldine was inviting. Amy had insisted on asking Kip, of course, though his sister was more or less confined to the clinic place, which Amy had not yet been to. She knew she ought to go see Kerry, for Kip's sake,

346

and out of simple American solidarity, but she still had not. Kerry had been so distant, so tired, on the train ... actually, Amy faced it, she hadn't liked Kerry. She scolded herself for this imperfect sympathy, and tried to put herself in Kerry's place.

Tonight she would wear the stunning French black dress Géraldine had made her buy. Amy had been more than docile on the matter of clothes, since Géraldine seemed to enjoy the expeditions to buy them. Probably she didn't have this vicarious pleasure with Victoire, who, though chic, was rather low key. Clothes here were quite pricey. Amy knew intellectually about the existence of, but had never confronted, dresses, off the rack at that, that cost four thousand dollars. There were no such dresses in Palo Alto, though perhaps in San Francisco, since the brand names were the same, Yves St Laurent, etc., names you could get anywhere. Amy was firm with Géraldine about buying only one of these imposing garments, an elegant sheath that could be worn over and over. She was shocked to realize this was a secondhand dress at that, from a smart shop in the Palais Royal that sold black dresses only. Two thousand dollars!

'But it is Balenciaga,' Géraldine had explained. When Amy mentally looked in her California closet, she realized that both of her dresses at home were black, too.

'It is ravishing on you, and you carry it well,' Géraldine said.

There was no time now to meditate on whether to follow Géraldine's instruction to get her hair cut off. She had refused, but now she did wonder if there was something hopeless about her hair that had animated such personal consternation from a relative stranger. She also wondered why Géraldine was so solicitous. She didn't think it was her money, entirely. She had begun to see that her entrance into French society was important to Géraldine, as if she were her daughter. Maybe the real daughter, Victoire, had not come up to Géraldine's hopes for social success – she seemed too unworldy and sweet for that.

They had gone to lunch the day before at a restaurant grand but unpronounceable, Carré des Feuillants. Near them, a table of beautifully groomed people caught Amy's eye. For an instant, she indulged the dream of being like them, effortlessly speaking French, effortlessly ranging over the menu, knowing what to expect. The women all wore designer dresses and were draped in scarves. The men, too, far more elegant than American men, wore dark suits, i.e., matching pants and coats, ties, their collars higher than at home, perfect haircuts. She thought she might be making progress in the awareness department, to be able to notice such subtle cultural differences as collars, though she wasn't sure she respected thinking about such subjects. Géraldine glanced at them too. Amy was stunned, as, when one woman got up and wended her way toward the bathrooms (*'toilettes,'* she had been instructed to say, though it sounded a little too frank), the other people at the table switched into English, with heavy Texan accents.

'*Bien sûr* Americans. What did you think? French people wouldn't go to the *toilettes* in the middle of a meal,' Géraldine pointed out. 'Also, the jewelry . . .' rolling her eyes as if something un-French about the jewelry was self-evident, though it looked okay to Amy.

She had noticed the frequent remarks people had made in Valméri about the American female voice. It had bothered her that she was herself unable to hear whatever it was they heard, but presumably her singing lessons were training it out of her own voice. She had other projects for self-improvement, too, but it often seemed impossible to think of organizing them all – she who had organized, practically, a whole corporation. Luckily, Géraldine, Tammy, and the others seemed to have endless connections and had summoned up a voice coach as easily as they had found the cooking school and the French teacher.

Géraldine had invited two other American women to lunch. Amy hated them instantly: Dolly Martin and Elaine Deutz, two well-groomed American divorcées approaching forty, recently arrived in France for reasons very much like Amy's own, with the added hopes of finding Frenchmen to marry. Dolly was from Connecticut and Elaine from Redwood City. These two women had become friends, were both protégées of Géraldine, and both wore smart suits, high heels, and buckets of perfume in the French style. Thus Amy realized that Géraldine didn't really understand Americans. If she did, she could not have supposed that she, Amy, could have anything to do with these cheerful, in Amy's view supremely dumb, women, who were also very snobbish about other Americans in Paris.

'I met an adorable boy, who does the flowers at the Georges Cinq; he has a budget of fifty thousand euros a month. He's doing the flowers for Dana Whittaker, too, on the side. Imagine! Really, the French have no idea who anyone is.'

'Have you been invited to the embassy? The paintings are okay, but the hors d'oeuvres are really tacky.'

'The Roaches have a château, but only a nineteenth-century château.'

'Oh, you bet she did the Etoile cooking school. Boy, can she prepare a *terrine de foie gras*. But she still can't boil an egg.'

The day of this lunch with Géraldine, the Joan of Arc affair had surfaced again. By some mysterious process, the French press, which as far as she knew could have no idea of where to find her, had obtained the American newsphoto, an old photo taken at the time of the Dootel sale, with Amy standing slightly behind Ben and Forrest, all of them holding up papers and grinning. The French caption translated to 'Telecom Heiress Implicated in Alpine Tragedy' and, like the American item, noted the filing of a civil process, while 'criminal investigations were ongoing.'

She had rushed to call Sigrid, and also Mr Osworthy in London, to demand to know what it meant, and he soothed her by saying he had not heard of any process involving any of them, and if there were such a thing, it was certainly not his doing. Probably her name was involved because of her hiring the rescue plane. Probably investigations were routine after accidents. Look at the prominence the papers and television had given to Adrian Venn, singled out among the other victims for mention by name. Amy was particularly galled to be called an heiress, since she had earned her money herself, but there didn't seem to be any way of setting this straight, or any other point either.

'Amy, are you sure you're safe over there? Are they – attacking Americans or anything?'

'Where?'

'In Paris. Where you are. The war – you read these awful things here.'

'Really? No, it's fine,' Amy protested. What on earth had Sigrid been reading?

As she had not yet visited Géraldine's apartment, Amy had no idea what to expect. She was slightly disappointed, perhaps surprised was a better word. Though large and comfortably furnished with antiques, it fell short of the grandeur she had imagined of French interiors. The ceilings were only slightly more than normal height, with beige curtains and wall-to-wall carpet, and a modern coffee table in the salon. Only the chandelier in the dining room and the pale walnut armoire said 'France' loudly enough for Amy, the rest could have been saying New York or London, not that she had spent much time in either place. She noted, however, that the tablecloth, of heavy linen, bearing no creases at all, might have come from the stock of the expert Herr Hoffmannstuck himself and had the air of having lain in some ancestral cloth press until Géraldine's day. Amy tried to picture how it could be ironed, but was unable to.

The doorbell rang again. The newcomer was Emile Abboud, clearly a cherished son-in-law, and one who obviously admired Géraldine. Amy noted their complicitous, affectionate greeting, so unlike the cliché sitcom renditions of the mother-in-law and son-in-law relation. Perhaps his nature had a sweet side. One must always be prepared to change one's opinion of someone one has judged harshly. Géraldine rushed to commandeer him before he stepped out of the foyer.

'Emile,' she said, 'Victoire is here, with the girls.' Her eyes slid around to indicate the direction in which Victoire could be found. The two ravishing, dark little girls came rushing into his arms, and even the barman hired for the night turned to look at him. It was impossible not to notice the little stir he seemed to cause whenever he came into a room, as he had at the Hôtel Croix St Bernard.

'There is nothing to say,' said Victoire loudly to her mother and Emile, behind Géraldine. '*Rien à dire.*'

'Salome and Nike, *les enfants, allez à la cuisine, je viendrai vous donner à manger,*' said Géraldine again. The two little girls again scampered away. Emile moved off behind them toward the bar that had been set up in the dining room. Géraldine said something to Victoire that Amy could not catch, though this was easy French to understand.

'Of course I love him, Maman, he is *l'homme de ma vie.*'

'Then try to understand men, chérie . . .'

'*Non,* Maman, you can only forgive a man if you don't love him,' said Victoire.

Amy, recognizing a drama of some kind between the Abbouds and Géraldine, began to retreat toward her coat, thinking this would be a good time to go buy flowers, as she had forgotten to bring any; she should not be a witness to a family discussion, though perhaps it was only some asperity because Emile had been late, had been told to come even earlier. Anyway, seeing him embroiled in domestic quarrels required her to contemplate Emile as a married man. As far as Amy had gleaned from Géraldine at lunch, the situation of Emile and Victoire was now financially promising – he had a new job and she would have some money from the château and the *vignoble,* unexpected good luck. Amy fled into the outside hall, hearing behind her the raised voice of Géraldine, who seemed to be scolding Victoire.

On the street she bought tulips and waited twenty minutes, window shopping at the antique stores, where the prices were too high to be mentioned. She knew she would never ever bring herself to enter one of these shops, nor, frankly, would she want these peculiar tables with talonned feet and mirrors with wings. Napoleonic, she knew. It was odd that a villain of history should have had such a large and deleterious influence on interior decorating. No doubt Mr Abboud would have an explanation.

When she got back, carrying her giant bouquet, the tension had diffused, and numbers of guests had begun arriving, greeted by Géraldine and a maid hired for the occasion whom Géraldine minutes before had been instructing in the operation of the interphone. Amy, too, hovered near the door, feeling it her duty to be introduced whenever new people arrived. Tammy and Wendi came in, also Elaine Deutz, of the lunch, and later, Elaine's friend Dolly Martin.

Here, too, were Mr Osworthy and with him a woman

who was introduced as Mrs Pamela Venn – evidently the mother of Rupert and Posy. Pamela Venn and Géraldine liked each other immediately, the one so sturdy and English, with her lovely white hair and flowered, slightly too-long dress, the other so adroitly dyed, wearing one of the tailored suits run up by a little woman behind the Madeleine. They made plans to lunch later in the week.

'But I had so hoped to meet Posy and Rupert!' cried Géraldine. Osworthy and Pamela explained that Rupert would be coming to Paris on the weekend. They didn't say they were uneasy about Posy's whereabouts. They did say she was to have arrived yesterday carrying Adrian's ashes, but had not been at the hotel just now, though it was quite possible she was already delivering the ashes to Adrian's widow. The two women grimaced their indifference to these ashes. Pam explained about the vicious revenge Adrian had taken on the restive Posy, the legacy of ten pounds.

'Thank heavens such things cannot happen in France,' said Géraldine.

Amy had not realized Emile was in politics, which would explain his relentless chauvinist criticisms of the U.S. Amy had heard him issue a number of dogmatic historical analyses in Valméri, always digging at Americans. Another time, of someone's medal, 'Of course it means something. It's a British medal. It's only the Americans who give out medals just for turning up.' Amy had felt rather cross that Robin Crumley had agreed with this.

Even now, as he moved around the salon, he was delivering one of his diatribes on the subject in answer to someone's question: 'You think Americans are bad now?

One can think as far back as the Algerian War – that war was really the Americans' fault. After the invasion of 1942, they distributed leaflets calling for the freedom of colonized people. Not that *un peuple colonisé* should not be liberated, but it was innopportune, and stirred up factions, and encouraged political developments Algeria wasn't ready for. Plus it was another blow at the French army, ostensibly an ally of the U.S.' Amy would have liked to stick up for America, but she didn't know anything about the Algerian War; had never heard of one.

'*Tiens,* I didn't know you were Algerian,' said someone else to Emile, at which he frowned.

'I'm not, actually.'

Amy could imagine that Victoire would be a perfect political wife, self-controlled and cultivated, and not interested in Algeria or medals. Amy could imagine being wife to a politician. In fact, anything less than such a challenge would hardly be worth the trouble of wifedom. It was suddenly what she most wanted in the world; did Victoire know how lucky she was to have this role?

She had not expected the baron Otto von Schteussel, who apparently was one of the large acquaintance of the amazing Géraldine. She was startled to see his familiar face, with its embarrassing associations, yet here he was, kissing her hand and clicking his heels. 'I'll see you home,' he whispered, with an imperceptible nod at the door. 'As soon as you can leave.'

'Oh, please don't bother, I'll have to be one of the last,' Amy quickly reminded him, but he said he would wait for her. She recognized that in some perverse way she was a little glad to see him; their intimacy, however regretted, was unlike anything she was likely to experience with anyone else present, which made him at least a friend. Her essential isolation struck her anew, a feeling of being alone in a crowd. Given neither to introspection nor self-pity, nonetheless she felt a stab of the notion that, favored by fortune though she was, there was something that was going to elude her, maybe, she just wasn't sure what.

Collectively, Géraldine's friends seemed the essence of France: animated, slender people in suits, the perfumed women carrying perfect handbags, the men in ties that gave meaning, Amy remarked, to the word *cravate*, though, since men in Palo Alto didn't wear ties at all, maybe any ties would impress her as ineffably European and elegant. Many of the men wore little badges or had tiny red lines in their lapels. The room had a sound in a different key than a roomful of American people would give off, different even from the international buzz of the Valméri guests as they gathered in the bar in a dozen languages.

A Frenchman kissed her hand. That this was still done! The rules of French mutual aid dictated a large place for politeness, which seemed to ooze out of the pores of Géraldine's friends. Amy recognized the French lawyer whom she had tried to talk to in Valméri – Antoine de Persand – who had in some capacity an interest in the Venn children and had been so unhelpful about Kip and Kerry. She caught him glancing at her, rather startled, not being able to place her as Géraldine's guest of honor, and not appearing to associate her with the intrusive meddler of Valméri. Now, however, he bowed over her hand. Of course, in her devastating dress, she felt quite unlike the woman in ski clothes he had seen. With him was a woman of his own age whom Amy had not seen before.

'Did his wife have her baby?' Amy wondered to Géraldine. 'In Valméri she was about ready to pop.'

Géraldine paused. 'Mmm, you must mean Clara. I did hear she was pregnant. She's the mistress. Whether the baby is Antoine's or her husband's . . . is not spoken of.'

Amy noticed that at one moment Victoire would be gazing with tightened lips at Emile, who was deep in talk with Antoine de Persand, or surrounded by the smart ladies, or if he extricated himself, he could be seen looking pensive, or talking intensely to his mother-in-law, Géraldine. It was plain that Géraldine's mind was half on her party but half, or in some other proportion, on something else, perhaps related to the new job taken by her son-in-law. Perhaps the family was not in agreement about it and that was the origin of the strains Amy had observed. These were only her fleeting impressions as Emile made his way around the salon. Like a political team, Victoire and Emile seemed to work opposite parts of the room, the one moving off to fresh territory as the other neared. Amy noticed that Emile and Victoire had not spoken to each other even once, like a perfect team in silent harmony.

Géraldine stuck to Amy and presented her relentlessly to every guest, like a Victorian mother, or so it seemed to Amy, who longed to hide in a corner and talk to Kip. She disliked being the focus of the party. She was aware that the rich American girl was a stock character in the

French imagination, or possibly in French experience, her boisterous vulgarity offset by her good nature and money, and Amy was vaguely afraid of fitting the bill. But each French person was more gracious than the last, and several proffered invitations to their châteaux, country houses, and favorite scenic expeditions. Amy, who had no wish to leave Paris, was obliged to accept several of these invitations, not that she didn't want to, but a future of visits extended uneasily before her. All French people wanted to visit Las Vegas – what luck she didn't live there! – but none expressed a wish to visit Palo Alto, though *Stanford* and *Silicon Valley* had for them a dim resonance.

Amy noticed that Géraldine prefaced each introduction of an English person by referring to *'nos amis les Anglais,'* our friends the English, in a tone that suggested that the English were even less beloved than Americans. But Géraldine seemed genuinely delighted to be able to present to each other such great literary figures as Estelle d'Argel and Robin Crumley, the latter of whose fame was known to her from her rententive memory of the names that appeared under small photos of guests at Paris parties, usually to do with fashion, in the front pages of *Vogue* or *L'Officiel.* Amy had found it strange that well-dressed French people seemed to attend a tireless circuit of commercial perfume parties to launch 'Mystère, *le nouveau parfum de . . .'* Or they flocked to buy diamonds! She had been to one such party at the Place Vendôme. Amy was amazed that Géraldine could think that she, Amy, would plan to buy a diamond, but the $250 donation went to preserving old windmills, a mildly good cause you could not regret.

Estelle and Mr Crumley might easily have met in the great world of letters, but had not. Neither of these writers showed the least awareness of the other, though they smiled warmly. 'Of course, I've never read a word of him,' Estelle said later. *'Un Anglais et un poet?'* Robin, though he said, 'What an honor, madame,' seemed irredeemably vague too. They were separated by the enormous gaps of nationality, of genre, and of sex, for male writers rarely read their female counterparts, poor creatures condemned to struggle in the wakes of the men racing to greatness like sailing yachts, and poets never read fiction, or vice versa. It went without saying that Estelle's novels had never been translated into English, though an ardent disciple of Robin's did produce translations of his poems into French and send them to French papers, which published them from time to time.

Emile and Robin Crumley were delighted to see each other. They exchanged cheek kisses and pounded each other's shoulders, which Amy thought very odd for men to do, and certainly un-English, whatever the French custom, or in Italian films where she had seen men kissing each other.

'Emile, my dear! How nice to see you, all of us in our city clothes, *alors,* as you say, and Amy has metamorphosed from an Alpine sprite into this *mondaine* creature we see here! Hello – so wonderful to be *en ville*, frankly – remember our snowy calamity – I see now we could have been killed – people are in droves during winter, driving off roads, freezing, exposure – what a near thing!'

'Crumley, you look very well. When did you get here?'

'Yesterday. Yes, yes, I am very well indeed. The warmer climate of Paris suits me,' Robin agreed. He seemed to radiate genial Francophilia and urbane goodwill. 'Look at Amy, doesn't she look citified?'

Emile had noticed this. Haloed by the soft lamps of Géraldine's salon, Amy did seem aglow, radiant in a way he had not noticed before, reflecting the attention, perhaps respect, implied by his mother-in-law's interest, and the presence of her most important friends. Perhaps a ski station has a levelling effect that dissipates in the ruthless inegalitarian light of the City of Lights. Here she shone with beauty, even glamor. He wished she wouldn't talk, but even there she seemed instinctively to know she was to say very little. She smiled, spoke a few shy words to each and every guest. It was not a bad performance. Really, Crumley – where was he? – was a clever creature, for an Englishman. How astute of him to recognize in the American a ton of money, with its peculiar reifying effect. Despite himself, he was a little dazzled too.

Yet you heard that these heiresses were always restive, unhappy souls, not to be satisfied, so it was as well, for his own sake, that Crumley had not persevered. Looking at her, Emile didn't detect restlessness, however. He shook himself out of his reverie, as he had other things to think about: the tiresome behavior of Victoire – which he assumed she'd get over – and the beginnings of an international incident that would have to be handled in the press. But there was a moment when politeness dictated he speak to the heiress herself.

'Are you enjoying Paris? How are you spending your time?'

She gave a demure smile. 'Monday Wednesday Friday French lessons, Tuesday Thursday cooking, *visite guidée* each afternoon, *musées* – assorted *musées* each afternoon but Tuesday, exercise between five and six . . . I'm hoping to add piano,' she said, only half facetiously.

'Your life is like an opera, in the first act, when the *jeune fille* is coiffed, receives her music lesson, learns a few words of French – the young woman people are trying to marry off.'

'Unlike me,' Amy said.

'What is the goal of all this effort?'

Amy was startled. Wasn't self-improvement an evident virtue? 'Well – to be better. Every day in every way. It's an American obsession.' She deliberately threw in the dreaded *A* word, which she had observed before to have the effect on him of garlic on a vampire. But he didn't flinch.

'Isn't your project of personal perfection rather self-indulgent? You don't need to have perfect stomach muscles and a complete working knowledge of *pâtisserie*. Most people have to learn to live with their own imperfections, or just work on them at the weekend.'

'Abs.'

'What?'

'Stomach muscles are "abs" to us.'

'Yes. It's an American self-indulgence. And it misses the point somehow.'

'Oh, well, we Americans always miss the point. I've come to understand that.' Her tone, ironic, didn't convince him she believed this. 'I'm not doing it for myself, anyway,' she added. Was she?

'Oh, for whom, then?'

'For others. It's a gesture of cooperation to the world, to be as informed and as fit as you can.'

'It is simple vanity disguised as Protestant virtue.'

'Many religions incorporate physical feats – fasting, standing on your head, the plow,' said Amy. 'Crunches, in my religion.'

'The religion of the self.'

He was really unendurably sententious, but this time she felt, at least, that he was making an effort to be friendly, he just didn't know how to be.

Robin Crumley was presented to Pamela Venn. The woman was in truth closer to his age than her daughter was, though he didn't dwell on that. A good-looking woman, a prediction of what Posy would look like. 'Of course I had the pleasure of meeting Posy and Rupert in Valméri,' he said. 'She's a clever girl, most impressive.'

'It was a hard thing for them. I am very proud of them both,' said Pamela. Robin had an instant of blankness before remembering what she could mean – the long coma of the father, the swine who had treated Posy so badly. 'I'm so pleased to meet you,' Pamela went on. 'I think we have a friend in common, Drusilla Able, the head of the North West London Reader's Society – I know you gave a wonderful reading at the Regents Park Mechanics Hall recently . . .'

'Mmm, oh yes indeed,' Rupert agreed, though he had no specific memory of that occasion and hadn't a clue about Drusilla Able.

*

362

Kip was going on to Emile about his school at more length than Emile actually wanted to hear. 'It's not so bad here, though. There are a lot of Americans. I'd like to go back to Oregon next year, though. I'm on the ski team. If I went back now, there's only another month of the season, and I think I should stay here with Kerry. She's getting better, but not that fast . . .' and many more details of Kerry's recovery and even of her mental state, described as very preoccupied with her supernatural vision.

Emile was puzzled to hear from Kip that the clinic found for Kerry was the well-known Clinique Marianne, an alcohol rehab and psychiatric facility made famous in the days of Cocteau. Was there more to her malady than had been acknowledged? Or was it simply that there was comfort (even luxury for rich clients), and space for baby Harry and his nurse? Emile could easily picture the private quarters and expensively cheerful staff of this legendary clinic, and it occurred to him to wonder if the American was paying for this, too, or whether it was coming out of the estate. He didn't care enough to raise this issue himself, but someone would, probably the English family, soon enough. Kip went on speaking to Emile, but seemed to be avoiding Amy Hawkins, his supposed benefactress. Emile noticed that when Amy would glance around for Kip, the boy would look down or away. Amy noticed this too.

Emile thought it was rather hard on Kip to be stashed in some school in Versailles – he was clearly happy to be here among familiar faces like Rupert and Crumley, and Amy Hawkins. Emile had known about her unfortunate interference in the matter of transporting Victoire's father, but hadn't known until Kip told him that it was she who had organized the school and offered to pay his way back to America if he wanted to go back to his former one.

All, but especially Amy, were surprised to hear of the continuing interest of Parisians in Jeanne d'Arc, whose apparition was being talked of either as a 'psychic aberration,' a true 'visitation,' or an 'American incursion,' though always *entre guillemets,* as if each speaker feared making the wrong choice among these possibilities, given the impossibility of such an apparition at all. In the American newspapers, Amy had been following a growing protest in America, localized for now in Washington, but with voices newly raised in California, over the government's lack of transparency when it came to military activities, now jeopardizing even Europe, which it had taken an Alpine tragedy to expose. In the teeth of a number of these small demonstrations, the President's press secretary had issued a flat denial that any American planes had been anywhere near the Alps, let alone flying low enough to start an avalanche. Activists had countered with statements of disbelief, and hypotheses about planned escalations of war in the Mideast or the Balkans.

The serious French press was also hammering this view, predicting random invasions, perhaps even of Europe, so extreme was their apprehensiveness. The very most left-wing papers predicted illegal cooperation by the French government with the nefarious American plans. The popular French press was more drawn to stories of the apparition of Jeanne d'Arc herself than to discussions of her political significance. It was the occasion for many essays on the 'mystery of the Alps,' and the manner in which it represented lingering superstition and symbolized national aspirations. 'An apparition in the mind of an appointed one, the witness, is no less meant for the rest of us,' opined Father Ruiz, the revered priest, in Lyon. Géraldine had passed on some clippings, which Amy, dictionary in hand, had laboriously translated.

'The sainted Jeanne, whatever one may believe about her material presence, retains her inspirational power – her courage and candor, her belief in herself,' Emile was saying to several admirers.

Apropos of Joan of Arc, Mr Osworthy had good news for Amy, gleaned from reading *Le Monde* on the train. 'There was nobody there, under the snow, at least that they can find. They don't rule out a grisly suprise in the spring.'

'Good news,' said Amy, wondering if he meant, as a subtext, You in particular will be relieved to hear there's no one else dead up there. 'How do they know?'

'I believe they do probes, or radio waves. But there is some bad news, too, or at least cause for uneasiness. But I will ring you tomorrow. Something rather appalling has happened, concerning Kerry and Kip. I'll ring you first thing in the morning.'

'Well, what? You can tell me now.'

'Kerry is acting strangely, combative, unhappy with the death of her husband.'

'Seems natural.'

'We'll speak in the morning.'

Amy drifted off to look for Kip. 'American culture, an

oxymoron,' Emile was saying in English to someone. 'However much they may want it, however flat their lives must be without it – hence the obsession with money – they mistrust culture in the European sense. Think of their inhuman treatment of their most brilliant writer, the neglected genius Poe.'

This was the first time Amy had heard the notion that Poe was the most brilliant American writer. The same Poe that had written 'The Telltale Heart'? It was true that she could still remember her elementary school reading of that tale, more than one could say for most stories. She resolved to ask Sigrid to find a biography of Poe and FedEx it over.

At nine, people began to drift off to their dinners. Amy waited till all had gone to thank Géraldine profusely and say a special good night to Victoire, for whom she had had a sympathetic feeling since the moment of Victoire's incipient tears in the hotel ladies' room. Tonight, as then, Victoire was a miracle of poise and *soignée* ('well-tended, well-groomed') prettiness, but, as then, was distracted though playing to perfection the role of daughter of the house *(jeune fille de la maison)*, leaving to her husband the task of talking to the serious politicians and businessmen.

Victoire's children, so unlike children at home, were models of some French concept of childhood, putting their little faces up to be kissed by the adults and saying, *'Bonsoir, madame,'* like fully functioning citizens of this party. Amy admired the way they weren't shuffled off with a baby-sitter and that they repaid the trust placed in them by behaving well. Though because of Harry, Amy was more aware of children than before, she was not sure how she felt about them generically, and was pleased to feel an actual affectionate impulse toward these pretty, dark little girls. The Abboud family seemed to embody some ideal not quite American but more in the Platonic sense of the way families were meant to be – sons-in-law cooperated in the family project, even when it was for some friend of the mother-in-law. On Sunday afternoons in Palo Alto, the guys would be watching football.

'It was a joy, *bien sûr*, and thank you for the lovely tulips. But did you think we didn't have enough flowers?' Géraldine said.

Kip had continued to avoid Amy, so that finally she accosted him. 'Why are you hiding from me?'

'I'm not,' he said.

'Is it something about Kerry?' Amy asked, remembering what Osworthy had just told her.

'I can't help it if she's weird' he said evasively, and she let it drop. Mr Osworthy would tell her soon enough. She insisted on inviting Kip to dinner after the party, partly because she guessed that he would like to stay away from his boarding school as late as allowed, and she wanted to cheer him up a little, and partly because she feared Otto's offer of seeing her home. Sure enough, Otto was waiting for her outside, and if he was chagrined to find Kip, he didn't show it, but took her arm and chatted to them both. They dined in a brasserie on the Ile Saint-Louis. Kip seemed uncomfortable – perhaps it was the presence of the baron – and hurried through his dinner. Amy knew he must be lonesome at his school without even Harry to talk to, which could explain his taciturn manner, as he talked about his French class and the problems posed by the fact that kids his age in France were farther along in math – though far behind in computers. He finally confided some of his worries about Kerry.

'They won't let her go home,' Kip said. 'Her château, where she lives – they say no one can go inside now.'

'Why not?'

'Because it won't be hers. Posy and the others get it. Maybe they'll let her stay in it, but it depends on what Adrian signed or something.'

'Doesn't Harry get a share? They can't just put Harry out in the street. Anyhow, they seem nice, it's hard to believe . . .' Amy said, very shocked. 'Let me find out.' She was thinking that perhaps Posy and Rupert didn't realize that Kerry had no place to go. 'I can call Mr Osworthy. He probably just hasn't thought.'

They put Kip on the metro at eleven, and Otto walked Amy home through the courtyard of the Louvre and over the Pont Royal. Lights on the other bridges were reflected in the black water of the river. A *bateau-mouche* washed them with its powerful lights. He came upstairs with her, not to her surprise and, in a funny way, in accordance with her hope; though she didn't plan to sleep with him, his familiar face at Géraldine's in the sea of thin, well-made-up, and crisply barbered unfamiliar French faces had somehow warmed her. She was lonesome herself. He admired her new apartment in effusive, slightly professional terms – 'Hmmm, north facing but you will have sun from the south in the kitchen and bedroom, and it is well that the bedroom is not on the quay. Quite a pretty color – what do you call it?'

'Robin's-egg blue,' Amy said. 'Something else in French; it's copied from the Grand Trianon.'

'We must talk,' he said, as they gazed reverently at this so meditated and authentic color.

'Drink?' Amy proposed. 'Sit down, please . . .'

'It's Fennie,' he began when they had sat down. 'My wife. As you know, she is very difficult. I do not see how we can go on, you and I. She is going to come to Paris with me in future . . . In fact, she is here now, at the Hôtel du Louvre. I told her I had a business engagement . . . I felt I must see you before – before our hearts become too entangled. More entangled.'

Startled, Amy began to protest that her heart was not entangled, but that seemed tactless, and not even entirely true. Now that he had ruled it out, she felt she at some level might have been watching to go to bed with the baron again, on his visits to Paris, not to mention during winter months in Valméri. She could see a future of occasional intercourse, coupled with reliable real estate advice, ultimately perhaps a chalet . . . After all, he was the only person to have presented himself. He wore his overcoat of loden green with silver buttons. She smiled to conceal her conflicted feelings and said she understood. Baron Otto brightened when he saw there was to be no scene, and accepted an after dinner *gennepi*, which Amy had brought with her from the mountains.

'Of course we will stay fast friends, and I will do everything in my power to help you, with property, or advice – I am utterly yours,' he said.

When he had gone, she thought – *brooded* was maybe the word – about the baron, about Géraldine's party, the various dressed-up people, the hors d'oeuvres of stuffed quail eggs and salmon on toast squares, and especially the way she could not compete – even if she had cared to – with Otto's married state. Someday she hoped to understand the peculiar institution of marriage, with its jealousies and proprietary emotions she never had felt, and did not wish to feel yet. Perhaps that was the trouble – her heart had never been broken or even grazed.

Still, husbands. What a bunch! She hoped Victoire, who was so nice, would be able to manage her handsome, doubtless troublesome, quarrelsome, probably – like Otto – unfaithful husband. You heard about philandering European men, and from the evidence, if Otto, Emile, Adrian Venn, and the French lawyer were typical, a low opinion of them was about right. Yet these men all seemed relatively blithe. Those of her male Palo Alto colleagues who were unfaithful to their wives suffered, went to shrinks, publicly discussed their anguish, and inevitably divorced, creatures of some American, Protestant form of the superego that wouldn't let them just get away with it. Was it ever wise to marry?

But there was something to trouble her about what had just happened with baron Otto, all the same. If she had been chagrined not even to get started with her ski instructor Paul-Louis, it was even more demoralizing to be dumped after one encounter, as if the initial tryout had failed to please, or that he had found her too American, lacking in some basic erotic skill or attitude. Had her episode with the baron in a way gone too well, too weddedly, perhaps?

Amy had never had doubts about her own sexual

adequacy, but now she began to fear that some chasm of cultural difference, of which she knew only the native tradition, made sexual intercourse something quite different in different countries. She thought of those odd Japanese prints where fully dressed people thrust their organs out of the folds of kimonos into the concealed orifices of others – was that the reality, or an artistic convention? She thought of the television film in which the naked French girls had stood on their heads. Or the Almodóvar film, shown in polite Palo Alto theaters, where the heroine receives cunnilingus while dangling from a clothesline. Was there something peculiarly Spanish there? Or not?

Or even worse – new thoughts chilled her – had Otto simply realized she was never going to buy a ski chalet? She didn't believe in being emotionally vulnerable – that was no way to be – but still these thoughts disturbed and worried her. One of the worries was that she didn't feel keenly enough her adventure with Otto.

Yet, she was troubled by an unnamed erotic turmoil. It was not midnight, and she felt the smallness of her apartment, a sense of confinement not to be looked at too deeply lest it lead to confronting her ambivalence about her whole project here. She put on her coat and went outside to look at the view up and down the Seine, as she often did. She loved the way in Paris a woman could walk around at night with no worries, unlike in Palo Alto. She had no explanation for the problem in Palo Alto that wasn't too politically incorrect to be directly thought of. She often felt, being here, that she had to censor some area of her consciousness to avoid certain pointed realizations she was not ready for about America.

Standing on the Pont du Carrousel over the black river to see arcs of lights on the bridges on both sides, like a scene and its mirror image in infinite regression – this was surely one of the most splendid sights in all the world. Was the beauty of the surroundings a positive value, like cooperation, for which society should bear the collective cost? The French apparently thought so. Prince Kropotkin had not been very interested in beauty, as she remembered.

She felt, rather than saw, someone approach, then made out Emile Abboud coming toward her, his collar turned up, his woolen scarf wrapped around his neck, walking briskly from the direction of Géraldine's. He raised a hand in greeting. It was somehow unsettling to run into someone she knew in the middle of the night in Paris, especially Abboud, whom she had earlier seen in the bosom of his family, and, despite her reflections about the safety of Paris, she felt a crawl of fear, as if he would menace her. Or was it a start of guilt, as if she had been caught at something?

'*Bonsoir, mademoiselle,*' he said. '*Est-ce que la soirée vous a plu?*' speaking absentmindedly in French.

'*Oui,*' said Amy. 'It was very nice – I hope there weren't a lot of dishes, I should have stayed ... it was a lovely party.' How stupid she sounded, of course Géraldine had had helpers, she wasn't doing dishes, what a banal remark.

'No, she enjoys giving parties.' A silence extended itself.

'Oh, good.'

He suddenly took her elbow. 'Why are you out here? Come and have a cognac, or some eggs.' It seemed an odd conjunction. Amy stepped passively along, walking toward St Germain on the rue des Saints-Pères, wondering why she was going with him. What was he doing here, for that matter?

'She knows a lot of Americans,' Amy said. 'I suppose she was making me feel at home.'

'Here, the Flore.' They walked into the café, still crowded at midnight, and sat on the terrace under the warmers. He ordered two cognacs, without asking what she wanted. Amy wondered why she should even sit here, having unwisely broached the subject of Americans, which would invite more criticism and involve having to defend her country yet again, even if she half agreed with many of the things he would probably say. There were lots of Americans in the Flore tonight, but also some old French women staring into their *pastis*, as in a painting Amy had seen of a greenish woman staring into her absinthe. She and Emile stared at each other, he perhaps wondering, as she was, why they were here, or what to say now? Yet she was not unhappy to find herself sitting with a handsome Frenchman at midnight in a café – surely that fitted somewhere into her dream of Europe? Why were her feelings always so contradictory? Was contradiction after all more conducive to growth than certitude would be?

'Are you familiar with the works of Prince Kropotkin?' she asked presently, for lack of any other topic.

'*Oui,* yes, why?'

She was startled. Though she had often tried to bring

up Kropotkin, this was the first time anyone had ever heard of him.

'I find him an interesting figure.' She heard herself telling him about her belief that Kropotkin's ideas should be promulgated.

'You are an anarchist, then. I had taken you for a capitalist,' he said. Was he speaking of her personal situation, or of the American way of life in general? Her wariness grew. 'Naturally mutual aid is a good idea, cooperation is a good, but principles are needed also,' he added.

'Oh, naturally,' she agreed, thinking in confusion that cooperation was a principle. What did he mean? 'It was so beautiful on the bridge, I was trying to remember what he said about beauty.'

'I can tell you. He said beauty was an "idea thought out in detail."' How surprising that Emile knew this! 'I can even illustrate. You looked very beautiful at Géraldine's – I've been told one doesn't say such things to Americans, they think you are insulting their seriousness. But what I mean is, when Kip told me about your kindness to him, I began to see your beauty. My idea had impeded my eye. It was a strange corrective to realize that. But why were you thinking about that particular abstract idea?'

'I was thinking that there is an idea behind the French treatment of the riverbanks and bridges, or maybe an assumption is a better word, that it should be beautiful, an idea we don't have at home. Usually we have factories along rivers.'

Emile evidently restrained himself from making some cultural slur. 'I should apologize to you. I didn't appreciate the extent of the help you've given to Kip. I heard that it is you sending him to the school in Versailles.'

'Yes, why?'

'That is very generous too.'

'Oh, I'm sure they'll pay me back,' said Amy. 'If not, I'll make him mow my lawn or something.' Mr Osworthy had not been sure how things in America had been left for Kip, or whether Kerry even had custody of her brother.

'They say Americans have a somewhat careless attitude to money.'

'Not me, I'm quite careful,' she said. 'Some things are just important, like school.'

'I didn't mean it as a criticism.'

'Really? Then that's the first thing you've ever said to me that wasn't . . . Why is Kip avoiding me? He hardly spoke to me.'

'I imagine he's embarrassed at the way his sister is acting.'

But she didn't know how Kerry was acting; to her shame, she had not yet been to see her. She thought again of how she had misguidedly helped them move Mr Venn, to his death.

'Anyway, I should apologize to *you*. I'm sorry about the way it turned out for your wife's father. I feel it was my fault.'

'The mysteries of culture. A French person would say, "It's not my fault."'

'I've noticed that,' said Amy. 'They often say *ce n'est pas ma faute*,' where we would think it polite to say, "It's my fault," even when we don't think it is. But I do think it was my fault.'

'*En fait,* it was the fault of the English lawyer. You yourself were generous and altruistic.'

She had no reply to this. 'You have a new job,' she came up with finally.

'Well, an additional job; I've kept my other jobs too.' But since she didn't know what his jobs were exactly, this also went nowhere.

'*En fait,* I find much to my surprise I am sometimes wrong about things,' he said. Looking at him, Amy didn't believe he often had to admit to being wrong. People would always indulge him. She would not, though. She saw that he was trying to be nice; she could not explain her growing discomfort with this conversation, banal and good natured as it was.

'I think I am too determined to think the worse of Americans in general,' he went on.

'Yes, I've noticed that. Do you actually know many?'

'You are almost the only one.' He laughed. 'Apart from Géraldine's voracious friends, the *décoratrices* and *facilatrices* . . . They do reinforce my low opinion of Americans. You go some way to redeeming them.'

'But not all the way,' Amy said, remembering the many things he had said in Valméri.

'In general, yes. That is what I am trying to tell you, that I have seen that you are not like the others, that you are something more.'

'Not at all,' said Amy, with a twinge of indignation for her countrymen. 'There's where you're wrong. I'm just a regular American, I'm totally typical. Maybe you should reexamine your ideas about us. You should examine your ideas about categorizing people. But I suppose you want to be congratulated for your marvelous flexibility, changing your mind about me . . .'

She heard herself say much more in this vein, delivering herself of a longer, pent-up patriotic outburst, and observed his look of astonishment, and his polite manner of rising, as she made her escape from this horrible, though handsome, man.

Emile watched her go, wondering if, at last, he could be in some danger.

35

Amy tossed in the night, slept fitfully, and woke still feeling strangely shaken by the events of yesterday, all on their surface so agreeable – a party, lots of interesting new French acquaintances, even friendliness from the distant and formerly hostile Emile Abboud. There was the wounding episode with the baron, to be sure, but Amy realized it had not been chagrin that had colored her restless dreams; that little episode had been a small blow to her self-regard, not more. No, it had been Emile Abboud and the peculiar encounter of late last night that had disturbed her. She ought not to have been so rude to Emile; he was after all Géraldine's son-in-law, and she owed it Géraldine to be civil.

It hadn't been entirely fair to attack him, he had a point about Americans. Thinking about Elaine and Dolly, and Tammy and Wendi, she could see where he might have got his bad impressions of her countrymen, unfair as this was, and he had been trying to be complimentary to her, even friendly. But his view that she was not like other Americans, if sincere, was insulting to typical Americans like herself. Perhaps he had been an emissary from the whole Venn family, to say that she was forgiven for the sad way Venn's trip to London had turned out.

But it wasn't the Venns, it was Emile himself she kept thinking about. She had not forgotten her own frisson when she had first met him – and the feeling she had whenever she had seen him since. And he could quote from memory the words of Prince Kropotkin – the only other human being in the world to share her enthusiasm. How bitter that such intelligence should be embodied in a man who hated such people as herself. How she longed to redeem herself.

Despite her declaration, of course Posy was obliged to see her siblings again, to discuss the château, a discussion she had been dreading. Though Trevor Osworthy had proposed the offices of the Paris branch of his firm, Osworthy, Park, and George, the French, with their propensity for having things their own way, insisted that this meeting was to be held at the *bureau* of Antoine de Persand, who was now an underminister of the economy, with an office in a government palace on the rue Solferino, remarkably luxurious for a public servant, with a Chagall and a Corot borrowed from the public collections, and serious furniture by Meisner.

'Only in France,' said Osworthy, as he often did about other social phenomena in this country, 'only in France would the functionaries be able to loot the national heritage for their own uses. The French are a docile race, despite their revolution. No doubt the energy, the spark, was guillotined away, no wonder they didn't resist the German occupation. Priest-ridden, to boot.'

Posy wouldn't have minded bumping into Emile, who had already taken up his duties with the ministry. She wondered if he could work his old magic, now that Robin had entered her life. But Emile had been aware that his wife and Posy would both be in the building and had stayed away in his office at Sciences Po for the day, so both Posy and Victoire were disappointed. Both women wanted to put themselves to the test of seeing him, to relish the feeling of indifference they were sure to have, and to enjoy the sensation of Providence being on their side, of things working out for the best. It was almost worth having had a bout of misery for the pleasure of knowing one had got over a destructive emotion. In addition, Victoire dreaded seeing Posy, though Posy didn't dread seeing Victoire.

Osworthy had convoked Posy, Rupert, and Victoire, and he himself was representing little Harry and the widow Venn, who was still too frail to venture out of the Clinique Marianne, a pleasant-enough place, he could verify. Mr Delamer, Venn's man of business, and the French *notaire*, a Monsieur Lepage from Saint-Gond, were also there. Rupert and Mr Osworthy were glad to see Posy turn up. She had managed to avoid them all week, and they had been worried about her.

Osworthy told them he had finally come to an understanding with the French tax people, to the effect that, most of the property being in France, most of the taxes were due in France, but other taxes were due in England on property there, which included, to his horror, Pamela Venn's house, which had never been properly signed over to her. France agreed to look the other way when it came to the English estate.

'She was very badly represented, poor thing, a result I myself was somewhat responsible for. As Adrian's solicitor against her, I was not overly concerned about her affairs. Of course her own solicitor was at fault.' He was sorry now, but there was nothing to be done, unless he could convince the Inland Revenue that it was a mere error of registration and the house was not part of Venn's estate. No fraud had been intended, God knew.

'One good deed I can take credit for. I have managed to prove that the Bonnard was bought in London, and there we might get an exemption on the condition it return to and not leave England. The French, of course, wanted it in lieu of death duties.'

Rupert and Monsieur Delamer stared. Even the suave Monsieur de Persand appeared startled. 'You told them about the Bonnard?'

'*Mon Dieu,* are you a fool, man?' cried Delamer. They had become abusive – that was the only word for it – at Mr Osworthy's declaration that he had listed it, for they had spirited it away out of sight of the French tax authorities, they thought safely. However, he wanted no part of chicanery.

'I remember when Adrian bought it,' said Monsieur Delamer. 'How he loved it, how he would want his little boy –'

'I believe it's called hiding assets,' Mr Osworthy said. 'Often done by people planning to divorce. Mind you, it's illegal. I'm not sure what Pamela Venn's claims could be against the estate, if any, if it came out he had these things at the time of the divorce.'

'There are two issues, then,' said Persand, quickly, not wishing to ignite any simmering divorce recriminations, 'now that the inventory and appraisals are finished. A valuation of the château at two million eight hundred thousand euros is conveniently low; it would fetch a bit more than that at sale; though not as much as if it were smaller, prettier, and in better repair. But the lower evaluation helps you reduce the tax basis.

'It has value to Harry as his home, and as a seat of the business Icarus Press, and for the vineyard enterprise. These two *affaires* have also been appraised, the press at a loss, which will diminish the tax liability of the entire estate, the vineyard at a profit, after the deduction for depreciation of the capital equipment. In France, by the way, it is the heirs who pay. You are individually liable. I believe it is otherwise in England.'

'Yes, in England the estate would pay the taxes, the heirs get what's left over,' said Osworthy, his tone leaving no doubt about which system he thought more reasonable.

'The upshot is that if the estate were liquidated, each of the heirs would receive about six hundred fifty thousand euros, and after taxes around three hundred eighty thousand – that is, each of you will owe around three hundred thousand in taxes, regardless of whether you sell or keep the building and businesses. Madame Abboud, your share is a little less because of the illegitimacy penalty. It was the philosophy of the French Revolution, and its triumph, that children conceived in free affection should not be penalized, love should not be constrained by the dead hand of the Church or the State, parental love should not be legislated, girls and boys be treated equally ...' The listeners were a little startled by a passionate tremor that had entered his voice. Of course they had noticed in Valméri that he was or was about to be a new father.

'Unfortunately there were revisions, and one was that a child conceived in adultery should not quite get an equal share because he has done an injury to his siblings – that is you, Madame Abboud. Your father was apparently married to Madame Pamela Venn at the time of your conception.'

Posy and Rupert contemplated this new evidence of Father's infidelity and unreliability, but without surprise. Victoire rustled with indignation.

'You are saying that if neither of my parents had been married, I would get an equal share, but as Papa was married, I thus must pay them for the injury of my birth?'

As if they had not injured me, said her expression, alarming Posy. Why was Victoire being so distant? Had Emile confessed or confided? Apart from this worry, the news was overwhelmingly wonderful to Posy. Relief and happiness sang in her ears. Even the hugeness of the tax owed came as something of a relief, in that there was no way on earth Rupert could get that much money together, either to buy her out, or even to pay his share of the taxes. He would therefore have to see the sense of a sale; it wouldn't all be her fault for demanding one.

But this was not the solution Rupert had by now set his heart on: 'We sell the vineyard, a profitable business involving land, it should fetch quite a bit, and use the money to pay the taxes. Thus we save both the château and Icarus Press. I would run it, with my sister – sisters – as investors. And Harry of course has a share, and Harry could go on living there with his mother. We would all live there.' Farewell England, rainy gloom, the bond market.

'Why would I agree to that?' asked Posy.

'You'd have a part of the château, an apartment in it or something like that, and be a partner in the press.'

'Mr de Persand just said the press is a losing business. Father's vanity press.'

'That scheme seems sound to me,' said Victoire. 'I could live there too, it would be lovely for the girls. Of course I've never seen it, but I'm sure it must be wonderful, and also for Madame Venn and the baby.' She was impulsively drawn to the idea of living in Provence, far from Emile, where she would organize anglophone play groups along the lines she had done in Paris, and play the flute, and the children would have fresh air, away from the lead-laden air of Paris, and perhaps her parents would help a bit with support. Also, she would not wish to agree in anything with the detested Posy.

'The press is hardly successful enough to support seven people, if I am counting correctly. It does usually run at a loss,' said Mr Osworthy. They all contemplated a romantic future of poverty and cooperative toil in a cold, leaky, rustic mansion, and it was not a vision that appealed, except to Victoire and Rupert. Osworthy had his own notions of a suitable future for the widow and her baby, but it involved her share suitably invested and a small but cosy flat in an affordable suburb of London, somewhere like Purley, and her taking a job as soon as Harry went to school. Three hundred fifty or so thousand invested didn't yield a living wage, or barely.

'I hope you will not sell,' said Monsieur Delamer. 'It was a labor of love for Adrian, he had poured so much money and energy into it, and it is doing rather well, much better than at the beginning, and in time –'

'I'm sorry, but I'll take the money,' said Posy. 'If that means selling, too bad. I just don't see there's any other way.' She recognized that she was frustrating the others, but she could not believe they were so impractical as to really want to bunk in together in a drafty château – father's widow, an infant half-brother, Father's ghost hanging about the place, three ill-assorted siblings, and Emile's dusky sprogs. Eight personalities, counting Father's ghost, living in what was hardly a crenellated medieval castle but only a poorly maintained seventeenth-century structure sitting on flat ground in the middle of a vineyard, boasting only one tower and a couple of crumbling outbuildings, exactly the kind of hopeless place starry-eyed Englishmen usually did buy in the south of France. She told herself that Rupert would be much better off without these encumbrances, that he had no turn for publishing, that it was her duty to save him.

'The press is just turning the corner – I think that is the expression?' Delamer was insisting. 'If only for the sake of Adrian's memory, you ought to try . . .'

Antoine de Persand didn't comment on any of this. He remarked that though he was not a tax specialist, except in aspects of national fiscal policy, it was well known that in such cases of disagreement among heirs, a sale was always called for. The only way to avoid a sale was for the remaining heirs – Harry, Rupert, and Victoire – to buy out Posy's share, and pay the taxes somehow; but that was up to them. The matter should be put into the hands of Monsieur Lepage, the *notaire*, as soon as possible.

Victoire drew her scarf around her shoulders. 'It would

be *trop triste* to let a beautiful château pass out of the family. I will sacrifice, if need be, to keep that from happening.'

'You've never seen it,' Posy reminded her.

'*Non*, but I have respect for *patrimoine*, for history. Perhaps it could become a *relais,* a little hotel ... ?' Osworthy noted for the first time that the two sisters didn't appear to get along. He also saw, too clearly, that it would not do to discuss this issue further at this time. It was obvious that for the moment there was a complete impasse, with his own views tending to support Posy's. He didn't know which side Kerry Venn would come down on in Harry's behalf, given that she was being cruelly done out of her own inheritance by the laws of France, nor did he know whether Victoire's view should have equal weight, given the bizarre French regulation about adulterous 'love children,' which diminished her share slightly. The others had accepted Victoire with such docility, Mr Osworthy observed to himself – for all they knew, she could be anyone. Shouldn't there at least be a DNA test?

'I suppose you should talk to Madame Venn about what she wishes for her little boy,' added Monsieur de Persand. 'Perhaps they will return to America. I believe Americans always do return to America.'

'On the contrary,' observed Mr Osworthy. 'They never seem to, once they taste expatriation. London is overrun with them.'

'Posy and I will talk over our possibilities,' said Rupert grimly. His rage at Posy had boiled up. What in hell was her problem? Why wouldn't she just listen to the various possibilities? He had been somewhat worried about her. He knew she was depressed, and this was how she got, combative and tired-looking. He wished that Pam could hear all this.

'We won't talk it over,' said Posy. 'I'm sorry, but I want to take the money. This is a great piece of luck for me, it will change everything. Anyway, I don't see how you could bear to live there, after all that's happened. You'd be better off with cash.'

'Obviously you don't mind ruining things for Father's other children. You've never cared whom you hurt.' They descended into uninhibited recriminations of this kind. Osworthy and Monsieur de Persand listened with fascinated foreboding at this confirmation of their fears, this textbook example of quarreling heirs.

'Stop, *arrêtez*, you are all horrible,' cried Victoire, beginning to sob violently. 'I should never have gone to see that man. *Comme je savais. Les Anglais, "Méfiez-vous des Anglais."* I wish I had never met any of you.' Her distress alarmed all the men, though not Posy. Victoire, she who had always seemed so light and composed, now thrashed them away when they tried to offer tissues and consoling gestures. Mr Osworthy, his eyes burning in an eagly way behind his spectacles, stood, shook hands with Rupert and Posy, and waggled his head to indicate that they should tiptoe away, they would speak later. The two English heirs stood, Rupert kissed Victoire on both cheeks, and Posy backed toward the door.

'Let's go get something to eat,' Rupert proposed to Posy as they walked along the quai.

'I can't, I'm doing something, I'll see you later,' Posy said, wishing at all costs to avoid a private discussion with Rupert.

'We have to talk about it. Let's go in here.' They turned in at a little bistro and sat in the corner. Rupert ordered pâté and salad, Posy, bowing to the inevitable, an *entrecôte Béarnaise*.

'I don't have to talk about it,' Posy said. 'It's clear. There's no way we'll be able to pay a million pounds of taxes.'

'Euros. It's not as bad.'

'Euros. You know we have no choice, it's just a matter of your recognizing it, we have no chance at all of finding a million euros.'

Rupert knew Posy when she was adamant and agreed that she was right, no point in discussing it. But he could not leave it alone. He burned with determination to find the means to keep the château. Even though on his recent visit to the *coffre*, he had been aghast at its shabby state, ungainly dimensions, and the menacing exigency of its hedges, it was becoming as they wrangled about it the most important thing in his life. Maybe it was because the place was so in need of him, and he of it, that filial emotion seized him now.

'Can't you at least try to see what it means to me?'

'Rupert! I'm not against you, I'm realistic. Our family will owe, we *do* owe, one million pounds to the government of France. Father's curse! Didn't you even hear Mr Osworthy?'

'Why do you always have to be such a bitch? Why is that your role? Why do you think Father punished you,

Posy, do you think he would have punished you if you had just acted like a normal, pleasant human being? It wasn't any of your business who he married.'

'Oh, for God's sake! I never commented on his pathetic vagaries, I never did, it was his own guilt, projected on me. Why am I always the scapegoat? Why am I in a family that hates me?' Their voices were rising, their faces flaming. 'You always were a silly ass,' 'Spare me your dramatics.' The waiter bent over them.

'One of the patrons has asked that you perhaps continue this conversation outside?' A couple at an adjacent table studied them to see how this message was being received.

'There's no need to continue it,' said Posy rising. 'Rupert, you're the rich brother, you pay the bill.' She grabbed her coat from the wall hook and stalked out, fighting with the sleeves as she thrust through the revolving door.

At about seven, Amy's telephone rang. It was Sigrid, in California, who said, 'Jesus Christ, Amy, I'm coming over there tomorrow afternoon. My tomorrow, your today, I'll be there your Tuesday morning.'

'Why? What's the matter?' There was no mistaking the urgency in Sigrid's voice.

'You tell me! What's going on? You haven't warned me of any of this.'

'You tell me what you're talking about.'

'This lawsuit. Your insurance called me this afternoon, to say it's way outside the umbrella. Have you been served there?'

'What? No. Suing me? Why?'

'Karen Adelaide Venn suing you for battery on her husband, I haven't seen the papers, I don't know – they said for thirty million dollars!'

This seemed so outrageous that Amy couldn't take it seriously, but her stomach constricted a little anyway. 'She thinks I was Joan of Arc?'

'It's to do with moving her husband to England.'

Amy thought a minute, then displayed her legendary corporate coolness under stress, as Sigrid would later tell the story. 'I don't think I owed Venn a duty of care, I've never seen the man – I doubt that a suit like that will fly, even here. Mr Osworthy ought to worry, though, and the hospital in Moutiers.'

'Yes, but, Amy, deep pockets. You have the deep pockets.'

Oh, bother, thought Amy. Bother, bother. She had planned her day: the Musée Marmottan, then to lunch with someone who had invited her yesterday, Mademoiselle Fouquet, a docent there; and she wanted to think about Emile and other things, and now she had to think about this. Bother, bother, bother, and injustice too.

'Sigrid, don't come here yet. Let me look into it first. Was it filed? Where?' Not yet filed, no one yet served, the venue was being chosen.

'Oh, bother,' said Amy. 'I'll call you later.'

She had the telephone number of Mr Osworthy's hotel. Obviously it was this development to which he had referred yesterday, this which made Kip so uncomfortable. His sister was suing his benefactor. It was only nine o'clock, and Osworthy was still at his hotel, in the breakfast room. The desk clerk went to find him.

'Yes, true, I'm afraid,' Osworthy said. 'No good deed goes unpunished, as the saying goes. I suppose we shouldn't be surprised. We should have remembered, the litigious Americans. Oh, sorry, not you, of course. I don't have details because I'm here. Suit was evidently filed in London on the grounds that the harm was there because Venn died there. How she has been able to move so fast I can't imagine.'

'The poor woman is upset, it's not surprising that she had to strike out. She wants someone to blame. Still, what a bitch,' said Amy, only now beginning to feel outraged. They agreed she had to go see Kerry, discover who her lawyers were, and take the thing seriously. Amy repeated her opinion that she herself was not liable, but the fact hung between them that Osworthy probably was, along with the doctors, and maybe the rescue people too. At least Kerry had a good case against someone. And this was France; who knew what weird laws might obtain? Amy had an uneasy feeling – no, it was more than that; she had a powerful wish to go home. She also had again the fleeting thought that maybe it was going to be too hard to be rich, that the complications in how one had to approach life were going to be too much for her. But it was only a fleeting fear. She would be equal to it. She knew she should go see Kerry, immediately, but somehow she put it off again.

36

Géraldine Chastine was friendly, even sisterly, to Pamela Venn, and arranged several pleasant occasions for the two of them. She confessed that it was a relief to get out of her apartment, which seemed very full, what with Victoire, Nike, and Salome all there, and poor Eric, after these years of middle-aged respite, had by no means adapted to the constant presence of small children.

Today she was extremely supportive when it came to Pam's worry about Posy. Madame, at the hotel, had that morning asked Pam where Posy was. Mademoiselle had left a parcel at the desk two days ago, saying she would come back for it – had she forgotten and returned to Angleterre? This simple query had chilled Pam. Posy was an independent girl and it was not unusual for her to keep to herself, or, especially right now with the inheritance unpleasantness, to avoid her mother and Rupert. But not to have been here for two days? Even if she had met the dashing Frenchman of her dreams, she would have stopped in her room to change, or come back to sleep.

'*Non, non,*' Madame had protested, she had not been there, had checked out two days before. Pam now found herself telling Géraldine about this, emphasizing how depressed and difficult Posy had been finding this time, how flighty Posy could be, how unfamiliar with France, and Géraldine had soothed her with observations about young women in general, even when they became mothers, like Victoire, who even as they spoke was sobbing and flinging herself about at her parents' apartment like a schoolgirl, and it seemed to them leaving most of the child care to Géraldine and Eric. The two women commiserated.

'There is no reason she can't be home in her own apartment,' Géraldine complained. 'Emile is apparently not there. At first I assumed she needed moral support, but now I think it is our babysitting that keeps her with us. It is clearly not my advice and counsel! That she ignores with impunity.'

The parcel Posy had left at the desk was the oblong cardboard box containing Adrian's ashes. This horrible discovery meant that Posy had not taken them to Kerry Venn as assigned. Pam discussed with Rupert what to do, but neither of them had any ideas. Rupert took charge of the box, and pledged to take it to Kerry. Pam was concerned about Posy, to the extent of ringing Mr Osworthy, who had not seen her since the meeting in Persand's office on Monday. Nor did he have any theories.

'Posy's in a very bad mood,' Rupert reassured his mother. 'Father, and then things generally. I don't know what's getting her down, exactly. The legacy, for sure. She's just avoiding us.' There was really nothing to say against this analysis. They left a message for Posy at the hotel desk and would wait to see.

Posy continued missing. Pamela Venn was more and more worried as the days passed, and even weighed calling the widow, at her clinic, to learn if Posy had telephoned or been there. But she couldn't bring herself to. She didn't really want to talk to the new Mrs Venn, and had no concern about Posy being in real trouble, that was silly. All the same, the more she reviewed the past weeks of death and disappointment, and thought of the huge financial uncertainties ahead for both of her children, the more uneasy she became that Posy might in some way have done something impulsive – her imagination shirked thinking what. To imagine her throwing herself into the Seine was ridiculous, but there were also serial killers, traffickers in women, and incommunicado French jails, the latter only a bit less primitive in her English mind than a jail in Turkey or Argentina. There was also sudden illness – she could be lying in a French hospital, their hospitals only slightly less dangerous than their jails. Pamela didn't like to share all her real fears with Rupert, lest she be seeming to accuse him of somehow being responsible for Posy's state of mind. How difficult it was to sort out the dynamics of a family. How simple everything would have been if it hadn't been for the wretched Adrian.

Rupert, for his part, was trying to find a way to avoid selling the château. The château and press had come to seem to him his whole future, his whole life. With every passing day, in Rupert's mind, the vines became more fruitful, the one turret of Father's castle more majestic, its shallow, dried-up moat a silvery pond stocked with little fish and lilies, and the publishing business a national treasure of selfless service to the arts, the whole a monument to Father's memory and a haven for his loved ones. Rupert was fairly sure Posy was lying low to avoid discussions because she was ashamed of wanting to blight this perfect, preordained plan.

He bore in mind his mother's offer to sell her house. Was the offer still good if the house truly hadn't been registered as hers, or was that simply a detail to be straightened out? They discussed it, tentatively. The house might not have been Pam's during all this time, but if it was, she was willing to sell, she said, between strolls with Rupert around the Louvre or down the Avenue Montaigne. She knew that he would never have gone shopping with her if these issues had not meant a great deal to him, but she could not see that selling her house would help. It might cover the tax liabilities of one, maybe even both, of the children, but where would Victoire and Harry get money to pay theirs? Pamela realized that she, Posy, and Rupert would have to go back to England; Rupert had to work, and Pamela had her normal life to return to. One couldn't stay indefinitely in a French hotel, as desirable as that seemed. Pam was torn about her duty to her children and still worried about Posy – part of her said that Posy must be all right, but part was frantic.

'You'll have to take the ashes to Kerry,' she said to Rupert. 'I'm not going to do it.'

'Mr Osworthy should do it, that would be more fitting,' said Rupert. 'He's staying here, we can leave – the box – here for him.' They uneasily decided on this course.

'Have you by chance heard from your sister?' Géraldine asked Victoire after talking to Pamela. Victoire had not. For all she knew, Posy was installed somewhere with Emile, but she didn't share this concern with her mother.

Géraldine also mentioned Posy to Emile, one afternoon as he stopped by to see the children.

'They don't know where she is. She has vanished from her hotel, leaving her father's ashes with the concierge!'

Emile had no reply, but felt a twinge of concern. He was always very fond of people he had slept with. He remembered Posy's agitation and sadness in Valméri, and hoped she hadn't done anything desperate. He wondered if he should confess his role to Géraldine, who always had an accurate reading of human, especially female, nature, and would probably reassure him. But he delayed doing this, would wait a few days longer.

Despite the shadow of Kerry's lawsuit, Amy's week returned her to the normal rhythm of her Paris life. Beyond the photograph in the paper, there had been no repercussions of events in the Alps, though she could not shake the feeling that word of her money was somehow coloring the way people saw her, in Paris as in the Alps, at the sorts of occasions Géraldine was taking, or, increasingly often, sending her to, or that she was being invited to by others as her acquaintance grew – posh charity cocktails, art openings, theater. She was always going somewhere; she could never just see a movie or have a hamburger.

She also couldn't escape the feeling that despite her meek cooperativeness, Géraldine didn't approve of her. Géraldine may have liked her all right, but when it came to her clothes and hair, and to her general presentation of herself to the world, she knew she was globally unsatisfactory. Géraldine had made her have various '*soins de visage,'* and leg waxes *(jambe entière)*, though these things were hard to work into her strenuous schedule of lessons and social occasions. On her own she had tried the method she had observed Victoire using, perfume between the fingers and, her own idea, why not toes?

Amy was certainly not the first American to feel inadequate to some concept of womanhood known to the French – Tammy and Wendi had reported still having the same abashed feelings, and between them they had lived in Paris nearly forty years. Yet it seemed to Amy that when you studied them objectively, most French people looked no better than Americans, just thinner. The clothes of people on their way to work or waiting on you in shops usually were the same slightly misjudged skirts and pants and jackets, the same last year's overcoats, as Americans would wear.

In fact, Amy had begun to find that Americans also looked odd to her now, when spied on the street or overheard talking, their clothes too casual and too brightly colored. She found herself dressing with care even to go to the Monoprix, as if expecting, even hoping, to run into someone she knew. In all, she felt daunted and confused by the general issue of culture and increasingly wished to go home, though she despised herself for it. She found herself calling her parents quite often – she could tell it amazed them. But talking to her parents also had the effect of stiffening her resolve to stay, as they conjured up visions of Ukiah, SUVs, and freeways, things she didn't miss at all. Though she loved her parents, she had resolved since about the age of ten not to live like them. She could remember resolving to have an unusual life, but

when she got older, she realized she didn't have a definition of life, if only because she didn't know enough. Her
definition was forming now, now that all was possible,
and that was why she must stay.

After a week of blissful separation from familiar things,
Posy had relented and called home; once back in England,
Pamela Venn found a message from her on the answering
machine that all was well, she was travelling, and she
would be keeping in touch with Monsieur de Persand
about the legal situation. She hoped her mother had
found a parcel at the hotel, and she apologized for not
dealing with it herself. Pamela was reassured, but Rupert
had less to feel happy about. Alas, hours spent poring
over the vineyard and press accounts and talking to
bankers in both London and Paris had produced no
feasible plan for saving the château – it didn't look like a
good investment to anyone. There seemed no way to
avoid having to sell.

37

Amy was looking out from her apartment at the Seine River, a scene in monochrome gray and brown of mud-colored water and bare trees, a scene in *grisaille*, a word she had learned looking at charcoal-colored pictures in the Louvre that seemed to render accurately the actual palette of nature in wintry Europe. Perhaps the sun never shone here in March, but she told herself it didn't matter, a small price for the pleasure of acquiring a word like *grisaille*, not that she would be likely to need it.

She could look down on the very spot where she had bumped into Emile. In recent days Amy had not stopped thinking about Emile. She tried to think about him calmly, but was conscious that she couldn't. She went over and over their coffee at the Flore, regretting her rudeness and remembering everything he had said, the very words and also his tone and expression. This was a severe attack of *esprit de l'escalier*, remembering every wrong word she had uttered.

Perhaps his sudden friendliness hadn't been what she hoped for, an attraction to her person – instead, he had congratulated her on her character. She had never been congratulated for her character before, that she knew of. People usually liked each other for more visual, superficial reasons – reasons that could describe her liking for Emile. She could no longer conceal from herself that he was the only person she had met in France she really wanted to talk to, let alone go to bed with. Yes. Nor could she refuse to recognize, alas, that of all the men she had met in France, he, the man she was most drawn to, was exactly the kind of bad-news man her aunts, mother, and an immense literature of those rich-girl tragedies warned her against – married, faithless, foreign. Maybe she was having the ultimate French experience after all.

Everyone found him attractive, even French cabinet ministers, why should she be any different? And she had refused his friendship, his apology, his overture, even though it was probably nothing romantic, though he had mentioned beauty ... She wondered if he believed that beauty was an idea thought out in detail, for this was also a definition of character. Waves of self-reproach made her almost dizzy. She had mishandled every relationship – her ski instructor, the baron, and now the one she really would like to have. The way a desire, once hardened into consciousness, becomes acute, so did her hindsight condemnation of her actions. She had ruined her own life by rudeness to the one man in France she wanted, and this failure symbolized the entire failure of her enterprise here. Defeat, in fact. She would never want the things she could have, and couldn't have what she wanted, even if she knew what it was. How American, Emile would say.

As the days passed, she had been trying to cure herself of her infatuation for Emile – for such she had come to call it – by thinking about his relentless, rather ignorant criticism of Americans, based on no knowledge, and about his suspicious knowledge of enlightened social thinkers like Kropotkin. Was he a communist? Not a category of person Amy had ever personally met, as they didn't exist in northern California, though of course there were Marxists at the numerous local universities, just as there were deconstructionists and new historicists – it depended on when you went to graduate school. But if he were a communist, he probably wouldn't be in this conservative French government.

Well, she didn't need to try to understand French politics, an impossibility, just as it was impossible to believe in French religious superstitions. She had heard that people were being taken to see the spot in Valméri where Joan of Arc had stood.

She had called Paul-Louis for the latest Joan news, and he'd told her that more than one hundred eighty people had now made the chilly trip by Sno-Cat, twenty-five euros each, an optional excursion they were offering at the Ecole de Ski Française. The saint herself had not been seen again.

She also called Joe Daggart. He had no news of Joan of Arc, but reported in a friendly way that a German town was petitioning to be rid of its American air base, citing the Alpine avalanches as evidence of their claims that the noise of American C-5 Galaxies had ruined their lives.

'Valméri is not on the normal flight path for those planes,' Joe said. 'But we don't know everything yet.'

Despite her belief that she was in no legal jeopardy, Amy was also unsettled by the daily phone calls from Sigrid, and now from the firm of San Francisco lawyers to whom her legal problems had been referred, affirming that Kerry's lawsuit had indeed been filed; they were talking to their overseas colleagues about who should represent her in France, if she insisted on staying there, instead of prudently skipping.

'Come home, Amy. With the changing world situation, we'd all feel better if you just came home.'

However she decided about that, perhaps she should accede to Géraldine's suggestions and cut her hair. She had not cut it since high school, since she had learned to braid it by looking behind her in a mirror. Her long pigtail suited her, she had always thought, and people had always affirmed. She had done other things Géraldine had hinted must be done to achieve a soignée perfection – for instance a sort of sandpaper massage, *gommage,* so like their word for damage: *dommage.* Géraldine was usually right about everything, so maybe Amy should listen to her about her hair.

She didn't think her plans were working. She didn't feel more cultivated and wise, though her skiing had improved in Valméri. She could make cream soups but would never speak French. The thought of home continued to draw her, and the negatives of staying outweighed the positives. A. in little more than a month she had found herself in legal jeopardy, B. she had contributed to a death, C. her heart was broken, or soon would be, D. she had no one to talk to, really, and was not making progress in those skills that had formerly seemed so desirable, or at least these were turning out to be nothing she couldn't learn at home. She herself was the same! She didn't feel herself to have changed. Still, would you know if you had changed, or was change a more insidious process imperceptible to the subject of it? She hoped she might have changed a tiny bit ... Yes, she would go home. And she would go see Kerry.

Once these courses of action were definitively decided, her heart lifted with an almost jubilant sense of relief. She would have a huge party – let Géraldine figure out how to do it – throw around a lot of money and leave, and never have to think about *grisaille* and *gouache* again, or, better yet, would have permanently acquired these useful art terms and lots of other terms and upgraded her skiing by quite a lot, and these would stand her in good stead forever. Nothing was a waste! Yet she knew that underneath her happiness at having taken a decision lay a core of misery, perhaps the most intense – and nearly the only – misery that she had experienced, life till now having given her little to complain of. Was she at last in the crucible of pain that would forge for her a fine, perceptive character, an infinite understanding – maturity? Well, she hoped so – she hoped this misery, this feeling of being close to tears at any minute, would net some benefit.

For Posy it was a time of heady delight. Days ago, after the scene with Rupert and Mr Osworthy, Posy and Robin had crept off for a few days in a slightly dingy hotel near the Gare du Nord until they could take up an invitation from Bette Maricheval at her country place. After Bette's, they had spent a few days at a sweet, ivy-covered auberge in Normandy. Now they were back in Paris, fulfilling an oath Posy had taken to perform a reverence at the tomb of Napoleon. Maisie de Contelanne, off to the country, had loaned them her apartment for the rest of the week, a luxurious place in the sixteenth arrondissement, where the maid was circumspect and let them sleep late – and nap impulsively. Otherwise it was a little desultory sightseeing or a social engagement in the evening. Robin's French acquaintance was nearly as wide as his English one, and he rather enjoyed the reactions when he turned up with a Miss Venn. It had begun to dawn on him that the hostesses weren't entirely pleased at the addition of Posy, but at least he had the fun of astonishing them.

'I have been coming to Paris since my schooldays, and yet I've never been here,' he remarked now, his face pensive, looking at Posy. How beautiful she is, he was thinking, so fresh and high-colored, so blooming, the epitome of the girl to tumble between the hedgerows, if hedgerows there had been in the seventh arrondissement of Paris. If he could not quite separate her from his notion of her family's château, it was because his idea of her as châtelaine was so stirring. She would know about gardens, about roses – two subjects he had already worked on with distinction. His lines on the rose were widely quoted. He and Posy of course would not live in a castle but in a cottage, and also in his flat off Kensington Road. He saw her warming milk, arranging flowers in a simple blue jug, the scene presenting itself to his imagination as if painted by Matisse in primary blues, reds, and yellows. So much younger! Eventually, her appetites would exceed his, if they didn't already. Never mind, it was possible that by blooming late, desire would last longer, like autumn chrysanthemums or asters.

'Oh, Robin,' Bette Maricheval had rebuked him at her drinks party on the Wednesday. 'I knew in my heart you'd choose an English rose eventually. As a *française* and as a hostess, I cannot but be disappointed with you. In fact I had already made a cross over you. He is lost, I told myself.' She smiled at Posy to show she didn't mean to be rude to her. 'I didn't even think of you for the Longchamps party you used to love so much . . .'

Robin too clearly had seen that his French circle was going to dwindle; for an instant he weighed the relative merits of *la vie mondaine* on the Continent and the domestic comforts of England, and had no question but that the latter were preferable, but anyway why should the French not also love his comely girl in her charming flowered dress, and – he knew, if they didn't – underneath, her red lace bra and suspenders?

So handsome, though thin, Posy was saying to herself. He's got to gain weight, needs some taking care of. They say he has a good chance of being poet laureate next time round. Posy loved to look at Robin thinking. She had been surprised by the transformative power of love, no matter whom you loved, evidently, since she could just barely remember being in love with Emile a few days ago. By love itself she was transformed, and the transformation in her perception of Robin had been sudden, too, almost like one of those electronically generated images on a police screen, his face morphing from thin and a bit older to handsome, sensitive, and in his prime. Never mind about Emile. Perhaps being in love with one man makes you more receptive to the next? Perhaps love is just a state of vulnerability, or receptivity, as in newborn ducklings. Is receptivity the same as 'the rebound'? No matter, she could see the healthy side of it, for the feeling was the same, of intense joy at being with the loved one, and unreserved admiration. By means of this emotion, she would be suddenly transformed into a good person, joined to a man whose work commanded admiration, and in English, thank heavens. Whatever the role of desire in her now almost forgotten feeling for Emile, her feeling for Robin included desire and was more intellectually involving. So there.

She was performing a promised pilgrimage to Napoleon's tomb, Napoleon, wise author of the law that had provided for her over Father's wishes. Gazing down on the *tombeau* of the emperor, she could not but think of Father's ashes, back at that hotel, and of how she had shirked the unpleasant, sad task of delivering them to his wife. She knew she was dilatory but so much had intervened, and Rupert could jolly well do it. Besides, ashes weren't Father, they were just matter, inert powder, the very enemy and opposite of life and memory.

There was a similarity in some ways, Posy was thinking, between Father and Napoleon. They were probably the same height, and Father had had a rather Napoleonic optimism, daring and restless. Maybe that sort of character wasn't such a bad thing. She felt a surge of forgiveness for Father, a feeling of love, along with the realization that she took after him. Had they cremated Napoleon or was he actually buried here? She thought idly of how suitable it would be to sprinkle Father's ashes here, on Napoleon's tomb, if only she hadn't left them for Rupert.

Amy, lost in thought, was also making her way to the Musée de l'Armée. Having decided to go back to

California, she felt an urgent need to see all the things she should, as if they were to be denied her forever, and she had arranged to meet a friend of Géraldine's for a special guided visit through the historic cannons, and the Thursday lecture on Austerlitz.

Paradoxically, her new interest in French history had been animated by a rising interest in American history. It was as if, having decided to go home, something told her she'd better learn where it was she was going. She had gone to see the grave of Lafayette, and the small version of the Statue of Liberty, for she had never seen the big one in New York. She had gone to two American museums, and gazed at rather limp displays of tarnished Revolutionary uniforms, three-cornered hats, small purses worn by the ladies of Jefferson's time, battered flags, and canteens carried by the soldiers of the First World War. These items didn't stir her very much, but she did feel a surge of patriotism that such a mighty country should have bloomed from such meager ingredients.

'Bunjer,' said someone next to her as she stopped at the corner at a red light.

She looked over to see embarrassingly dressed people, their fat bodies, plaid pants, and sneakers marking them unmistakably as Americans. But the strange iteration, bunjer, might be some other language altogether.

'Bunjer. Bunjer Bunjer.' They were looking at her. Why? She resolutely refused eye contact in case they were Americans after all. When they had moved on, she heard the woman say, 'See, they are so arrogant and rude, she can't be bothered. It's like everybody says. They hate Americans, as if they didn't have a stupid little socialist country here where lots of people don't even have cars.'

Shame shot through her. Oh, my God, Amy thought, they are talking to me, they are saying *bonjour*. They think I'm French and that I've been a typical rude French person! 'Oh, excuse me,' she ran after them to say. It wouldn't be fair to let them think ill of the French on account of her own behavior! 'I was just so lost in thought, I didn't hear you speak to me.'

They stared, embarrassed in their turn to have been overheard by this French person who obviously spoke English perfectly well, almost like an American, and who – it was dawning on them – actually *was* another American.

'Can I help you?' Amy asked. 'I live around here . . .'

When they had chatted a few minutes and she had oriented them, Amy went on her way, only by chance seeing Emile Abboud stepping into a taxi outside the Invalides. He saw her see him, and gave a little wave. Her heart lurched. Probably he had observed the whole encounter and thought these fat people were her best friends. One's countrymen are always a humiliation for the traveler, whatever the country, but this was especially bad. It appeared there was to be no end to her mortifications. If only she knew what her crime had been. Ah, but that was American for sure, not to know your crime.

She was used to the fact that tourists in Paris, congregating at a handful of monuments, are apt to run into each other, so she was not too surprised to find herself facing Robin Crumley and Posy Venn across the round pit where the poor emperor was entombed, like her gazing down on his nested coffins. She was somewhat surprised, though, to see them together. Like Emile, they waved, and after a few minutes she walked around to where they were. They had been holding hands, she noted, but unlaced their hands and embraced her joyfully, and asked for an account of her week.

'We've been in Normandy. I'm sorry I didn't go to the party at Victoire's mother's, but I didn't feel like it,' Posy said. 'Wasn't feeling well, I mean.'

'It was very nice, of course,' Amy said. 'Lots of French people, but since I can't speak a word, practically ...' They agreed on the charm of being Anglo-Saxons with no French people present, the three of them now chattering on in English with no feeling of shame.

Posy's eyes fell on the book Amy carried. She carried it everywhere, to read on buses. 'I see you are reading *The Red and the Black*,' said Posy. 'It's so unbelievably French, don't you think? Even reading it in English. An absolute celebration of hypocrisy.'

'I was always afraid it was an American specialty,' Amy admitted. She was above feeling stung by Posy's noticing she wasn't reading in French.

Amy noticed that Posy and Robin seemed on very good terms. Posy tugged on Robin's arm and looked up at him to affirm this or that statement. They all exchanged cell phone numbers.

When Robin and Posy had gone, Amy stayed awhile to meditate at the tomb of Napoleon on the themes of history, and whether it was wise to be too mindful of it. Were you indeed condemned to repeat horrible mistakes if you didn't keep history in mind? At the moment, she felt that whatever her country was involved in now, and her ancestors had done back then, made no difference, for they had no power to lighten her feeling of isolation and self pity, emotions so new to her that she had no reflexes for dealing with them – unlike people who were used to them, and might take brisk walks. Though both Napoleon's own history and the apparent conjunction of Robin and Posy pointed to fortune's tendency to change rapidly, either for the good or the bad, Amy derived no intimation from the inert bronzes entombing forever the once vital emperor, that hers would change any further and that she would not remain forever just shy of personal happiness.

Robin and Posy were invited to the de Ditraisons' for a cocktail buffet. Madame de Ditraison had mentioned to Robin how pleased they would all be if he read a few of his poems aloud before dinner, preferably some of his translations from the French. Robin was accustomed, as he said, to singing for his supper, and would be happy to oblige. He was no more unwilling than any other poet to read aloud.

Now, in the drawing room, all gilt and white paint – rather overdone, in her view – Posy listened, her mood a confusion of affection, admiration for Robin, and a deep wish to escape, though there would be no escape, there would be dinner.

She was oppressed by how patronizingly the French ladies had praised her flowered dress, saying, 'How English!' 'How like a garden!' *J'adore* Laura Ashley,' 'How original,' and several other such comments.

She was also oppressed by the poem Robin was reading, a translation from Beaudelaire to do with seeing a female corpse by the side of the road being picked at by crows. No doubt it was a meditation on mortality, but still, like mortality, it was revolting:

'Yes, such shall you be, O queen of heavenly grace,
Beyond the last sacrament,
When through your bones the flowers and sucking grass
Weave their rank cerement,'

intoned Robin to the attentive, well-dressed people standing around with glasses of champagne.

Well, ugh, thought Posy, but it was wonderful how Robin's light voice had picked up authority and sonorance as he read. The French people nodded with solemn concentration, determined to discern the Frenchness of the old poem in its new guise of clumsy English words.

'How delicious,' said Madame de Ditraison as he finished, 'and now, some dinner!'

Posy could only dart imploring glances at Robin during dinner, as she was seated between two Frenchmen who twinkled at her in turn in the friendliest way, but gave up after their first moments of gallantly speaking English to her. She tried to think of a French phrase or two to bring herself back in, but lines of French poetry were all that came to her.

'Où sont les neiges d'antan?' she said to Monsieur Brikel on her right, hoping he would take it as bringing up the subject of Villon. But he simply looked astonished and turned to the French lady on his other side.

'Ah, *nos amis les Anglais,*' said Monsieur Requart on the other side.

Perhaps Robin, too, felt, even if for the first time, this sense of estrangement with his *amis* the French, for as they walked home, he said, 'Posy, we should think of the future.' Posy agreed without reflection, and later, upon reflecting, found that everything she thought about the future was better than it had been.

Kip was permitted to visit a parent figure until eleven P.M. two nights a week, so tonight Amy had invited him to go to a movie and have dinner. Though they spoke often on the phone, she wanted to reassure him in person that she was not blaming him for the behavior of his sister, and she also just sort of wanted to see him, a familiar face, a companionable American, though young.

He still had the reserved air he had worn since Géraldine's party, owing, Amy now understood, to Kerry's lawsuit, which still embarrassed him. Amy planned to bring it up, to reassure him, saying she wasn't worrying about it, her lawyers were confident, and so on. All this was true. Whatever Kerry's case against the hospitals, it was weak against Amy. She also had to tell him she was leaving Paris for California, soon. She worried about this, because Kip depended on her, and seemed to be fond of her, hardly surprising with the poor boy so alone in the world.

'What do you want? *Croque-madame?* That's what you usually have. Something different?'

'*Croque-madame,*' Kip agreed.

'We need to talk about what will happen to you. I'm going back to California soon. Do you want to come back with me, and go to your old school next semester? Do you want to stay here? You'd have to learn French and the whole bit if you stayed.'

'Why are you going? I thought you were staying for a while, you've got an apartment and everything.'

'Oh, I think it's time for me to move on, and get on with my life.' Amy smoothed her napkin *(serviette)*.

'It's Kerry's lawsuit, isn't it? That is so fucked.'

'Not your fault! Anyhow, that's not why I'm going. It's because, I don't know, I'm an American, so that's where I ought to live. And I have my foundation, I want to get started with that ...' She couldn't tell him the other reason – why burden a person of his age with an intimation of erotic and intellectual setbacks to come?

'It isn't Kerry so much as her lawyers,' Kip said. 'They're making her do it.'

'I know,' said Amy, though she wondered why Kerry had gotten new lawyers when after all she had had Mr Osworthy; and who were the new lawyers? Sigrid knew.

'I don't think they should have had a service for Adrian without Kerry,' Kip said.

'Did they? I don't actually know. Just the cremation, probably. Wouldn't they be waiting till your sister was well enough?'

'Kerry wanted to talk at it, but they did it without her. I would have talked too. About how he was. Adrian was nice. He was nice to me. I feel really sad for him.'

'Mmm, I'm sure he was nice.'

'He was funny, he made you laugh. He made French dishes – cassoulet and some kind of French pot roast. Kerry can't cook worth um – anything. I wish you wouldn't go!'

'I know. I have mixed feelings,' Amy admitted.

'What I wish is you would buy the fucking château, Amy. You're supposed to have all this money, why wouldn't you like a nice French château? That's what rich people are supposed to buy.'

'Right, just what I need, a French château.' Amy laughed, shocked that he should know she was – well off, though of course she was.

'Anyway, it'd be cool. I could come there at Christmas, you know, summers. You could have a horse.'

'I don't want a horse.'

'What's it like to be rich, anyhow?' Kip wondered.

Amy thought about it. She didn't know. She hadn't really faced her mixed feelings of guilt and pleasure or the duties she saw were coming. She had been trying to behave as though everything was the same. Running away to Europe had been part of her escape. She quickly changed the subject – they caught up with Kip's news as if Amy were family. How was Harry? How was Kerry's recovery? She was sorry to learn that Kerry would never walk correctly.

'You should go see her, Amy. No one goes but me. Rupert and Posy haven't been out there at all, or anyone but Mr Osworthy. Mademoiselle Walther has gone back to Valméri – there's some new nurse, Farad, and Harry misses Mademoiselle Walther. He'd be glad to see you too. Harry has feelings like everybody else.'

'You don't always need to lecture me, I'll go,' Amy said. 'I know I should.'

In the night, she had one of those moments of dream clarity that rise to consciousness as you are waking up. The complete plan occurred to her as if she had thought of it herself, a solution so perfectly in accord with her inner wishes and social principles, a textbook example of mutual aid so obvious, that she wondered why it hadn't occurred to her sooner, and to everyone. Well, it had occurred to Kip. It was he who had suggested she should buy the château. Well, depending on the price. This would accomplish a number of ends: she would let Rupert run his press, and Victoire do whatever she wanted to do there, and Posy would get her share of the money, and little Harry could scamper in the grounds and corridors, not that she knew if it would have corridors.

Further advantages swirled in her head: the publishing business, a huge tax write-off. With luck the publishing business could pay the overhead, though a profit was unlikely – she'd look at the books – so there would be no ongoing expense ... Kerry – it would be stipulated – would withdraw her lawsuit against her, which didn't have much chance of succeeding anyhow, in return for this haven for her child.

The château, at a couple of million euros, was miles cheaper than many, if not most, houses in Palo Alto, California, it was even grotesquely cheap – and who has not dreamed of a château? The idea was archetypically alluring. She would take a tower suite for herself, for when she visited – she hoped there would be towers, perhaps a moat. Of course she would go down to see it, but her mind, she knew, was fixed in advance, there was almost no need to. Then, they could market some products, maybe a line of cosmetics made from grapes, or dishes with a crest. She would visit from time to time, an annual write-off trip to France, the prospect of which sweetened the idea of going back home, and almost lightened the anguish of her silly crush on Emile Abboud, and her general feeling of having been defeated by France, two subjects somehow connected.

38

The Clinique Marianne occupied a couple of hectares of the forest between Saint-Cloud and Versailles, in an imposing nineteenth-century house and stables, with a circular drive and very secure hedges to confine those of its inmates who needed confinement. Halfway between a madhouse and a luxurious spa, it had served the drying out, the breaking down, the tired, at a price, for a hundred and fifty years. Amy took a taxi from the end of the RER line, with some feeling of trepidation at finally meeting Kerry Venn under awkward circumstances. She reproached herself that if she had been normally, responsibly, civil and gone to see Kerry in the beginning, she might have headed off this lawsuit. Now it was too late to pretend to be paying a concerned call on her countrywoman as she should in decency have already done.

Evidently it was not madness that accounted for Kerry's long stay here, for the woman at the desk in the foyer indicated that Kerry would be found in the garden with her baby, through that door, unconfined and no doubt pleased to receive visitors. Amy wandered out into an extensive garden, somewhat shabby at this season, with some new pansies just put in, and the gardener's implements stacked on the steps.

At the bottom of the garden, across a stretch of the bare, impacted earth that Amy had learned was included in the French idea of a garden, she saw a thin, tallish woman with a toddler – Harry, if she was not mistaken – pushing a wheeled toy. The woman, Kerry, was strangely lopsided, one shoulder higher than the other, and her legs twisted oddly. How horrible! On the train she had been sitting down, so Amy had not noticed this. Had she always been handicapped? But no, she'd been out skiing.

She approached, thinking maybe she should just pretend she hadn't heard about the lawsuit yet. 'Hello!' Amy had learned that her own person was nonthreatening, benign, and was usually met with smiles, so she was surprised when Kerry looked unwelcoming and dour. 'I'm Amy Hawkins. We met on the train? I'm very late in paying you a visit, I'm afraid. I hope Kip has given you my good wishes? He is such a nice boy, we've become friends . . .'

'Yes, he's mentioned you.'

'Harry too,' feeling thankful that Harry had seen her and was running over to her with a big smile and his little arms outstretched. She bent over to give him a kiss, genuinely thrilled that he seemed happy to see her, though she knew it was probably because all his experiences with her had been food-related. Amy's affection for Harry didn't erase the expression of hostility on Kerry's face. Now Amy saw that Kerry was bandaged around the middle under her loose blouse, and one of her legs was stiffish, so that when she moved to pick Harry up, she listed to the side, and she seemed to be in pain.

'Do you have someone to help with him while you're getting better?' She picked him up.

'Yes, there's a woman who comes in.'

'How long do they say . . . ?'

'They say I'll always walk like this. Unless I have some operations in the future.'

'Do you have enough' – Amy thought of things Kerry might need – 'books, things to read? I can go the English bookshop. Tell me what you'd like.'

'I know you're here because of the lawsuit. I suppose you want me to drop it,' Kerry said. Perhaps embarrassed at her confrontational tone, she turned away. Amy tried to think of the right thing to say. She couldn't deny, of course, that she wanted Kerry to drop the lawsuit. But that was not altogether it. She was filled with sympathy and chagrin about her own bad behavior, and horror at the power of the snow that had battered this woman's body, taken her husband, left her in this state.

'Of course I'd prefer that,' Amy agreed, 'but I understand the legal situation. I really just came to see how you and Harry were – to pay a call.'

'Do you know anything about my situation?' Kerry asked, and without waiting for an answer began volubly to explain about what Adrian's horrible children were doing to her, the sealing of the château, inventories. 'In France, the spouse is just dirt, the children are everything, but all Harry gets, basically, is a lot of taxes and debt. This is a police state that decides what happens to a person's money. I'm not allowed in my own house.' Amy had not heard any of this. It was clear that Kerry included Amy in the list of people who were harming her.

'Briggs, Rigby, Denby, Fox, say I have a huge case.'

Amy did not utter the retorts that occurred to her, but she could not keep from a reproving tone. 'You must feel lucky to be alive,' she said. She was rather shocked by Kerry's not feeling her good luck along with her disappointments.

'Oh, sure. I feel that St Joan was looking after me. How can I not feel that? She must have been the one that called the rescue team. A woman called them to dig us out. Someone who saw where we were buried. Of course I feel the miracle of that.'

Amy now noticed that Kerry was wearing a religious medal, presumably St Joan – had Kerry become a crazy votary of Joan of Arc? She tried again for a mollifying tone.

'I wanted to discuss something with you. My idea is to buy the château, that is, your château, but then make it available so you and Harry could live there, and the others.' She went on to explain her plans for the château, the press, the vineyard.

'Oh please! Get real! I'd have to be crazy to live with Adrian's children. Look what they're doing to me! I truly don't give a shit what happens to them, or the press, or the vineyard, I'd like to live in my own house, yes. We'll see, when the suit goes to court.' Amy had been about to apologize for her role in sending Venn to London, but thought of what Sigrid would advise and didn't. She couldn't resist saying, with asperity, 'I'm afraid you don't have much of a case, but time will tell,' and taking her leave as quickly as she could, shocked at how wrong her idea of Kerry had been. How odd that Kip should love this disagreeable woman! As she calmed down, though, she tried to imagine how she would feel in Kerry's shoes.

*

The same night, Géraldine took Amy, Wendi, and Tammy to the *Comédie Française*. Alas, the play was in French, but Amy bore up, dreaming of one day being like the two other American women, who apparently were able to follow the words. As it was, her inability to understand forced her back into her own thoughts, which had been increasingly restless and disturbed anyway. Behind the rhythmic declamations of *Phèdre*, a chorus of self-reproaches took the stage of her consciousness: meddling with Mr Venn's medical fate; not applying herself at French; being rude to Emile Abboud; being slow to visit Kerry Venn; possibly starting an avalanche ... Her self-reproach about her rudeness to Emile was the sharpest among these faults.

At her French teacher's insistence, she had been reading (in English) Stendhal, *The Red and the Black,* one of their seminal texts, she had been told. She found it slow going, and didn't really like reading novels anyway, but she had been struck by one of the characters, Madame de Renal, saying something like 'Poor me, I am rich, but what good does it do me?' At first Amy had thought Mademoiselle de Renal stupid and selfish not to be happy when she had so much to be happy about, and inwardly directed her to perform charitable activities. But was it so easy? Here she, Amy, was, living her dream and not happy, and not knowing why.

Other things gave Amy the feeling she was living in Stendhal's novel. For instance, Géraldine, beside her at the play, had been unhappy earlier for a reason that had seemed to Amy very French, though she could not have said why. Just as in the novel, where the heroine Mathilde had made her mother go to the opera 'despite the unsuitable position of the box which a humble hanger-on of the family had offered them,' so a friend of Géraldine's, the director of the play, was to have left tickets for them at the box office, but when they got there, no tickets had been laid aside for them. Géraldine expostulated, and Tammy and Wendi didn't seem to think she was making a scene, though Amy shrank.

'There must be a mistake. Look again. "Madame Chastine ..." Go, then, and find Mr Elias. I talked with him only this morning ...' But Mr Elias could not be found. There were no seats left, except perhaps in the distant *balcon*.

'It is not possible to sit in the *balcon*,' Géraldine fumed. 'Someone might see us.'

Literature was a guide to life. In the end they did sit in the balcony, but Amy could still sense the warmth of Géraldine's indignation radiating around her, and since anyone would be embarrassed at having invited friends and then not having tickets, there was nothing specifically French about this that she could put her finger on ... But she herself would not have chosen such an issue, seating arrangements, to focus unhappiness on. Her own incipient misery was more intrinsic.

After the play, at supper, Géraldine partly apologized for having put them through a scene and given them bad seats to boot. She explained that the reason for her unusual testiness had been, as usual, Victoire. Tammy and Wendi nodded, from long experience of hearing about Victoire's woes. The separation of Victoire and Emile was apparently not going to be complicated either by Emile or

Victoire with any of those discussions, second thoughts, and outbursts of emotion that usually characterize breakups. Fait accompli, it seemed.

'Perhaps it is some idea of kismet in Emile's North African background,' Géraldine said. She was exasperated with both of them for not trying harder to stay together. 'In America you have marriage counselors. I hope the idea will catch on here. I would pay for them to see someone like that, but both of them, separately, refuse. He comes by, he telephones, he takes the children out, but he makes no effort to patch things up, and neither does Victoire. If she knows he's coming over, she leaves. And now I think he's back in their apartment, so she won't go home.'

'It's the money,' Wendi guessed. 'She feels more independent since her inheritance. She knows she doesn't have to put up with what she had to before.'

'She hasn't got the money! Not until the chalet is sold, and she owes more than three hundred thousand euros into the bargain, and rather soon. The government is *impitoyable*. I fear that she just can't deal with his condescending attitude anymore. Even I, who adore him, can see he treats her as if she were the dumbest girl walking. To say nothing of his womanizing ... he is a *cavaleur impénitant*.'

Amy was alert to these revelations. Géraldine described Emile as an unrepentant *cavaleur*, which Amy at first supposed to be a reference to his horsemanship, a strange objection for Victoire to hold. But she quickly understood that this was not what was meant, and made a mental note to look it up, though as a metaphor it was rather obvious.

'Victoire is far too romantic, and she understands

nothing about men. But I think that's only part of it,' Géraldine went on. 'She is in love with the idea of living in Provence with these English people, her new brother and sister, in Adrian Venn's château. She talks of it as her real home, as if she had never been happy with Eric and me. After all Eric has meant to her. He feels it keenly . . .'

Wendi and Tammy, being American, tended to side with Victoire. They, too, maintained that a modern woman should not have to bear such provocations as Emile offered her; Victoire – so principled, so adorable, so contrary – was right to stick up for herself at last, and to maintain her self-respect. Emile, incorrigible womanizer even though a rising figure in the French pantheon, was no one to be married to. 'Better to have him as a "friend" than a husband,' Wendi said. 'Victoire is simply in the wrong position.'

'She should just tell him to shove it,' Tammy summed it up. 'She's so beautiful, she'll find someone else right away, just like you did, don't forget.' Amy could see that Géraldine did not like to be reminded of the unpleasant episode in her past, the conception of Victoire.

As the women nattered philosophically on, Amy saw one thing clearly, to her great discredit: She could see that she had been actively hoping for the interesting, handsome Emile and the romantic Victoire to split up. Just now, she had been holding her breath listening to Géraldine talk about it, because of the way she herself was horribly drawn to him. It was wrong to ill-wish his marriage, of course. She felt torn between self-reproach and wanting to enter the discussion, to go on talking about him, to make a kind of claim on him by pronouncing his name.

'Emile has his defects, but he is amusing,' went on Géraldine, 'and I'm sure in private, very amusing. Of course Victoire does not say. I so wish Victoire would be more, I don't know, more calculating.'

Did women have a right to expect men to be amusing? The idea had never before occurred to Amy. Was this a French idea? American men were expected to be strong, responsible, and solvent, certainly, and sensitivity had been urged on them in recent years, and the ability to talk about their feelings, something Amy had reservations about. When people talked about their feelings, others were bored. Such talk also encouraged egotism and violated the tenets of mutual aid in some way she had not examined. No, she preferred men to talk about subjects, not subjectivity, and she preferred to talk about subjects herself. Amy blamed women for the gap that seemed to exist between male and female conversation. It was women's fault, she had always believed, that men usually reserved their talk about interesting subjects for other men. Still, these women were talking about a very interesting subject, Emile.

'I know one thing,' said Géraldine, when Tammy and Wendi had said good-night. 'Anglo-Saxons are very *complexée* about being female. We all feel the superiority of women to men, *bien sûr* – what heroines we are really – but, why worry so much about it? All that agony about motherhood, and whether to work or stay home – not you, Amy. But Americans in general, et *les Anglaises aussi*. Not so much the Swedes . . . I have seen it time and again.

Luckily Tammy and Wendi have been here long enough to overcome most of their role conflicts, but it is amazing how their reflexes have stayed *américaine*.'

As Amy walked home across the Louvre with Géraldine, she brought up the subject of the château, at first saying she might know someone who wanted to buy some property in the French countryside, would Victoire's be suitable?

'I told my friends I could go down and look at it. Where is it? Is there a train?' asked Amy.

'I'll find out,' Géraldine said, not taken in by Amy's talk of the American friend.

'In fact, it's me,' Amy added, recognizing Géraldine's comprehension, and anyway not given to lies. 'It makes a certain sense – I would love to have some French property, I could come stay in the summers. And the Venns could run their press there, all the things they wanted to do.' She outlined to Géraldine the nature of her thoughts on this.

'You should certainly see it, but it might be a bit more than you want to chew off. Is that the American expression?' Géraldine did not seem overcome with pleasure. Amy had thought she would be pleased.

'Yes, we bite off more than we can chew,' Amy said.

'Yes,' said Géraldine. 'These leaky old places . . .' Her heart speeded up with anxiety as she realized how Amy's plan would mean that Victoire would have even less reason to reconcile with Emile. She weighed the duty of a loyal mother – was it to help Victoire, or to impede Victoire? – according to Géraldine's idea of Victoire's own good, and decided her higher duty was to discourage

426

Victoire from any harebrained scheme involving the Venns, the château, anglophone play-groups, and the rest. But of course this meant that Amy must not get involved. And for Amy's own good too. These leaky old places, shaky collaborations with basically unknowable English people, and even if she booted the Venns and the press out, she'd be stuck with a drafty ruin, no doubt in bad repair, much too large and so on. Géraldine didn't know Venn's château but had experience with the general category. She ventured a couple of these ideas, but Amy was carried away with the reasonableness, even brilliance, of it all.

'Of course there will be terms. For example, Rupert would buy into the press, I'd be the partner. The vineyard – I'll have to see. I'm a good businesswoman, this isn't philanthropy. I'd make it pay.'

Géraldine agreed, against her heart, to telephone Antoine de Persand and find out what Amy must do next. She made haste to call Persand the next morning, and was given the name of the *notaire*, a Maître Lepage, and of Monsieur Delamer, the man who ran the vineyard, who would make arrangments for Amy's visit. Persand thought it all sounded like a perfect example of American acquisitiveness and fecklessness, qualities he didn't totally object to, but was wary of. He had a more serious objection.

'I'll organize it, but frankly, I'm sorry to see all these fine old places pass into the hands of foreigners. Especially anglophones. The English already own half of southern France, and now the Americans coming in droves. These disastrous tax policies ...' Géraldine listened patiently while he ranted a bit on dissuasive French tax policies that obliged legitimate heirs to sell to foreign opportunists, and pointed out that he might himself soon be in a position to influence positively some aspect of the tax situation he deplored. He hoped he would.

Amy would go down on Wednesday; Maître Lepage would make a hotel reservation if she wished to stay the night, since the château was not heated at the moment and the water turned off, so there was no question of staying there.

Now in a flurry of meddlesome anxiety (the adjective was her own), Géraldine made other phone calls seeking support for her general belief that Amy should not buy Venn's château. She had some misgivings about obstructing Victoire's hopes, and in some ways believed that her daughter would find a happy way of life beyond marriage, if that was how it was to be. She could not entirely judge the depth of Victoire's rage at her husband, but she could see that Victoire was not happy staying at home with her and Eric – had regressed, was dependent, fretful, and restless, so unlike her.

Nor had Victoire revealed to her mother what the final straw had been that broke her patience with Emile. Géraldine assumed it was infidelity, maybe one too many infidelities, which Victoire's pride would not let her mention.

'It was so many things, Maman. Today's woman is not like your generation . . .' For Victoire to begin in this irritating way with a reference to her age would vex Géraldine and blight whatever confidential mood she had hoped for. Yet she was sure that Victoire loved Emile, and, if things could be ironed out, would return to him. He remained inscrutable, didn't appear to have found a new partner or to be looking, was infallibly sunny when he came to see the girls, and in general seemed a little more uxorious than when they had been together. She was sure this was his way of demonstrating his hope that all would be well between him and Victoire eventually.

First she telephoned Pamela Venn. Was Pamela in favor of Amy's scheme? She was disappointed in Pamela's passive acceptance: 'Oh, Americans are always dreaming of castles, their own country is quite poor in them. English castles are always being dismantled and carted off. But when it comes to the financing, and the actual disadvantages of the plumbing, most have second thoughts. On the whole, I think it's wonderful that there's a buyer for the place,' Pam said. 'Is something wrong with it?'

'She doesn't plan on evicting the children. She'd lease it back to them on good terms, or let them use it if they take care of it. Or they make some business arrangement by which they are part owners . . . I'm not sure. My own fear is that having the money will make it easier for Victoire to leave Paris, she will never see the folly of leaving her husband, the children fatherless . . . but I suppose that is not to look at the big picture.'

'How generous! I think it's a quite remarkable chance.'

'She sees herself as a sort of savior, Joan of Arc or something . . .' Géraldine's voice could not conceal her disapproval and concern.

'I know that Posy just wants the money. Rupert? I

don't really see him as a publisher, but I would never tell him he shouldn't try, if she offers to let him. That would be wonderful.' Pam thought Rupert very well situated in the City, and realized the contradiction of hating to lose him to the same life in southern France she had found pleasant enough when she was married to Adrian.

Others had other observations. Tammi and Wendy thought it was a lot for a woman alone to take on, Amy would come to see it that way, and so on, but in the face of what was mostly mild approval of Amy's plan, Géraldine felt isolated in her disapproval, and, after some reflection, made two further phone calls, first to Emile.

'I'd welcome your advice, *mon grand*. I've told you of Victoire's latest dream, wanting to live in the country with her new siblings and so on. Venn's château must be sold, she will have a share. But you know all this. My concern is that my American friend Amy now wants to buy it and give it back to them to let everyone do as they please in it, the brother would run the publishing, the widow and baby would live there, and so on.

'But I cannot see that it would be a good idea, not that it is up to me. I'm thinking of Amy, of course, of protecting her from this impulse – for impulse it must be; it was suggested to her by the young boy. I know nothing about her finances, but – but you also know how much I hope that Victoire will see sense where your marriage is concerned, something far less likely if she leaves Paris and takes the children off down south – it just sounds like a terrible idea for everyone concerned.'

'I'm afraid I have no influence with either my wife or *l'Américaine*,' said Emile. 'In fact, they both think ill of me. The American has no particular reason to think well of me, but it's rather a more wounding attitude from one's wife.'

'I'm sure she would listen to you,' Géraldine said. 'Telephone her. Just explain to her it's haunted, or needs a new roof, it can't be in her best interests to buy it, a single woman.'

The other phone call was to Otto von Schteussel. 'You remember my young friend Amy – the party in her honor last week? I feel she may need some expert advice.' She told him of Amy's unwise idea, and suggested that the impulsive Californian had need of counsel that could result in him finding her a more suitable property. It was a challenge no real estate agent could have ignored.

'Give me the name of the *notaire*. I may have a client myself for a property such as that, but I will need more information.' Otto assured her, 'I'll talk to Miss Hawkins. I think these Americans often don't know what they're getting into.'

39

Amy took the train from the Gare de Lyon, excited, charged with dreams of doing a really amazing thing, whatever the château turned out to look like. A country property in France! It could even become the seat of the Mutual Aid Foundation. Would there be a swimming pool? Monsieur de Persand, so rude at first, now so solicitous, had telephoned the *notaire,* who would be waiting for her at the train station, and had booked the hotel so that she could have a good look around the village and countryside and see the château at various times of day and evening. The price? Sigrid had refused to believe that, at a price so low, it could be anything worth having. She also had strong reservations about the wisdom of buying foreign property with war shadows and international misunderstandings rampant. Amy paid no attention to these last objections.

'Amy, just get out. The situation is changing fast.'

'Really, everything's fine.'

The landscape was flat and welcoming as they left Paris, streaking by at twice the speed of little autos on the freeways they passed. She was struck by the simplicity of the villages, the country train stations gone in a wink as they hurtled by, too fast to read their names. Heaps of old tires and junked cars marred the byways – it might be America, it might be anywhere. Hills and rocky cairns developed, stately aqueducts with Roman arches were glimpsed snaking onward, electrical pylons loomed above, and an odd ruin lay atop every conspicuous hill. Her heart yearned toward each of them, any of them, castles. One to be hers. Perhaps mere acquisition could indeed overcome defects of character and yearnings of the heart – she who had never cared about real estate.

She was making a mental list of the advantages of French over American, and American over French, civilization: France had trains, *fromage frais,* the garbage was collected every day ... America had Quaker Oats, and the stores were open on Sunday ... The agreeable dreamy mood she had fallen into was abruptly interrupted by arrival, a voice announcing that there would be one minute's stop. She picked up her little case and leapt out.

Maître Lepage and Monsieur Delamer were standing together on the platform and had evidently been alerted to look for a tallish American blonde. In any case, she was almost the only person to alight, and they confidently presented themselves. Maître Lepage was roundish and wore a knitted vest. Monsieur Delamer, gaunt and attractive, wore an overcoat. It was clear that they were delighted that a posssible buyer had appeared so early in the estate-settling process.

'Thanks so much for letting me come down on such short notice,' she said.

'Merci d'être venue,' they said. Would she like some coffee? To leave her overnight case at the hotel? In the event, they drove directly to the 'château,' as she thought of it, or 'Mr Venn's house,' as they called it in their careful English. It lay outside the village of Saint-Gond. Amy had

not thought for months of her original intention to learn something about her European heritage, but now it occurred to her that her forbears could have come from someplace like this village of small stone and stucco structures, with tile roofs and ivied courtyards, a stream running through, a mill, all reminding her of jigsaw-puzzle scenes of country life. A few stout citizens stood around in front of the *mairie*, a pair of elderly men chatted outside the rather self-consciously charming small hotel, where Delamer indicated Amy would be staying. Details of gentrification began to consolidate under her closer scrutiny – antique shop, boutique of La Perla lingerie, pâtisserie, real estate office.

The house, or château, didn't conform to Amy's idea of a castle, certainly; it was a rectangular three-story structure with a mansard roof of slate tiles, and a tower at one corner that appeared to be older. She inadvertently thought of Gatsby and William Randolph Hearst, Americans with castles, icons of acquisitiveness and delusions of grandeur. Luckily, this place was somewhat smaller than certain houses recently built near Palo Alto, and the price was lower – a modest place, really, for a girl in her situation, more of a big house than a castle. Its modesty was a relief.

'The tower dates from the fourteenth century, the rest from the seventeenth,' Maître Lepage was saying. 'The other tower fell down.' Small weeds had everywhere begun to volunteer. The walls gave off a smell of damp stone. History! In truth it looked somewhat bleak, but Amy knew at once that she would buy it, no matter what it was like inside. How bad could it be? Maître Lepage sorted out his keys and they advanced across the gravel to the door.

Amy went through the rooms in something of a daze, room after room, none very pretty, some without furniture, some in disorder, with little appraisers' tickets dangling from chairs and picture frames. The wintry March light flowed in through the tall windows, the fireplaces were empty of ash or andiron. Harry's toys in the corner of the dining room, an ugly table, the kitchen bare and large, innumerable bedrooms where books were stacked in boxes – unsold back stock from the press, Delamer explained – and several office rooms, Adrian Venn's desk, his books. This was her first impression of Adrian Venn as he had been when he was a living person, someone who had looked at these pictures on his walls, his newspaper still folded on the sill where he must have stood to gaze out on his vineyard. Or perhaps it was his ghost she was feeling now. If she believed in ghosts, she would have to agree, one lived here, and it must be his, or that of some earlier inhabitant who had died, like Venn, discontented. She could feel the clammy breeze of his presence through the leaky window frame.

She, of course, would have the tower, Harry his room again, Kerry (the horrible) her old rooms, Rupert and Victoire – but they would decide, it was not up to her, she was not making the same mistake again of interfering with their lives, she would just raise the possibility that they might want to carry on the press, the vineyard. She followed the two men out to the vineyard office, through the barn and tiny tasting room, into the low modern metal building that held the press. To a person of her general

435

administrative competence, it raised no warning flags of difficulty. The peculiar form of desire aroused by real estate had begun for the first time in her life to course through her blood.

Mr Delamer had made a reservation for lunch at Amy's hotel. She took her case up to her room, washed her face, and came back down again into the tiny bar–dining room. Mr Delamer and Maître Lepage stood at the bar with snifters of something, but Amy was riveted, stupefied by what she saw beyond them in the doorway, the baron Otto coming in, looking almost ludicrously Teutonic in his loden coat with its shiny buttons and his Austrian green hat. Though he had looked very natural in the Alps, here he seemed a figure from an operetta.

He seemed as surprised as she, but delighted, and greeted her warmly, but formally – 'Miss Hawkins!' – and ceremoniously introduced himself to Maître Lepage, with whom he had an appointment. Of course he would join them for lunch. He could see the château after lunch, and Miss Hawkins might want to see it again too.

Throughout lunch, a slow sense of anxiety began to dominate Amy's emotions. What did the baron want to see the château for? Unless by some chance Géraldine had sent him to give her his expert opinion, it was his profession of real estate developer that worried her. Visions of schools, hotels, spas, deluxe apartments remodelled as weekend time-share condos, nearly spoiled her appetite for a delicious *blanquette de veau*. It didn't escape her that this feeling about the château was stronger than her memory of her connection to Otto; did acquisitiveness trump discomfort after all?

She returned to the château in the afternoon with the notary, Maître Lepage, and the baron, who inspected with minute interest each corridor and closet, shaking his head and deploring the things he found. Ominous water stains had drawn him to the roof; she had not noticed them. He had a knack for discovering broken panes and walls deteriorated down to the lath. Amy watched from the window as he climbed partway onto the roof, resisting an impulse to hold on to his shirttail.

'Missing an enormous number of slates,' he reported. Maître Lepage agreed that things had been neglected, but not, he insisted, to a dangerous degree. All of Otto's reactions seemed to Amy too negative – he shook his head over the spool and wire electricity in parts of the building, the inadequacy of the radiators, which had been installed in the thirties, and at the age of the furnace. She was happy there was one. In Amy's tower he pointed out that there was daylight to be seen through the ceiling. He seemed impervious to the charm of the main staircase and the little chapel room.

'There is a one-star restaurant a few kilometers from here,' he said at the end of the afternoon. 'I propose we not eat at the hotel. I have my car.' She recognized the car, still with its ski rack, and spattered from the melting snow.

Over dinner, he said, 'I have considerable experience with these older properties, I know what to look for, and I would advise you to avoid this one, Amy. The roof –'

'So nice of you to have a look,' she said.

'The roof alone a crippling investment. I think you can find something for the money with considerably more charm. There is a lot on the market much better; I have a couple of listings myself. You should look at comparable properties, not just grab this one. I think it's no bargain.'

'I'm sure I ought to look at other things,' Amy agreed.

'Then, Amy, as your friend I suppose I can advise you, it's not something for one person to take on. I have a group, builders, construction people – I could think of it, but for you, not knowing France – frankly, folly.'

'I'm sure you're right,' she said, certain he was right, her heart fastening on the château with more determination.

'It's a terrible idea. More wine?'

'Thank you.'

'Also, no bank is going to lend you the money for it. Not without a business plan. Why do you want this building, by the way?' Amy could not say, and now had begun to wonder what he foresaw for after dinner. Fennie, after all, was not here. 'And your budget? A mortgage? Private terms? What did you envision?'

'Perhaps at the right price . . . ? I thought I'd offer less than the asking price, on account of the roof,' she said. 'Would you advise that?'

'I commend the principle, of course, but not here. Rarely have I seen such a lack of distinction in a château. I would hate to see you make a mistake by buying it, at any price.'

Could Otto be sincere? Perhaps he didn't want it for himself as a school, clinic, small hotel? Perhaps he only wanted to spare her? In fact, she decided, all his dealings with her had been kindly meant. Though she had been drawn to her image of him as worldly Eurotrash aristocrat, he was only a kindly, if portly, normally sensual businessman, if that was not an oxymoron. She began to feel friendlier toward him again. Still, as they drove to the hotel, Amy again began to think once more about how to handle any possible awkwardness, unable to formulate any actual objections to another little passage with the baron, but most unwilling to face one all the same. She would tell him how he had wounded her the night after her party. These concerns were drowned in astonishment, however, when they walked from the little gravel parking lot behind the hotel toward the front door just in time to observe Emile Abboud getting out of a taxi.

But of course, Emile's visit must have something to do with the château and the estate. He seemed surprised and not particularly pleased to see them, recognizing the baron from Géraldine's party if not from Valméri. Amy was embarrassed to think he must believe she and the baron were here having a romantic weekend in a little country inn. Her color rose to think what he must think. 'Yes, I have some matters to see the *notaire* about,' he said. 'And you?'

'I came down to see about, um, investing in the château,' she said.

'Investment seems such a puritan justification. Can't you just want something and buy it?'

'I don't understand why you're always talking about me and my national characteristics as if Americans were all puritans and all the same. Have you ever been to America?'

'Certainly not,' said Emile.

'I have,' remarked the baron Otto. 'Several times to New York and once to Florida.'

'I'll get them to give me some supper, if it's not too

439

late,' Emile said. 'Won't you join me, the two of you, have a *digestif*? I suppose you've dined already.'

Amy, seeing her chance to escape being alone with the baron, eagerly acceded. Seeing Emile had animated every conclusion about him that had plagued her during the past weeks, sexual turmoil and also her disturbing sense of a person she wanted as a friend. They took a table in the bar, and Emile waved for Madame the barman/cook. Otto and Amy had brandies, Otto handing Amy hers from waitress's little tray with an almost proprietorial assurance. Amy's heart began to pound with the desire that Otto go to bed and leave her alone with Emile, to whom she had as usual already said something combative – to whom, she could understand very clearly, she wanted to be very nice indeed. She wanted to sleep with him. Was there a chance of this?

'Falling down, a ruin, a catastrophe,' Otto began to describe his professional opinion of the state of the château, she supposed, but it could be a description of her uneasy mental condition. Otto settled in for an elaborate real-estate chat.

'We should have a bottle from the estate vineyard, I'm afraid I don't know what it's called,' Emile said. He asked the woman, who brought a bottle, conducting a jocular discussion in French that Amy couldn't follow.

'I wonder whether in general Prince Kropotkin would have approved of your project of buying the château and establishing the Venn heirs there. This would not be unlike Godwinian anarchism, but more like a monarchy,' said Emile, with a smile. The words and the smile smote her heart directly. She knew he was intending them to, the allusion to the prince a direct message. She felt jubilation and panic in about equal proportion.

'I hope she will not buy it. I have strongly advised against it,' Otto said. Fortune hunter, he said to himself indignantly of Emile, guessing what he thought was Emile's game, to influence Amy to buy the château and set his wife up there. And he was probably trying to sleep with Amy into the bargain – why else confront her here in an isolated hotel? Shameless. His chivalrous nature, such a natural part of his métier of real estate man, was stirred, and of course his affection for Amy.

Of course I won't buy it, Amy was thinking. Cold rooms, bricks, moats, are not for me. It was suddenly clear what she wanted, or, rather, clear that the château would never provide it, things would probably go wrong the way her other forms of helping had gone wrong. Instead of disappointing her, this moment of realism and self-discovery – could it lead to others? – was liberating, exhilarating, and told her that the heart has its directions you did ill to disregard, even if you must occasionally overrule it. Her heart was fixed on Emile, so that it could be broken, and feelings, sadness, passion, all could rush into the breach. Her excitement grew.

'Communal living was an approved form of mutual aid, but he would have wished us to own the property in common, which is going a bit far,' she said. 'I'm too much a capitalist for that.' Go to bed, Baron Otto. Emile, too, was gazing with something like exasperation at Baron Otto, who was calling for a beer. The baron for his part had begun to respond rather coldly to Emile and Amy's prattle, clearly irritated by the presence of Emile and baffled by it, too, as by the appearance of a rowdy dog or importunate child.

'*Grand ou demi?*' the waitress asked.

'*Grand.*' The baron began to discourse on the state of the roof, and drainage problems inherent in old moats, however dry. Thoughts of Emile kept intruding on Amy's concentration. She distracted herself by going room by room through the château in her mind.

He would never leave Amy to the mercy of this predatory con man, Otto thought. Americans were naive and ambitious, always overestimating their powers. Women were always being taken advantage of by men of this type. 'The pipes alone, almost entirely lead, fifty thousand euros at a start.' He could not repress his private recollections of Amy, lovely creature, whom he remembered himself to have satisfied satisfactorily, as far as he could tell. 'To say nothing of the eave drains, which should be lined with copper . . . Amy, you must be tired. You musn't let us keep you up. We can discuss all this tomorrow.'

'Oh, I'm fine, I was just thinking of having another glass . . .' she protested. Emile poured her another glass.

'Géraldine is so hoping everything will work out for all the Venns and – your wife – and everyone,' she said. 'Did you see the press? Those beautiful old machines, the old-fashioned typefaces? There is something so romantic about fine printing . . .'

'On the contrary, I think my mother-in-law is rather of the same opinion as the baron,' said Emile. 'She thinks you would make a mistake to buy it, and she thinks I have powers of persuasion. Dissuasion.'

'I think you probably do.' Amy smiled her sweetest, dimpled smile.

'She wished me to dissuade you.'

'Just so, Madame Chastine was concerned about you making a mistake,' the baron agreed.

'I on the other hand tend to think you should buy it, if you can afford it,' Emile said.

All this seemed confusing; she had thought Géraldine approved of the affair. 'Did she ask you to come down here?'

'Géraldine suggested I have a talk with you,' agreed Emile vaguely.

'I told her I'd come have a look,' said the baron.

'You came all the way because of me?' Amy began to find this irritating. After all, she could make her own decisions.

'I wanted to see the place. And Persand suggested I come down, since I had to see the *notaire* anyway. Persand is opposed to Americans buying French real estate,' said Emile. 'I suppose I am, too, in general. But there are Americans one would want to see more of.' Both Emile and the baron, seizing on that happy turn of phrase, beamed at Amy. The combination of beauty, a big fortune, and enlightened social thinking was an assemblage of qualities Emile had never before encountered; he couldn't blame himself for being dazzled. If he could get rid of this Austrian.

Fortune hunter, lecher, this was deplorable, thought Otto.

It was hopeless, Amy saw, these men were going to keep each other in view till midnight. 'Good night!' she said, and got up. 'Thanks so much. It's incredibly sweet of you both.' She hoped her glance at Emile would be readable. She smiled again and left them.

'Would you like a cigar?' the baron was saying to Emile.

In her room, Amy, putting on her nightgown, weighed whether to leave it off entirely. Europe! where she could behave as she pleased. In a high state of excitement, she wondered what she would do if after all it was the baron who should tap on her door. She didn't think it would be. Her excitement was more than sexual, it was a sort of sense of being on a life cusp, between what and what, she had no idea, but she had glimpsed it earlier, strands of self-understanding knotting into a strong frond that she could depend upon without giving it a self-indulgent amount of thought in future.

Fortunately it was Emile who knocked at the door. Standing modestly aside, despite herself she glanced down the hall, half expecting to see Otto also tiptoeing toward her door, as in the play she had seen by Feydeau, one of the few theatrical events Géraldine had sent her to which she had understood – people tiptoeing down corridors carrying their shoes, and hiding under beds. Emile came in and took her in his arms.

After some time, when neither of them had anything more to wish for – the phrase was Stendhal's – Emile said, 'I was trying to explain how I fell in love with you – in a way. It could have been either your air of mystery, or the fascination of your alien tribe, but in fact it was when I saw you being nice to some fat Americans in front of the Invalides.

No, not love "in a way," I fell completely in love with you. You were concerned to save the honor of the French. Well, it was actually before that. Once, in Valméri, you wore your hair down at dinner. Do you remember? It was then I saw your beauty for the first time.'

Amy did remember, it was the night she had slept with the baron. So, evidently Géraldine was right about the importance of hair as about everything, including how amusing Emile would be in private, as she had just learned.

'Well, of course I had remarked it before, at that lunch and even before. You are "noticeable," after all,' Emile went on. Amy was quite content to be praised for any attribute by such a perfect creature.

'For me, it was when you didn't kill the lobster,' she said. 'But I didn't know it right then. I only let myself know it when I heard Victoire had left you – you see how scrupulous I am. So you don't think I should cut my hair?'

'Perhaps shoulder length,' he agreed, as if he had given it some thought. That was when she knew he was truly French, member of an alien tribe.

'Do you think it's too late for us?' she wondered. 'I'm going back to California.' Tears sprang to her eyes, surprising her. Emile held and kissed her with considerable conviction. Amy clung to him, but a shred of self-preserving instinct remained to her to protect her heart. Emile seemed to feel the same wariness.

'Must you go back?'

'Yes, I don't belong in France, I know that.'

'Any more than I do, I suppose. We are both outsiders. That's our opportunity.'

'You should go back to your room. Being together just makes it harder,' Amy said. But he stayed the rest of the night – it was irresistible after all – both of them firmly agreeing that what they were doing didn't count, and would not interfere with their various real-life resolutions.

'What is your mysterious secret?' Emile asked at some point.

She wasn't quite sure what he meant; she was boringly transparent to herself. It could be her money, she knew – it was the one thing she couldn't talk about, a kind of shameful secret.

They were never sure they didn't hear the baron – or someone – outside her door in the wee hours; whoever it was must have heard the noisy moans and cries within.

40

Back in Paris, Amy had walked around for a few days in a dream state, wandering through the Jardins de Luxembourg or the Bon Marché without looking at anything, her resolutions wavering. At moments she dreaded going back to Palo Alto with a visceral panic. Once she heard herself give a great hiccupping sob in the Monoprix. She knew the future, unwelcoming and bleak: she would never again see Emile; the love of her life was behind her; the years to come held nothing in particular to look forward to but good works, which she didn't find as satisfying as she ought. Was her unhappiness relative, because she had had little to trouble her in life? Her eyes filled with self-pity that she would always be outside, excluded, and that by her riches she had put herself beyond deserving any form of consolation. Who could feel sorry for her, one of the luckiest people on earth?

She knew she didn't really want a château. It had been a stupid idea. She was not a châtelaine, and not even a European, she was someone who hadn't even got around to furnishing her condo. Her authentic self was not an exile in a tower; like it or not, she was an American person from Palo Alto, there was no getting around this. A château would be a burden far from her interests and abilities, a sort of pretentious diversion from her real life.

She thought of her colleague Ben, stranded on his vast tracts in Patagonia, and of the forlorn, bored expression in his eyes when he came back to California, as he rarely did now.

What was the fine line between boredom and depression? Could whole nations be depressed? Bored? Walking along the Paris streets, looking at the thinner bodies of French people and thinking about their longer lives: were they less bored than Americans? Was it because they could see things at eye level, walking along, instead of being trapped in cars? Or did they feel limited, shackled by the lack of wheels?

Of course she bore in mind the disappointment she was causing to Victoire, Posy, Rupert, Kerry, and Harry, and even herself, though the decision not to buy lightened her, too, routing the specter of the leaky, giant, cold edifice reproachfully looming in her consciousness, if not also in her unconscious, where the primitive real estate gene still emitted its disturbing dream influence. She was going against her own principles of mutual aid, not to do something so clearly for the general good.

Amy had been reassured by Emile that Géraldine would be pleased that she wasn't buying the château. Nevertheless, she explained her decision to Géraldine with some trepidation. 'Baron Otto says not to buy it, everyone seems to say it would be unwise,' she apologized.

Géraldine had heard this already – had had phone calls from Emile, Baron Otto, the consternated Pamela, and the desperate Rupert. She had asked Emile if it was he who had talked Amy out of the château affair.

'I? No, I haven't talked to her about it,' he said, not quite untruthfully.

'I'm sure you are right,' said Géraldine to Amy now. She was relieved but didn't wish to seem too pleased.

'I have mixed feelings. I can imagine so many people happy there, little Harry, Victoire ... In so many ways, I can see it ...'

'I'm sure you're longing to be at home,' said Géraldine. 'It must be lovely, all those palm trees and beaches.' She was thinking that Amy didn't really look like she was longing to go home. There was now something about her, at once a glow and something triste. Géraldine would like to keep her a few months longer. Amy was on a cusp, clearly, and could fall either way, but probably would fall back into California's simple, even barbaric ways; she had told Géraldine about take-out food, for example.

'Not really,' said Amy, thinking of freeways, Burger Kings, gas stations, traffic, garage door openers, resentful Salvadoreans doing the hedges, war, religious fundamentalists in A-frame churches with vinyl siding, all the anger and ugliness she knew she would find at home these days. She thought of the Ukiah of her childhood, hot and dusty, where you could ride your bike everywhere, and of Palo Alto today. But you couldn't escape, that was the probability, you could only try to become better at being where you were. Roots were nonsense. What a lot of trouble she had gone to, to discover only this rather banal and simple truth.

'You will visit often, you have your apartment,' Géraldine reassured her. 'It will not be a disappointment to Victoire not to live in the château – she would not after

449

all have lived there. She has decided to take her husband back, I'm happy to report. Perhaps she listens to me more than I supposed. *A mon âge,* I think I do know a few things.'

Amy did not know how to feel about this news. In principle, she believed in stable social relationships like marriage. Géraldine began to air her views about marriage. 'Somewhat conventional, I know,' she assured Amy. 'But the point of folk wisdom, is it not, is that there is so much experience behind it?' She emphasized that it was Victoire to whom her strictures were directed.

Géraldine had been relieved, though somewhat baffled, that Victoire had decided to patch things up with Emile and go on leading the life she had led before. She suspected it was because Victoire had seen him in his glory at her party for Amy, handsome and surrounded by admirers, treated collegially by the rising Antoine de Persand, reverently by the grandest of her guests, and with the new prospects of earning a better living.

Géraldine had not expected to find in Amy such a glowing, changed person, someone altogether in the kind of altered state that often meant its wearer had fallen in love. At least Amy's transformation didn't seem to be related to real estate. Of course she wouldn't pry, but the sight of the girl's enhanced radiance led her to contemplate, and dilate upon, the subject of love in general. As she spoke, she watched Amy to see if Amy understood that she, too, could profit from the motherly wisdom Géraldine dispensed.

'Victoire is so idealistic. She is so apt to neglect the very ordinary things that make love last,' she said. 'The old recipes suffice – the negligee, the candlelight, should not be underestimated. Perfume – so important. Even, dare I say, a change in – sexual positions – from time to time? I wish to say, physical love is the basis of all.' She went on discoursing about womanly wiles, and the fitful nature of Eros, so apt to displace himself when the tiniest bit bored.

Wiles did not interest Amy greatly; she disapproved of them. Anyway, Géraldine's wisdom was no more than what any ladies' magazine would say. Why was Géraldine telling her things like this? For a moment Amy feared she had guessed something about Emile and her, and wanted to warn Amy off with descriptions of how happy Victoire and Emile were going to be in their perfumed bed. But Géraldine didn't appear even to know that Emile had gone to Saint-Gond, so no doubt she was speaking only as a disinterested representative of her generation, bound to convey vital information to younger women coming up.

It was occurring to Géraldine as she spoke that another plausible explanation for Amy's changed manner and stylish shorter haircut – thank heavens she had got rid of the Heidi braid – was her relief at going back to California. Géraldine was not sure she could count Amy among her successes. Two of her real successes had involved American divorcées achieving marriages to Frenchmen, though only one of those marriages had lasted. In comparison, what had Amy accomplished, really? Still, she was intelligent and observant, and perhaps had evolved some in her few months here. She looked smarter in her clothes now, seemed to appreciate art and food, and had referred to reading several books! Géraldine had also overheard her mention the *grisaille* French weather.

The most likely explanation for Amy's present happiness, she decided, was that Amy had fallen in love, and it suddenly occurred to Géraldine that the lover could be Baron Otto! That must be it! They had both been in Valméri, and were both in Saint-Gond, Otto dutifully doing Géraldine's bidding by going down there to look at the château. She certainly would not have proposed he seduce the girl. Perhaps Otto saw a ski chalet in her future? Géraldine found this idea somewhat annoying, but refrained from asking him about it later. What she did, whom she slept with, what she bought, were Amy's concerns.

Amy's radiance was love, it was clear to herself, but it was also relief at having settled the issue of love, found an object for her heart. She had a grateful sense of having got life's principal drama behind her. If loneliness, misery, and unbearable pangs of desire got the better of her from time to time, well, she would fly to Paris. It was these insights that gave her a glow of inner calm. She had broken through to the raw edge of something, felt it, and would suffer – and this new intensity was after all, maybe, what she had come for.

'I've never seen you look so well, Amy,' said Géraldine. 'Just when I've made a Parisienne of you – what a pity that you're not staying longer.'

41

Amy had decided the menu for her farewell party would be tiny caviar tacos, lobster enchiladas, nachos, quesadillas, rare roast beef chili, giant prawns marinated in lime juice, champagne, and margaritas. Géraldine had tactfully added some items to the hors d'oeuvres and proposed two versions of the chili. For those – almost every French person – who weren't fond of spices, it would be chili without chili powder, more of a *boeuf bourguignon* with beans. For the music, there would be mariachis. Amy had brought two of her tablecloths to cover the long buffet, which the waiters were spreading as she watched, their snowy perfection and distinguished monograms invoking a venerable tradition of hospitality.

The white ship *Elba* lay at anchor in the Seine, with a metal gangplank leading to it from the quay, festooned with ropes and life preservers. The feeble afternoon sun had set, but the weather was still mild. Géraldine had known whom to call to hire this *bateau-mouche*, which would leave its dock in the yacht basin Henri IV at nine-thirty and make a circuit during dinner of the splendid monuments along the Seine, fixing them in the powerful battery of lights it swept along the darkened banks. For Amy, this was almost a metaphor of her French experience – a dark and shadowy reality momentarily illumined with flashes of clarity.

At nine, her Paris acquaintance began to climb the gangplank to the *bateau*. She was surprised at how many people she had come to know in a few months, counting her singing, cooking, and other teachers, American advisors, French people who had invited her, friends of Géraldine, the whole Venn clan – for Pamela and Rupert were coming over from London again, as was now so easy on the Eurostar. Here came the Valméri contingent, Joe Daggart, the prince and *princesse* de Mawlesky, and Madame Dové-Chatigny. Perhaps Baron Otto would be in town; he wasn't sure.

Assembled, it was a handsome, even glamorous group, which Amy mentally contrasted with her friends at home. How was she going to find them? Changed? Would they find her changed? No matter, parties were mutual aid at its sweetest, proffering pleasure, each guest acceding by his presence to the principle of human sociability. As they arrived she greeted the various American women who had helped her and their French husbands. She expected Géraldine and Eric, Victoire with them – a hundred people in all.

Posy Venn and Robin Crumley were among the first, tripping up the gangplank hand in hand, Robin almost dapper in a nautical blue blazer, Posy in a windbreaker and white trousers. They hardly noticed Amy in their absorption with each other, but were delighted when they spotted her, and rushed to her side.

'You will be amazed,' Robin said, kissing her on both cheeks like a Frenchman. 'We want you to know we are going to be married! You are the first to know! It will be announced. We've written to *The Times*.'

They did seem to project a bridal radiance that confirmed this surprising development. Amy was as amazed as they could have wished. Surely the lunch in Saint-Jean-de-Belleville was the first time they had ever been in each other's company? Amy asked herself whether she could imagine being married to Robin Crumley, but it seemed far from any imaginative leap she could make. She concluded that Robin and Posy had not heard of Amy's projected purchase of the château, hence had not known the disappointment felt by Victoire and Rupert when she decided not to do it.

'You must announce it tonight. An engagement is so much nicer than a farewell,' Amy said as they moved happily along the deck toward Emile, who had arrived separately from Victoire and Géraldine and stood at the rail gazing solemnly down into the water. Perhaps, Amy thought, he felt as forlorn as she did. They almost didn't dare to look at each other for fear that anyone could see their emotions.

'Abboud, dear fellow! Providence works in wondrous ways, as one is always being told. Posy and I are to be married! All that one could wish from a romantic escapade – we're off to Monaco tomorrow, you know, on these wondrous French trains. We've sent word to *The Times*. You'll see it one of these days . . .'

'Congratulations, Crumley. A very intelligent choice.' Emile pumped Robin's hand with hearty sincerity. He could easily see in Posy the sturdy mother of Englishmen she was destined to be, could envision the little rosy blond tots, Posy knitting woollies and making trifle, or other elements of their odd cuisine – she was perfection for

Crumley, for anyone. He embraced Robin, and kissed Posy on each cheek with an admirable detachment and genuine affection.

Victoire had come up to him and put her hand on his arm. Amy could not but notice the proprietary gesture. Victoire embraced Posy and kissed her. 'I have a confession. Oh, you will think I am an idiot,' she whispered to Posy. 'I *am* an idiot.'

'Don't be silly,' said Posy reassuringly. There was nothing idiotic about her. What was she talking about? Victoire drew her away from Robin and Emile to walk along the deck as the deckhands began to loosen the ropes, and the noise of the engines drowned their conversation from the others.

'I know I've been distant and crazy, but it is over. All along I thought – you will laugh – that you and Emile felt something for each other. I was so angry! At you and Emile both, but especially Emile. I thought That's it, *j'en ai assez*. Not even Maman could make me listen to reason. I must just tell you and clear the air – that is why I've been so horrible to you, darling Posy, can you forgive me?'

'Well! there's nothing to forgive,' Posy said enthusiastically, after an imperceptible beat. 'Of course, I do like Emile tremendously, but you are my sister, after all. I want you to be happy.' She thought God would probably not strike her dead, because this was a sincere statement. Next to Robin, of all her new acquaintance it was Victoire she loved most. She would always feel a certain hardness of heart for Emile, not enough to damage family relations, just a spark of spite, but she sincerely knew she had been spared, her anguish erased, by the great good fortune of meeting Robin. She'd narrowly escaped being in love with a two-faced North African seducer; how much better it was to marry a famous English poet, an artist, an intellectual, a man of letters with entrees everywhere, in love with her and soon to be her husband. She would get an M.A.! Even have a child! They would often come to France, where Robin had such incredible connections, and perhaps use some of her inheritance to buy something small in the Dordogne or the Midi. For somebody or other would buy the château and the money would be hers. Posy's happiness was perfect.

Pamela Venn and Rupert had run up the gangplank just before nine-thirty when the boat was scheduled to pull away. Each had a little agenda. Rupert had come to Paris in some hope of changing Amy's mind about buying the château, a long chance, he knew, or in case of failure to convince her, he could try to persuade her to invest in Icarus Press. Amy was surprised to see that they were followed by Kerry Venn, walking up the gangplank with a stick, bent over to one side like a leaning branch, her legs encased in metal braces, with Kip supporting her. Amy had not herself invited Kerry, though she had said to Kip that it was okay if he brought her, given that her case against Amy was being settled for a face-saving small amount.

'She needs to get out,' Kip had told Amy. 'She's at the clinic all the time, and these crazy Joan of Arc people come to see her – she's becoming their goddess or something.'

'Their saint,' Amy had corrected. But who were the Joan of Arc people? Would there be a special awkwardness, even a scene, with Pamela Venn, whose house Kerry was expropriating? When it came to the rest of her lawsuits, Kerry's emotions had been reported to be savage; if she could not live in her own home, she had resolved to occupy Pamela Venn's house, which now, in law, belonged to her. Amy had her own issues with Kerry – the lawsuit – but had not realized the extent to which Kerry's appearance at the party was like that of the bad fairy at Beauty's christening. Everyone on deck reacted, all in some way betraying their dismay, though perhaps only at seeing the poor thing so handicapped and so brave.

At the moment Kerry wore a tentative expression of resolute sociability, perhaps making an effort because of Amy's generosity in taking Kip back to California with her. He would go back to his old school, but the great thing was that Squaw Valley was just a few hours away from Palo Alto, so they could visit each other often, and Amy would oversee Kip as a kind of sister surrogate. Kerry did not speak to anyone but was settled in a deck chair forward, eventually to behold the marvellous sights along the banks.

Rupert Venn managed to take Amy aside to ask whether he might come to see her with his business plan. He was going to invest his own inheritance in the press, which would move from the château to some other French structure; but he would need a partner. He would show her the numbers. Amy said she would very much welcome the discussion. She could imagine that Icarus Press could produce handsomely printed copies of Kropotkin's *Mutual Aid* and no doubt other worthy titles.

Rupert and his mother had already spoken to Kerry Venn on several matters. They knew they had little hope of changing her mind about taking the London house, though Pam hadn't given up hope, and meantime Trevor Osworthy was trying to straighten things out legally. Pamela was curious at last to see the younger Mrs Venn; so was Géraldine. They also had already raised another delicate issue with Kerry. They had brought the ashes.

Almost silently the big boat pulled out of the yacht basin and cruised along the banks of the Seine, headed under the first of the beautiful bridges. The guests stayed on deck a few minutes, but it was cold, and they soon consented to go down to be seated for dinner. In the central cabin, tables were set along the windows so that from either side the diners could see the marvelous sights. Amy regretted the mariachis; though they played delightfully – 'Cielito Lindo,' 'La Cucaracha' – the music didn't seem to go with the ghostly splendor of the buttresses of Notre Dame as the lights played over them, invoking the medieval bones interred within. However, the guests seemed to enjoy the pudgy Mexicans, or pretended to, and their spangled costumes and sombreros certainly accomplished the mood of New World ebulliance with which Amy had hoped to signify her mood at leaving. Of course it was a lie; her heart became heavier and heavier as she looked at Emile, and thought of Palo Alto. Like Pamela Venn, she had in some way become homeless, fitting neither here, nor, she had a suspicion, there, if ever she had.

She saw she should have put place cards on the small

tables. She would have liked to have Emile, Kip, and Géraldine at her table, but as people shuffled around and paired off to sit down, she was only able to organize for herself Géraldine, Victoire, Joe Daggart, the awful Dolly, and another woman she had never seen in her life. Kip sat at the next table with his sister, Emile, Géraldine's husband, and a French couple whose name Amy had forgotten.

Amy could not be with Victoire without suffering a pang; but Victoire's simple sweetness, pretty blue eyes, and unsuspecting nature ensured forgiveness. Amy told herself she respected Emile for not leaving his wife and children, and that respect was almost as important, and much less mysterious, than love. She tried not to be sorry that the day-to-day disappointments of life with Emile would be left to Victoire. But it was hard.

She was glad to talk to Joe Daggart, though, for he had a bit of news: in the midst of escalating tensions between the U.S. and France, though the United States had officially denied its role in causing an avalanche in the French Alps, it was compensating certain of the victims nonetheless. Nothing to do with airplanes, he said. Someone had seen American snowmobiles on the ridge above the place the Venns had been swept away, and had come forward with accusations. He himself had been with the snowmobile party, Daggart said.

'No damn way we caused the avalanche, but they were right that it was a woman who called the rescue patrol on her cell phone. It was someone called the baroness von Schteussel, who was skiing opposite. We saw the avalanche from above, where we were, on the ridge in our snowmobiles. We couldn't get down there, and we ourselves didn't have the equipment to search for victims, but I confirmed what she had already told them, exactly where to look – two people under the snow, relatively shallowly buried, as it turned out.

'You didn't go to help?' asked Amy, very shocked.

'Well – no, we had no gear, we'd have had little chance of finding them. The professionals found them much sooner. I'm certain we didn't actually dislodge the snow, though. Up where we were, the cornice was intact. They must have done it themselves.'

'Why were you there?' Victoire asked.

'We were looking for a bit of wreckage, something belonging to our satellite program that was thought to have landed just about there.'

'Will Kerry and Harry get compensation?' Amy wondered. He was negotiating it now, Daggart said. The widow would get something, but he didn't think it would make a difference to her plan to go to England. She had decided Harry should be brought up an Englishman, like his father. On the other hand, she was under a lot of pressure from the Joan of Arc votaries to remain as their symbol and treasured, important presence in France, so maybe she would change her mind.

'I'm glad they're getting some money. America always does the right thing eventually,' Amy said, though she was less sure of this than she had once been.

'I like to think so,' said Joe Daggart, without irony, it seemed.

After the dessert – chocolate sundaes – the tables were pushed back and people began to dance. Amy observed

Rupert and Posy Venn, with their mother and Kerry Venn, leave the dining room together.

'Let Kerry do it,' said Posy, helping Kerry undo the parcel.

'We should read something, or say something, I suppose, Posy?' said Rupert.

'I could say Robin's poem "Go to the Dark Starling,"' she said. Goodbye, Father, she said to herself.

'Let's do it silently, each with our thoughts,' Kerry said. After a moment, she opened the box and abruptly dumped the contents into the starboard breeze. Little stinging grains flying back at them made them blink painfully, but tears soon washed them away. Rupert looked around to see Pamela, withdrawn at a distance, watching them, making a little sign to say that she was with them. Goodbye, Father, said Rupert in his heart.

'All right?' Kerry asked, turning to Posy and Rupert.

'Fine,' they said. Posy wished Robin had been there, he had such a sense of occasion; but he had been deep in conversation with Emile.

Under cover of the music and dancing, Emile and Amy found a furtive sexual opportunity in what looked like a chart room, their passion proving to them it was not going to be so easy to say an absolute goodbye forever. 'Kip and I leave Thursday,' Amy sighed. They smiled insouciantly, neither feeling reassured, but neither quite believing in the entire unkindness of fate, to part two lovers so perfectly suited in every way, and both so generally favored by fortune. Was this to be the punishment after all, to miss the love of their lives? If so, it would not be without a struggle, a fortune spent on airfares, tears, a Hoover fellowship for Emile, silent financial backing from Amy for some of his projects, torrid lovemaking in San Jose motels or Provençal hotels – or in Amy's new house in Tahoe, not far from Kip's school – they saw it in prospect, probably underestimating the ways in which it would preoccupy them for years to come, desire increasing with the trouble they had to go to to gratify it. It would not be so bad.